# NUMBER TWO

## 32 Horror Tales Best Read Over Water

### Compiled & Edited by
### Gerri R. Gray

A HellBound Books Publishing LLC Book
Austin TX

HellBound Books

Download on the
App Store

# Also by Gerri R. Gray:

*The Amnesia Girl*
*Gray Skies of Dismal Dreams*
*The Graveyard Girls*
*Blood and Blasphemy*
*The Strange Adventures of Turquoise Moonwolf*
*Madame Gray's Creep Show*


# Contributor to:

*Ghost Hunting the Mohawk Valley*
*Beautiful Tragedies*
*Demons, Devils & Denizens of Hell 2*
*EconoClash Review*
*Deadman's Tome Cthulhu Christmas Special*
*Mixed Bag of Horror: Vol. 1*
*Night Picnic: Vol. 3*
*Coffin Bell: Vol. 2*
*Dig Two Graves: Vol. 2*
*Mixed Bag of Horror*
*Jitter: Issue #7*
…and others.

# CONTENTS




INTRODUCTION                                    7
*Gerri R. Gray*
THE CADAVER ARTIST                              11
*Carlton Herzog*
WHY I DON'T DRINK                               21
*Sarah Cannavo*
BEST FRIENDS                                    31
*Mark Towse*
ALI BABA AND THE SOUL THIEVES                   39
*John Kojak*
BITE                                            46
*Hayden Gilbert*
THE LAST SLICE                                  56
*Vivian Kasley*
TIME FOR CLASS                                  68
*David Rose*
THE 'MOLE PEOPLE'                               75
*Jay Baird*
EDGY AND DULL                                   88
*Wolfgang Potterhouse*
THE BALLAD OF MR. BUDOKAI                        92
*Matt Martinek*
THE TAPHOPHILE                                  101
*Gerri R. Gray*
BROKEN                                          116
*Joanna Koch*
DEAR DIARY                                      125
*J. Tonzelli*
SHE SPEAKS IN STATIC                            130
*Tim Mendees*
ANY PORT IN A STORM                             144
*Matthew A. Clarke*
IT'S WHAT'S INSIDE THAT COUNTS                  153
*Frederick Pangbourne*

THE UNLIKELIEST OF HEROES                164
*Carlton Herzog*
A CHRISTMAS CAROL KILLER                180
*J Louis Messina*
'SIRIUS' MATTERS                195
*Rob Santana*
PILGRIMAGE TO THE RANGE                202
*Jay Baird*
DARK AENEID                210
*J.B. Toner*
MEDIUM RARE                219
*Ken Goldman*
MANOR OF BONES                234
Thomas K.S. Wake
THE BLACK MARKET PROJECT                243
*Chisto Healy*
HASTINGS                257
*Drew Nicks*
MONSTROUS LOVE                267
*Pamela Scott*
BLOOD RED ORANGES                283
*Barbara Jacobson*
SHADE                295
*Joe Palumbo*
THE WAITING ROOM                307
*Jameson Grey*
FRONTIER FAITHS                320
*Henry Myllylä*
YOU NEVER CAN TELL                332
*Matt Bliss*
GLASS BODIED WOMAN                343
*Josh Darling*
ABOUT GERRI R GRAY                356
OTHER HELLBOUND BOOKS                358

# INTRODUCTION
### *By Gerri R. Gray*

You're traveling through the unknown, hellbound, with no roadmap or stars to guide you. The light around you fades as you descend into a shadow realm where supernatural terrors make their lair and evil lurks at every turn. Here, good doesn't always prevail and dead things don't always stay dead, for this is a place where things that shouldn't be, are... and the things that should be, are not. The blood in your veins turns to ice. Your gut instinct warns you that danger is afoot. But it's too late to turn back. You are about to step inside another dimension...

When the publisher asked me if I'd be interested in editing the second volume in *The Toilet Zone* series, I was all too happy to take on the project. Who wouldn't be? Delighted to be working on my fourth horror anthology for HellBound Books, I set about the first task at hand, which was to read through a plethora of submissions and select the ones I felt best represented *The Toilet Zone: Number Two*. Contracts, proofreading, and editing followed, and in less than one month's time, the book was completed and ready to go!

So, imagine, if you will, over thirty blood-curdling tales crafted by some of the finest writers of horror fiction to emerge in recent years. Tales that unlock the door to imagination and transport you to strange and terrifying dimensions existing outside the four dimensions known to man. Imagine nightmares from which there is no waking and worlds where unspeakable horror reigns supreme. Each story in this standout collection makes an ideal "sit-down read" for those times when the porcelain throne calls.

Watch out for that signpost up ahead...

You've just crossed over into…

*The Toilet Zone: Number Two*!

# NUMBER TWO

# THE CADAVER ARTIST
### By Carlton Herzog

A thing of beauty is a joy forever. I can look for a whole day with delight upon a handsome picture, though it be but of a corpse. Perhaps, because it is an instant arrested in eternity and imprisoned in a tangible dream. It represents life in another world, whose inhabitants have no speech, no motions but frozen gestures. It completes what nature cannot elaborate. And when I gaze upon it, I am free from the tyranny of conscious thought.

But I am no mere dilettante. I paint lost souls to enchant this world with their passing. Turn your head up please. Here, let me help you.

See, that is my first wife painted on the wall, looking as if she were alive. I call that painting a wonder. It captures her depth and passion in its earnest glance. Sadly, I was not the sole source of all that joy. Her heart loved everything and everyone in equal measure. It was all one: the diamonds I gave her, my family name, the rising sun, the painted rainbow, her snow-white horse, the butterfly. All basked in the rays from her beatific smile.

Knowingly, or perhaps not, she stabbed me with her incessant joy until my love for her bled out. Like Othello with Desdemona, I wanted to tear her all to pieces.

So, one night as she slept, I wound her hair three times around her little throat and strangled her. I'm sure she felt no pain. As she lay there, I opened her lids again and stared into her laughing blue eyes. I untied the tress around her neck and kissed her blushing cheek.

Immortal bird, she was not meant for death, for she walked in beauty like the starry night. So, I braced her rosy head, glued wide her smile and her eyes, slathered on the blush, and painted her as if she were alive.

Thus done, I needed not her cold kisses and icy blank stare; my rendering so much the warmer. I gave her body to the rutting swine that made a meal of her then lurid frame.

Ere the worms had pierced her winding sheet and the spider had made a thin curtain for her epitaph, I had remarried. My second wife is pictured here. To mine eye and heart, a Madonna pure and good. Our hearts beat the cadence of true love each to each. But then I caught her making the beast with two backs. The gardener, a swarthy Mediterranean type, was having his way with her whenever I left for my official duties.

It happened that the Sybil, a fashionable fortuneteller, known to be the wisest woman in the world, told me of her infidelity. She wanted to trade that knowledge for freedom, since I keep her in a cage lest she fly away. But she is too valuable to lose, so I endure her persistent lamentations. Soon, there will be no need for a cage; in time her wings will wither to stumps.

I had Tom the Dwarf creep up on the two illicit lovers while tangled in a passionate embrace. He clubbed them silly and dragged them to my studio. I injected them with a narcotic to make them sleep as I posed and braced their bodies upright. Once entwined again in each other's arm, I applied the molten wax. Thus prepared, and later solidified, I added the bronze glaze. Now she will always be mine to admire, albeit in the dead metallic arms of another.

Shake your head if you think me mad. My apologies, for your head is bound to that block. I am quite sane. Would a madman take such meticulous care? Would he have the foresight and imagination to transform such a lethal endeavor into an enduring piece of art? Assuredly not, for when a woman stoops to folly, her man should correct her.

I think of myself as a good husband, the sort who protects his wives from the ravages of moral decline in a decadent world. In return, I ask only for unflagging fidelity. For without marital solidarity, no union can hold against the rising tide of evil in the world.

Blink your eyes once if you agree. So good of you to concur I am no fiend. My so-called wives were not women at all, but dark ladies of the stratosphere sent to beguile me with their Circean wiles. You cannot correct such monsters. You must kill them, and to do so, you must become one. On that point there can be no compromise. No turning of the other cheek, no praying for their redemption, no self-sacrifice to win their heart and soul. The disposal of monsters is as much hot-blooded art as cold-blooded science.

On this side of the grave, the shadows of the dead remain to walk with us, ever reminding us that only a thin veil separates us. When I walk with another, there is always a third who glides beside us. There are more dead about than I can count. Who would have thought death had killed so many?

But we can do more than plant flowers and sing sad songs when death is near. And that is what I did. I married again. At the wedding, bats with baby faces thronged about the ceremony whistling and beating their wings. My guests said it was an evil omen. To be certain, I asked the Sybil what that meant. She warned me not have a child with my wife, for she had been cursed by gypsies. I did not listen.

My son came forth as an abomination, old before he was young, a disgusting thing, proto-human and neurasthenic. I gave him to the circus. Years later, as I walked along the river meditating, I heard the rattle of bones and a chuckle. I turned and saw an old purple man with wrinkled female breasts dragging his slimy belly along the bank. He had flippers for arms and hands, and a long serpentine tail.

He said, "I am your son. I come from the place where the dead men lose their bones and witches drink the blood of children. All your dead wives so meticulously planted in your garden have begun to sprout. They will bloom this year."

I asked, "Why?"

He said, "One of your many wives, Ulpian, shared a bloodline with Sycorax, queen of the witches. She wants vengeance on you for burying Ulpian alive beneath the rose garden. Know those wives do not rise as thin shades like the multitude around you. They are gaunt cadavers with revenge boiling in their rotting veins, a fiendish platoon of ravenous corpses bent on devouring you. Get thee hence."

Then he slithered into the muddy water, never to be seen again.

That would not do. I rode back to my estate. I looked everywhere for the Dwarf, my sole confidante and accomplice. But I could not find him. Normally, he is hard to look upon with his odd-shaped head and hanging nether lip. But how I craved the sight of that hideous face as I pondered the possibility of an attack. With that brute by side, I might survive. Without him I was surely doomed.

I ran to my study and retrieved my shotgun and pistol. Then I remembered the Sybil. She was a lady of intrigue; she knew all the situations.

She said, "Even now that ghastly tribe shuffles about your estate like beasts of prey. They are like a great creeping vine that would wrap around you and drag you into the earth. You must go to Sycorax, the witch who controls them, and kill her. She lives in the hut beside the river's bend. Only she can disunite those tendrils."

I made for the witch's lair posthaste. I found her stirring a great cauldron. The hag was muttering to herself.

"Let us look at the Garden of Time and see what weeds may grow. Look there: the mare doth eat her foal. And over there: the graves yawn and yield up gliding ghosts. I see here: the heavens rain blood on the worlds below. And over there: babies born without heads. These signs bode well for witches. Soon we shall gather in great numbers and retake this world."

I hit her from behind. As she lay there sprawled before me, I raised my pistol to her head.

"Here me, crone. Call off your dogs or I will splatter your brains. Wait, better yet. Give over control of them. Not just their mephitic will, but the power to reshape their bodies into something more suitable to my broader purpose. I am an artist, you know."

The witch did her incantation. No sooner had she finished, than eight listing pestilential corpses appeared before me. From their lipless mouths, they groaned with the anguish of the marrow. I saw their skulls beneath their skin. Weeds stared at me from the sockets of their eyes. Their hands bereft of flesh, frail and brittle, ill suited to seize and clutch, showed the fever of the bone. With skin as white as leprosy, they were fit to crew a Death Ship or dance about a cemetery in a dead land.

I had made them all, each with a unique death-stroke. Some with poison, some by rope, one with axe, one with adder, two by water.

Yet, for all my delicate attention to their final moment, they were incomplete, as much from missing limbs as from my own aesthetic. Alone, each could freeze the blood of the sternest man. But fear alone is not enough. I needed something stronger. So, I asked myself what might this heap of broken women—neither alive nor dead—do together as one, accomplish together what they could not do alone?

What, I mused, could they become if the crone tongued them with the language of resurrection and joined them into one mighty creation?  A giant, I reflected, one formidable and puissant.

Satisfied with my answer, I demanded the hag, "make them into one fiend that will do my bidding."

Sycorax waved her hand and all the rotting bodies joined into a hellspawn with a body for each arm and leg, three for a torso and one for a head. As tall as three men, its head punched through the straw roof. The other heads snarled and snapped as mucilaginous strands of gleet oozed and dripped off the body. It reeked of death and decay and all things foul belonging to the grave.

It asked, "What would you have us do first, Master?"

I said without hesitation, "Kill this putrescent conjurer."

My Ostrobog unceremoniously ground the witch into the dirt floor with its massive foot.

With the witch gone, I was free to ransack her library of magic tricks. I found several grimoires. I used one of the spells therein to whisk my new creation and me back to my estate.

I thought the worst was over. But Tom the Dwarf came running from the house. The Sybll had told him that Sycorax's extended coven had been alerted to my efforts by the Hanged Man, another seer. In life, he had been known as Bagby, the shifty gravedigger often cited as proof that evolution runs backwards as well as forwards.

He had robbed a family outside of town, cut up the bodies and stuffed them in the pantry cabinets. Before the hangman had dropped the door, he had appealed to Hades to save him. And save him he did with a black bargain that liberated Bagby from death but imprisoned him in the noose for all eternity.

Now he hangs between life and death on the very gallows of his execution. Needing neither food nor drink, nor air, nor any other vital, he will offer his services to those who can relieve his suffering, if only for a time.

I learned that Crazy Jane, of the Darkling Thrush, had gone to the Hanged Man to make inquiry into Sycorax's whereabouts. With his crypt a canopy of clouds and the wind his death lament, Bagby, shrunken hard and dry with ancient pulse, named me her assassin.

Jane sent her ancient thrush to assemble all the covens at my home. When I learned of the imminent attack, I searched the witch's books to find a useful spell.

As I did, the sky above turned black as the broomstick horde blocked the mid-day sun. I sent my new monster to keep them at bay. The behemoth swatted them to the ground and then crushed them.

I clutched the grimoires and ran across the green dodging and parrying bolts of eldritch lightning. Cackling as they zoomed about me, the witches cracked trees and cratered my lawn. Bolts of natural lightning crisscrossed my path, as did eruptions of fire from the very ground.

I made the house, even as fire bolts shattered its façade into marble splinters. Once inside my studio, I fumbled through the grimoires until I found the right spell, the one that would end the witches once and for all and make me the greatest cadaver artist of all time.

I returned to the battlefield. I found my Ostrobog being cut down to size by blue lightning. First, the ankles, then the knees. That was followed by the amputation of its hands and arms. The last bit of surgery consisted of a combined strike that severed its multiple heads. The poor thing squirmed on the ground like a worm caught on hot pavement.

Even so, I invoked the gods and spirits of architecture:

"Hear my prayer, Athena and Hestia, and in the name of the Basilica of San Vitale, the Cathedral at Notre Dame, and Galerius of Thessaloniki, let these witches be gathered up by the earth. Let them be rendered useful sculptures on the end of flying buttresses to adorn my estate."

No sooner had I uttered those words, than the earth shook, and great spikes of stone and soil shot from the ground and ensnared every witch. I could see the earthen influence spread throughout their bodies, turning them first to stone and then into brilliant polished marble identical to that adorning my now shattered facade.

Emanating from the ground and fusing with my house, those marble tentacles formed great looping buttresses capped by witches frozen in mid-flight. It was a Gothically grotesque sight, those fifty or so broomstick witches with their mouths agape in shock and terror.

Yet, in its ugliness, it exuded a subtle beauty of form and verisimilitude found in the monumental sculptures of Raphael and Michelangelo.

Originally, I had intended to do something similar with mermaids, nymphs, and Nereids. Thankfully, necessity forced me to discard those hackneyed tropes and push the envelope further into the black frontier where the gruesome and the vile are elevated to new aesthetic heights.

I created a colossal, deviously complex Ostrobog to guard my estate. From a distance, it looked like a bulky muscular figure trapped in a geometric armature from which its bodily elements struggled to emerge. Its frenzy of dynamic motion conveyed the appearance of living tissue made of metal. The fluid, rippling planes of that body connected, intersected, and swirled in mysterious, reciprocal sympathies.

I also repurposed some of the witch buttresses. Now the crones emerge from and plunge into the ground. Likewise, on the roof, the she-devils penetrate the roof from above and others emerge from below. I peppered the grounds with witches exploding from the earth and others diving into it. I even have some on spokes colliding in mid-air. Still others intertwined in intersecting trellises.

Now my estate is the talk of the town, if not the world. Amazing is it not what a little determination and magic can do in the right hands?

Now, as for you, my silent friend, I must thank you for being patient and not struggling with the bindings. I can appreciate how uncomfortable it can be since my wives never liked it much. Nor the gags. Certainly, your being hog-tied to this chopping block with the sight of my newly sharpened axe mere feet away is likely to make anyone nervous. The mere thought of losing one's head to an axe stroke makes even an aesthetic assassin like me tremble.

The question is: What am I to do with you? You never understood my art. My work is nearer heaven than you could ever be. For I paint of myself to myself, unmoved by others' praise or blame.

To crown the issue, you proclaimed me amateur and fraud to our city's elders. But I could not abide an angry mob massing at my gates provoked by your slanders to hang me next to Bagby. When your slanders failed, you tried to kill me for murdering your sister. Lamia was it? I can never keep the names straight having dispatched so many.

I am leaning toward cutting out your tongue. Harsh yes, but I was not above burning out my own sister's eyes for giving me the evil eye. Now she walks around with two grisly craters where her eyes used to be.

If I could not stay my hand for her, then, how can I, in good conscience, do that for you?

I like to think of myself as the soul of civilized intellectual gentility with a taste for the better things in life. To you perhaps, my thought moves from the learned to an insane reasonableness leavened with a nightmarish conviviality.

Lunacy is the mark of all great souls. So naturally, great art, like great music, is mad with itself. I would sooner let my wife starve and my children go barefoot than renounce its call.

But enough of this one-sided palaver. That tongue of yours must go. We cannot have you stirring up the groundlings again. If, instead, you prefer a quick beheading, then know I have been practicing my swing, so it would not take more than two strokes to get the job done. In that event, I would bronze you holding your own head and stick you at the main gate. Your epigram would be: "I died cured of my disease."

The choice is yours.

# WHY I DON'T DRINK
*By Sarah Cannavo*

My dad was a mean drunk. Not that he was a peach to be around when he was sober, either, but shit, when he got some booze in him, watch out. Whiskey was his poison of choice—Old Number Seven, if he could get it; rotgut if he couldn't, and that was never hard to find in our little patch of Georgia. Sometimes, when he was really feeling bad, he'd send me out to get it for him, even when I was too young to legally set foot in the local liquor store. Pop Carlyle, the owner, knew who it was for and sold it to me anyway, just like the couple of neighbors with backyard stills did when I came knocking on their doors. Everybody knew Creighton Donnelly's boy would never touch a drop of it; I'd sworn off the stuff pretty damn early.

It went in cycles with my dad. He'd pick up a job somewhere and things would steady out a bit (which doesn't mean he didn't fly off the handle anymore, just that when he did he'd confine the beatings to bare hands instead of his belt or a birch switch, at least until I hit my growth spurt and dished it right back at him, spoiling his fun). Then he'd lose that job somehow—he was a great one for that; my old man lost jobs like toddlers lost milk teeth—and his collective shit along with it, blowing whatever he'd earned on whiskey and heading out to find a woman to try to make things better, though when he inevitably stumbled or stormed home I never saw much improvement in him; whatever good his lost nights did him he must've carried in his heart, making it impossible for anyone else to find. Most people, including me, doubted its existence. But what was undeniable were the times I called his black days, when he swung between sullen and snarling to raging and restless, all on some incalculable whim, when everything and everyone were his enemies and survival meant keeping your head down and staying the hell out of his way. And bad as it was when there was alcohol around, it was a thousand times worse when it ran out, trust me.

Eventually he'd find another job, and the cycle would start all over again. Occasionally, it wasn't getting fired that would set him off; it could be getting a court summons for his traffic violations, or getting locked up for a while for fighting or stealing, or getting turned down by some woman he'd been eyeing for awhile but who had too much of a brain to shack up with the likes of him. Creighton Donnelly didn't like folk telling him no, or standing up to him, or calling him on his bullshit. Not many people did, which is partly why he blew his stack so bad when someone finally would; the other part is that he was just a sonuvabitch, plain and simple, and the world would've been better off if someone had put him down when he was still young, the way you do with a dog that bites without provocation.

Anyway, like I was saying, whatever it was that set him off, eventually it'd pass and things would go back to our normal, which meant he'd be an asshole instead of a monster. Sometimes the in-between periods would last a while—one, when I was sixteen, lasted almost a year, a record by my reckoning—and sometimes I'd blink and he'd be slamming the screen door and revving the truck, roaring and ready for a hunt. You never could tell from one day to the next what was going to happen, just that it'd be ugly as the ass-end of Hell. It was, as you can probably guess, not an ideal way to grow up.

It was also the reason my mother was gone. I was eight when it happened, and I'm a grown man now, and I'd hoped at some point it might hurt a little less, but it doesn't. Not really. It's not exactly something I can blame her for, but it's sure as shit another in a long list of things I can hate him for.

And not to play the martyr or anything, but who do you think had to help clean up his messes when he got through making them? Not just the smaller ones, like the shit he broke around the house when he was raging, the holes in the walls, the screen door ripped off its hinges, the busted windows, but the big stuff, too: scrounging up bail when Warner Bailey or one of his deputies picked Pop up on drunk-and-disorderly or DUI or for picking another fight somewhere (Sheriff Bailey always gave me this sad look when I'd show up with the money, like he thought I deserved a better life or something, but I knew one way or another my dad was always gonna get out of jail, and it'd go worse for me when he did if I hadn't). Then, of course, there were the *really* big things, the late-night shake-awakes with his hot booze-scented breath hissing in my ear, "Linc, *Linc*, get your ass up *now,*" with a heavy-handed smack upside the head if I didn't obey fast enough.

Those nights he'd tell me to "keep goddamn quiet" and half-drag me out to where he'd crookedly parked the truck— a battered old Ford whose black paint helped it hide better at night. When I was real little, seven, eight, nine years old, and my dad first started using me as his little helper, the truck always seemed to me to be some kind of creature crouching, lurking in the darkness, haunting the woods around our house, and as I grew up I never fully lost that feeling, though even back then a part of me was well aware the truck wasn't the monster in my midst. The real one would open the truck door and pull a long, bulky shape wrapped in a tarp or blanket or sheet from the cab or, grunting and cursing, pull it from the bed, and snarl at me, "Get the shovel."

"Dad, what the—" I asked the first time it happened, rooted to the ground and staring at the black-wrapped parcel in utter confusion, wondering what it was. Dead deer, maybe; it had the size and looked to have the weight. But the truck was too together to have collided with one, and besides, if it *was* a deer Dad would've been trying to get as much meat as possible off its bones, not aiming to bury it.

My dad had looked at me with this horrible flat light in his bloodshot blue eyes, a look like I'd never seen even when he was getting ready to whip me a good one, and said, "I been huntin' tonight, boy, and if you don't get me that shovel, or you wake your momma up, I swear to holy Jesus you'll be goin' in that goddamn hole, too."

I got the shovel. I pissed myself a bit, but I got the shovel from the crawl space under the porch (which I'd been well and truly afraid of ever since a swarm of red-eyed rats had flooded from it and attacked my dog Bonham so badly my dad had to put him down, but right then I would've happily curled up there all night rather than spend a second longer in my dad's company), and we laid it on top of the tarp-shape. Each of us grabbed an end—I remember thinking for some reason Dad had the head and I was down by the feet, though there was absolutely nothing to indicate that—and the weight nearly dragged me down, but I did my best to keep up as my dad led us deeper into the pitch-black woods, moving along as if by memory.

*Deer,* seven-year-old me kept telling himself as we went. As Dad dug a hole a few feet deep in the clay and we rolled the tarp-shape into it with a thump that nailed itself to my brain. As we covered it back up and the crickets chorused in the black brush in counterpoint to each shovelful of earth that rained down on the hidden form. *Deer deer deer.* Why my dad would wake me up in the middle of the night to help him bury a deer was a matter for discussion, but my dad did crazy shit sometimes. He was, after all, a dirty stinking drunk.

*Deer. Definitely.*

Yeah, yeah, I know. You're sitting there reading this going, "How fucking stupid are you, Lincoln Donnelly? How could you not realize what your daddy was doing when he went out on his black days, and what exactly he and you were doing out in those woods? You either don't have the sense the good Lord gave a gopher or you just turned a blind eye to the whole thing, which makes you just as bad as your old man." And I totally get why you'd say that. But... fuck. That first night, I was *seven.* Ripped out of bed by a man with a temper like an active volcano but not as stable and led on some whacked-out errand at well past midnight— honestly, by the time I got back to bed the whole thing already seemed like some strange dream, and the next morning only the dried piss-stain in my shorts and the fresh clay caking the bottom of my shoes hinted it hadn't been. Whenever it happened, and that was irregularly, it had that unreal, nightmare-like quality to it, maybe my young mind trying to protect itself, maybe just ignorance, but there all the same.

And in case you couldn't've guessed, I was scared shitless of my father. Fucking terrified. This was a man who'd take a belt to my ass if I dared ask when he'd be home from Ol Joe's, the local bar where he did a lot of his troublemaking, and you wanted me to ask him exactly what we were burying in his personal graveyard in the woods? Maybe you could've; props to you if that's the case. You probably would've earned yourself your own plot in Creighton Donnelly's Eternal Rest in the Pines, but maybe to you it would've been worth it.

So no, I never pressed the issue too hard. Some questions are like dead skunks lying in the middle of the road: They're ugly enough on the outside, but poke 'em long enough and something a whole lot worse is bound to burst out. Better, it seemed for a while, not to ask.

One of the most fucked-up things about the situation (I know, shooting fish in a barrel) is for the longest time I thought it was normal. I mean, I had friends whose father and/or mother drank, whose father and/or mother beat whoever was handy or got picked up on the same charges that littered my dad's rap sheet, so for my young/naïve/stupid-as-stone brain it wasn't too far a leap to assume at least some of them did the same things at midnight that he did. None of them ever mentioned anything like it, but hell, we never mentioned any of the rest of it, either, just put it together from who showed up at school with a black eye they didn't get on the playground or whose mom passed out in front of Ol' Joe's on a Friday night. So who was to say they didn't?

Then I turned seventeen, and the name on the news, on the tongues of everyone that still had one, was the Silencer, which is just about the shittiest name for a serial killer I've ever heard, but I guess his methodology didn't leave the press much room to maneuver (though Internet trolls had a fucking field day, that's for sure). A jogger out with her dog, because these sorts of discoveries are always made by a jogger out with their dog, came across the corpse of a woman in a stand of trees on the edge of a public park, the mound of earth above her having been dislodged by a week of heavy rain. The body had begun to decompose but was intact enough for her wounds to be on full gruesome display: throat slit open like an envelope, the part of her that used to be between her legs relocated to her mouth—it took them a bit to realize her tongue'd been cut out, too, and the cops deliberately neglected to mention the neck of a broken whiskey bottle retrieved from her rotting rectum, hoping to weed out any false confessions that might get made.

She turned out to be Debbie Lambert, a twenty-six-year-old waitress who'd vanished two weeks before after finishing up a night shift. She also opened a floodgate once it was determined the method of her death matched the M.O. of the Silencer, a serial killer with a string of cold cases in his wake spanning the last thirty or so years—sixteen victims so far but more suspected, scattered erratically over the decades and the state. I was four the last time one of his victims had been found, too young to remember any hype, but now I sat and watched the news, amazed and disgusted by the depravity one human being, to use the term loosely, could enact on another. They had a criminal profiler on, who said the Silencer preferred to get up close and personal with his kills, suggesting a kind of twisted intimacy, and also harbored deep resentment and/or hatred of women, which apparently he needed a college degree to figure out.

Debbie was found a county over and there was nothing that suggested a connection to my father until the newscaster mentioned the name of the bar where she'd worked, which I remembered my dad mentioning he'd hit up recently. Not that there was a bar in Georgia my dad hadn't set foot in at one time or another, but what jolted me up on the couch was remembering *when* Dad had gone: a couple weeks ago, right when Debbie had gone missing.

And sure, a lot of guys had gone there then—hell, maybe the bartender had done it, or one of the regulars. But then the TV flashed a 'before' picture of Debbie onscreen, and though I'd never seen her before in my life she was stunningly familiar. With her dark curls, delicate features, and bright wide smile, she looked eerily like my mother.

My vanished mother. My departed mother. The mother who, I'd come home from school one day at eight years old to discover, had packed her things and left—because, my dad had explained, already half a bottle deep, she'd wanted her freedom when all she'd ever done was begrudge him every bit of his. Even then I'd read it as her being tired of the rages, the drinking, the days and nights spent away with other women, and I'd understood her desire to escape, just wished she'd taken me with her. But looking at dear departed Debbie and the parade of past-victim snapshots marching across our cracked TV, all of whom bore a resemblance to the former Marie Donnelly in some way, faint or distinct, even in the victims that predated my parents meeting, I wondered for the first time if maybe she hadn't had a choice.

I was surprisingly calm and methodical about it. My dad was at Tugger Welk's, one of our neighbors, enjoying a taste of 'shine fresh from the still, and I knew I had time. I got pencil and paper and, in that reeking living room, listed all the murders and disappearances the Silencer was suspected of, then, best I could remember, my dad's own disappearances during his black days, and compared them.

I'll spare you the suspense. Like my mom and Debbie Lambert, they were disturbingly similar. Some of the older disappearances happened close to home ("Linc, get your ass *up"*) and murders that happened farther away, like Cori Graham's up near Decatur, coincided with my dad staying away for days at a time. Some of the dates I was fuzzy on, but most matched, and if it looks like a pig, et cetera.

I sat there for a good long while, thinking things over, and when I regained sensation in my legs I went and did what dear old Dad had several times ordered a terrified child to do: got the shovel.

I'd tried, once or twice in the past, to retrace the paths my dad had led me down with his burdens between us, never with any success. Child-me had kept his focus mainly on making one step, then the next, then the next, and avoiding any action that could make the ogre ahead of him angry, not mentally marking the way, and in daylight the woods had always seemed so different. I also might not've tried too hard, full disclosure—that whole poking-the-dead-skunk thing again.

But that day I did. It took a while, and even when I reached a spot I thought we might've visited, I was never more than half-sure and had to space my digging out to cover as much area as possible. That took a while, too, but like I said, I had time; Dad never pulled a drive-by at Tugger's. And while he was out getting blitzed I dug and dug and dug until my muscles were on fire and I could hardly see for sweat, dug until, in the third place I tried, my shovel tore into a rotting white sheet, and a human hand, half-bare bone articulated by leathery muscle, flopped free, as though the occupant of the undignified grave was waving, glad to see me again.

Third time's the charm, I guess.

I remembered five trips into the woods with my father; later, when the investigators took over the area, they exhumed six bodies. Mom hadn't gone too far after all. The graves weren't packed close—once-pretty maids not all in a row, but spread out over a mile or two, all killed, it was determined, in the Silencer's favored way.

After I'd dug up that corpse (Ariel Kooning, a stripper who worked a pole a town over), I lost a bit of time. I know I vomited at least once; the evidence was on my boots when I finally found myself at home. I think I screamed; my throat was hoarse enough. Trying to remember, all I get is illness, rage, a fever of guilt and shame—if I'd told someone, if I hadn't spent years cowering like the frightened child I admittedly was...

Memory clears when I heard Dad's truck in the drive, heard him stumbling to the door and skittering the key over the lock several times before managing to fit it in. That's when I realized I was in our filthy living room, still holding the clay-caked shovel. And when that door opened, admitting my father and a cloud of booze fumes, as if he'd bathed in Tugger's still, I swung the shovel hard as I could and connected squarely with his face.

I remember *that.* I remember the crunch of bone, the hot burst of bright red blood from his ruined nose, his thick garbled cry of surprise. I remember him wheeling, sputtering more blood from between broken teeth, and lunging at him like an animal, tossing the shovel away in favor of my fists as we rolled on the floor, me dishing back every blow he'd dealt me over the years and more for those women with the misfortune to have crossed his path on the wrong damn day.

I made him suffer—not as badly as he should've, maybe, but I did my best. I didn't kill him, though. I left him lying there, bloodied and broken and abruptly sober, and called Warner Bailey (why, of all the times the cops'd pulled my dad over, it'd never been when he'd had a body in his trunk I'll never understand) to come scrape him up.

Half of you are demanding to know why I didn't do it, pointing out it's what he deserved. Half are congratulating me, saying I'd be no better than him if I had. But that's not why I didn't.

I'm not saying drinking made my dad a killer. That was who he was. Whiskey didn't put those vile urges in him, just brought out what was already there. That's true of everyone who drinks, though with my dad it was to a more extreme degree than most. He could've sought help but chose not to, chose to surrender to both his compulsions no matter who got hurt, because they made him feel good. He was responsible for every drink and life he took.

But I've heard problems like his can run in families, and, to bring all this full-circle, I didn't kill my father when I was standing over him, watching him snivel and whimper and bleed, though every fiber of my being was screaming at me to *do it, do it, do it,* for the same reason I long ago decided never to drink.

Because I'm worried I might like it a little too much.

# BEST FRIENDS
*By Mark Towse*

Waiting for his big moment, Arthur stood patiently at the back of the room with his hand thrust deep into his shorts' pockets. Momentarily, he wished his ex-wife, Janet, could be there, just to see him achieve something for once; to demonstrate he wasn't a complete failure. But Janet left him for some flash prick from the city just under two years ago. What made it worse, the guy was even older than him.

Gold digger.

*It's nearly time*, he thought, surveying the crowd to make sure all the important people were there. He even had a speech planned. He was going to devote it to Gerald, his best friend. It had been a year to the day since his death, and Arthur found it hard to believe it had been that long since they were at his barn, celebrating Gerald winning the rosette for biggest marrow for the fourth year in a row. The speech was going to be a nice touch, Arthur thought—sure to bring tears to many eyes. Arthur loved giving speeches. He enjoyed being center stage when the rare opportunity offered itself.

Adrenaline induced an involuntary shudder down his spine as the speaker, Fat Pat, took to the stand.

"The next category is for biggest marrow," Pat announced, eyes directed towards Norma on the front row and giving her a sympathetic nod. "It's still hard to believe our four-time winner, Gerald, is no longer with us," he croaked, loosening his collar with a chubby finger. "Just not the same."

*Fuck off, Pat*, Arthur thought. *You won't spoil this for me.*

"Each contestant will bring theirs to the front when announced, please," Pat said. "Kicking off with—let me see—Tom Stevenson. Come on, Tom!"

One by one, the contestants wheelbarrowed their offering to the large wooden table where they were assisted by Big Tony. Arthur knew even before Tony lifted each of the marrows onto the scales, that they were all far inferior to the beauty that he had nurtured over recent weeks.

"And finally, last year's runner-up, Arthur Pinkerton. You have eighty-six pounds to beat, Arthur."

Arthur grimaced as he lifted the wheelbarrow. People turned. It was his big moment.

As he began to push, the wheels squeaked noisily. He enjoyed the gasps and chatter as he made his way through the centre of the crowd. It choked him up a little, triggering memories of escorting his daughter down the church aisle. That was a proud day. But this was going to be even more special, he thought.

When he got to the front, he took pleasure in watching Tony's mouth drop open. The guy was six-foot-three with arms like tree trunks, but it took the two of them and Fat Pat to drag it onto the table.

"Wow. I think we have a winner," Pat said. "Could be a new record even. Let's find out. Tony, over to you."

Necks craned, and the room came alive with murmurs of excitement. Arthur ran his eyes over the audience and was pleased to see all eyes were aimed at him and his marrow. Norma, Gerald's widow, had a stoic look on her face that gave nothing away.

"Tony, when you're ready," Pat announced, following up with a nervous giggle.

"I'm bloody trying, Pat," Tony replied, face as red as the beetroots on the table behind.

*Come on*, Arthur thought. *Get it on the bloody scales, you big chunk of uselessness.* He knew Tony was going to find it a struggle, though—the only way he could get it into the wheelbarrow was to use his tractor.

And then the marrow pulsated. Only once, but it was violent, loud, and unmistakable—a temporary network of dark green veins lining the skin of the vegetable. And that sound, it reminded Arthur of the first time he heard his daughter moving inside the womb, but with dread replacing excitement. And—had it got even bigger?

The crowd went quiet. Arthur, Pat, and Tony gave each other a look to verify they had all seen the same thing.

*Get it on the scales*, Arthur thought. *Quickly.* "Come on, Tony, after three," he said, enthusiastically.

Warily, the three of them began to count down, eyes wide and fixed on the marrow. Another pulse, and this one even violent—veins more exaggerated and a loud whooshing sound that lingered in Arthur's ears for seconds afterwards.

Another pulse. Louder, more urgent.

And another.

The chatter started again, but this time it was nervous and frantic. People started getting up to leave, clumsily brushing against each other as they backed away, struggling to take their eyes from the giant marrow that appeared to be expanding in front of their very eyes.

The marrow was now maintaining a consistent pulse, as though it had developed a heartbeat.

"No, wait!" Arthur screamed. "We have to weigh it. It's going to be record-breaker!"

But it was too late; the crowd was all but gone. Norma remained seated on the front row, though, face unchanged and emotionless.

"I'm sorry, Arthur," Tony mumbled as he began to follow Pat out the tent. Arthur took a few steps forward and grabbed Tony's arm, pleading with him to come back so they could weigh the marrow. Tony snapped his head around and raised one large bushy eyebrow. Arthur immediately let go.

A smile crept across Norma's face then, and Arthur thought it to be a not particularly warm one.

The pain was instant and explosive as the first green vine wrapped around his waist, large razor-sharp thorns embedding into his sun-damaged skin. As he let out a garbled yelp, another vine locked around his legs, lacerating them with deep cuts that sent crimson spilling down his sagging brown flesh.

"Norma! Help!"

The next one lassoed around his neck and began to squeeze.

"Norma, please!"

She finally got up and made her way towards him. "I'm sorry, Arthur. This is what he wanted."

More green shoots fired out, hooking into his skin. Slowly, they started drawing him back towards the marrow.

Arthur flailed at his neck, trying to desperately to get his fingers between his skin and the vine, but it began to squeeze even tighter.

"You see, he knows what you did, Arthur," she said, stopping a few feet in front of him. "As do I."

Arthur's body felt like it was on fire, nerve endings singing in unified agony. Suddenly, from behind, a different sound emerged—a chunky snapping sound that sent his heart rate pounding even faster. Stomach lurching, eyes wide with fear, he turned to see the crack developing across the middle of the giant vegetable. All the time, the thick green limbs pulled him closer towards it.

"I remember it all so well—Gerald asking if you had anything stronger than beer, and you sending him into your barn for vodka and two glasses."

"Norma, it was an accident; you know that. Gerald was drunk and used the wrong bottle, that's all," Arthur croaked. "It was just—unfortunate." Blood pounded in Arthur's ears as the pressure around his neck continued to increase.

"When Gerald began to writhe on the floor, you pulled out your phone without a second of hesitation. There was no surprise or shock in your eyes. Your actions were too urgent, Arthur. One might say, almost planned."

Arthur began to scream as the vegetable opened slowly like a mouth to reveal multiple layers of saw-like thorns and a marshy tongue made up of soil and roots. It reminded him of something he'd seen on a late-night horror movie, only this time he wasn't laughing. He started to scream again, a high-pitched blood-curdling effort that was cut short by another green limb that whipped across his face and slipped inside his mouth. Its taste was bitter and earthy. But there was something else. What was that smell? Dank, vegetative, with a whiff of—Old Spice? *No. No way.*

The smell unleashed images of his old friend, Gerald. Only, there was no sentimental nostalgia, only renewed feelings of jealousy and rage. Gerald had it all—the good-looking and faithful wife, the big house with endless land, the boat, and the prize-winning reputation. And with it, the ego. The underlying hatred seethed for decades—Arthur always in the shadows, second best. But Arthur knew Gerald was really just a drunk that had come into family money. Countless evenings spent drinking together in their houses and barns resulted in covering his friend with old blankets and helping nurse the hangovers the next morning. Gerald got worse towards the end, ostentatiously rowdy and sometimes quite abusive.

"You didn't plan on me following you into the barn through, did you, Arthur? I saw you take the label off that bottle full of weed killer and put the real vodka on the bench. You knew it was only a matter of time before he went to the harder stuff, him being a drunk and all."

"… accident …" Arthur croaked, saliva leaking down his chin.

"I guess the drinking got to you, too. Or was it the fact that your life fell apart and that Gerald's seemed so perfect in contrast? I guess it doesn't really matter. I must say, though, you continued to play the part of the best friend very well. You even looked genuinely upset when you gave your speech at the funeral."

"Please, Norma," Arthur tried to say, but his words were muffled and inaudible.

"You have to understand, Arthur; Gerald was a bastard to me. Did you know he used to beat me—after he'd been drinking? I wouldn't leave the house for days sometimes, waiting for the bruises to fade. Nobody knew. He said he would kill me if I ever ratted. I lived in fear, especially towards the end—even thought about it doing it myself. That's the only reason I concurred it was an accident, that he'd simply poured from the first bottle he could get his grubby little soil-stained hands-on."

Arthur was now only a few feet from the jaws of the giant vegetable and its swirling tongue. The veins of the marrow pulsated intensely, and the whooshing sound had developed into something even more sinister—loud, alien, not of this world. He tried desperately to plant his feet firmly into the ground, but the limbs continued to reel him in; they were just too strong. Suddenly his head was snapped back, and he let out a muffled scream as the bottom row of thorns pierced the back of his neck. His eyes focused on the swirling tongue above and the top layer of sharpness that now loomed only inches from his face.

"I thought I'd got a free pass, Arthur. But he came back, you see. That same night when I thought I could finally lay my head down and not dread getting up the next day, he came to me from the dark recesses, liquor on his breath, and Old Spice leaking from his pores. He told me that the Devil showed him what you did; said that he wanted his ashes sprinkled on your field and that vengeance would be his. I'm sorry, Arthur, but he threatened to never leave me alone if I didn't. I made a deal that I wasn't proud of, but I hope you understand that I had no choice."

Arthur felt the warm trickle running down his leg as observed the workings of the organic machinery within the marrow. It was alive—there was no doubt. Shades of green pulsated and writhed against each other, creating wet sounds that humanized the marrow further. He tried to scream, but the limb occupying his mouth slipped down his throat. Instinctively, he tried to suck in some air, but panic immediately set in as his chest tightened. He could feel the green root working its way down his esophagus, thorns tearing at vulnerable muscles.

"When I woke up, I thought at first it might have been a dream, but then I saw the footprints of soil next to my bed. I couldn't stand the thought of him lording over me in death after all these years of praying for it to happen."

Arthur felt life ebbing away from him. Each failed attempt at trying to suck in the air increased the pressure across his chest. He felt like he was going to explode.

Norma watched as Arthur raised his hand weakly towards her. She was surprised at the lack of guilt she felt, but then again, the man with his head in the marrow had murdered her husband. As she turned and walked away, she hoped that she would be able to finally put it all behind her. "Best friends," she whispered under her breath as she shook her head. It prompted a giggle that even surprised her.

She heard the sound of Arthur's skull being crushed and the subsequent chomping sounds as she neared the exit of the tent.

# ALI BABA AND THE SOUL THIEVES
*By John Kojak*

My name is Martin Ficklin. I used to be a Euthanasia Technician with the Dignified Departures Company. Some people called what I did murder, but I told them those stiffs were dead already. They had the cancer, heart disease, lupus—everything but hope.

That's what I brought them. Hope. It was called the EM5000. The EM was short for euthanasia machine—like the one Jack Kevorkian built: the Thanotron. But his death machine was a piece of crap he built in his garage out of broom handles and Erector sets. If it were a car, it would have been a Ford Pinto.

The EM5000 was a Ferrari.

The work wasn't bad, like people think, and I never had a problem with any of my clients until the morning I was dispatched to a home in Breyerville—an old, well-to-do neighborhood on the west side of the city. It should have been a quick job, in-and-out in under an hour, and as I pulled up to the house I was already thinking about grabbing some food and heading downtown to watch a ball game—but that never happened.

I parked on the street, grabbed the EM5000, and walked up the long, winding brick path to the white, two-story home's column-lined porch. I rang the bell, and a few moments later a tall, slender black woman in a colorful green and yellow flowing dress answered the door.

"Hello, I'm Martin from Dignified Departures."

"Hello, Mar-tin. We've been expecting you," she said in a sweet Caribbean Creole accent.

"Are you the nurse?"

She ushered me inside a large foyer with white marble floors and a big dusty crystal chandelier. You could smell the money. "I'm Alma. I take care of Miss Norma."

It looked like she was taking pretty good care of herself as well. Her hands were dripping with big shiny rings, and she had on a long gold necklace that hung down to her waist. I didn't know if she had been ripping the old cooze off, or had worked herself into the will, but she looked downright giddy I was there.

"She's in the back; follow me."

Alma was light in front but heavy in the rear, like a lobster, and she walked with a slow island sashay that mesmerized me with its hypnotic rhythm as I followed her down a long corridor toward the back of the house.

"This be Norma." Alma waived her hand dismissively toward the bed as we entered the back bedroom. The easy smile she had flashed at the door was gone, replaced by a contemptuous scowl.

Norma, or what was left of her, was barely visible under the heavy duvet that covered the bed. All I could see of her was her face, which looked like an old peach that had been drying in the sun for a hundred years. She had bright blue eyes though, like a little girl's that still sparkled out from beneath all of those wrinkles. A large, heavy framed picture hung on the wall across from the bed. A statuesque blond with pale skin and delicate looking hands, was sitting next to a proud looking bald man with round wire-rimmed glasses. There were two small children kneeling at their feet. They looked happy, but the photo was old. Everything in the house was old.

I checked my paperwork: Norma Bernbaum. Widow. 98 years old. Paid in Full. "Mrs. Bernbaum, my name is Martin. I am with the Dignified Departures Company."

"She don't talk no more. But she knows why you're here. Best to just get on with it."

"Sure," I said. I knew how it worked. The families and caregivers were usually just as tired of my clients being alive as the clients were of living. "I just need someplace to set up my equipment."

Alma walked over to the nightstand and swept the half dozen or so prescription bottles off the top of the nightstand and onto the floor. "She won't be needing those anymore."

I swear the chill in her voice lowered the temperature in the room a couple of degrees, but it was true. Norma Bernbaum wasn't going to need anything soon, except a good mortician.

I placed the aluminum case containing the EM5000 on the nightstand.

"Is that it? I thought it would be bigger."

Half-a-dozen crude jokes flashed through my mind. I always tried to maintain a solemn demeanor at times like those; sometimes I was more successful than others. "That's what my ex-wife said," I replied flatly.

The scowl Alma had worn since we entered the room cracked into a grin.

I flipped the latches and opened the clamshell case. The upper half of the case held the vaporizer chamber, a small rectangular box that worked like an e-cigarette, but instead of vaporizing vials of cherry-cola flavored nicotine, it vaporized Dignified Departures' proprietary death juice concoctions. Beneath the vaporizer, were four rows of small surgical steel cartridges, each about the size of an AA battery, which contained the drugs and snapped into ports on the front of the vaporizer chamber. The bottom half of the case contained the oxygen tank, mask, hoses, and a small pulse monitor that attached to the client's wrist.

I reached under the covers and felt around for Norma's arm. It was as thin and frail as a child's. I pulled it out, attached the wristband, and turned on the monitor. Her heart rate was low; barely registering fifteen beats a minute. I placed the mask over her nose and mouth, and turned on the oxygen. Norma's eyes followed me silently as I worked, but she never moved so much as a finger.

The vaporizer chamber had three output ports along the top, and one input port on the bottom. I took a cartridge from the first row that contained sodium thiopental, a barbiturate that ensured the patient would feel no pain, and inserted it into the first output port on the vaporizer. Next came a cartridge from the second row containing pancuronium bromide, a paralytic that induced respiratory failure, and then one from the third row that held the kicker, potassium chloride, to stop the heart. I placed an empty cartridge from the fourth row into the input port on the bottom of the unit— I will tell you more about that one later—and looked over at Alma. "It's ready. Did her children, or anyone in her family, leave any final instructions?"

Alma scoffed. "Her children dead, no family neither. All she had left was me."

"Once I start the machine, there is no going back. Do you have anything—a prayer, or final words—you want to say to her?"

Alma reached into a dresser drawer and pulled out a large doll, about eighteen inches tall, wearing a white silk dress with a purple lace veil. It had a ghoulish looking porcelain face, tangled gray wooly hair, and a small chain around its neck with a silver cross and skull hanging from it.

She walked over to Norma and placed the doll beside her in the bed.

"What's that?" I asked, although I was pretty sure I knew what it was—a Voodoo doll.

"That be Madame Bridget; she gonna help Norma on her journey."

I can't say I was surprised. A lot of the caregivers I worked with were Haitians or Dominicans, and I couldn't get through half my jobs without someone waiving around a chicken's foot or some crazy thing.

Alma wrapped Norma's right arm around the doll, and then bent over and began whispering a strange tongue into Norma's ear. I couldn't make out the words, but it sounded more like a curse than a prayer. After Alma was done, she stepped back behind me. "She ready now Mar-tin."

I checked Norma's pulse again. It had slowed to a catatonic ten beats a minute. Norma was just about dead already, but someone had paid a lot of money for her to have a dignified departure®, so that is what she was going to get. I pressed a button on the front of the vaporizer and held it down until a small red light began to flash. It only took a few seconds for the heating element to reach temperature; then there was a low hissing sound as the liquefied barbiturate in the first canister was vaporized and fed into the oxygen tubes. Thirty seconds latter a yellow light came on, and the paralytic entered the system. Her breathing became strained and her heartbeat dropped to six beats a minute. A few moments later the green light flashed, the last canister was vaporized, and her pulse flat lined.

After her heart stopped, I pressed another button on the vaporizer unit. This one engaged a small fan inside the device that pulled the remaining air in the mask back into the chamber and across a cooling element that condensed the vapors back into liquid form. The company called it residual vapor retrieval, and said it was necessary to ensure that some poor slob like me didn't suck in a mouthful of potassium chloride when he took the client's mask back off and disconnected the tubes. It made sense, at least to me, but there was a rumor floating around the Internet that the fan's real purpose was to suck out the person's soul and capture it in the empty canister. Once the media got wind of the rumor, they started calling Dr. Alfonso Babano, the inventor of the EM5000, 'Ali Baba,' and guys like me 'soul thieves.'

"Is she gone?" Alma asked.

"Yes, she's dead. There are a few papers I need you to sign, and then—"

"Did you get it?"

"Get what?"

"Her soul…" Apparently Alma had heard the rumors.

"You shouldn't believe everything you read on the Internet," I said, leaning over to remove the mask from Norma's face. As I turned to place it back in the case, I saw Alma moving towards me with her hand cupped in front of her mouth, as though she was about to cough. Suddenly a cloud of white powder shot out toward me.

"You not the only one with magic, Mar-tin." She said as I collapsed onto the floor. "Dat some zombie powder, same I gave Miss Norma this morning. It not gonna hurt you, just make you lay real still for awhile."

My body folded over on itself, with my left arm twisted awkwardly behind my head and my right knee pushing into my chest. I tried to lift myself up, but I couldn't move.

"I don't know what that old goat was holding on for. Everyone she ever loved was dead. I was going to kill her myself a few months ago. But death would have been letting her off too easy for all the things she done to me." Alma's almond-shaped eyes flared with anger. "That damn woman treated me like a slave!"

I watched as Alma walked over to the EM5000. "But then, I heard about you soul thieves…" She removed the bottom canister, and slipped it into a small clay jar. "Now she gonna be my slave." I heard something shatter against the wall. "Me and Papa Legba gonna show her what Hell *really* is!"

I waited for something to come crashing down on my head, for the lights to go out forever, but they never did.

"Goodbye, Mar-tin." Alma said in the same sweet Creole accent she had greeted me with. "Never let anyone steal your soul," she said before calmly sashaying out of the room. A few moments later the front door slammed shut.

I had heard of zombie powder. It's made from the glands of puffer fish, which contain a poison called tetrodotoxin, a paralytic similar to pancuronium bromide that shuts down the nervous system and slows breathing. Some of the big pharmaceutical companies have tried to harness the toxin, but its effects are too unpredictable. It was just as likely to kill me as turn me into a zombie, but I got lucky, and by the middle of the next day the effects of the poison began to wear off. I was eventually able to untwist my body and gather up my equipment. The first thing I did was drive back to the office and turn in the EM5000, then I packed up my belongings and moved as far away from Breyerville and the Dignified Departures Company as I could get. That was two years ago. I have tried to scrub Alma out of my mind every day since then, but her words still haunt me. *Never let anyone steal your soul*—that's goddamn right.

# BITE
### By Hayden Gilbert

Greg Smalley woke up to a good sight. It was one he was sure would be the first and, if the last few years of his life were any sign of what was to come, probably the last warm and cheerful moment of the day. His dog, the red heeler named Charlie, stood over him on his bed and, after seeing the old man's eyes creak open to greet the morning, furiously began to assault Greg's face with his soft, wet tongue. Greg groaned sleepily and managed to push Charlie to the side after a few pats and scratches.

Charlie whined, hungry for his morning meal and Greg rose from bed as fast as he could, his back and legs straining and pulling, sending fire up and down his muscles.

Greg poured the dog a bowlful of chow, topping it with a leftover chicken breast from the fridge, and was hit with the sudden urge to go to the restroom, shuffling for the toilet on aching feet, and a few minutes later when he wiped, there was less blood than had been there the day before, so he considered that a good thing. As good as it gets.

He turned on the television, where he would probably sit and read—not paying enough attention to the TV because of the book, and not paying enough attention to the book because of the TV—and made himself a bowl of oatmeal.

When he finally sat down in front of the TV, Charlie was by his side, laying on the ground and staring toward the door.

"In a bit, buddy," Greg said. "Promise."

His phone buzzed across the room and he rose once again, ankles trembling, and shuffled painfully across the floor. He hoped it might be his son Bill calling for anything, even to shoot the shit about the weather, but his head told him better. Greg wasn't healthy or wealthy or lucky, but he was intuitive, and when he reached the phone where it lay on the bookshelf by the hallway, the screen did not read *BILL*, but *UNKNOWN*. Greg shook his head and hung up before answering.

Since he was already up and the oatmeal was tasteless anyways, he looked to the door and then to Charlie.

"Well," he said. "Whatcha say, buddy?"

Charlie leapt to his feet, barked twice, and spun in circles while Greg fetched the leash.

* * *

Charlie wheezed as he choked himself against his collar. Greg huffed and puffed as he struggled to keep up with the old dog. These walks were good for both of them. They were also really the only time they left the house.

"Hold on there, boy," Greg said.

Charlie did not hold on; he never did.

"You wanna coon dog it, do you?" Greg asked and at that threat, Charlie eased up slightly.

The heeler lead by his nose, sniffing the side of the road as it wound around the block searching for new scents and smells to enrich his palate.

Where Greg lived had once been far more remote than it was today. They walked by a clearing where several houses were being built, the foundations laid out but not much else. Pretty soon there might be plans to develop a subdivision around them. Pioneers, they must have fancied themselves. But the real pioneers were Greg and Angela before them, who built their house out here on Hickam Road when it was nothing but a dirt path leading to the national forest. Back then it was only a bunch of trees, a real mess of them, tall and towering pines and the creatures that lived amongst them. They had many fond memories back here before Billy and before the accident, and until, that is, the trailer trash had moved in.

Greg held his breath while he passed the first trailer of the Sader family like he was passing by a graveyard. They had moved in a few years after Greg and Angela and had brought their extended family with them, all in identical Airstream trailers. After they moved in, the road became very busy at all hours of the night as visitors and "friends" of the Saders came by for who knew what. The Saders' teenage kids were in and out during nighttime as well. Their headlights cut through the trees and into Greg and Angela's windows, stirring them awake constantly. They didn't think much of it until years later when Angela was on her way home from a late shift and the Saders' older kid came peeling around that corner in their brand-new, jacked-up Jeep Wagoneer.

Greg bit his tongue and tried very hard not to think too much about it when suddenly Charlie struggled harder against his leash. There was a squirrel in the road ahead, seemingly teasing Charlie, whose muzzle began frothing and whose whines became erratic.

Greg's arm popped as the dog thrashed against its collar and with a twist and jerk; the leash came free of Greg's hand and Charlie bolted.

"Charlie!" Greg yelled.

*Shit*, Greg thought.

There on the stoop of the furthest trailer, growling low, was the Saders' young but big Rottweiler, Brawler.

As Charlie raced ahead toward the fleeing squirrel, Brawler stood up, his large shoulders poised to launch him from the porch at any moment, and once Charlie had reached the tree across the road from their driveway, launch he did.

"Shit!" Greg said. "Sader! Dammit, Sader! Get a hold of your animal!"

Greg trudged ahead as fast as he could but the Rott was much faster. The big, black bull of a dog barreled through the air between it and the little heeler and tackled Charlie, who sat at the base of the tree, unsuspecting. They tussled on the ground and Charlie thrashed his maw forward, ripping at Brawler's neck, but the big animal simply shoved the heeler's head aside, took Charlie by the throat, and whipped him back and forth. Charlie let out a high-pitched squeal and Greg felt like his stomach fell out of his ass.

Greg bent to the ground and scrabbled for anything, managing to snatch up a few rocks and hurled them at the frothing beast. The first flew clear past, striking the knot of a tree, but the second thudded against the Rottweiler's broad side and bounced off like it was nothing.

Greg threw his hands in the air, trying desperately to shoo the animal away, but it only turned its attention on him. It was then that Greg's anger was overcome by fear as the dog growled again. Its mouth dripped blood and it steadied itself to rush forward.

As darkness crept at the edge of Greg's vision, the Rottweiler bounding forward, he heard a sharp whistle and, at once, the big dog stopped in his tracks and turned its head. Leighton Sader stood on his front porch and called for his dog: "Get back here!"

The dog obeyed immediately.

Greg stood there in the road, his knees weak, his ankles and eyes on fire, and he rushed the rest of the way to his dog. Charlie lay in a bloody heap but still breathing.

Despite the pain, Greg fell to his knees at the dog's side and laid his hands on its auburn fur, feeling the rise and fall of its slow breaths.

The dog whimpered but Greg managed, "It's alright, boy. It's okay."

He looked over and saw one of the younger Sader boys, Luke, emerge from the trailer.

"What happened?" the boy asked.

"Get back inside," Leighton said as he wrestled with the Rottweiler, trying for the scruff of its neck with his hand,

"Dad, what happened?" the boy repeated.

Leighton raised a hand, about to strike the boy, but the young boy Luke fell back inside quickly and without another word. The man, lean with muscle, led the dog inside the trailer. When they had disappeared inside, Greg heard the animal make a horrible, sharp noise, and then it began to whimper.

Greg looked back to Charlie who blinked at him, slowly.

Leighton returned outside and spat tobacco from his mouth over the porch railing. He made his way down the driveway at a casual pace.

"What's the damage?" Leighton said.

Greg looked his dog over and wiped a tear from his eye.

"It doesn't look good," he said, "but he's breathing."

"Lucky."

Greg regarded his neighbor with the same eyes he had many years ago.

"Seen him take down dogs bigger than that. Hell, seen that animal take down a young deer before, out there by the fence."

"That dog shouldn't be off a leash," Greg said, stroking Charlie's coat.

"Hell he shouldn't," Leighton said.

"Your dog is dangerous, Sader. I should report this."

And then Leighton Sader did something, intentional or not, that Greg could not believe.

He smiled.

"You want to call the cops because my dog bit up your dog after he was trespassing?"

Greg looked at him more sternly.

"What did you say?"

"Your dog ran up here trespassing, and we ain't got no use for animals of the like."

It took all he had not to throw a punch at the man. Not only was Leighton Sader younger and in better shape, but he had the air of a man who would feel no shame in sending an old man to the hospital.

Leighton spat again then walked inside.

Greg held his head in his hands, then managed to collect Charlie in his arms, and walked home.

* * *

A week had gone by and Charlie still couldn't walk or "talk" well.

In the mornings, instead of whimpering in that gleeful way for his food, the heeler would instead just hiss, as his voice could not collect, only escape. The vet had inadvertently agreed with Leighton Sader. Charlie was lucky, indeed.

As Greg regarded his dog, his buddy, lying there on his side unable to sleep or do anything else because of the pain, he thought, *what great luck.*

The new routine was helping the dog eat, watching the dog try and drift off to sleep, and holding the shivering dog at night as that mongrel from down the road barked outside their window.

With Charlie out of commission, Brawler had taken ownership of the road and would often sneak over in the middle of the night and growl or bark that incessant, repetitive bark for hours and hours. In the morning light, the dog would be gone, but there would be several massive piles of droppings on Greg's front lawn, just a reminder.

At the end of the week, Greg—feeling Charlie quiver in his arms at the familiar sounds of that sinister snarl right on the other side of the glass, picturing that face in the darkness, drool pooling at its paws, its tongue lapping for the blood it had tasted enough of to leave a thirst unquenched—had begun thinking of the day he and Angela had built their first house. It had turned out to be their last house as well. The day their power went out after the hurricane and they made love all night to drown out the sounds of the wind. They were so secluded it had taken two weeks to get the power back on, but they had fucked each other silly every night until that air conditioner kicked back on and began to cool the sweat on their bodies. He remembered Billy scribbling on the walls in crayon and turning seven and wanting to be called Bill. He remembered having to tell Bill that his mother wouldn't be coming home from the hospital that night, or any night afterward. He remembered making macaroni and cheese for Bill for a month straight because it was the only thing he would eat. And he remembered the day Bill had gotten his father a puppy for his birthday so that he wouldn't be so lonely and would stop "blowing up my phone all day."

So the next night when Brawler came back, waiting for him outside the bedroom window was a meat patty stuffed with rat poison. A lot of rat poison. And in the early morning light, Greg was delighted to find, instead of a heaping pile of dog shit, the shit dog himself, lying on his side, his eyes open and staring into nothing. He looked at it for a long time, waiting to see the rib cage rise, waiting for the realization that this thing had somehow deceived him. It would have been one last trick, and a fine one at that. Imagining that the beast would come for him, biting at him with pearl-white teeth and stripping him of his flesh and probably his testicles.

But that didn't happen; the dog did not move and its eyes did not blink.

For good measure, and because poisoning the animal hadn't quite given him the satisfaction he felt he deserved, Greg stepped on the dog's head until he couldn't feel his ankle anymore.

Taking an old shower curtain, Greg wrapped the dog well and drove it to the creek, swollen with late-summer rain, where he dumped the body.

That night, he and Charlie were able to enjoy their first night of restful sleep in a week.

* * *

A few days passed and there was a knock at the door.

Foolishly Greg thought for a second that it might be his son, but only for a second. His head won out again and it was not Bill, but Leighton's son Luke.

When Greg saw the boy on the doorstep, he was surprised to see that he did not wear the slightest hint of anxiety.

"Can I help you?" Greg asked.

*…find your dead dog?*

"Probably not," Luke said. The boy didn't look sad, just curious.

"Well then, did you want to talk about anything?"

*…as long as it isn't about your dead dog.*

"Did you kill him, Mister?" he said with no hint of shame.

"I don't know what you're talking about."

*Yes.*

"My dad says you did. But he says it's not a big enough deal to come over and call you out."

Greg said nothing. He only looked at the boy. A boy that should be wearing a smile, or even a frown given the circumstances, instead of the death-like, grim *nothing* he bore now.

"I wouldn't be mad if you did," Luke said. "He was a mean dog. He always was. He always picked fights with anything. He took out my sister's eye when we were little."

"I'm surprised your pa didn't kill it, then."

A half-smile crept into the corner of the boy's mouth, but his eyes were dead all the same.

"I am too."

They both stood in silence for what seemed like a very long time before the boy began to walk away.

When Greg began to close the door, the boy turned and said, "I'm sorry about your dog," and Greg stared, saying nothing, and closed the door.

That night, as he lay in bed, he felt Charlie tense up against him, shivering. Greg rose a bit in bed and thought he heard something shuffling around outside his bedroom window. He convinced himself it was only his imagination, that he was only *imagining* those sounds of something sniffing the air and settling down for the night. He almost got up to look outside the window, but, he told himself, his feet hurt too much for that.

* * *

For several nights after that, Greg would wake from a nightmare to the sound of barking right at the edge of his hearing, but once he was awake, waiting in bed for the sound of more, there was only silence.

In the morning he would go outside to find the grass outside his window matted down where something had been lying in the night.

* * *

That night, Greg lay in bed with Charlie in a bundle lying on his feet. He wanted to nudge him off, knowing his ankles would be throbbing in the morning, but he was gentler with the dog now after the incident. He was spoiling the thing.

He lay awake for a long time, staring at the ceiling (not the window) wondering if he would hear those noises, that sniffing outside, that inimitable and ceaseless bark. The bark that had made him kill the dog who owned it. The bark that had driven him crazy.

His eyelids began to feel very heavy when, cutting through the silence, there was a low growl. Only, the growl was not coming from outside but in.

He stilled himself, every muscle in his body frozen in fear as the realization dawned on him that *this is not dream, this is happening and it is happening now.*

He hoped it might be a waking nightmare; good God let it even be sleep paralysis, because Charlie had not stirred at his feet.

He mustered all the strength left and turned his head to see what was growling in the doorway.

It was Charlie. Good boy Charlie.

And it was then that Greg felt how very cold his feet were.

And when he turned to look at them, he saw what lay there was the dog from before.

It had its head bent back around to regard him with red eyes and red teeth.

# THE LAST SLICE
### By Vivian Kasley

Wilbur Neelan was unlucky with women, always had been. He'd been engaged once, but it didn't last long, and modern dating was like fishing from a cesspool—every nibble was hopeless. It wasn't that he was horrible to look at; he was just socially awkward and lacked a certain confidence. An electrician by trade, he joked that most of his shocks came from work. His hobbies included puzzles, model building, and woodworking. He particularly enjoyed making his own walking sticks and selling some of them. All the extra money was put away with the hope that he might one day share his life with someone other than his pet parrot, Tally-Ho.

Wilbur loved Tally. He had gotten him from a local rescue and named him after the only phrase the parrot seemed to know. On the nights he didn't go for a beer, he enjoyed dinner in front of the television with Tally on his shoulder. Even though he enjoyed those moments; having his ear nibbled and kissed by a bird wasn't exactly his idea of a steamy romance. Hell, he couldn't remember the last time he'd been touched by anyone other than Rosie Palm and her five ugly sisters.

He didn't go out much, and when he did, he frequented the same place he always had and nursed a few beers. One night, he sat on the same stool he'd been sitting on for years and chuckled as he observed the tipsy college girls throwing darts. Wilbur finished his third mug of beer and put money down on the bar, but before he could get up to leave, a hand covered his. Startled, he looked down to see milk white, slender fingers with long, red-painted nails. A woman's voice purred, "Such strong, rough hands. You must work with them a lot, huh?"

Wilbur gulped and looked up. The woman he saw made him feel flushed, or like he had a full-body rash. For some reason, his bowels started to twist and turn and he struggled not to rip a fart. She was tall, raven-haired, with emerald eyes, and was the most stunning creature he had ever laid eyes on. A skintight red dress clung to her curvaceous body and her bosom spilled just enough out of the top to cause his heart to protest.

He had to peel his eyes from her cleavage and find his voice. "Uh, well, yeah. My hands are very important for my work." Wilbur felt sweat gather in his armpits and nether regions. It was like the whole room became a broiler.

She smiled, showing her pearly whites, then chirped, "I knew it! What kind of work do you do?"

"I'm an electrician. I work mostly with—"

"That's interesting. I'm Laura." She took her hand from atop his, and held it out.

Wilbur felt tipsy even though he'd only had three beers. He shook her hand and struggled not to lick it. *Such beautiful hands,* he thought. "Name's Wilbur, but you can call me Will. Most people hate the name Wilbur, on account of the pig and all."

"I like the name Wilbur. It's sweet. I'll call you, Wilbur. And if I remember correctly, that was *some* pig." She winked.

Wilbur jumped in his skin. This woman was way out of his league and he knew it. People were staring at them and a few were even snickering. He stood up and put his head down as he pushed his stool in. He wanted to give up before it got any worse. "Well, I was about to head out before you came in, so… it was nice to meet you, Laura. Have a good night."

"Now hold on, Wilbur! Don't you want to buy me a drink and stay a while?"

"I, uh, well, I mean I reckon I could. I ain't got nowhere to go in the morning—not that you'd be with me in the morning! I didn't mean…"

"I'd like a very dirty martini, with extra olives." She settled onto the stool beside him.

Wilbur blinked absently, sat down, and ordered himself another beer and a martini for her. She swirled around to face him. He drank in her long-crossed legs. The whiff of her perfume thrilled him. It was as intoxicating as she was. She bit her luscious bottom lip, and smiled at him in a way that told him she was game for anything.

"So, tell me, Wilbur. What do you like to do for fun around here?"

"You're looking at it. I work and come here sometimes. That's about it I reckon."

"That's it? No wife or girlfriend?" She looked at his left hand.

"No. Just my parrot."

"Interesting… I figured you for a pussy man."

"Wh—what?"

A laugh bubbled from her throat. "Cat—Pussy cat! So, a bird, huh? How odd."

"Yeah, my mom always had parrots and I grew to love them too. They're really smart and just as loving as a cat or dog really. Mine sits on my shoulder while I'm doing dishes, watching TV, and… well, he's quite the fella. He doesn't say much, though. I've tried to teach him—"

"He sounds delightful." She was examining her nails as if bored.

He tried not to look taken aback by the fact that she had cut him off again. "What do you do for fun? You don't seem the bar type."

"I do lots of things, Wilbur, lots of things. What type do you think I am?" She tilted her head, raised her perfectly plucked eyebrow, and smirked.

"Well, this bar here is mostly full of college kids, old drunks, and people like me. Not women like you, though. I reckon I never seen a woman like you in here. You should be in a fancy high rise somewhere, looking down on all of us or traveling on a private jet to some place like Bora Bora."

"Bora Bora? Ha! You're too adorable! I'm here for business though, actually." She sipped her martini, skewered an olive onto her nail, then trailed her tongue around it. Wilbur never saw someone eat an olive more provocatively.

"What kind of business you here for?" Wilbur stared down at her legs again.

"The usual kind, Wilbur. Look, who gives a flying fuck? Let's finish our drinks and get the hell outta here."

"What? You mean, leave… with me?" He nearly fell off his stool.

"Yes, Wilbur, with you, you silly little man." She poked him in the rib.

"Um, yeah, sure, I can do that. Where'd you want to go?"

"Let's pick up pizzas and go back to your place!"

"My place? Pizzas?" Wilbur shook his head in bewilderment.

"Yes, your place, Wilbur. I haven't eaten in forever and I'm famished. I love pizza—I adore it more than anything else in this world! Don't you?" she asked.

Her excitement was infectious and Wilbur didn't want it to end. "Why, yeah, I reckon it's really good, but I don't eat it often 'cause it gives me heartburn something fierce. Even just one slice, but—"

"Perfect, let's go! Don't you want to get to know me and have fun? I don't get to have fun very often. I just want some pizza and a good time, that's all Wilbur." She grabbed his hand and squeezed.

Wilbur paid the tab and tried to control his breathing. This was a gorgeous woman and he had no idea what to do with her; well he had an idea, but he hadn't had it in so long he was afraid he'd forgotten how. *Maybe it's like riding a bike; just hop on and start pumping*, he thought. *If I fall, I reckon I'll just get back on again.* He was never very good at analogies. Everyone looked at them as she hoisted her arm though his and dragged him out the door. He asked if she had a car, but she said she walked from where she was staying. This puzzled him since there were no hotels nearby, but he kept his mouth shut. They got into his car and he apologized for the mess, but she waved him away and told him to just drive.

They went to La Russo's Pizzeria and she practically hopped out of the car. She almost tripped in her stilettos as she ran into the restaurant. Without even asking him what he wanted, she ordered two large pizzas with sausage, pepperoni, and extra cheese. How on earth they would eat that much pizza was a question he burned to ask but didn't. She went on and on in the car about how much she loved sausage and pepperoni. Wilbur's heart palpitated and when he looked over at her, she was grinning from ear to ear. *Why on earth is this heavenly creature interested in me? And why is she so damn giddy about pizza?*

"Mm, Wilbur, it smells sooo good! I just wanna rip into it—it's making me so hot! We need to get to your house, now! Doesn't this car go any faster? I looove going fast!" She put her hand on his thigh.

"I reckon I'm going as fast as I can without getting a ticket. Kias aren't really known for their speed." His thigh was on fire where she had touched it.

Wilbur was embarrassed that he'd gotten a hard on and tried to will it away by thinking of unpleasant things, but it didn't seem to be working. Then he began to worry that he hadn't scrubbed his balls well enough earlier or when was the last time he'd trimmed his pubic hair. He reckoned he probably had muttonchops down there or what his ex-fiancée used to call, Disco Dick. *Why should it matter? This woman isn't going to be near my balls, right?* He glanced over at her again and gasped. She put the window down and was leaning halfway out of it.

She shouted, "I love the wind in my face! I hardly ever get to feel wind in my face! It's so dull where I live!"

Wilbur had to raise his voice to be heard over the air rushing in. "Where're you from, exactly?"

"Wilbur, you ask too many goddamn questions." She pulled herself back in.

"Too many questions? I reckon I haven't asked enough!"

She moved closer to him and he could feel her breath on his neck. She traced her tongue into his ear, nibbled the lobe, then whispered, "Are you going to look a gift horse in the mouth, Wilbur?"

He thought about that for a moment and then sped the car up a little more. "I guess not, no."

"It's good for the soul to live once in a while." She slid her hand further up his thigh and then rested it on his crotch. "My, my, what have we here?"

Wilbur pulled into his driveway and Laura swung the door open before he could even turn the car off. He grabbed the pizzas and used them to conceal his hard-on. He watched her ample backside as he followed her to his front door. *Oh, Lord, help me now!* "It's not fancy and may not be super tidy, but I wasn't expecting company—"

"Just open the door! I don't give a shit about any of that!"

As soon as they entered, Tally-Ho skidded to the back of his cage. "He's not used to anyone but me. He's just being shy," Wilbur said.

"He doesn't like me?"

"He doesn't know you, that's all."

"Well, neither do you and you like me."

He ignored that, and said, "He's an African Grey… they're real smart birds. He'll warm up."

"Whatever. Got any adult beverages—what about music?"

"Yeah, sure." Wilbur turned on the radio, found some classic rock, then turned the volume down. "I got some beer in the fridge. La Russo's makes a big ol' greasy slice, so you'll need a plate too, I reckon."

"I don't want a plate, Wilbur, just hurry the hell up!"

Wilbur rushed to the kitchen and grabbed a couple beers from the fridge. He noticed his hands were shaking, so he hung his head in the cool air and lingered there. When his heart slowed, he leaned against the counter and sighed. *A strange woman is in my house, beautiful, but damn strange.* But he was odd too and he had no idea what to do with the situation. *What if she wants to actually have sex with me, what then?* He turned on the sink and splashed some water onto his face, grabbed the beers, and walked back into the living room.

Wilbur was surprised to see Laura finishing a slice of pizza when he came back. The grease was dripping down her chin. "Sorry, I couldn't wait," she giggled.

"I have—here's a napkin. You have a little something right there."

"I'm good. You can clean it off me later. That is, if you want to?"

She licked her lips and swayed to the music. Wilbur gulped as he saw her unusually long tongue reach down to her chin and clean the grease. She moaned and he could see her nipples through her dress. A voice screamed inside of his head, *Holy shit, that's hot!* Strange or not, he decided to go with his dick's idea and excused himself to go to the restroom.

Once the door was shut, Wilbur took his socks, shoes, and pants off. He squatted in the tub and rolled his shirt up and did his best not to get it wet. He gave his undercarriage a rub down with a washcloth. His erection came back as he combed his hair and he hissed at it, "Down boy!" He looked down at his briar patch and eyed his razor, but decided against it. After a spritz of cologne, he rinsed his mouth out, put his pants back on, and smiled at his reflection. He looked for some condoms, but couldn't remember if he even had any. He scolded himself, *Shit, you bumbling buffoon. Maybe she has one? I reckon women are very savvy these days, ain't they?*

Wilbur stood with his hand on the doorknob and tried to pump himself up before heading back out. The music began to blare and vibrate the walls. *Wow, she must really like this song.* He turned the light off and went back to the living room. He gasped when he saw Laura's dress ripped open. She swayed with her eyes closed and held a slice of oozing pizza in each hand. Tomato sauce covered her nose and mouth. Her face was slick with grease and it dripped down her neck and onto her exposed breasts. "What the fuck," he mouthed.

As much as he wanted to appreciate her glistening bosom, he decided sex was out of the question. After a slice of pizza and a beer, he would call it a night, and then call her a cab. He didn't want her in his car again and thought, *Gorgeous or not, she looks like a savage!* A shiver racked his body when she turned to face him.

"Wilbur! I didn't see you standing there. This's so good! I could eat it for eternity! Oh, and I love this song! What is it?"

"It's uh… it's Hall and Oates. *Man Eater*."

She looked rabid as she twirled around. Tendrils of mozzarella hung from her mouth and chunks of sausage and pepperoni clung to her cleavage. She kicked her heels off and danced seductively back over to the boxes of pizza, then grabbed two more slices and forced them into her unhinged mouth. Wilbur was speechless. *How does she manage to shovel such large slices of pizza into her mouth like that… is she even chewing?* He tiptoed around her and walked over to the pizzas.

He lifted the lids and his eyes widened in surprise. One box was empty and the other had only one slice left in it. *Holy freaking crap! She ate two entire large pizzas? What the hell is wrong with this woman? Does she have a tapeworm?* Wilbur shrugged and took the last slice of pizza. Just as he took a bite, she stopped dancing. The radio shut itself off, and then she flung her crust at the wall like a boomerang and howled at the ceiling.

Rage dripped from her eyes like the grease on her chin. Her arms hung at her sides with her hands balled into fists. The beautiful face he saw earlier was gone. It was a tomato sauce covered monster looking back at him. Pizza flecked drool dripped from her mouth and her nostrils flared like an angry bull. She planted her feet like a sumo wrestler and let loose a string of guttural noises.

Wilbur froze, afraid to blink or swallow. The beautiful woman that he brought back to his home was gone. Her eyes were no longer emeralds, but two fiery coals that cut into him like a hot knife through butter. Every strand of raven hair had disappeared and was replaced by a bald dome covered in festering sores with long gnarled horns curled atop. The red dress that had clung to her perfect body, now lay in shreds beneath a revolting beast that was covered in dark bristly hairs. Her hands were catcher's mitts with claws and her legs looked like tree trunks with large hoofed feet.

She howled again, then cracked the tiles as she angrily stomped toward him.

Her voice echoed around him. "You troglodyte! You. Took. The. Last. Slice. Of. Pizza. The last one? THE LAST FUCKING SLICE!"

Wilbur held out the limp slice of pizza with a shaky hand. Her large arm swung out and knocked it across the room. She let out a roar that shook the entire house. Pictures fell off the wall and shattered, and then the TV and radio exploded.

Fetid spittle flew into his face as she snarled, "Look what you made me do! I get one day, one fucking day, to do whatever I want and you ruined it! You fucking ruined it! You're all so greedy! You always were, with all of your Earthly pleasures! But you, you measly pathetic worm, just had to have the last slice, didn't you? I just wanted to eat pizza—but no—you took that from me! You will pay!"

"I... I didn't know! I swear! It was just one slice... you had all the rest! Here, take my wallet! Get another one!"

"You imbecile—it's too late now! I'd rather have your soul!"

Wilbur panicked. He slowly backed away toward the front door. She laughed a horrible laugh and quickly followed, reaching out and putting her claws through his shirt. He gagged at her hot breath. It reeked of decay and pizza. Vomit crawled up his throat, but he swallowed it.

"Aw, what's the matter Wittle Wilbur—is it my breath? Is it not sweet enough for you anymore? Or maybe you don't find me attractive now? I'm not pretty enough for you?" She batted her eyes and pursed her peeling cracked lips. "Stupid flesh bags. You were always so dim! Whimpering and whining little shits! Oh, look, you pissed your panties! Ha! Could be worse, you could've shit them, Wilbur! What a stupid fucking name. That's some pig! Some big dumb last slice eating fucking pig!" She started to squeal and snort.

"Tally-ho! Tally-ho! Tally-ho!" The cage rattled as Tally repeatedly flew against it with all his might.

She let go of Wilbur's shirt and turned toward the bird. While she was distracted, Wilbur opened the storage closet next to the front door and pulled out one of his unfinished walking sticks. He stood tall and gripped it tight. She turned back toward Wilbur, began to cackle, and do a jig.

"Oh, what? You're going to stab me to death with one of your sticks? How original, pig boy! I didn't see that coming—I'm a fucking demon for Christ's sake. This night wasn't so bad after all. You sure are making me laugh. Sadly, it must come to an end and yes, I must take you with me. I'm still kind of hungry, so your puny soul will have to do. It won't hurt too much. Put the stick down, pig boy. Don't make this a thing."

"This stick is… it's made of olive wood!" Wilbur held it out like a sword.

"Oh really? Please, tell me more," she cackled.

Tally-Ho screeched as she lunged toward Wilbur, but he lunged back and pushed the stick as hard as he could into the demon's chest. She growled as she flung Wilbur against the front door, then backed away. She looked down at her chest and tugged on the end of the stick.

"You fucker… that hurt." She choked up what looked like coppery mud and fell over.

Her eyes fluttered and the house began to quake. A large hole began to open up in the floor beside her. Acrid smoke filled the room, flames darted up from beneath, and Wilbur heard a blood-curdling chorus of screams. Arms like burning logs came up out of the hole and hands reached out with smoldering fingers. They grabbed her hooves and swiftly pulled her toward them and down into the flames. When he saw her clawed hand rise back out, he ran back out the front door, but then turned back. *Tally. I can't leave him! He saved my life!*

Wilbur ran back inside and almost collapsed when he saw the hole was gone. He grabbed another walking stick from the closet just in case. Other than the odor of shit-covered rotten eggs that lingered in the room and a shredded red dress, there was no trace of the demon. He walked around his disheveled living room and took it all in. Red sauce and pizza grease covered pretty much everything. There were broken glass and tiles, and cracks ran down the walls.

Despite everything he just witnessed, he put his hands on his hips and whistled. "Great. How do I explain this to my insurance company? Yes, I had a demon in my house who got angry at me for eating the last slice of pizza and it destroyed my home. It could work; Farmer's has seen a thing or two. Maybe I could just say it was an earthquake… or a tomato tornado!"

He went to the kitchen, chugged a beer, then went back to his living room where he peeled the half-eaten pizza slice off the wall and brought it over to Tally's cage. The bird pecked the crust. Wilbur felt the heartburn he feared finally make its debut. He burped several times and choked back the acid. "I reckon I'm never eating pizza again, Tally. What a night!" He rubbed the bird's head with his finger.

Crumbs burst from Tally's beak as he screeched, "Last Slice! Last slice!"

# TIME FOR CLASS
## *By David Rose*

We were both sixteen, but he wasn't in any of my classes. I knew about his tragedy. The whole school did. Hopeless cases were always abandoned here. Voices began just two days after he had arrived. Rumors swirled around the classrooms like dandelion clocks. The walls were good at tales; hushed half-truths and murmurs about past accidents persistently wafted through the halls.

"Follow me."

We followed Mr. Sullivan, still wearing his tracksuit, down the stairs into the entrails of the building. We shuffled down the lofty, empty corridors. The school, like a hollowed-out church, stood free of purpose and belief, seemingly kept erect by its drive to inflict order. Jason was taller than me and healthier. He walked confidently, obviously someone from the city and not this small, rural backwater. He and his father had arrived, according to the voices, a couple of months after his mother had died. His uniform was pristine and new, its colors vivid and bright, shaming my worn and dulled clothes.

The sun set early this far north. The fluorescent light strips flickered as we passed and shadows congregated in the unseen spaces. We descended more stairs down to the basement. As we walked, I kept my eyes fixed on damp stains on the cracked walls, cruel memories bleeding through.

An old door lamented as it painfully opened.

"A bit dusty, I know, and the lack of windows doesn't help, but the librarian set the detention, not me."

Mr. Sullivan pointed out the hidden computer, meekly and timidly humming in the center of the bookshelves. He tapped the keyboard to turn the blank screensaver off and light stuttered into the room. "She told me to say: tick the books against that database-thingy there."

As Jason bent over the computer, I turned and looked at the old dusty shelves and the imposing leather bound books huddled aloof on their perches, indifferent to my attempts to read their titles.

The door slammed behind us, making me jump slightly. Mr. Sullivan had gone, his hurried, scuttling feet sounding like a whole class.

"God! He's not very clever, is he?"

I started. We were the only two in detention, but I just wasn't used to being noticed. I was rubbish at sports, certainly not that bright and never wearing the right clothes. I faded to magnolia in the corners and alcoves of this redbrick, Victorian schoolhouse with its dark spaces and echoey, cavernous corridors. And he wanted to speak to me. To me. No one ever spoke to me. I tried desperately to put the words in the right order in my head, "Y-y-yes. B-b-b-but, he is only a P-P-P. E. teacher."

He smirked at my joke, "My dad dragged me to this shithole. He thought the change would do us good and stop me fighting. Obviously not a success. Why are you here?"

The fight had started because of the whisper of the word 'motherkiller.' Just more anguish, more pain and hard, relentless cruelty seeping from the crumbling walls of the malign building. "J-j-ust the n-n-normal." I said no more, too aware of the sting in the words, *stutterboy, dunce, robot*, and the shame that nestled in me.

"Normal? No homework, I 'spose," he mimicked my rural accent, "What's your name?"

"Oliver," and then I lied to be more interesting, "My friends c-c-call me O-o-olly."

"Well, O-o-olly, I'm Jason. I'll read out the titles and you tell me whether the books are here."

He looked at the computer screen, its irreal light cast obscure shadows on the walls. The lightstrip flickered irritatingly, so Jason turned it off, smothering us in a fragile, vulnerable ball of light at the center of the basement.

A slight scratching noise in one of the dark corners caught my attention. It sounded like a shrill giggle and the draught from under the door seemed to purr, "Boys." Jason put his hand down flat to stop the rustling of discarded papers on the desk.

He began reading and I would say 'yes' when I found the book, squinting in the dark. We did this for ten minutes before I asked about his mother. The masters had always said I had no manners. He stopped and looked at me.

"I suppose I should tell someone. I've heard some ridiculous versions."

I looked at his face; his eyes weren't fixed on me, but on an avaricious shadow in the far corner of the room consuming the light. He began narrating, his voice emotionless and flat, "I found her on the bed. Six months ago. Her lips were blue. Really blue. Pills were littered on the bed."

I looked at his eyes. The screen mercilessly picked out the tears.

"I'm f-f-f-fostered," I said in the hope that my own misfortune would build a sympathetic bridge between us. The room embarrassingly shivered and the pipes suddenly cracked like a cane, making me flinch and Jason jump. He looked into the corners of the room and reached to turn the light on.

The light flickered feebly, and then died completely.

Jason began reading out names again.

The books leaned in on us oppressively, apparently waiting for him to speak and me to look. He tapped away, vainly trying to ignore their heavy presence. When I walked to the fourth of the impossibly long shelves, I could detect a scuttling in the walls, a rasping, a scratching. In one of my temporary homes, when I was really young, birds had nested in the walls, and the noise was the same. I imagined a small chick breaking out of its shell. Abandoned. No mother to feed it. No exit from the cavity. The mother bird, lying near, its beak blue.

Jason jumped, littering books on the floor.

I followed his gaze. When I tried to fix the thing, I could see nothing. "I thought I saw a boy," he breathed out. "Must be the screen reflecting off something."

The giggling began immediately. Jason swung round. It stopped. I turned quickly as a shadow shot across the corner of my eye. Shorts. Bare legs. We stood breathing deeply, "How long have we still got?"

"Another forty minutes," I answered.

"Fuck this, I'm off."

The room went dark.

Jason banged the keyboard to relight the screen.

"I'm looking for a certain book."

The voice was unearthly and tore layers off the skin in my ears. We spun round. A woman, elderly but of indistinct age, stood before us. A cane rested in the palm of her hand like a barrier across her chest. Her prim and precise clothes weren't so much pressed as cast in iron. Her lupine face was stern and unforgiving. Her eyes fixed me with a greedy stare, insisting I think of the word 'formidable.' Jason looked incredulously at the unnoticed, closed door behind her.

I had a thin yet immensely heavy book in my hands.

"Are you the librarian?" Jason nervously asked.

"I'm a teacher," she exasperatedly sighed. "I need you to bring that book to my class. Both of you!"

And then she added, "It is obvious you do not have mothers."

I noticed Jason was staring at her lips. They were blue. No doubt a trick of the computer screen's light.

The book in my hands fell to the desk and opened. Pages flicked like a fan, too many pages for its thin body. My fingers traced the lines of the spidery letters, but found it impossible, my wrist often bending in the wrong direction and my fingers knotting dangerously. I could see they were a mix of symbols, words and doodles.

It went dark. Scuttling, breathing, a rasping. A voice. Words I could not understand.

The screen of the computer came back on as Jason aggressively banged the keys. The scratching shadows scuttled under the shelves and behind the books once more. The door was open. She had gone.

"Come!" commanded the voice. "Time for class."

The book was still open. I could make little sense of it, but Jason scanned the pages. "The school used to be an orphanage," he said, "for children from bad homes. This is one of their workbooks. The boy..."

It went dark again. A thousand sharp feet scratched menacingly at the hardwood floor. I sensed a rasping breath on my neck and what felt like a claw on my shoulder. I heard the banging at the keyboard. Light slapped my eyes.

The book was open at a different page. An arc cut through a triangle, although I found it difficult to count the sides. Words, scrawled by an angry child, read: "She hurts me." And below, in blood red ink and a neat, exact hand: "F-. D-d-dunce."

Jason's fingers massaged a scratch on his neck. It was bleeding.

"Now!"

I saw him walk through the door and a deep foreboding wrung the inside of my stomach like a wet rag. I wanted to stop him, bring him back. I ran after him and found him sitting at a desk. The classroom was dull with grey walls and large black windows, mocking any attempt to see out. Scratching, wailing and hail buffeted their weak frames. About twenty blond boys, short trousers and faded uniforms sat silently and eerily straight, seemingly all cast from the same mould. At the front, the teacher rhythmically tapped a free desk with her cane. Above perched half-moon glasses on her aquiline nose, her cruel eyes indicated the empty seat: "Time for class Oliver. Sit!"

I shook my head and looked at Jason. There was terror in his eyes. I could see fear forming the word 'help' in his mouth. He seemed fixed to the chair, his hands glued to the desk in the same position as all the others.

"S-s-sit Oliver," the teacher said, each syllable a whip of her cane on the empty desk. "We're your family now. Let's help him, class."

"Yes mother," flatly voiced the class in unison, as they mechanically rose to their feet.

"You must call me 'mother.'" She slapped the cane into her palm, "You boys really need a mother. It explains so much about your behavior."

The schoolboys slowly began to turn at the same time. Their eyes were dark pools of fury, deep wells of hate. "D-d-dunce," they chanted in unison.

I turned to run, but the door was no longer there, only a damp, crawling wall. My fingers found it viscous to the touch, its give swallowing my palms to the wrist.

I heard her heels play a painful staccato on the parquet. She was coming nearer. I vainly pushed at the wall. She was dragging the cane on the floor, the sound of a thousand pleading children's voices.

I began to sob. The cane gently touched the naked back of my neck, torturously bending back the small hairs. I could feel her breath now. I could sense her bony, hooked hand nearing my shoulder.

Light blinded us and we found ourselves in a cupboard.

"How did you get here?" Mr. Sullivan asked.

Jason opened his mouth and pointed. He began to say something, then stopped and closed his mouth tight. He looked at me.

"Look, I'm sorry. The headmaster explained I should cut you some slack. No more detentions, but no more fights, all right?"

Jason shuddered. He shook his head. He tentatively touched the wall.

"Your dad is here. Are you okay?"

Jason rose and followed Mr. Sullivan. "Wait," he said. "What about Olly?"

"Who's Olly?"

"Oliver?"

Mr. Sullivan looked at Jason and noticed how the blood had drained from his face and his pupils were tiny. "There's no Oliver at this school."

I watched them go and felt a claw on my shoulder. "Time for class," the voice hissed. "Mother's waiting."

# THE 'MOLE PEOPLE'
## By Jay Baird

The rain fell in harsh torrents from the gray Nevada sky as Sam Norrick made his way home. Home being an intricate series of concrete storm tunnels beneath the city of Las Vegas. In the case of Sam Norrick and the people he shared his home with, beggars couldn't be choosers.

Sam entered through the south entrance and made his way into the dark labyrinth. He could navigate his way around the earlier series of tunnels with ease. He soon arrived at the camp, a small living area he shared with others not too far in the sewer.

Terry was rambling to the others. Sam was used to Terry's ramblings and it was odd if Terry didn't come out with at least one new conspiracy theory every other day. A poor substitute for TV, but entertainment nevertheless, Sam believed.

"No… I'm talking about real "mole people.' Deep in the center of the sewer…" Terry punctuated his ramblings with raised hands that didn't really indicate anything, but they never stayed down all the same. "I heard from Leon, you know Leon? Over on the East Side. Well, he said to me that him and a couple of other people over there, they'd seen some 'mole people.' No, I shit you not. Said they crawl on the roofs of the tunnels and hiss like some kind of fuckin' snake or something."

Sam believed that he and the other sewer dwellers being called the 'mole people' by the public was another source of entertainment.

"Oh bullshit," retorted Lucas. He was enjoying Terry's story, but felt the need to shoot down the more ludicrous parts. He gained nothing from doing this, but did it anyway. Nobody expected Terry to suddenly have a reality check due to Lucas calling bullshit on his sewer fables.

"Let him finish," said Yua. Her head was resting on her open palms while she looked on at Terry.

Sam walked over to his mattress and sat down, placing his rucksack that contained a miscellaneous amount of snacks and cigarettes among other things down next to him. Sam didn't smoke, or rather hadn't for some time. He collected cigarettes so he could trade them with other people in the sewer for better things. He once bartered a couple packs of cigarettes for a pocketknife. He felt the hilt of the folded blade rub against the side of his leg through his trousers as he adjusted himself on the mattress to get more comfortable.

"This is almost as batshit as the one you told us about the aliens that like to wear people's skin." Lucas said, flippantly, even though it was obvious he was invested in whatever story Terry had to tell.

"Let him finish, for goodness sake," Yua shot back with rising annoyance in her tone.

"Jeez, sorry," Lucas replied meekly.

Sam snacked on a chocolate bar while watching and listening from his mattress. Yua turned her head towards him. "You gonna share the loot?" she asked. Sam smiled, rolled his eyes and dug into the rucksack. He pulled out a chocolate bar had tossed it over to Yua. He pulled out another and tossed it to Lucas because of the wounded puppy expression that came over his face when he tossed Yua one.

"You gonna give me one?" Terry asked Sam with a stern look on his face.

"Depends if this story is any good old man," Sam replied with a wry smile.

"You cruel sonofabitch," Terry said in a mock forlorn way that made Yua laugh.

Sam pulled out a chocolate bar and shook it in his hand like a prize. Terry's expression fell flat and he returned to his story, even more determined to tell it than before.

"Leon said people in his tunnel started disappearing. Said people who lived deeper in the sewer would disappear without a trace."

Sam, Yua and Lucas were all silent. They had all heard rumors about people disappearing in the tunnels. People they had known had suddenly gone and disappeared. The three of them came up with their own ideas on how or why these people were no longer seen around the sewers. None of them involved wall crawling 'mole people' though.

Terry finished his story in the usual fashion, adding his own reasoning as to why he believed what was happening was happening. Lucas sighed.

"Why? Why is it always aliens with you?" He said in an exasperated voice.

Yua laughed.

Terry grunted and turned his gaze toward Sam. A chocolate bar sailed through the air and came to rest in the Old man's lap.

"You beautiful sonofabitch," Terry said as he began to undo the wrapper.

Sam bought two packs of cigarettes with what meager amount of money he had. He made his way over back to the sewer. The rain from yesterday hadn't let up and this concerned him. The sewer tunnels were built as storm drains and when it rained, like it did now, a miniature version of the river Nile would soon take form in the tunnels. The only defense against this was a pair of green and red plastic beach buckets that were used to try and get rid of the rainwater. They weren't really all that efficient though. Sam considered seeing if anyone else in the sewer tunnels had anything better to use against the rainwater, like sandbags, which he could maybe get by trading some cigarettes.

Sam approached the south entrance and trudged through the water, resting atop a half mile of concrete. Sam reached the camp and was taken aback when he saw Yua resting against a wall. The left side of her body was covered in a combination of fresh and dried blood. Lucas was kneeling next to her. He noticed Sam and ran up to meet him. Sam had a lot of questions on his mind and was about to speak, but Lucas spoke first, in a panicked and shaky voice.

"Terry's gone... Yua's hurt. Oh fuck, oh man. Yua's hurt pretty bad man."

Sam approached Yua and knelt next to her, examining her. She was pale. Really pale. Her skin complexion somehow looking whiter than a fresh sheet of snow. She held a limp hand to her shoulder. Sam took her wrist gently and began to move her arm away.

"Let me see." he said in as calm a tone he could manage.

Yua winced as she relinquished pressure on the wound.

"I tried to help. I tried to..." Lucas said meekly over Sam's shoulder as he lifted the dark burgundy-saturated bandage from Yua's shoulder. Blood bubbled from her wound and fresh rivulets began their slow descent down the left side of her body. Yua's head was turned away from her injury, looking down at the damp floor on her right. Sam examined the wound. Blood hemorrhaged from a series of punctures in her skin that seemed to be in the form of a semi-circle. There was one big puncture in the middle that bled more than the others. It looked like she had been attacked by a rabid animal or something. Sam placed the bandage back down on her shoulder and held his hand atop it.

"What happened?" asked Sam, incredulous of what was going on. "What—who did this to Yua? What—where the fuck is Terry? What…"

"I don't know man, I don't know… Some girl came through here. She was hugging herself and like… muttering to herself, I don't…" Lucas was interrupted by Yua as she groaned weekly. A tear ran down her face.

"Terry tried to speak to the girl. She starting saying stuff that me and Yua couldn't make out. She walked past Terry and starting making her way to the south entrance. I went after her. I recognized her; it was Shannon from further down."

As Lucas spoke, Sam replaced Yua's bandage with a fresh one from the medical kit that lay open next to her. The bleeding seemed to stop abruptly. Sam didn't know if that was a good or a bad thing.

"I grabbed one of her arms and tried to talk to her. She was covered in like blood man… I didn't have much of a grip on her but she scratched me with her other arm." Lucas presented his left arm; four distinct bright red lines ran the length of his forearm.

"She ran away after that. I figured that Phil had done something to her."

Sam remembered Phil. He lived with Shannon further in the sewer. He had a temper about him. The crystal he smoked didn't help it. Just made him paranoid and violent.

"I came back here and both Terry and Yua were gone. I sat around and waited. Then Yua came back."

"Terry…" Yua muttered. She raised her head slightly and looked weakly at Sam and Lucas.

"Where, Yua?" Sam took hold of her by the arms gently to support her slumped body. "Where is he?"

Yua swiveled her head slightly and looked off into the darkness of the sewer. "Terry went to Phil's… Confront him…There was blood… There was…" Yua spoke softly and seemed to be on the verge of fainting.

"We gotta get her to a hospital, man," Lucas said with a desperate plea in his voice.

Yua's eyes started to roll in her head. "Terry… Terry… TERRY!"

"Oh God, oh man, oh God…" Lucas was running his hands through his thick strands of dark brown hair. Sam moved his arms up to the side of Yua's head and held it in place. Her frantic eye movement ceased.

"Did Phil do this to you?" Sam thought about Phil, high on crystal, attacking Yua and biting her on the shoulder. Sam wouldn't put it past the mad bastard. Yua shook her head that was clasped between Sam's hands. Sam's confusion was intense.

"Then… who did this to you?"

Yua was looking at Sam, but Sam felt like she was looking through him. He let go of her.

"M-M… Monst… M-Mol…" Yua couldn't say whatever it was that she was trying to. She gave up and rested her head against her good shoulder. She seemed to be drained of everything.

Sam stood up and walked down the tunnel a couple of paces.

"TERRY!" Sam bellowed, his voice reverberating down the tunnel and into the darkness.

Sam moved over to his mattress and rummaged through his belongings.

"What are you doing?" Lucas asked while alternating his gaze between Sam and Yua.

"Going after Terry."

Sam brandished a torch and shone its bright white beam down the tunnel. "Get her to a hospital," he said to Lucas as he made his way down into the maze-like network.

Sam walked for some time. He knew the layout of the earlier parts of the network quite well, but the deeper he went, the more his sense of direction became skewered. He walked for some time until his light fell upon a makeshift campsite. *This must be where Shannon and Phil had set up*, he thought. As Sam approached, the light from the torch scanning over the camp, he noticed blood splashed along the wall and floor. He stopped in his tracks. The scene before him was evidence of something awful. What had happened? Whose blood was this? Sam moved forward cautiously. He shone his light on the ground and saw that a thick trail of blood went farther down into the bowels of the tunnel. Sam contemplated turning back, meeting up with Lucas and helping him with getting Yua to a hospital. He looked at the blood trail and thought of Terry. Thought of the worst. Sam dug out the pocketknife from his pocket and moved onwards.

"Terry?" Sam asked in a low voice as he progressed forward. He was afraid to shout now.

Terry followed the blood trail. He was deep within the network now. The atmosphere felt heavy and a foul odor became increasingly potent. More so than the usual smell that permeated the sewer. Sam thought he heard movement around the next corner. He turned it warily and followed the trail. It came to an abrupt stop.

Sam's frustration grew to meet his confusion. Neither came close to the amount of fear he now felt. He shined the light around the floor where the blood trail ended. The light began to flicker.

*Fuck*, he thought. The light flashed rapidly and then cut out. *Shit*. Sam stood in the darkness. He fiddled with the torch, flicking the switch on and off and lightly whacking the torch against the side of his leg. Sam heard something. He turned his body towards the sound, instinctively pointing the torch towards where he heard it. His grip tightened on the knife. The sound seemed to be in response to him whacking the torch against his leg.

Something wet hit Sam on the face. He flinched and brought his hands to his face in a protective stance. The torch came back to life, shining upwards. Something small and barely noticeable fell through the line of the torch beam and then dropped to the floor. The same wet thing that hit Sam hit him again. He brushed the spot where he'd felt the sensation with his thumb and brought it into the light. The tip of his thumb was red.

A red glob fell on the glass surface of the torch, turning what little light that shone through it a dark shade of pink. Sam looked up.

The pale, white glow from the torch fell on something as equally pale. Phil hung from the ceiling. His legs were bound to the ceiling by a mixture of ripped fabric. His arms hung limp, like they were reaching out towards Sam. His eyes were open but saw nothing; they had a glazed glassy expression that met Sam's eyes and conveyed the terror that he had experienced in his final moments. Oval-shaped skin punctures were present all over his body and were the source of the blood that fell down in random intervals over Sam. The sight brought to mind thoughts of livestock hanging upside down with their throats slit.

Looking up, Sam stepped back and was aghast with horror. He was hyping himself up to turn and run when he heard the same sound he had heard whilst standing in the dark. Sam froze. He slowly moved the torch over to where the sound was coming from. It fell upon Terry. His head was resting against the ground, his eyes staring up at the ceiling. He looked gaunt and pale, his skin tight against his skull. His upper body gyrated from side to side with movement. The torch beam moved from his head and down his body. Something was hunched over Terry. Something pale. Something thin and skeletal. The vertebrae of its back pushed against what thin layer of skin it had.

Sam held his breath. All his hairs stood up. His first thought was that the thing was some kind of animal, but he could see from its hunched posture that it was bipedal and had the build of a human. Its head was hovering over Terry's abdomen; the sound that Sam had heard was coming from whatever it was doing to Terry. Wet smacks followed by the sound you get when you suck hard on a straw. Sam took one step back but lost his balance. His boot made a squelch in the coagulated pool of blood where the trail had ended. He steadied himself but it was too late. The thing that was hunched over Terry swung its head around and stood to attention. Sam could feel his heart beating against his chest as the thing stood, illuminated by the bright torch beam. Sam looked on at the vile thing before him. The features of its face were sharp and rodent-like. Its ears and nose pointed, its mouth a cave of sharpened horrors, stained red from whatever it had been doing to Terry. Its eyes looked cataract, no pupils visible in the whites except for the circular reflection of the light from the torch. Sam looked down briefly at Terry. His shirt had been ripped open; the semi-circle punctures were present in a plethora of locations all over his abdomen. His stomach was practically non-existent and his ribcage looked like it was about to rip through the thin layer of skin that clung to him.

Sam's attention shot back to the thing. It sniffed at the air with its slit nostrils. Its hunched legs began carrying its gangly frame towards Sam. Its fingers were extended outwards and a pointed nail protruded from each tip. Sam was frozen to the spot. He felt like running but couldn't, a clash of thoughts and instinct telling him to run or be as still as a statue. The thing's nose probed the air; its pointed bat ears pricked spasmodically. Sam deduced the thing was blind. If it had any sight it would have most certainly seen him already. Instead, it seemed to guide its way forward through smell and sound. Sam held his breath to the point of feeling faint. The thing stopped edging forward all but five feet away from him. It bore no expression but cocked its head from side to side as if trying to decipher signals in the rancid air of the sewer. The light from the torch flickered on the creature. Sam felt like a bolt of lightning was coiling down his spine. The light flickered more rapidly, casting the thing in a strobe light effect, its shadow large against the sewer wall behind it. Then both Sam and the thing were in darkness.

Sam closed his eyes and did something he hadn't done since he was a child. He prayed. He prayed to open his eyes and find himself on his mattress, and all that had happened in the last hour being nothing but a nightmare. He opened his eyes. Darkness. Then a light.

The torch now seemed to shine brighter than before, and in its full light giving glory, it presented Sam with the sight of the creature's face all but seven centimeters away from his. Sam would have gulped if he were not afraid to even blink. The thing's warm, rank breath blew in Sam's face; his unblinking eyes felt red and raw. Sam hoped no tear would fall. A dark gray tongue slithered its way out of the thing's mouth. The tongue seemed to be barbed in sets of miniature needle-like teeth. It slithered through the air, translucent strands falling from it as it extended towards Sam. Its reflection grew bigger in Sam's pupil as it grew closer to his face. A sudden rush of movement in the air between them. Both were still. Sam's firm grip on the blade hilt released.

His hand pulled back to his side. The hilt of the blade stuck out of the side of the thing's neck. Sam took a couple of steps back as the thing began to twitch. The tongue started to thrash through the air like a wounded animal. Then it suddenly slid back into the mouth in a rapid motion. A shrill scream escaped from the thing's mouth just as the tongue returned. Sam covered his ears. The thing's hands swiped at its neck. One of its hands brushed violently against the hilt, breaking it away from the blade. It fell to the floor and started to roll violently, its elongated limbs flailing out in every direction. Another noise broke through the sound of the thing's pained wailings. It came from a tunnel connected to the room they were in. Sam shone his light over the creature and down the tunnel. The beam presented nothing but cement and stone. But then Sam noticed something: Two circular, white dots reflected the torch beam farther down in the tunnel. The two dots were joined by another pair. And then another pair. And then another. The black void of the tunnel soon resembled a night sky full of stars. The stars grew brighter and bigger, the sounds coming from within the tunnel picking up in their intensity. Sam knew what was coming. He didn't know how many though. It didn't matter. He turned and ran.

The screaming of the wounded creature became fainter as he navigated his way back through the tunnels. But this was soon replaced by a cacophony of other shrieks and screams. The splashing Sam's boots made in the rainwater as he ran wasn't as loud, it seemed, as the scratching sounds echoing from the tunnels behind him. Sam ran until it felt like his heart exploded in his chest, and then he ran some more.

He recognized the tunnel he was in now. Home wasn't far. He made his way round the turns and followed the tunnels in the area based on his sense of direction and memory. The sounds behind him seemed less intense. Still, Sam ran. His trousers wet from the rainwater that had splashed against him as he sprinted through the sewers beneath the city of sin. The front and back of his shirt were wet from perspiration.

He made it to the camp. He slowed down his pace slightly. He looked around and saw that both Yua and Lucas were gone. He took a moment to relish in their safety. Sam arched his back and rested his hands against his knees. He threw up. Sam wiped his mouth against the sleeve of his jacket; the torch in his hand flickered once more. *Fucking useless thing*, he thought. He threw it against the floor, where it spun and came to rest against a wall. Sam had no use for it now. He knew the way out from here. The sounds from the darkness began to rise in volume. Sam ran once more.

Not long after Sam's exit from the camp, the torch he discarded flickered to life a couple of times. The beam spluttered and shone down the tunnel from the camp. A series of lank silhouettes were pressed against the wall and ceiling of the tunnel; they each ran through the flashing light in rapid succession. Then the light gave out.

Sam made it to the edge of the tunnel leading to the south entrance. He could have cried with joy. His stomach ached as he jogged his way towards the entrance, evening sunlight hanging over it like a drape. Nearly half way down the entrance tunnel, he saw two figures slumped against the ground. It was Lucas and Yua. Sam panicked. He saw Yua slumped in Lucas' lap; he had an arm wrapped around her. Sam heard something in the distance behind him.

Lucas looked like he was trying to get to his feet.

Summoning what little energy he had left, Sam made his way over to the pair. He'd help Lucas and carry Yua out of this hell. He made his way to them.

"Lucas… Yua…" Sam said in a barely audible and exasperated voice.

Yua grabbed Lucas' shoulder and tried to support herself. Her head rose so that the top part was visible over his other shoulder.

"Yua…" Sam said, once more. He moved forward by three steps and then stopped.

Yua's eyes were different. They had no pupils. Her head rose over Lucas' shoulder. Her mouth hung open; rows of jagged teeth lined her mouth; fresh blood was smeared all around her lower face. Lucas turned his head to the side. His face was drained of all its color, his cheekbones as sharp as the corners of a wooden table. His eye looked pleadingly at Sam. His body shook a little and his gaze dropped; his eye lolled in its socket like a marble. A grey, forked tongue protruded from Yua's mouth; it brushed against Lucas' neck and a suction cup-like tip at the end of the tongue attached itself to him, making a wet sound as it did. Lucas let out a weak gasp. The tongue pulsated as something passed through it and into Yua's mouth. Then her head made its way towards his neck, the tongue pulling it forward like a motor. Her mouth clasped against him and blood soon poured out from around her lips.

Sam watched in stunned horror. Time froze; he didn't know what to do. He took a step forward and his boot made a splash in a large puddle of rainwater. Then something hit him in the back and he fell forward on the hard-concrete ground. His face breached the surface of the large puddle. He brought his head back up and drew a sharp inhale of air. The pressure that rested on his back made the task of breathing almost impossible. Just as he drew breath, something clasped the side of his neck. The air felt stuck in his throat, unable to travel further. He suddenly felt the same pain on his leg, and then on his arm, and then on his thigh. Within seconds, it felt like every square inch of his body was being penetrated by dozens of needles. He knew then and there that the creatures were chomping down on him from any space they could find. The pain was ineffable. He didn't scream, but he wouldn't have been able to if he had tried. Amongst all the pain, he felt like he was deflating. The pain, though always present, soon subsided into a lightheaded state of euphoria. Sam was conscious but not quite all there. Still, he recognized he was getting dragged deeper back into the sewers based on how the light from the south entrance became smaller and smaller.

# EDGY AND DULL
## By Wolfgang Potterhouse

I wake up with the sheets soaking wet again, my chest heaving and tense, shirt collar clenched in a two-hand death grip, pulled a foot away from my throat so I can breathe, my head throbbing from the freight train running through it.

My sweat smells like fear, anger, and blood—blood that christens a new set of dreams, hungers, premonitions, fantasies—I can't perceive the differences anymore; my conscious and subconscious minds have mingled and blurred—I can't tell what to focus on, to value, to validate. I don't know what I'm going to do, but I know how I feel. I'm tortured, straddling my breaking point. My soul, my heart, my head, there's heat, a lot of heat coming from somewhere deep, somewhere dark.

It's all I can do right now to not go over there and rip him apart. I let go of my shirt and try to ratchet the electricity down a notch. My hands ache, I run them through my hair, wet with torment. My anguish trickles through the filters of my mind and drips into the mason jar of my lizard brain. Drip, drip, drip. I want to kill them both.

I have to be free of this. I have to do something.

Love at first sight is a bitch when it pulls out in front of you on a one-way street. She was the new girl at school, and I knew the instant I saw her, man. She was it—the one. She was so beautiful, her smile, her walk, even her voice; they simply melted me. I'm not shy. I tried to talk to her; she instantly seemed to pull back, get small, tiny, point her eyes at the floor. Was she playing hard to get? My friends encouraged me. "Take it slow, she's new, give her space; you come off a little intense sometimes, dude…" Whatever. I knew from the first second that I was in love. It wasn't what I expected, but is love predictable? It was surprisingly joyless, hard, edgy and dull. I accepted this. Every time I saw her, it was like a knife carving a six-inch valley through my skull. There was always fear and longing and desperation mixed in with my desire, my inspiration.

I liked those feelings, I needed them, but I never felt fucked up until I met the love of my life.

When we were seniors in high school, she was still acting distant and coy, so I pulled back. I overheard her friends at lunch teasing her that she liked "authority figures"—I guess she said that some cop was cute or something, so I tried to impress her by joining the Marine Corps right after graduating high school. I thought it worked for a while; I emailed her every two days, like clockwork, and she wrote back. Every time that inbox chimed, I became lighter than air. My Marine buddies gave me shit, "There's your girlfriend again!" What a rush it was to have her actually think of me. I would have emailed her every two goddamn minutes, but I knew that would not come across as the stable, confident man that I was trying to portray, or become. I don't know. Before I met her, I thought I was normal. One look in those blue eyes, seeing her smile, things got foggy. It short-circuited something. I didn't know whether to swim against the tide—fight it and try to calm my thoughts and emotions, or embrace it and ride that wave of desire and love and terror. I will say, I felt alive, man, on fire.

She emailed me back and forth for a few months, like friends, you know, getting to know each other. I thought it was working. I thought I was playing my role to a T. Then she stopped, disappeared, went dark, started ignoring me. My friends back home said she got upset at something she heard about me from one of my ex-girlfriends. Then she started posting pictures of her and some guy. Huggy, lovie, cheek to cheek photos. They got an apartment together. I said nothing. I did nothing. That was two years ago, but my hatred has not abated; it has intensified with the relentless drip, drip, drip like I'm sleeping under a leak in the roof of my sanity.

How dare she? How can she do this to me? Why does she have this power over me? Why am I such a weak-minded piece of shit?

I want to call her right now and show her that I can affect her too. I can get inside her head. Sarcastic and slow: "Hey little girl, is your daddy home? No? Wanna see what kinda things I can do? I bet I can do to you things he can't do. I can take you lower than dirt, I can take you high." I spent a lot of time in the desert pretty fucking high. I told myself I needed it to cope, to make the mysteries seem a little less intimidating, a little less oppressive. When I shoot up, those are times when I feel like all these thoughts are someone else's and I get a little reprieve, then I wake up in a pool of hot sweat and sticky blood again.

Thinking of her, thinking of THEM, it's that freight train again, churning through my head. It obliterates everything in its path and leaves waste and destruction, noises of grinding metal, sparks, heat.

"Did you kill anyone in Iraq?" These are fucking supposedly smart people asking me these idiotic questions. Yeah, Dummy, I did. It was my job, and I was good at it. I actually lost count of my kills, and yes, there are women and children in the mix—you couldn't tell who the fuck to trust over there. It's not my fault; I didn't decide to invade that place where they hated us, where they hated me. I see their faces every time I close my eyes, mixed with hers, mixed with his.

The cutting helps. I know I deserve harm. I can balance my mental torment with some physical pain; the scarlet blood pouring down my chest somehow eases the urgency of my anguish; I know delivering and absorbing pain is my destiny, so when I cut myself I feel honorable; I feel like I'm playing fair. Things just make a little more sense when I'm bleeding; I seem a little less frantic upstairs, if you get me. Everything slows down and thoughts stop ricocheting off every surface. The therapist at the VA wants to give me a diagnosis, a label, calls it PTSD; he doesn't know I felt like this before the government made me a killer.

I was glad to kill people. Before that, SHE couldn't even see me. I was invisible. I was nothing. I was garbage. Bullshit. Now I'm the Grim Fucking Reaper.

I loved her. I thought about her every second; she thought I was creepy? She moved in with some dickhead with a fucking ponytail?

I'm getting dressed; my uniform still feels good, feels right. Authority figures. This rage, this heat; I'm going over there. I got a bad desire.

I'm on fire.

# THE BALLAD OF MR. BUDOKAI
*By Matt Martinek*

He seemed the gentlest of creatures, almost like a cartoon mouse or an Asian Charlie Chaplin, complete with black bowler and cane. His gait was a little awkward… kind of a stutter-step on the verge of severe drunkenness, with the cane saving him from the pavement at every curb or crosswalk. You would see this tiny fellow around town, clomping about, minding his own, always with a big smile, which always overshadowed his pencil-thin moustache. He was just one of those characters… the ones whose histories were created for them on the lips of bemused children or bored housewives. I had no issue with him. But my friends… they did.

You know how kids are. Especially kids in a group. They called us the Three Musketeers around town, as we were never seen alone. The group consisted of yours truly (Charlie), Ricky, and Dom, which was short for Dominic. Amongst the group, however, Dom was referred to as "Dumb" instead, which was funny because he was the smartest of the group, kind of a nerd, really. I guess it's like calling a big fat motherfucker "Tiny" or something like that.

Dumb was also skinny as hell, and had the reddest hair you could imagine. He always said he was Italian, but I don't know too many Italians with flaming red hair and freckles. The other kids would pick on him constantly, but Ricky and I always had his back. Ricky, on the other hand… he was dumb for real. He was held back in kindergarten and struggled ever since. But the girls loved him, and always followed him around school. They always said he was a cutie, and sometimes we would catch him at school in the coatroom making out with some starry-eyed little girl. He just had those good genetics… jet-black hair, tan skin, and a little muscle to him, too. As far as good old Charlie goes, well, I was pretty much a nobody. No looks, no smarts, no talent, nothing. Dry as a popcorn fart. Invisible as the plague.

It was that one particular summer, the summer of '88, when everything started to change. Me and my buddies, we were all twelve… that weird puberty shit was kicking in and we were all getting moody as fuck. Every day felt like 1,000 degrees outside, and boredom was always the enemy. Unfortunately, in an attempt to ease their testosterone-fueled frustrations, my friends began to turn their attention to Mr. Budokai. It started innocently enough with Ricky and Dumb making noises towards the man or flipping him off as we passed, but it progressed as the heat of the summer intensified. I was never one to pick on a person… it just didn't feel right. But, as they say, peer pressure is a bitch. So I followed, as a lamb to slaughter.

The act that pushed things over the edge took place at the fruit market downtown. We saw Mr. Budokai there nearly every Saturday, and Ricky told me they had a plan. I didn't like the sound of it one bit, and I tried to get them to go with me to see the new Freddy Krueger movie instead, but they just wouldn't have it. I tried to make up excuses why I couldn't go, but my friends knew me too well. "Oh come on Chuck, why do you gotta be such a pussy about it?

You got a hard-on for this weirdo or something?" Ricky had such a way with words, God love him. I was stuck.

The night before this plan was supposed to take place, I thought at length about this mysterious fellow and all of the stories I had heard about him. There were so many possibilities floating around… that he was retarded, that he was an ex-ninja, that he had bodies buried in his back yard, or that he might even be some sort of war hero from his native country. All bullshit, I was sure, but I just wished my friends hadn't taken an interest in harassing this person that we really knew nothing about. I even asked my parents what his deal was, and neither of them had the slightest clue. It seemed Mr. Budokai was a puzzle no one could solve.

That Saturday started out with a lump in my throat because I was nervous as hell. I didn't know what was going to happen… my only hope was that Budokai would simply not show. Unlikely, but not impossible. My friends and I made it to the market at around noon, and to my relief, our target was nowhere to be seen. I tried to speed up the process and suggested other dastardly things to do on such a beautiful, sunny day but Dumb just replied, "Don't worry. He'll be here. He's always here." So we waited, and watched.

Fate would have it no other way, it seemed. At around 1, we spotted the little fellow stumbling his way up the street about a block away. The largest smile grew upon Ricky's face, and he walked away from us into the vendors' stands. "Where the hell is he going?" I asked. Dumb replied, "To get ammunition, of course. It's gonna get messy!" I watched Ricky as he bought a bunch of tomatoes, put them into a plastic bag, and quickly made his way back to us, grinning uncontrollably. Fuck. So this was their plan.

Everything seemed in slow motion as Mr. Budokai neared the market, step-by-step, heartbeat-by-heartbeat. Ricky and Dumb each took a few tomatoes as they perched behind one of the stands, like snipers in wait. I stayed a few steps behind. I wanted no part of it. Even at that moment, I didn't think Ricky or Dumb had enough balls to go through with it. Just as that thought entered my mind, Ricky yelled, "Hey Budokai, you weird little fuck, check this out!" A tomato sailed through the air, as Budokai froze in mid-step and spotted the little red orb coming for him. *SPLOOSH!* Right on his black vest it smashed, as everyone at the market looked in his direction. The man made eye contact with us, but his smile never wavered, which I thought was the strangest thing. That singular tomato opened up the floodgates, as Ricky and Dumb pelted the man with more and more. The tomatoes' entrails engulfed this poor man, and everyone started to laugh. Dumb motioned to me and yelled, "Come on, you pussy!" I wanted to walk away, but I didn't.

I came up behind my friends, put my hand in the bag, and pulled out the largest, juiciest tomato I could. One would be enough, just so they couldn't say I wussed out. I cocked my arm back, and wailed that fucker right at the little man. Unfortunately, my aim was a little different than my friends'. My tomato hit Mr. Budokai, square in the face with a force that knocked him to the ground and sent his bowler cap into the street. His face was drenched in the gooey juice and dripping seeds (mixed with a bit of blood, I'm sure), and everything stopped. The laughter stopped. Hell, there was no sound at all. There were just the stares of the people, including my friends, aimed squarely at me. Mr. Budokai sat there, frozen, looking quite the mess, and he stared at me as well. But again, somehow… his smile remained.

I ran from the market with a speed that could only be born of embarrassment and shame. My legs burned like fire as tears streamed down my cheeks the whole way to my house. I could not believe what I had done, but I also cursed the kind of luck that would allow my action, over everyone else's, to turn a prank into something more. My parents knew that I was upset but there was no way I could tell them what happened. How could I have been so stupid? I didn't want anything to do with it, but I took part anyways. I hurt that man, and he had done absolutely nothing to me.

For the entire week after, I kept replaying the event over and over again in my mind… I wanted to take it back, to somehow make amends. I didn't want any part of the Musketeers, either… those fools were the ones who got me into this whole thing in the first place. They kept calling me on the phone, but I told my mom I didn't want to talk, that they were no longer my friends at all. I just sat in my room, alone with my guilt. What could I do?

It would take some nerve, and a whole lot of balls, but I settled on making an apology to Mr. Budokai. I had to… it was simply the right thing to do. I knew where he would be on Saturday, if he weren't too embarrassed. Again, at the market. I would follow him until we got away from the crowd, and tell him how sorry I was… that it just got out of hand. It was my only option.

And so the day came, and just like the weekend before, that same lump in my throat appeared, but with nervousness that was much stronger and debilitating this time around. I was sweating and my hands were shaking. I did not want to face this man… not just because I was embarrassed but because the guy was strange as fuck and I didn't know how he would react. For all I knew he could bop me with his cane and beat the living shit out of me. Still, I probably deserved it.

I made my way to the market, thinking of what I would say and how I would approach him, dreading the moment. Budokai was not there yet, so I set up shop… another sniper in waiting. It seemed forever, and my heart beat faster and faster, with my nerves as raw as a rotting tooth. And, eventually, there he was… waddling up the street. I felt like I was going to have a fucking heart attack. I stood by, out of site, and watched him as he began to browse. He was so polite to everyone he came in contact with, and always with that damned grin! Another thing I did notice, however, was a small bandage on the bridge of his nose… remnants of my stupidity. After about a half hour, he finished up his shopping, and made his way up the street, with a few bags of groceries. I followed, about ten yards behind. It was the moment of truth.

As I continued behind this man, my curiosity began to get the best of me. All of these stories about Budokai began to enter my mind… were any of them true? I could've approached him and apologized right away, but something told me to keep following. Where on earth does a man like this live? What of his family? Is it a nice house? I was going to find out. Mile followed mile, and just as I was getting ready to abort the mission, Budokai stopped at the gate of what was apparently his home.

The house was meager, yet well kept and clean looking. A two-story brick; more than enough for one person. The yard was perfect… flowers and shrubbery out front. Nothing stood out. A part of me was disappointed. What a usual surrounding for such an unusual man. And so, with my heart in my throat, I yelled, "Mr. Budokai!" He was startled, and actually dropped his bags. I quickly went up to him, and he looked afraid for a moment until I spoke. "I'm Charlie, and I'm that idiot who hit you with that tomato last week. It was a stupid prank and I just wanted to say that I'm sorry. I was going along with my friends and things just got out of hand." I was relieved to get this off of my chest. I waited for what seemed a lifetime for some type of response as he stared at me confusedly. But then, it came.

"Ah! Charlie! Apology accepted! Believe it or not, I was that age once, too! I have to say, you cut me up pretty good on the nose, here." He pointed at his bandage. His accent was nearly nonexistent, but you could still tell he wasn't born in the States.

"I'm sorry, sir, I guess my aim was a little off." I retorted.

"Oh no, I'd say it was dead on!" Budokai laughed, as did I. "Do me a favor, my son… make an old man happy. Come inside and have some tea with me?" He seemed so genuine with his words. I smiled at the old man, picked up his bags, and followed him inside. There was a warmth about Mr. Budokai… it felt like I was talking with my grandfather.

So there we sat, at Mr. Budokai's kitchen table, sipping tea and talking about everything and anything. He was one of the nicest men I had ever talked to. Had a sense of humor, too, which is rare for an older fellow. I was glad that things had gone so well.

"I have to say, you always seem so happy… you always have that smile on your face. Even when my friends and I were making fun of you, you still smiled at us. How do you keep your cool?" I had to know his secret.

"Oh, Charlie, don't mistake the smile for happiness… I simply smile because I can't frown. You see, back in the war all those years ago, I was shot in the neck, and the bullet destroyed some nerves. The damage was quite severe. It entered at the neck and lodged into my face. Now my smile cannot be wiped off." A tear fell down the man's cheek as he said this. My eyes redirected to his neck as I did spot the remnants of a scar. Apparently he had seen battle, like some of the stories I had heard about him. "But don't fret! I did my duty, and I do have my share of medals and trophies!" Budokai's eyes gleamed as he spoke of his victories. "I must show you, Charlie! Come see what I've done. I have it all set up!" Budokai already started for the stairs, and I must admit, I was intrigued.

I followed my new friend up the stairs, but as I began to climb, I noticed a peculiar scent… almost like a piece of rotten food that was forgotten about. Mr Budokai climbed the stairs excitedly, almost to the point of perfect health. The cane no longer seemed necessary.

At the top of the stairs, he showed me into his bedroom. Everything was neat and tidy, unlike the conditions your regular bachelor would keep. He pointed towards the wall, and I did not understand what he was trying to show me. It was just a stark, white wall. What was this? A joke?

Mr. Budokai slid his fingers around the left side of the wall, and I heard a barely audible *click*. As he was doing this I noticed the scent of rot growing, almost burning my nostrils. I was becoming more than uneasy. Something… was wrong. He slid the façade of the wall aside, and I could not believe what I saw. Lined up in two rows, on shelves, resided six shrunken, mummified heads. The hideous smell rocked me backwards as my eyes attempted to take in the grisly sight of these skulls… the writhing looks of pain, the differing states of decay, the stringy white hairs that reminded me of the silk of a corncob. I believe I was screaming, but I don't know for sure, as it was all so very surreal. As I attempted to get my bearings, I noticed the shelving underneath the heads… six matching pairs of shriveled, twisted hands.

"See, Charlie! My trophies! These men were great, but I was greater! And look… I have some recent additions!" Mr. Budokai gestured towards the corner of this hidden room, where I saw… my friends. There, in the dim light, I could make out the faces of Ricky and Dumb, both in their own container of pale green liquid, streaked red from whatever blood was still present. Their features were distorted, their mouths frozen in their screams, but it was definitely them. It was at that very moment that my bowels let loose, and I messed my pants. I looked at Mr. Budokai, whose smile had transformed into something a bit more ghastly and devious.

"Charlie!!! It seems you have dirtied yourself!!!" Budokai chuckled as he raised his cane and brought it down onto my head with a great deal of force. I fell to the floor, in disbelief of the situation. I knew I was bleeding badly… I could feel the warmth drip from my scalp. I was dizzy, but still conscious, so with all the strength I had for a boy of twelve, I rushed the old man, knocking him down in the process. I ran/fell down the stairs and busted out of his door into the street. My legs were on fire again, with tears streaming down my face. I sprinted home, covered in my own filth, with the visual of my friends' decapitated heads floating through my mind.

When everything was said and done, the police found Mr. Budokai waiting patiently at the bus stop, with his everlasting grin still stretched across his face. As they approached him, he asked only about his newfound friend. "How is Charlie? I hope his head is all right. Such a good boy he is!"

# THE TAPHOPHILE
### By Gerri R. Gray

I am a taphophile, and have been for many years. Perhaps you've heard of the word before… perhaps not. At any rate, it literally means "a person with a fondness for, or is attracted to, graves, tombs, and/or funerals." As a taphophile, one of my passions is visiting old cemeteries to photograph the tombstones, mausoleums, and funerary statues. I realize there are some who would regard my unusual interest as a rather morbid pastime. But that's only because they don't see the *beauté de la mort* – the beauty of death – through the same eyes as mine.

It was in the early springtime, on the kind of day when little islands of melting snow cling to the awakening hills, and winter's slowly dying breath lingers stubbornly in the air, that the cemetery known as Primrose Hill called out to me. As I was parking my van on a patch of level ground, alongside the gravel-covered road that wound its way past the graves of corpses from another century, a news bulletin came over the radio, reporting that a search was underway for yet another local area woman who had gone missing. There had been so many over the past few months, I lost count. I switched off the ignition and set off on foot with my digital camera in hand.

With the exception of the occasional cawing of an unseen crow and the crunching sound my boot heels made as I walked upon the loose aggregation of crushed stones, the place was blanketed in a peaceful silence. There appeared not to be another soul around, which was fine by me since I'm hardly what you'd call a 'people person.' Solitude is one of the things that I cherish dearly, yet one of the things I never seem to get enough of.

For a small town cemetery, Primrose Hill was fairly large and bordered on three sides by the wilds of a sprawling forest preserve. Its oldest section dated back to the mid-nineteenth century and was dotted with weathered gravestones into which were engraved poetic epitaphs. Mausoleums with Gothic, Grecian and Art Nouveau architectural details sprung up from the hillsides, and larger-than-life statues – some with missing hands, and others, entire arms – stood like motionless sentinels with perpetually mourning faces.

After about fifteen minutes of walking about and snapping pictures, I came upon a small mausoleum situated alongside the main road. My eyes were instantly drawn to its ironwork doors, which featured an elaborate Egyptian-themed design. Unlike the chained and padlocked doors of all the other mausoleums I had seen and photographed, these were unlocked and stood invitingly ajar. My taphophile heart jumped for joy!

I had photographed many mausoleums in the past, but never their interiors. The unlocked doors of this one were beckoning me to enter, and I was unable to resist the temptation. The unexpected and rare opportunity to photograph one from the inside was too good not to take advantage of.

I took a quick look around to ensure that no one was watching, and then began to ascend the mausoleum's slab-like steps that lead up to its entrance. But just as I reached the top, the crunching sound of tires on the gravel road stopped me in my tracks. *Damn it!* I cursed to myself, dreading that it was the cemetery's caretaker in his rickety, white Ford pickup truck, for I'd had a few unpleasant run-ins with him in the past. A cantankerous old louse whose mouth bore a slight droop from a long-ago stroke, he had made it quite clear that his feelings for "morbid weirdos" like me were anything but amicable. All I needed was for him to accuse me of breaking into a mausoleum and call the police, which I had little doubt he would do, given the opportunity.

The vehicle turned out to be a black, late model Corvette, and I exhaled a sigh of relief. As it slowly crept past me, the driver – a dark-haired man in his mid-to-late thirties – turned his head in my direction and flashed me an overtly flirtatious smile. I found it to be a rather odd thing, considering he had an attractive, blonde-haired woman sitting right next to him. She stared straight ahead at the road, avoiding eye contact.

After the car disappeared from sight, I took a peek through the open doors of the mausoleum and then ventured inside with camera in hand. Curiously, the air within the mausoleum was noticeably colder than the air outside. The walls at each side contained several crypts, and on the back wall a colorful stained-glass window depicting a winged hourglass encircled by a wreath of lilies radiated in the sunlight.

I had taken at least a dozen pictures when, all of a sudden, a bone-chilling gust scattered some dead leaves across the marble floor. I was sure I heard, within the moaning of the wind, a faint and ghostly voice telling me to go home. I chuckled at my over-active imagination and then proceeded to snap a few more photos, including some "selfies." With my curiosity satisfied, I exited the mausoleum, shutting the doors behind me. I then continued strolling through Primrose Hill, stopping periodically to capture with my camera a particularly interesting gravestone or the haunting beauty of a weeping stone cherub.

I was photographing vistas from the top of a pine-covered hill at the other end of the cemetery, when my ears were suddenly filled with loud rock and roll music. I instinctively turned my head in the direction from which the sound came and observed the same black Corvette that had passed by me earlier pull over to the side of the road at the bottom of the hill. It sat there for several minutes with its engine running and radio blaring before the door on the passenger's side flew open and the blonde-haired woman bolted from the vehicle, screaming wildly on the top of her lungs. The driver's door swung open and the dark-haired man jumped from the car and took off after the fleeing woman. He quickly caught up to her, and then, to my absolute horror, I watched him place what appeared to be a long, white extension cord around her neck and began violently choking her with it. She struggled for a bit, kicking and clawing at her assailant, and finally collapsed upon the ground. The man stuffed the cord into the front pocket of his jacket and then started dragging the woman's limp body into the nearby woods.

I could scarcely believe what my eyes had just witnessed. It was surreal, to say the least! Terror assaulted me, like a monstrous bird flapping its wings within the confines of my chest, throwing my heartbeat into disarray. My palms broke out in a cold sweat. My blood pressure shot up, and I could feel an increase in muscle tension as my fight-or-flight response kicked in.

Terrified, I took off running as fast as I could, my feet stumbling over grave markers and tree roots that protruded from the earth like gnarled fingers. All I could think about was getting out of Primrose Hill as fast as possible and notifying the police. I scolded myself for not getting the license plate number of the Corvette, even though I was too far away to make it out clearly. And then I regretted not heeding the warning of the ghostly voice in the mausoleum. I was convinced beyond the shadow of a doubt that it was portentous in its nature. *Oh, why didn't I listen to it and leave when I had the chance?* I grilled myself.

I had been running for quite some time and felt as if I were going in circles. I then realized I had managed to get myself lost. I paused to catch my breath and collect my thoughts by a granite sarcophagus guarded by a large metallic angel whose copper alloys had oxidized to blue-green. My lungs felt as though they were on fire and a cold sweat beaded up on my forehead. I ordered my trembling body to calm down, and tried to convince myself that everything would be all right; I would surely find my way back to my van, sooner or later. I gazed around and was relieved to see no sign of the Corvette. I took a deep breath and then once again broke into a run.

The road eventually forked and I had to choose whether to go left or to go right. A gut feeling – call it 'woman's intuition' if you like – prompted me to go right, so I did. The scenery began to look familiar, which imparted a slight sense of comfort to me. I then spotted the mausoleum with the unlocked doors just up the road and knew I was heading in the right direction.

"Yes!" I shouted with a temporary burst of glee. I could feel a smile form on my lips despite the dread and panic raging deep within me.

I began to run faster and, within a few minutes, my parked van came into view. Nothing could have been a more welcome sight at that moment! I suddenly felt overwhelmed by a flood of emotions, and tears welled up in my eyes.

I unlocked the door to my van, rushed to get in, and then quickly locked the door. With my hand shaking, I inserted the key into the ignition and turned it. Like a scene out of some godforsaken horror movie, the van wouldn't start. *This can't be happening.*

"God damn it!" I screamed at the instrument panel.

I tried to start it again, but the engine still refused to turn over. And then I spied the black Corvette ominously approaching. A wave of dread washed over me.

The car pulled up alongside of me and the driver got out and casually walked up to my door. I instantly recognized him as the man who had strangled the blonde. He rapped on my rolled-up window with his knuckles and asked if I were in need of any help.

*Maybe he doesn't know that I saw what he did to that girl*, I said to myself, trying to calm the terror that was rising up from the pit of my stomach. I turned to him and forced a smile upon my lips. "I'm fine, thank you," I lied, trying my utmost not to sound as though I had just witnessed a cold-blooded murder. "I'm just waiting for my husband." I gazed down at the watch on my wrist and then turned back to the man who was peering at me through the window. "He should be showing up any minute now."

"Oh, you don't say?" he asked me. The tone of his voice told me he didn't believe my story. (I guess I never was very good at telling fibs.) A frightful scowl contorted the muscles of his face. His watery blue eyes glared at mine, filling me with uneasiness. They were cold and empty eyes, like those of a predatory animal... and he was stalking his prey.

I nodded my head, straining my face to maintain the smile. Panic was clawing at my insides, but I had to keep a calm exterior. If I exhibited even the slightest sign of fear, he would surely know that I had witnessed his unspeakable crime.

He turned and began to walk back to the Corvette. I exhaled a sigh of relief. However, it proved to be premature, as he stopped after taking a few steps and then returned to my window. His face was now aglow with an eerie, feigned smile, as though he had slipped on a friendly-looking mask to gain my trust while he had his back to me.

"You wouldn't, by any chance, be lying through your teeth to me, would you?" he inquired.

"No," I lied through my teeth. "Of course not. I have no reason to do that."

The smile on his face dissolved back into a snarl. His eyes turned menacing. "Women are always lying! It's what bitches do best!" he yelled in an insane voice. "Filthy lying whores! Every fucking one of them! And you're no different from the rest!"

"My husband is going to be arriving any second now!" I reiterated, hoping it would prompt the man to leave. But it soon became apparent to me that he had no such intention.

He went over to his car, opened the door on the passenger side, and retrieved something from the glove compartment. To my horror, he then returned to the spot where I was parked. His right hand was wrapped tightly around the handle of a black, steel, expandable baton. I blared my horn, but it didn't faze him in the least. With his teeth clenched, he swung the baton against my window, taking out a small chip of glass. I frantically pumped the gas pedal and tried the ignition key again and again, but the van stubbornly refused to start. There came another swing of the baton and a crack resembling a spider's web fanned out with a loud thud. Shielding my face with the back of my hand, I let out a scream, and then another swing of the baton completely shattered the window, showering me with pieces of broken glass. I scrambled across to the passenger seat as he pulled up on the lock and opened my door. Like a wild animal, he lunged at me, but I managed to open the passenger door in the nick of time and fled from the van into the adjoining woods.

Branches and prickly weeds scratched at my face and body as I ran like a doe from a hunter. The forest grew denser and darker, and I felt like a small, helpless creature being swallowed alive by some giant monster with a voracious appetite.

I don't know for how long I had been running. It felt like an eternity. My leg muscles were on fire with pain, my stomach was cramping up, and my pounding heart felt ready to burst. The terror-stricken little voice in my head told me I had to keep moving, but my fatigued body demanded a rest. I paused for a brief bit to catch my breath, all the while keeping my ears alert to the sound of the killer's approaching footsteps. But all I heard was a loud droning coming from beyond a fern-guarded outcropping of low rocks. I don't know why, but I felt strangely compelled to follow the sound, as if my will was no longer my own.

The buzzing grew louder as I climbed over the ferns and rocks, until, all at once, it became intense, filling my ears with the rapid beating of a thousand swarming wings. Gazing down, my eyes were met by the sickening sight of six dead bodies. The maggot-infested carcasses all appeared to be female and were arranged in disturbingly obscene poses. Some were partially clothed, while others were completely nude. All had been grotesquely mutilated. Hordes of flies and bees and other winged insects crawled upon them, feasting on their remains, while others circled in the air above them. The eyes of one of the fresher-looking corpses were being pecked at and consumed by a trio of contentious crows.

My brain reeled and my stomach churned. I turned away and vomited onto a carpet of moss and fallen branches. The spell was broken and once again I sprinted as if my feet had suddenly sprouted wings.

Through a thicket of trees, I could make out the shape of a building in the near distance. I ran towards it. However, as I drew nearer to the structure and realized that it was nothing more than the derelict ruins of an old chapel that had long ago been abandoned and boarded-up, my short-lived spark of optimism extinguished like a burning wick in a rain storm.

Part of the wall at the rear of the chapel had crumbled away over the years, leaving a small opening at the bottom that was partially obscured by a clump of dead, thorny briars and brambles. It appeared to be large enough for me to squeeze my body through it, so I decided to venture inside and hide from the killer that was pursuing me. And then a thought ran through my mind. *Perhaps I'd get lucky and find something within the building that I could arm myself with should he discover my whereabouts.* Using a thick stick as a primitive tool to keep the thorny branches at bay, I crouched down in front of the opening and then crawled through it on my hands and knees, taking care not to damage my camera. My back, on the other hand, did not make it through unscathed. A jagged piece of stone protruding like a stalactite from the upper part of the hole ripped through the material of my jacket, slicing open my flesh from between my shoulder blades down to the small of my back. I clenched my teeth and forced the pain out of my mind, daring not to make a sound in case the killer was within earshot.

I was now inside the chapel, which was lit by hazy rays of sunlight that beamed through random holes where the rotting roof had fallen away. I stood up and, with my hands, dusted off the dirt and webs from my clothes. I gazed around at my surroundings, keeping my eyes peeled for anything with potential as a weapon for self-defense. The floor was buried under years of dirt, bits of broken plaster, and splintered wood. Filthy wooden pews, some broken, were strewn about, and a rust-encrusted, wrought iron chandelier that had fallen victim to a crumbling ceiling and gravity, sat idly on the ground, enshrouded by long-forsaken spider webs, thick with dust.

I made my way across the rubble to the altar, hoping to find some heavy brass candlesticks that could be used to bash a man's skull in, but there were none to be found. Upon the altar were nothing but a dusty taper candle and an equally dusty box containing a single wooden match. Looking around, my eyes caught sight of a large, round object on the floor, which I estimated to be roughly six inches in diameter. Using my foot, I cleared away the debris around it and discovered it was the iron pull ring of a trap door in the floor. I grabbed onto it and lifted up the door. Ten stone steps leading down to what appeared to be an ancient crypt came into view. At the bottom, a large rat scurried by and vanished into a veil of shadows.

My instincts were strongly advising me not to go down there. But rats or no rats, I felt I was really left with no other alternative. In the likely event that the killer came looking for me in the chapel, the underground chamber afforded me the best, and only, hiding spot. It was my one and only chance to survive.

I struck the match against the side of the altar. No flame... not even a spark. On the fourth try, its sulfur head ignited and I lit the candle in preparation for my descent into whatever hell awaited me below. I began to climb down the steps, shutting the trap door over my head. The dim glow of the candle's flame cast flickering shadows upon the walls of stone below, and gave the room the ambiance of a medieval dungeon. The crypt itself was long and narrow, abundant with cobwebs, and deathly silent except for the slow and steady sound of dripping water. On the cobblestone floor, in the center of the dank, subterranean chamber, sat six dust-covered, wooden coffins. They were rather plain in appearance and looked to be extremely old.

On any other given day, I would not have hesitated to raise their lids and capture some postmortem shots with my camera. However, I couldn't risk the sound of squeaking coffin hinges giving away my hiding spot in case the killer was lurking nearby.

The flame on my candle suddenly sputtered and then met its demise, and I was swallowed up by the immediate ensuing darkness. I stood motionless. Waiting. Listening.

Drip...

Drip...

Drip...

And then the sound of something scratching at wood came from somewhere in the black void that surrounded me like a sea of pitch. It stopped for a few moments and then continued; only this time it was louder than before. My thoughts flashed back to the not-so-small rat I had seen dart by earlier and I felt a panic attack brewing. My fear of rats started in childhood after watching the 1970's film, *Willard*, and far outweighed my other phobias, which were spiders and heights. I listened with dread in my heart as the sounds of tiny claws intensified. Soon, they were joined by other scratching noises coming from different locations around me in the dark. I envisioned myself surrounded by an army of hideous, gigantic rats. I struggled furiously to restrain myself from freaking out.

Suddenly, I felt something sharp, like long fingernails, pierce the flesh of my right upper arm. The pain was searing and caused me to scream and drop my camera. It hit the stone floor with a crash and the impact activated the flash and the fingernails immediately withdrew from my arm. The bright light that momentarily illuminated the confines of the crypt unveiled a terrifying scene that seemed too nightmarish to be real. Yet it *was* real.

Standing around me were half a dozen corpses in varying states of decomposition. Rotting faces, some more skull than flesh, gazed upon me hungrily from all directions. To my ultimate horror, these things that should have been dead and lying still in their graves were alive as if by some power most unholy.

The light from the flash died away after a second and the inky blackness once again consumed the crypt. I could hear the horrible breathing noises emitted by those undead things, followed by the sounds of their dragging feet moving closer to the spot where I stood, paralyzed from head to toe with fear. My blood instantly turned to ice in my veins. I let out another scream that was loud enough to wake up the dead; however, it was quite evident that they already were. I turned to flee, but my escape from the crypt was impeded by the long fingernails of other hellish hands that dug into my flesh like razor-sharp talons. My screams ricocheted off the damp walls of stone and echoed throughout the crypt and the chapel above as I struggled to free myself.

At last I managed to break away from the living dead things, which were now emitting high-pitched shrieking noises that were as horrible sounding as they were inhuman. Rushing towards the steps that lead out of this chamber of horror, I knocked one or two of the foul creatures onto the ground. The sound of their brittle bones cracking and their skulls shattering assaulted my ears. It was like a sound straight out of a nightmare… a sound that will never leave my memory for as long as I continue to live.

Running as quickly as humanly possible, I made it half the way up the stairs before tripping. I fell facedown, twisting my left ankle and banging up my knees and forearms in the process. Patches of my skin had been shredded by the rough texture of the stones, and from my stinging wounds my blood dribbled out, exciting those abominable things that I could hear getting closer. My heart was thumping furiously in my chest. I thought at any given moment it might burst and that would be the end of me. A quick death would certainly be preferable to being devoured alive by these decaying things that, by all accounts, should have been dead; yet, in defiance of the laws of the natural world, were not.

All at once, I felt a skeletal hand wrap its bony fingers around my injured ankle and attempt to drag me back down into the crypt. A surge of panic-driven adrenaline provided me with the strength needed to kick myself free from the monstrous grip. Ignoring the pain from my injuries, I picked myself up and made a mad dash the rest of the way up the stairs and out of the ruins of the abandoned chapel.

My ankle was rapidly swelling up and the pain was growing in its intensity. However, I dared not stop to rest. I had to keep running, no matter how great the pain. Through the leafless branches of tangled trees and shrubs, I could see glimpses of the winding road up ahead. I then heard the sound of tires rolling over loose gravel and could make out a vehicle. It was the white Ford pickup truck belonging to the cemetery's caretaker. *Oh, thank God*, I thought, and then almost chuckled out loud. Never in my wildest dreams would I have thought the day would come when I'd be pleased to see that man. But that day was today. As I continued to run towards the road, I began to shout for help and wave my arms wildly, hoping that he would hear my voice or see me and stop.

And then, I felt something slip around my neck, stopping me in my tracks and cutting off my supply of air. Without seeing it, and even before clutching at it in an attempt to rip it away from my throat, I knew right away it was the killer's garrote. As I fought tooth and nail to regain my freedom, as well as my breath, I could see, through the branches, the white pickup truck drive past and disappear around the bend. My hope for being rescued vanished right along with it.

"You didn't really think you were going to get away from me that easily, did you, bitch?" came a man's raspy voice from behind me. It was void of humanity and filled with a cruelness that ran deep. "Stop struggling and just accept your fate," he demanded. "Don't you understand? You have to die. I can't leave any witnesses."

I was certain that my demise was but minutes away and I became panic-stricken. However, with my throat being crushed, I was unable to scream or even plead for my life. A frightful gurgling noise was all I could manage. My heart was pounding. My vision was getting blurry. I could scarcely believe what was happening to me. It had to be a bad dream. It just *had* to be.

I had always heard that it was a common thing for death to be preceded by the flashing of one's life before their eyes. However, the only thing I could see in my mind's eye was the horrifying image of my strangled corpse decomposing in the woods, alongside the dead bodies of the madman's other victims.

Confusion and dizziness were now setting in and I found that I was rapidly losing the strength to struggle. My arms were going limp. The cord around my neck tightened and its fibers cut deeper into my flesh. I could feel my face puffing up and I somehow sensed it was turning a shade of beet red or perhaps even purple. I then heard my assailant's voice taunting me with his twisted plan to rape my corpse.

I wasn't a religious person; but, at this point, I found myself praying inside my head to God, or to anyone else who would listen, to stop my agony. I just wanted my inevitable death to be swift and mercifully bring this living nightmare to an end. I suddenly began to slip into a drowsy, almost dream-like, state and my panic melted away into a strange peacefulness. I knew my death was rapidly approaching.

My body was starting to slump to the ground when I heard the man behind me wailing out loud like a demon. He released the cord from my neck and I landed on the wet leaves that carpeted the floor of the woodland. I immediately gasped to refill my lungs with air and then coughed and panted like an overheated dog. My head was pounding with pain that was far worse than any migraine headache I had ever experienced and it hurt like hell to swallow. But there were no words to describe how wonderful it felt to still be alive.

Just before I descended into unconsciousness, my eyes beheld the horrific sight of the six undead creatures from the chapel's crypt savagely ripping the head and limbs from the killer's torso. His blood sprayed in the air in every direction, and some of the splatter, still warm to the touch, landed in my hair and on my face. His wailing ceased and the creatures began to feed on his bloodied body parts.

When I came to, I found myself sitting on the glass-covered front seat of my van. My dented camera was sitting on the seat beside me, and there was no sign of the black Corvette. Confusion flooded my brain. *How did I get back to my van?* I wondered. *Was it all just a horrible dream?* Nothing made any sense. I examined my throat in the rear view mirror. It was badly bruised, and a dark red mark left by the extension cord confirmed the reality of my nightmarish ordeal.

With curiosity eating away at me, I picked up my camera and switched it on. I was pleasantly surprised to find it still in working condition after having been dropped on a cobblestone floor. I set it to playback mode and scrolled through all the pictures until the last one taken was displayed on the LCD screen. It was a tilted, low-angle shot of an empty crypt.

# BROKEN

## *By Joanna Koch*

She woke, smeared with stains from another fecal demon that had suckled at her breast. Eighty-five degrees and humid, the smell of excreta pervaded Camille's ancestral mansion. Heavy curtains kept the daylight out. Sunlight damaged the conjured manikins. Though they hugged the moist cellar walls by day and ventured forth only after dusk, Camille wasn't going to take any chances. Her ritual had to work.

She'd been warned. The loyalty of fecal demons surpassed all other spirits made flesh. They slid into the world through an unholy tract, mingled delight with disgust, and bonded with their mother by mutual arousal during multiple virgin births. The sensation was addictive; thus the spell was forbidden.

Camille had confidence. She knew when to stop.

She came into the practice cognizant of the legend of the black priest who performed the rite at age ninety-three. Rather than resurrecting his beloved partner as planned, he awakened a whole lifetime of defecations. They fought their way back to him over decades and distances. Decayed fecal matter, steaming sludge, and deteriorated chemical gasses clung to him with noxious affection. It was unknown in the coven whether he perished from bacterial poisoning, intestinal disease, or from suffocation under the devoted caresses of his own reanimated waste.

The coven assured Camille that her sister's kidnapping, torture, and death would evoke a natural karmic correction in the sacred circle of life. Camille called their passive acceptance bullshit. She wasn't willing to wait for revenge. She'd waited already, and it had ended in her sister's violent death. She'd waited while the police gave their useless advice, waited while her exorbitant attorneys flailed at futile prosecutions, and waited while more than one hired hitman succumbed to a powerful defensive curse. Extreme measures were required to infiltrate the enemy cult. The bastards had stolen Camille's sister and wasted her unique soul as a common human sacrifice.

Camille burned with tremors of revenge. Midsummer heat drew a veil of sweat across her brow as she pulled a robe over the fecal stains on her body. The smell of occult waste from her bowels possessed an emotional resonance more potent than the citrus body-wash fragrance that replaced it. She almost hated to shower. Purified inside and out, adhering thrice daily to the demands of the rite, she toweled off and descended naked to commune with her maturing horde.

Nonverbal lessons reinforced the fecal demon connection with Camille's gut. Her deepest instincts and desires directed her abominable children with no need for her to issue commands. They were part of her body, one with her visceral ambitions.

Camille traced the cellar walls as she felt her way in the dark, waiting for her eyes to adjust. Her demon children no longer bulged beneath her fingers and juddered at her touch. Smears of filth led her deeper into the root cellar, a space unused for years. Little more than a hole carved into the dirt,

Camille crouched low to enter it. The smell of ancient turnips assaulted her. Though her senses were jaded, the acrid odor of decayed vegetation spilled from the cavity, rotten and unearthed.

It was a good sign. The infants had moved on to solid food.

Within, manikins of brown, black, and muddy yellow huddled in a circle under the sagging dirt ceiling. Some were soft, some firm, some peppered with red and green flecks. They'd worked together, an army of half-formed, putrid dolls who now gathered around a shallow pool of sewer water diverted from a rusted drain. Camille crawled into the small cavity and took her place at the edge of the murk. Warmth wafted from the fecal bodies gathered close together in the dirt hole.

Gazing as one, the demons waited until the man's face manifested in the fetid pool. Camille focused on the details to be memorized by the horde: his thick, black moustache, his acne-scarred cheeks, and the pudgy bags ever-present under his clever, mocking eyes. Most important, Camille envisioned the tattoo on his neck, a bastardization of the Coptic cross. Sacred symbol of his high ordainment as the Beast of the enemy order; no other member received it.

Her bowels churned with hatred at the sight of the culprit. Her fecal horde trembled wetly in sympathetic fury. One by one, the fecal demons slipped through the scum of the gazing pool, down the rusted drain, and out through the nocturnal pipes to enact the demands of Camille's insatiable revenge.

* * *

Fiduccio slammed his sanctum door. He was sick of making all the decisions and taking all the risks. Minions made every moment worse. Must they simper and watch him like foolish cretins? He didn't want to be their role model.

Yet no matter how much Fiduccio hated the work and burdens of leadership, he'd never stopped fighting to reach the top. Ascension compelled him like a drug, a curse.

Ordainment as the Beast had taken all the ecstasy out of torture, all the joy out of death. He'd never thought it possible until his last sacrifice. He'd sensed a curious connection to the girl that he was unable to explain. He suspected more power than he was supposed to glean from a minion's filial gift. Had he been a brother or practitioner or anyone other than the Beast, he'd have been able to keep her alive long enough to learn more. But Fiduccio must now be infallible, the expert, unmoved. He was not allowed to explore.

He heard her unwavering voice challenge him: *Descend, my soul, beneath the depths of glory, below our mother Earth. I fear not, for I am become Fear Herself. I am the goddess Below All.*

To kill and eat the enemy was his order's holy writ. Since ingesting the girl's flesh and swallowing her palpitating heart, meat had disgusted him. It was a dangerous secret to keep. Fiduccio now took his meals in private, claimed some arcane research for a new teaching demanded his continued isolation, and flushed away leftovers to avoid censure or suspicion.

With a listless hand, Fiduccio uncovered the warming tray left in his quarters for another dinner he didn't want. An unexpected, seductive smell seeped upwards and intoxicated him. The rich, dark, tang encircled Fiduccio like strong incense before he caught a glimpse of his meal. He tossed the cover on the floor. It clattered. The sour and savory odor of irresistible enticement arose from a thick consommé. Its dense texture was perfect. Fiduccio raised a spoonful with reverence. Unctuousness enveloped his tongue. Fiduccio rolled the stock around his mouth and appreciated the slow, measured skill of a chef who stewed such a dish. Exquisite patience was required to accomplish the complex, subtle effect. He scooped deeper for the next mouthful. The stewed meat had become so tender that it melted into a rich paste. The seasonings were fresh cut, balanced by a master, as evidenced by the green and red flecks that peppered the surface of the dark brown stock.

Fiduccio ate with genuine relish for the first time in weeks. He gulped down ladles full of the rich brown liquid and gorged his gullet, dwelling on the sensation of slick chunks squeezing with little resistance between his teeth. Visions of the sacrificed girl swelled in his head like a fever. He felt drugged, ravenous, and ill with hunger. He ate more. His heart—or was it the heart of the girl struggling for vengeance inside him—thudded in heavy monotone as he labored with desperate ardor to complete his meal.

He must finish. At all costs.

Near the end of the dish, the sensuous smell reverted to a sudden stench. Fiduccio balked at the onslaught of sulfur. He was helpless to pause and think, eating like a starved animal. While a muted part of his brain recognized some sort of filth was splayed on his plate, a dominant and mindless compulsion forced him to shovel more food into his mouth. He saw his feast was unclean. It was a bowl of sewage water and fecal waste. Yet his will reveled madly in perverse persistence. Fiduccio chewed, swallowed, and shuddered with savory repugnance and delight. He glutted, uncontrolled. The delectable softness of stool riddled with surprise clumps of undigested bits made him giggle and retch. Unbearably thirsty, Fiduccio gulped down the last drops of foul liquid until one final treat lay coiled at the bottom of his plate.

A headless, snake-like defecation curled through the dregs of brown juice. The slow, deliberate movement left no doubt it was a living thing.

Fiduccio's face, clothing, and tablecloth were spattered brown and yellow from the ferocity of his feeding. The room stank. Fiduccio's mouth watered with anticipation at the same moment he felt the need to vomit. The luxurious coil of filth slithered onto his spoon, curled through his fingers, and slid upwards around his arm. His gorge rose to meet the tip of the feces as it probed his lips and entered his gawking mouth. Conscious he was insane not to resist, stupefied into submission, Fiduccio let his throat go slack and accepted the moist excretion that wormed its way inside of him. Gasses and thick sludge bloated his chest, stomach, and lower gut until he felt full enough to burst.

The spongy tail of the animated waste left its fecal slime smeared on his lips and tongue. Fiduccio wanted to gag, but his reflex had gone numb. He was helpless. Or worse, maybe he wasn't. Maybe he didn't want to gag at all. Maybe he thrilled that he was enslaved to a sensation he'd never experienced. He longed to taste it, feel it, bath in the smooth and suffocating mystery of human sewage like rancid mother's milk, swallow it and drown and—

Fiduccio ran from the sickening images and urges, roused too late to prevent ingestion of the long coiled snake of excrement. He shoved his fingers down his throat over the toilet bowl. Purging was harder than he thought. He used a toothbrush to no avail. Though his eyes watered and his sides cramped, the filth inside him nested, curled, and clung tight.

He battered his throat until his capillaries burst and his tonsils bled. At last, he gave up. Fiduccio sat on the toilet with his head in his hands, rocking back and forth, waiting for digestion to run its course and rid him of the possessing, animated waste. Fiduccio could not venture forth until the abomination was out and he recovered control. The mire inside him swelled up from his stomach and glazed his tongue with the soft slime of temptation. He imagined saving the damp waste after expulsion, fishing it from the bowl when it seeped out of his feverish anus and hiding the stool in some safe place for further exploration. He giggled in spite of himself.

Fiduccio sobered at the sound of his unbalanced laugh. Vulnerability equaled death for a man of his standing in the cult. He must wait for as many hours as it took for this crazed idiocy to pass. After an hour or two, Fiduccio drifted in and out of sleep. A calming sensation of internal warmth pervaded his dreams. The fullness of the sliding thing inside him stimulated and satisfied his nerve endings from head to toe with a writhing, twining, erotic pulse. He rocked in rhythm with the strange, unseeing eyes that searched his bowels with massaging motions and stretched new pockets of pleasure within his sensitive internal mesh. The only comparable sensation was the saturating glow of first love.

Fiduccio gasped awake. He didn't want to feel this.

He was horribly, visibly aroused. He cried. He stroked himself. He cried some more. He heard a splashing sound. He hadn't relieved himself. He stroked harder. When the second warm coil swam up out of the toilet and snaked its way into his rectum to join its brother, he cried and laughed in ecstatic defilement, a babbling monkey, a worshiper of shit.

* * *

Empty nest syndrome hit Camille doubly hard. Her sister was far away in the next world. Her fecal children had gone off on their mission and expired. She'd been banished from her coven for heresy and left to practice alone. Even though she was beautiful, wealthy, and young, Camille felt lost. Revenge had turned out to not be the palliative she'd expected.

Morose, Camille mused about the possibility of travel, about closing the mansion for a season or two, or perhaps even selling it. Never before had she entertained the idea of leaving her ancestral home, or the land she and her sister had known and cherished. The girls had communed with the native spirits since childhood, growing together in knowledge and power. As sorceresses and sisters, they'd discovered and shared every novel aspect of each other's lives. Camille regretted leaving behind her memories, but what else was left here besides memories and loss?

Clanging bells interrupted Camille's thoughts. It took her a moment to realize the sound was the mansion's doorbell. In a home so distant from the majority of the population, it was rare for a stranger to entreat admission. Camille hadn't heard the bell in years.

She wasn't expecting guests, or she'd have been outside to greet them.

Camille went down to answer the bell. No maid or gardener worked that day, as far as she could recall. A confident sorceress, Camille had no fear of assault. She didn't check the peephole or pull back the curtains before she threw the door open wide.

A muddy man crouched on her steps. He stood at an unsteady angle and shuffled closer. He was caked in black and brown muck. He reeked of the sewer. His filth-stiffened clothing boxed in his frame as though he'd been starved since he last got dressed. Beneath the monochromatic dried sludge, his eyes shone in a dim jaundiced yellow, shot through with broken capillaries of red. He smiled at Camille, breaking open his skeletal head. Green and red flecks peppered his rotten teeth. The grin loosened some of the fecal matter that coated his face. As chunks fell away, they revealed a thick black moustache and traces of acne scars pockmarking his cheeks.

Camille hissed an inward breath and prepared to smite her enemy, grabbing hold of the charm she wore at her throat. The man or creature waved his hands, bowed his head, went down on his knees, and then further down on all fours. His head hung like a beaten dog. The tattoo on his neck was scratched away, in its place a suppurating infection. *The Beast indeed*, Camille thought. She raised her left palm high to end her foe's life, and then paused.

The sight of his humiliation and complete regression pleased her. Camille felt a twinge in her belly. It radiated outward through her extremities when his barely human voice pleaded:

"Feed me."

The twinge inside her grew. Camille had been alone for a long time. She recalled the addictive sensation of birthing fecal demons that suckled on her desire and enacted her will. The smell and slickness of the filth she released into an unseen, greedy mouth. Perhaps symbiotic pleasure was better than revenge. Perhaps this abomination had found his true use. She led the babbling, half-human creature to her root cellar where it hid from the dreaded sun to await its next meal.

# DEAR DIARY
## By J. Tonzelli

## MONDAY

Dear diary,

First night in the new house! Not sure what to think yet. Mom and Dad seem to like it. My room is twice as big as my old one, so that's cool, but something about it seems... off. I don't know how to describe it, but it feels like someone is watching me. I guess that's normal for living in a new place, though. Plus, it's been an exhausting day and that's probably not helping. I'll write more tomorrow when my mind isn't so fried.

Good night, diary.

## TUESDAY

Dear diary,

Okay, well... it's my second day in the new house and I am not sure I like it. I know we're not even finished unpacking yet, but I don't think I'll ever get used to living here. There are weird noises at night, and I keep seeing something flutter in the corner of my eye, and when I look real quick, it disappears. I told Mom about this and she said it's going to take time to get used to the new house, and all its sounds and creaks and stuff. I guess she's right. But will I ever get used to the feeling that I'm being watched? Because I feel that almost all the time.

Even right now.

Diary, here's hoping tomorrow is better.

**WEDNESDAY**

Dear diary,

Not getting much sleep. I toss and turn all night, and when I do manage to fall asleep, I have the worst nightmares. Luckily school doesn't start for another two weeks, or else I would be falling asleep in class!

Met the neighbors today. They have a son. His name is Brendon and he is cute! He seemed really nervous for some reason and only stayed in our house for a few minutes when he and his parents came over to welcome us to the neighborhood.

We went outside and I could tell something was bothering him. I asked him what was wrong, but he was hesitant to tell me. I finally convinced him to spill—now part of me wishes I had left it alone.

Brendon said the family who lived in our house before us... died. He had been friendly with the boy who lived here—his name was Todd. They had gone to the same school together and had known each other for years, and they were both overjoyed to learn that, by sheer coincidence, they were going to be neighbors. Soon after Todd and his family moved in, Todd began to complain about these really bad nightmares that he couldn't fully remember. After that, he began to act really strange, like his personality had changed in just a few days. Brendon said that Todd became very quiet and brooding, almost as if he had been possessed.

I wasn't sure if I should've laughed at Brendon's story, because he seemed upset, like he really believed it, but come on, diary... possessed?

But then Brendon said something that really gave me the creeps. He said that the night Todd and his family died, Todd had called Brendon late and whispered to him just five simple words: "Around and around we go..." He hung up, and then the next morning, Todd and his family were dead.

I'm sure Brendon was just picking on me. You know, the new girl on the block. Isn't that what kids do? Make up scary stories about the new kid's house?

Still, Brendon said Todd was having nightmares, like I am now, and I *never* told him that.

But nightmares are common... right?

Things will get better, diary. They just *have* to.

## THURSDAY

Dear diary,

I had another nightmare last night. This one was the worst yet.

Some black fog, or something like it, seems to rise out of my bedroom floor. It hovers over my bed, like a cloud, and then—and this is the only way I know how to describe this—it meshes with my body and vanishes, like it was disappearing inside me.

I woke up, wanting to scream, but I couldn't. I just lay in my bed staring at the ceiling until eventually falling back asleep.

This house is the pits, I swear.

If this keeps up, I'm going to BEG my parents to move out. I don't care what I have to do.

## FRIDAY

Diary,

I don't know what's gotten into me. Tonight at dinner, for no reason, I pushed my plate onto the floor after my mother handed it to me. Food splattered everywhere. My mom screamed at me to go to my room, and I did. But here's the weird thing about it... I don't feel bad about it. Not at all. Is it because I'm secretly mad at my parents for making me move in the first place? It's hard to tell. I want to believe that, just so I can stop thinking about Brendon's claims that Todd had seemed "possessed."

## SATURDAY

I am furious. I can feel the fury billowing inside me like a disease. I am furious at my idiotic parents for making me move to this crappy house, and I am furious at that little piggy, Brendon, for filling my head with all those scary thoughts. You know what I did today, diary? I was walking through the woods and I saw that a baby bird had fallen out of its nest. It chirped in pain—I think one of its wings was broken—and at first I stepped up to see if I could put it back in its nest, but then instead, I stomped on the bird and killed it. I wanted to feel bad. I wanted to be disturbed by what I had done. But I couldn't stop laughing.

## SUNDAY

I dreamed of my parents bleeding to death. I dreamed of Brendon lying on the floor, his arms and legs broken, burning to death from the fire I set.

I awoke from the dream and smiled. I went to the kitchen and looked at all the shimmering knives in the drawer. I touched one's blade. Pressed my finger so hard against the steel that it slit through my flesh. I could hear their screams already.

# **MONDAY**

Around and around we go...

## SHE SPEAKS IN STATIC
### By Tim Mendees

*"And now we go to the newsroom for a round-up of all the top stories."*
Joe crushed the empty beer can and tossed it across the kitchen. It landed perfectly in the open bin. Joe was a crack shot at beer can basketball. After all, over the last year, he had had enough practice. He ripped the cellophane off the top of the frozen lasagna for one and threw it into the microwave.

*"A serious road accident on the A3075 just outside Penhallow has claimed six lives."*

"Poor bastards," Joe slurred, looking at his battered radio. He was a long-distance lorry driver. Nobody knew better than he did how treacherous the roads around Cornwall could be.

He set the timer on the microwave and hit go. The appliance hummed as it set about nuking his food. Planting his flabby backside against the counter, he rolled a cigarette and lit it off the gas hob, nearly singeing his eyebrows.

*"The perpetrator of the robbery is still at large and the public is urged to report any sightings of the suspect to the Betyls Cove police station."*

The microwave crackled as it cooked the build-up of spilt food on the microwave's glass plate. Joe cracked open another beer. The microwave let rip with a sharp *beep,* announcing that dinner was served. After opening the door, he nearly burnt his fingers getting the flimsy plastic tray onto a plate. It was frazzled at the edges... as usual.

*"Joe? Answer me, you bastard."*

Joe jumped in surprise and instinctively brandished his fork at the radio.

"What the fuck?" The radio had gone to static. A high-pitched sound that sounded like the cry of a child burst forth amidst the crackles and pops. He leapt backwards again, clipping his elbow on the counter.

*"... heavy showers and gale-force winds overnight that should have cleared by morning."*

The ponderous tone of the newsreader was back. Joe stood there, slack-jawed, with his pulse racing and his elbow throbbing. After a second or two, he shook his head briskly and rubbed his eyes. He must have been hearing things again. His doctor said that he had been hearing things for months. He said it was understandable under the circumstances.

Joe reached out and switched the radio off. This wasn't the first time he had heard *her* voice on the radio. PTSD the doctor called it. After more than twelve months, his wife, Mary, was still missing. The police hadn't said as much, but it was clear that they believed her dead. Potential suicide, apparently.

To be fair to the local constabulary, the evidence of suicide was more than compelling. Her car had been found, parked near the ruins of the old lighthouse with the keys still in the ignition. Her bag, containing all of her possessions, was on the passenger seat. What made his wife's alleged suicide that much worse was the fact that she had taken their four-year-old daughter, Sam, with her on her last ride.

Sam's favorite teddy was found on the cliff edge...

* * *

The TV flickered with jarring images. Joe didn't even know what he was watching. He didn't even care. He only had it on to fill the silence. After his freak out with the radio, he had tried not to think about Mary and Sam. Even the beer wasn't helping tonight.

He picked up the remote control and hit the standby button... Nothing happened.

He tried again... Still nothing.

"Bloody cheap crap batteries," he grumbled, slapping the back of the device with his open palm and shaking it vigorously at the screen.

*"Daddy?"*

The screen jumped and sound hissed from the speakers before finally switching off.

Joe dropped the remote control on the knuckle of his little toe and cursed.

He would have to make a doctor's appointment on Monday. The pills clearly weren't working. If anything, the aural hallucinations were becoming more and more frequent.

Two days ago, while out shopping, Joe had heard his wife scream his name, followed by two seconds of ear-splitting static, over the supermarket radio during an advert for baked beans. He would never look at a can of veg in the same way ever again. It was blood curdling. He had clamped his hands over his ears and crashed into a fellow shopper with his trolley. It was clear from the other guy's face, that he hadn't heard a thing. So, not only did Joe feel like he was going bat-shit crazy, but he felt like a prize plum to boot.

With a grunt of exertion, Joe stood up and stretched. He had spent much of his time on sick leave sitting in his favorite comfy chair. So much time, in fact, that his spine was developing a definite kink. The clock on the wall said that it was just after 2 a.m.—Bedtime.

Outside, the howling wind whipped fat globules of icy rain against the bay windows. It was a savage night. It was just like *that* night...

That fateful day had started as usual. He had been out on a job for twenty-four hours straight and arrived home at around six. He always planned his arrival home at this time. It was perfect. He got to see Mary and Sam as they awoke. He would have a steak and chips while they ate cereal. Then, he would kiss Mary goodbye before she went to work, and drop Sam off at nursery school...

Once his family was gone, Joe would crash out for seven hours before heading down his local for a few jars... Bliss.

While he had been enthusiastically imbibing with pals, one hell of a storm had set in. The wind hammered at the coastal town. The crash of the waves near the coast was deafening and almost hypnotic in its steady rhythm.

Joe stumbled through the driving rain and arrived at home just after nine. He was so drunk that he didn't notice that his wife's car wasn't parked in the drive. After fumbling with the lock, he finally made it inside and was surprised to see that the house was in darkness.

Unease started to scythe its way through the alcoholic fug. He called upstairs but there was no response. He plonked himself in his chair and called his wife's mobile phone. It didn't even ring; it cut straight to voicemail. Joe cursed. The signal in Cornwall was atrocious at the best of times, never mind during a storm.

He quieted the gnawing panic by surmising that Mary must have popped out to the shops or something and would be back soon. The booze quickly took hold and he fell into a doze.

Joe had terrible dreams:

*Snap!* He saw his wife's face contorted in rage. *Snap!* The images flashed like Polaroids. *Snap!* Next, it was Sam crying. *Snap!* Now, Mary with a look of abject fear. *Snap!* A look of pain. *Snap!* A trickle of blood. *Snap! Snap! Snap!* Fear. Pain. Blood. Fear. Pain. Blood. Round and round. *Snap! Snap! Snap...*

*Ding-Dong!*

Joe fell out of his chair screaming blue murder. His vision drifted around the room and he had to hold on to the carpet for dear life.

*Ding-Dong!*

The doorbell snapped his brain back on track.

"Hold on a minute!" he growled, rubbing his head and slapping his cheeks. He didn't suffer nightmares often, but when he did, they were corkers. Outside, he could hear the rain bouncing off the driveway and the wind howling and rattling far off dustbins.

These noises galvanized him into action. It must have been Mary and Sam at the door. They would be soaked to the skin. The daft woman must have forgotten her keys. After all, who else could it be that late at night?

When the door creaked open and he was confronted by two police officers, his mind went into free-fall. The police don't turn up on your doorstep that late at night unless something was wrong. You never get neighborhood watch calls during the hours of darkness.

"Mr. Sunderland?" the young female officer asked in an ominous voice.

"Uhh..." Joe was still trying to get his addled brain and his mouth to work together. "Yeah. How can I help you?"

"May we come inside?" her male colleague replied.

That was it. That's how Joe found out the terrible news. The officers' explained that they had found his wife's car abandoned at a spot notorious for suicides. The Coast Guard was searching the rocks below the cliff, but as it was high tide during a storm they didn't hold out much hope. The remainder of the conversation was a muffled blur. Nothing they said sunk in. Joe just kept seeing his dream images repeating over and over, faster and faster, until merciful oblivion took him and everything went black.

Joe had relived that moment every night for the last year. Still, he couldn't answer the question that the police asked him: "Can you think of any reason why your wife would take her own life?"

* * *

Joe went to the bathroom and splashed cold water on his face. His eyes were bulbous, bloodshot, and stung like buggery. He looked about fifty-years-old, despite only being thirty-seven, but then, grief is supposed to age you.

Joe plugged his electric toothbrush into the shaver adapter and rinsed the head under the cold tap.

*Crackle!*

The lights flickered as he flipped the switch and a flash of current made him drop the device. It fell to the tiled floor and shattered. All the hairs on his body stood upright and he yelped in alarm.

"Bloody electrics," he chuckled, desperately trying to calm himself down. The local grid was notoriously twitchy, especially during a storm.

Brushing the debris to one side with his foot, Joe took a manual brush from the medicine cabinet and squirted a large toothpaste slug on the bristles. He put the head in his mouth and started to brush.

*Crackle!*

*"Daddy!"*

Joe jumped and raked the brush across his gums, drawing blood. The plug socket, the source of the distorted voice, sizzled and flickered intermittently. With a towel around his hand, Joe flicked the switch off. The light bulb popped at that exact moment, plunging him into darkness.

Groping around for the door handle, Joe put one of his size nines on a piece of jagged plastic, lacerating the arch of his foot. He swore and bellowed as he crashed through the door and into the opposing wall.

Trailing blood on the nice cream carpet, he hopped towards the bedroom. Lightning flashed outside the house, jolting his already frayed nerves. The electric candles that lined the hallway flickered and surged, making a noise like each one had an angry wasp trapped within.

The high-pitched whine of a television test signal burst from the living room to his right. The room was dark except for the garbled multi-colored glitches on the HD screen. Joe forgot all about his injured foot and stepped into the gloom, leaving a perfect bloody footprint on the threshold.

Feeling with his palm flat against the wall, he located the light-switch and flicked it on...

*Bang!*

All the bulbs in the hall and living room popped as one. The screen flashed a deep red and the whine rose in pitch. Joe clamped his hands over his ears as a trickle of blood trickled slowly from his left nostril.

The screen started to flicker and roll. Images merged and distorted. A face was forming. *Her* face. Mary's face.

"Why did you do it?" he screamed at the screen. "Tell me why?"

The whine distorted into an unnerving series of blips and hisses. It sounded like speech but he couldn't make out any words, only fragments.

Then the screen went blank.

Joe stood staring into the darkness. All was still now except for the noise of the storm and the ticking of the clock.

Standing there, hyperventilating, he tried to get a grip. The comfort blanket of inebriation had dispersed and all he was left with was panic. Finally catching his breath, Joe fumbled around in the drawer by the door for his torch.

He switched it on and swung the beam in a wide arc around the room. The light flickered, dimmed, and then died. Damn cheap batteries again. He gave it a sharp rap against his palm and it burst into a blinding flash.

Mary screamed in his face.

Joe threw the torch in the air and screamed. It landed on the carpet with a heavy *thud*. The pounding of his heartbeat in his ears sounded like a jackhammer. Tears started to stream down his face in thick salty trails. He stood there in the darkness, gently sobbing, waiting for Mary to strike...

Nothing happened.

Mary was dressed in her favorite red dress. It was the one she always wore when they went out together on his days off. He couldn't remember why they hadn't *that* night. It must have been something trivial.

Her face had been ghastly. She was pale and bloated. Her lips blue and cracked. Blood vessels had burst around her cheeks and her eyes bulged from their sockets. The visage was bad enough, but the worst thing was her expression. It was one of sheer rage.

Trembling, Joe crouched and felt for a large cylindrical object, his torch. Confusion joined his battling emotions when he located two. One was definitely his torch, but he couldn't fathom what the other one was.

He picked up both objects and, with a great deal of trepidation, switched on the torch...

Mary was nowhere to be seen. He was alone.

Breathing a sigh of relief, Joe focused the beam on the mystery object. It was that odd statuette of Mary's. At least he thought it was hers. The first time he had ever laid eyes on the thing was the day after the awful news. After drinking heavily he launched into an episode of grief-stricken rage and had lashed out, kicking the sideboard where their wedding pictures stood. The base panel below the bottom drawer had splintered and as he reached down to pick up the debris, he found the object underneath.

He never liked it. It was decorated with what looked like a surrealist nightmare vision of arachnids. It had been crafted out of some strange kind of alloy that he couldn't place. It always felt cold and clammy. It made his skin crawl. For the life of him, he couldn't figure out why his wife would own such a bizarre object, let alone keep it hidden.

Sweeping the room with the torch, he was stunned to see that all the glass in the picture frames housing their wedding photos had shattered. Each one had a web-like design radiating out from his smiling face. This couldn't be put down to either hallucination or dodgy electrics. What caused identical damage to all pictures was one mystery too much.

Joe could feel his knees buckling under him. Quickly, he shambled to the bedroom, crashed through the door, and fell instantly unconscious.

There is only so much the human mind can take before it shuts down completely.

* * *

Joe's eighteen-wheeler barreled down the A3075 on a direct route towards home. It was a cold and frosty evening and visibility was poor. His foot was down to the floor despite the treacherous conditions.

He couldn't remember why he was in such a hurry. It must have been something important. Something to do with Sam perhaps? Whatever it was, he knew that he couldn't afford to stop for anything.

Not even when he clipped that Land Rover pulling out of the last layby.

He knew he didn't hit it hard. He barely touched it. The lorry disappeared into the fog...

* * *

Joe sat upright on the bed, startled by a loud thunderclap. His head pounded and the under sheet had adhered itself to his bloody foot.

*"The stolen crate was en route to the local museum and is believed to have contained items worth in excess of a million pounds."*

"What the hell?" Joe groaned and shook his head. It was the radio in the kitchen. He was sure that he turned it off earlier.

Wincing with pain, he peeled the sheet from the wound. It looked nasty. It was probably going to need stitches. Remembering that all the bulbs had blown, Joe grabbed the torch off the floor, where he had dropped it on the way to bed, and headed towards the kitchen.

Static blared from the radio. He didn't know the damn thing went so loud. Every rasp made his teeth vibrate and his sliced gum sting.

*"... Caused by a hit-and-run... Knocked into oncoming traffic..."*

Every now and then, the newsreader broke through the cacophony. Joe stumbled towards the kitchen, using his free hand to balance himself against the wall.

*"... Avoid travel unless absolutely necessary..."*

Joe approached the receiver and reached his hand out...

A spark shot from the aerial and zapped him between the eyes.

* * *

Joe was in a dimly lit room with a man dressed in a sharp suit. He recognized the man but his brain wouldn't spill the beans and tell him why.

"I knew I could count on you, Mr. Sunderland." The man grinned widely. His face was strangely proportioned. His lips wide and fleshy, with a snub-nose and a narrow forehead. He held out his hand.

Joe shook it. His skin was revolting. It felt slimy.

"Here's the money as agreed," the man continued, "and, as a special reward for a job well done, take what you want from the crate."

Joe reached down and picked up the strange metallic object with the spider designs.

The mystery man chuckled. It was a grotesque, rattling, gurgle of mirth that made Joe cringe.

"The Atlach-Nacha totem. A fine choice. A fine choice, indeed." The man smiled a toothy grin.

Joe turned and started to walk from the room.

"Oh, Mr Sunderland?" the man called after him in a playful tone. "Do be careful with that thing, won't you? Once you are in his web, he seldom lets go."

The dream faded with the horrible laugh ringing in his ears.

* * *

His car alarm broke the silence.

The radio was now dead. All power in the house had shorted out when he was electrocuted. The mists in his memory were beginning to clear. What did these memories mean?

The car alarm abruptly stopped.

Almost instantly it was replaced by static from the car radio.

Joe knew what it wanted. It wanted him to go for a drive.

Almost like a somnambulist, he threw on some clothes and, ignoring the pain, his shoes.

*"Come,"* the radio beckoned. *"Come! Come! Come..."*

He knew he would never get any peace if he didn't figure out what was going on. He had to do what the voice on the radio said. What *she* said.

He grabbed the keys and stepped out into the night. The inside driver's light pulsed like a heartbeat. Slowly, he walked over and climbed inside. Sam's teddy sat grinning on the passenger seat beside him.

*"Do you remember now?"* Mary asked as Joe turned the engine over and pulled out into the road.

Turning out of the small suburban cul-de-sac, he accelerated away from town and towards the lighthouse. Where else? Joe should have felt mounting jubilation that he was about to find out the truth. All he felt, however, was guilt and fear.

*"Think."*

As Mary spoke, a vision passed into Joe's mind. It was *that* morning. It was nowhere as idyllic as he remembered. Mary was frosty with him from the get-go. She said that they had to talk later.

When she had gone, he noticed that she had been reading the newspaper. The front page was all about the crash on the A3075. It had a description of the truck believed to have caused the tragedy.

"Oh, God!" Joe cried as images of flaming vehicles in his rearview mirror danced in front of his eyes. "Was that?"

*"Yes,"* Mary whispered.

Another flash, another memory...

As he turned the page, the radio talked about the recent robbery. Joe hated the newsreader's voice. He sounded so smug. On page two was an artist's impression of the thief. It could have been his twin. Thank God he had woven a good alibi. He stroked the metal totem in his jacket pocket and dropped the paper into the bin.

"Oh, shit," he blubbered like a baby as he carried on driving towards his destiny. "You knew, didn't you? You found out?"

*"Yes."* the voice on the radio hissed. *"Can you remember what happened next?"*

Yet another flash unearthed long subdued memories. Memories he had wished long buried.

Joe had been awakened from his slumber by a scream of "You bastard!" He rushed to the stair landing and looked down over the banister. Mary was wearing her red dress. She was ready for their night out. But something was wrong. In a flash he got it. In one hand she held the soiled newspaper and in the other the totem. She screamed at him to "rot in hell!" and reached for the telephone.

She was going to turn him in.

In a split second, he was down next to her. He ripped the phone cord out of the wall, looped it around her neck and squeezed. Spiders' webs flashed in his vision as he extinguished his prey.

As his wife fell to the floor, as dead as dead could be, Sam came out from the kitchen and screamed.

Joe looped the flex one more time and advanced...

"No!" Joe screamed. "I couldn't have. Could I?" Tears blurred his vision, making driving through the rain even trickier. "I... I killed..."

"Yes!" Mary bellowed in his face. She appeared from out of nowhere on the seat beside him. Her face showing the clear marks of strangulation.

"Why, daddy?" Sam appeared behind him. He could see her bulging red eyes in the rearview mirror.

The car swerved as he jolted the steering wheel in terror. The front wheels mounted the curb and the car slammed into the metal barrier at the side of the road. The car flipped end-over-end over the cliff and down into the sea below.

As the taillights disappeared below the waves, one sharp burst of static announced that Mary and Sam had gone, finally at peace.

* * *

Nobody ever did find out what happened to the Sunderland family. A series of tragic suicides, most people said. And with no bodies to examine, nobody would ever know otherwise.

Police found the Atlach-Nacha totem and finally put two and two together. Joe had been the one that stole the crate from the depot and, in his flight, caused the accident that claimed six lives. It was easy to surmise from there what caused Mary to take both her and her daughter's lives. Nobody ever dreamed that Joe was, in fact, a double murderer.

He probably never would have been if he hadn't got himself caught in an inescapable web of criminality and guilt. He had no choice but to silence his wife. She would have ruined everything.

The Sunderland house was sold at auction for a tidy sum. The new occupants were very happy there. Even if the electrics were dodgy and the radio signal was crap.

# ANY PORT IN A STORM
## *By Matthew A. Clarke*

My relationship with Georgia Flint had become a little tense. The arguments started small but were spiraling out of control in the weeks following our dinner with her father, Terrance.

The old man, some big shot at a high-tech correctional advancement facility, didn't take well to me from the get-go. He didn't have to say it outright; I could see it in the way his narrow eyes were stripping me down to the bone. He was a big man, all muscle and moustache, which made me even more uncomfortable to meet his eye.

Georgia's mother was dead, and although I'd never said it to her, I wouldn't have blinked an eye if it turned out Terrance had a hand in her supposed suicide. That should tell you enough about what kind of presence this man had.

I don't know what he said to her after I'd left his place on that cold October night, but the next time I saw her she was all *where do you see us in five years,* and *maybe you should find a more stable job.* It was almost as if the old guy was talking to me directly, albeit through a younger, sexier body.

On the morning of Georgia's thirty-first birthday, I took a trip to the discount store to pick up a few groceries and I figured I'd try to smooth things over between us with a generous helping of chocolate and icing. I added butter, eggs, and flour to my basket, planning to surprise her with a birthday cake when she got home from work.

As I left the supermarket, carrying my shopping in a single groaning plastic bag that I was just *daring* to split (I couldn't afford to purchase a second bag after buying all the additional ingredients), a suspicious black van pulled up alongside my moped. I'd seen enough movies to know what that usually meant, but there still wasn't much I could do about it. Before I'd even put my shopping down on the cracked tarmac, the side door was open, and I was hit across the back of the head with something solid. My vision blurred as I was lifted off my feet and was tossed unceremoniously into the back of the van with all the grace of a child throwing out the trash. Sometime after they put the sack over my head I must have passed out, because the next thing I remember is waking up in this prison. I've spent the last four years trying to find a way out.

* * *

Every day, I wake up in a small supply cupboard out the back of a large amusement arcade, regardless of where I was when I fell asleep. I can't explain how. I don't even want to think about it; I'm not sure my brain could handle the answer at this point. It doesn't matter if I spend three, four days on my feet, constantly traveling in what I'm sure is a straight line, poking myself in the eyes, trying to force my body to keep moving. As soon as I inevitably fall asleep, I always end up right back here. But that's not even the strangest part, oh no. Although I've never seen another living soul in this cruel parody of my country, things move. On one of my first days here, I found a can of yellow spray paint, used it to mark my route at staggered intervals. The following day, after waking up back where I'd started, I attempted to find my way back to the first marker. The buildings were all different. They'd had a game of musical chairs in the night, I was but a song they were merrily dancing to. The off license that had been across the street the day before was gone and had been replaced by a laundromat. Not so much as a single blemish on its pristine brickwork.

I woke up perhaps an hour ago, I'm not sure what time (*does it even really matter anymore?),* wearing the same clothes I have done for many years—white T-shirt with red sleeves, loose navy jeans and black socks. If I'd known I was going to be stuck with the same outfit for eternity, I like to think I would have dressed a little better for the occasion. I did, at one point, have a pair of black, lace-up leather boots. I lost them a long time ago, though, I don't remember how. Every day seems to blur into one here, and I often find myself wondering if those guys from the van hit me too hard, accidentally killed me, and this is my own personal hell. Where are all the people? And why can't I ever escape this *damn* arcade? These questions run through my head now as they do every morning. I force them to the back of my mind, as I always do, and leave the store cupboard for a piss.

Today, the overhead speaker system is playing a love ballad from the eighties, and visions of my childhood come flooding back to me as I flood the single bowling lane with something else. I shake off and figure I might as well head outside to start my never-ending journey to find my way home.

The double doors swing shut silently behind me and I'm hugged by the comforting embrace of the rising sun as I step onto the parking lot, the only constant I've had for a long time. Today, there's a boarded-up pub, *The Haggard Hare,* planted across the street. It's one I recognize from a while back; I'd passed it during a two-day hike a year or so ago. I contemplate turning around and going back to sleep, but something inside me drives me forward. Perhaps it's my sense pride. Possibly it's some deep-rooted instinct, the human need for survival when faced with overwhelming odds. Whatever it is, I'm not ready to give up just yet.

I'm not far past the pub when I spot a small newsagents, *Barry's*. I pop inside and help myself to a coffee from the machine, a bottle of water, and a cheese sandwich from the refrigerator. Another peculiarity—there's always a single cheese sandwich in each shop I pass, and it's always fresh. At first, I'd been a little wary of consuming anything in this strange new world of mine, but I soon got over that fear when my skin over my ribs became alarmingly taut. There are no newspapers on the racks, but a flip-calendar on the front counter reads: 18 SEPT 2024. Almost four years exactly to the day I first arrived. I shout my thanks to the proprietor of the shop, of whom I will never meet, and head back outside.

By early evening I'm starting to get a little weary, and the great ball of fire in the sky has almost sunk behind the tall buildings to my right, and a chill is sneaking up on me. My water is long gone, so I decide to take a quick break from walking. In the last hour I've passed an old cinema, three empty husks, which were once restaurants, a large park complete with swings, and a pond with no ducks. All of which I have seen countless times before, sometimes more than once in the same day. A two-story house is ahead and to my right and I suppose that's a good a place as any to take a break; maybe I'll get lucky and find another cheese sandwich. I knock before entering, as I'm a man of respect, and pull off my socks in the hallway. The thick pile carpet is the color of honey and is almost as soft. It feels good against my aching feet, and for a moment the urge to strip off and lay down on it is overwhelming. My jeans are already halfway down my thighs when I see her, and freeze.

She's thin. Incredibly thin. I think back to when I first arrived here. She either hasn't found any food or is too afraid to eat, as I was. Her long hair is a thick mop of tangled yellows, almost dreadlocks, but not quite. The woman stands in the kitchen, leaning back against the corner of the worktop, unmoving. Our eyes meet and lock onto one another, and it's as if neither of us can believe the signals they are sending to our brains. Slowly, I pull my trousers back up to my waist, not wanting to alarm her any more than she already is, and raise my hands to show her I mean no harm. It is then that she allows her face to relax a little, her shoulders drop, eyelids lower.

"Hello?" I croak. It comes out as a question, and I suppose, in a way, it is.

"Hi," she says.

For a moment, my brain ceases to function as I try to think of what to say next. It's been so long since I've seen another person that I've almost forgotten how to interact with a real human being.

Finally, I manage: "Who are you? How did you get here?"

She stays where she is, propped against the counter, stiff as a rake, but her blue irises brighten a little when she seems to realize I'm not going to hurt her.

"I've been here for as long as I can remember," she says, smiling a little now, "I always thought I was alone."

"Me… me too. My name is David," I say. I step forward a little and extend my hand toward her, but she's still unsure, doesn't move.

"My name is Molly."

Finally, she stands a little taller, away from the counter, and takes my hand. It's warm, a little moist. I want to cry.

Four days. I managed to stay awake for four whole days with Molly before the sandman took me. I made the mistake of blinking for just a moment too long. After that my eyelids may as well have been made of quick-drying cement.

* * *

I woke this morning with the taste of salt in my mouth and the crust of dried tears on my cheeks. I spent my waking hour on the hard floor of the store cupboard, cursing until my throat was raw. Then, I went outside and cursed a little more. I managed to find a newsagent's shortly after leaving the arcade and have since had a bottle of water and a cheese sandwich, which helped a little; after lining my stomach I've started to feel a little less sorry for myself and a little more positive about my situation.

I'm not alone in this place. Molly is out there somewhere, waiting for me; I just have to find her again. (*And then wake up right back where you started again.*) My brain can be a real dick sometimes. I give it a mental thrashing and continue in roughly the same direction I had been heading when I found her. Although none of the buildings I pass are the same as they were a few days ago, I do eventually come to the large park with a set of empty swings and a duck pond with no ducks. I figure Molly might like to come here with me. If we're both going to be stuck here for eternity, shouldn't we at least try to have a little fun?

It's been another hot day, as they always seem to be here, and I peel my shirt away from my chest with my thumb and forefinger, desperately trying to cool off, to stop sweating so much. I realize I've never cared about this before. I care what this woman thinks of me. I'm not blind. I can see that she's been here for a long time, too, but she's still beautiful. It wouldn't stop me from fuc-

I'm pulled from my daydream just as it's about to get interesting by a familiar building on the horizon. Molly's building! I break into a run, forgetting about the heat, and my body's secretions. I'm worried that if I don't get there fast enough, I'll lose sight of it again.

It still stands as it was as I approach the crazy-paved footpath outside. I hop across the neatly cut stones and rap twice on the front door. This time, I get a response.

"David?"

I let myself in, aware that I'm crying but unable to do anything about it. When I enter the kitchen, I see that Molly is crying too. She's standing with her back against the corner of the worktop, as she was when I first laid eyes on her, only this time it's joy in her eyes rather than fear. I run to her and we embrace each other, fall to the floor laughing. Relief, joy, love?

I don't know how long it was before we fell asleep in each other's arms, but it was a lot faster than it had been the first time we met. We'd spent hours making love, barely saying a word to one another. Just pure, animalistic instinct taking over. After being alone for so long, it was incredible. For both of us. Molly made me promise that I would come and find her the next day, and the day after that, too. I told her I would, every day for the rest of our lives, no matter how long it took each time.

And so, waking up today, alone and on the cold, hard floor of the store cupboard, my life doesn't seem all that bad anymore. Regardless of how I ended up here, or the fact that I will probably never get back to my old life, I will always have Molly.

* * *

"You see, Georgie? I told you this man was no good for my daughter."

Georgia ran from the observation room, tissue clutched in her hand, mascara streaking her cheeks. She wore the tired face of a nightmarish clown.

Dr. Terrance Flint turned to his assistant, Joey Maplin, and held out a meaty palm. A clipboard was placed in it abruptly. It appeared comically small in the big man's grip, not that Joey would dare say anything of the sort to his face.

Dr. Flint removed a black dictation machine from the breast pocket of his white jacket.

"Subject D-12. Day three, o-nine hundred hours. VR Program 332142. David shows total lack of awareness for the reality of his surroundings. Signs of complex delusions present. Program will need further tweaking to accommodate. Subject witnessed engaging in detailed conversation with a kitchen mop. Subject later witnessed making love to aforementioned floor mop."

"Sir." There was a trembling undertone in Joey's voice, as if he were afraid to speak up. "Do you think the board would approve this as a safe alternative to conventional correctional treatment?"

Dr. Flint thumbed the recording device off and slid it back into his breast pocket. "Of course, my boy. You've seen the extent of the overpopulation in our prisons first-hand."

"Yes, I suppose you're right," he said, catching the clipboard as it was tossed back to him. "Shall we release D-12 now?"

"No, not yet. Let him stew a little longer. Send him to sleep, then run the program again." He turned to walk away, then stopped. He spoke over his broad shoulder to the smaller man, "In fact, another four days in our facility ought to do him good. No one's going to notice if this sad sack goes missing for the rest of the week."

"Sir."

Joey took a seat in front of the control panel as Dr. Flint left the room. He killed the lights in the chamber, released a little gas. The subject fell asleep almost instantaneously. Joey hit 'reset' on VR Program 332142 and watched as D-12 woke once again in the virtual arcade. He wasn't sure how he was going to get through another four days of watching this poor guy making love to a virtual mop. But then, he smiled, and took comfort in the fact that it could be worse. It could be *him* that Dr. Flint had selected as his guinea pig.

# IT'S WHAT'S INSIDE THAT COUNTS
*By Frederick Pangbourne*

**D**espite the disapproval of my wife, Peggy, and my own objectionable feelings at the time, I never the less surrendered to my ancestral calling when my only living grandmother called on Wednesday and damn near pleaded that I stop by their farm out in Nowata County. My grandfather, of eighty-three years old, had taken ill and my grandmother insisted that a doctor be left out of the situation for financial reasons and that I personally stop by to give my own diagnosis; even though I have no professional training in any field of medicine. My professional skills lie in the supervising of a Medical Supply Warehouse in Bartlesville. That unfortunately is the only extent of my medical knowledge.

So, despite Peggy's displeased badgering about missing bridge night at the Fowler's on Saturday, I told my grandmother that, because of work, I could not make my way out there until the weekend. My verbal commitment to showing up seemed to ease the tension in her voice as we spoke on the phone. When questioned about my grandfather's ailment, she only stated that he had been plagued with nausea, abdominal cramps and little to no appetite that rendered him helplessly to the confines of his bed for close to a week now. Constipation came to mind in my unprofessional opinion. I reassured her I would leave first thing on Saturday morning and that she should try pumping plenty of fluids into him.

Saturday wound up being warmer than usual for October, and I had the ole' 62 Ford Galaxie 500 on the road and taking on the forty-five-minute ride by 9:50 that morning. I leased the car brand new back in May after I was given a long-deserved raise of twenty-two cents.

I had the windows down and the radio blaring as I cruised along East Highway 60 en route to their old farmhouse. Their farm at one point was alive with peanut crops, and an assortment of small barnyard animals. Now, the acres of peanuts are long forgotten, and nothing more than weeds and tall grass grow where the multitudes of shelled nuts once thrived, and the animals are all but a handful of chickens and geese. Maintaining a farm of that size in your eighties is just plain impossible, and now Ross and Gwen Meredith simply putz around and enjoy their golden years. My folks, along with other relatives, used to gather there with their own families for the holidays. My father had three brothers and a sister who all grew up in the large two-story house. My father passed away three years ago and for whatever reason those holiday gatherings are far and in between nowadays. The last time I was out there was two years ago when Peggy and I had taken a vacation weekend out at Oologah Lake and we swung by on the way home to pay our respects. I wish I could make this trip more often than I do but life has a well-known tendency to unknowingly and easily fill the hours in one's day.

Mick Jagger was singing about not getting any satisfaction when I turned off Oklahoma's Highway 60 and started downgrading roads until I eventually found myself on the all too familiar dirt road leading to the farmhouse. I glimpsed the rearview mirror and watched as beige clouds of dirt billowed out behind the car as I neared the farm. On either side of the dry, earthy path that led to the house were the green waves of tall grass that now occupied the acres of unused farmland as it swayed in the breeze like the rolling tide of an emerald ocean.

I gave a quick couple of blasts of the horn as I pulled up to the front of the house just to allow my grandparents some forewarning that I had arrived. No one had yet appeared to greet me on the wrap-around porch as I ascended the stairs. Through the old screen door, I could see that the front door was closed. Being that it was my grandparent's home, I gave only a trio of hard raps upon the door's paint peeling surface before letting myself in.

"Grandma! Pops! It's Jack! I'm here!" I called out as I left the front door open, allowing the breeze from outside to enter through the screen door and into the home's shadowy interior. No one replied as I made my way through the first-floor hall, peeking inside each room as I passed. All were void of both Ross and Gwen Meredith. "Hello?"

From the kitchen up ahead, the squealing sound of the back screen door was heard, and I quickened my pace to investigate. I found my grandmother laboriously making her way into the kitchen from the outside steps with noticeable difficulty. I hurried to the door and held it open for her as I guided her inside the kitchen.

"Grandma, what are you doing?"

"Oh, Jackie, I didn't know you were here," she replied with a forced smile.

"I laid on the horn when I pulled up. Didn't you hear it?" I carefully escorted her to one of the chairs at the kitchen table.

"My hearing ain't what it used to be. I was out there looking for Buster. Haven't seen him in days." Once she eased into the chair and adjusted herself, she looked up and smiled again. This time not as forced. "I'm so glad you could make it, Jackie."

"Yeah, of course. Can I get you anything?"

She motioned to the sink. "Could ya grab me a glass of water? Walking around out there looking for Buster got a thirst going." Buster was their older-than-dirt golden Labrador Retriever. When I was a kid I considered it old.

I nodded and went to the cabinet where I drew two large glasses and filled them from the sink's tap, then handed her a glass and sat next to her. "You don't look too good yourself, gram. You okay?"

She drank deeply from the glass and set it down in front of her. "Oh, I'm good. Think I may have caught a little of what your grandfather has."

The water was cold and refreshing as I finished half my glass in one swig. "What's he got, the flu or something?" I reached out and placed the back of my hand against her forehead. She was unusually warm.

She lifted the glass to her lips again. "If we got anything good from this farm, it was that well water. It's so good and cold," she said ignoring my question.

"Yes, it is, now where's pop at?"

"He's upstairs in bed. He's hurtin' so bad, Jackie, that he can't pull himself from that bed." Her face released its previous smile and donned a worried look.

"You stay here and rest a second." I finished my glass in another single swig and took both of our glasses to the sink for a refill. I set her filled glass in front of her and sipped from my own. "I'm going to take him up some water and see how he is. I'll be right back." I leaned over and kissed her heated forehead, then departed the kitchen and went upstairs.

In their bedroom, I found my grandfather lying awake under his covers. The windows were closed; the shades and thin faded curtains were closed. The room was gloomy and smelled like a high school locker room. "Pops, why are you lying here in the dark?" I moved to the windows where I drew the curtains, lifted the blinds and opened the windows. Sunlight basked the room and the breeze from outside casually blew in and whisked away some of the odor.

"Jackie?" he said wearily from beneath the covers.

"Yeah, it's me, pops." I set the water on the nightstand near him and sat on the edge of the bed. "I hear you're not feeling too well." I placed the back of my hand on his forehead and his skin was hot.

"Got me some god damn stomach virus. Killing my guts." He grimaced as he spoke.

"Laying sealed up in here and in the dark isn't helping you, pops. Come on and sit up if you can. I brought you some water." I carefully leaned him up into a sitting position and stacked some pillows behind him. He moaned painfully as he sat up, and his pajama top was nearly soaked through with sweat. After a bit of attentive maneuvering, I had him propped up and handed him the water. At first, he politely refused the liquid but after a bit of coaxing, he eventually drank half the glass.

"So, when did all this start?" I asked, taking the glass from him.

"The hell if I know. Two weeks ago, I guess? Started getting these pains in my gut."

I pulled back the equally saturated covers and lifted his pajama top. "Let ole' Doctor Jackie take a look here," I joked and flashed him a smile. Funny how, in their eyes, just the word *medical* already proclaimed me as a certified physician. For a man of eighty-three he was obviously gaunt and pale, especially if he had been in bed all week and having hardly eaten, but to my dismay his belly was bulging and rounded.

"Let me know if this hurts," I said as I pushed slightly on the swollen stomach. He flinched and groaned in pain. "Okay. Sorry." I now placed my open palm of his belly. A loud gurgle emitted from somewhere in his innards and rattled the extended flesh. I quickly withdrew my hand and pulled his shirt back down. "You eat something that may have disagreed with you?" I asked, pulling his cover up.

He only shook his head and groaned as the gurgling sounded out again from beneath the blanket. Loud and very audible. Like my grandmother earlier, I was now forcing a smile to hide my concern. "I'll be right back, pops. I'm going to go downstairs and see gram for a second." I got up from the bed and walked to the door. I stopped before fully walking out and turned to him in bed. He looked so frail and weak at that moment. It pained me to see him in that condition and in pain. "Sounds to me like you ate something that may have been spoiled," I lied and forced another smile. He nodded in agreement and let out another groan. This time, as I turned to leave the room, I could have sworn I saw a slight movement from under the covers where he laid. I shook the obvious illusion off and went downstairs.

Back in the kitchen, I found my grandmother again at the screen door to the back porch attempting to leave the house. I hurried over and guided her back to the table by her feeble shoulders. "Gram, I can't leave you alone for two minutes. Where are you going now?" I asked as I seated her back in the same chair.

"I just wanted to have another look for Buster," she explained.

"You just stay here," I said as I noticed her glass was partially empty and took it to the sink. I grabbed myself another glass and fill them both. I placed a glass in front of her and proceeded to drink mine. "I'll go out and look for the dog. You stay put, please, and I think something is really wrong with pop. We should call a doctor. Have him checked out. You too," I suggested as I finished my glass and placed it in the sink.

"You know we can't afford a doctor, Jackie," she said in a distressed manner.

"I'll pay for the doctor, gram. It's not a problem." I kissed her heated forehead once more and exited the house by the back door.

Outside, I made my way around the house calling out Buster's name. There were a few Shumard oak trees in the surrounding yard, and past them the abandoned peanut crops began and stretched out to a distant tree line. If the dog had gone missing for a few days now and considering its age, it had mostly likely wandered off and died somewhere in that far off line of trees and woods. I decided that I would swing around back and look around the barn before calling it quits.

The barn, unlike the surrounding crops, had been maintained for as long as my grandparents could keep up with it and still held together pretty well considering. Still calling out Buster's name, I figured I'd walk around the outside before entering the interior, which was probably the abode to a number of hornets' nests and spider webs. It wasn't until I rounded the back of the barn that my search ended. Buster was indeed dead. Probably for the days he had gone missing. A swarm of black flies hovered and crawled across his matted yellow carcass. The smell of death lingered with the flies. I squatted near the body and covered my nose and mouth with my hand. There appeared to be no external injuries, and I surmised the cause of death to simply be from natural causes. Ole Buster had finally bought the farm, no pun intended. I was preparing to stand back up when I noticed something peculiar. Buster's dead eyes remained wide open, as did his mouth. As if he were screaming out as his life left him. From his stretched out jaws a trail of black blood, mixed with some type of slimy residue had poured from his mouth in a line that ran off into the grass until it eventually faded. The liquid trail had long since dried but left me with an eerie feeling that I could not shake. I decide to return to the house and find a garbage bag and give old Buster a proper burial.

Back in the house, I found my grandmother at the kitchen pulling a can of tomato soup from a top cabinet. She was wincing in pain as she stretched up into the cabinet, one hand on the can and the other on her stomach.

"Gram, I've got that," I said as I hurried over and took the can from her. "Are you hurting that bad too?" I asked.

"I'm okay. It comes and goes," she moaned the false words.

"Listen, you go sit in the parlor and watch some TV. I'll make you guys some soup, Okay?" I was already ushering her out of the kitchen and into the hall.

"Did you find Buster?" she asked. I stifled a laugh. In her ill condition, she was still more worried about that old dog than herself.

"No, not yet," I lied as I gently sat her down in a plush armchair in the parlor and slid an ottoman beneath her feet. "I'll look again after I make you two some soup." Once she seemed comfortable enough, I turned on an episode of *The Andy Griffith Show* on the TV and returned to the kitchen.

Once in the kitchen, I opened the soup can and poured its contents into a small pot on the stove. As the soup slowly heated, I poured and drank another glass of water before opening the cabinets beneath the sink in search for a garbage bag to use as Buster's death shroud. What I found under the sink was a drenched mess. A puddle of water had formed at the cabinet's floor from a slow but steady drip from what appeared to be from their well water filter. An odor of mildew rushed out to attack my senses. The water had soaked anything constructed of cardboard boxes and their contents. I looked over my shoulder and was preparing to yell out to her how long this had been leaking but, in their current conditions, I'm sure anything under the kitchen sink was the least of their concerns.

With my attention back to the leakage, I turned off the water lines by hand and found that the filter itself was so loose that I was able to disconnect it with little difficulty and without the aid of any tools. The PH neutralizer/filter was olive green and cylindrical. As I held it in my hands, I wondered how long they had been consuming the untreated water. With a good amount of elbow grease, I unscrewed the cylinder and pulled it from under the sink and into the sunlight for a better look. My mouth fell agape at what it contained inside. Caught in the filter and squirming about in the calcite bed were numerous tiny black worms. The worms were as thin as sewing string, and the longest ones were the length of my pinky nail. Mixed into the wiggling profusion were minute, semi-clear specks that were barely noticeable with the naked eye. Eggs? I dropped the filter into the sink in disgust. They must have been ingesting these translucent eggs for as long as the filter became loose.

I rushed from the kitchen and passed the parlor without glancing at it as I ascended the stairs two at a time to the second floor. In the sunlit bedroom, my grandfather, Ross Meredith, was no longer awake. At a glimpse he would appear to be very much alive, as he stared up into the ceiling with his bulging eyes and his mouth wide open in a silent scream. His limbs were frozen in contorted positions. A trail of fresh blood and the same slimy mixture dripped from his lips as its remnants ran down his chest and underneath the covers. I stood rooted to the wooden floor planks as the image of Buster was suddenly displayed in my mind's eye. I pictured his water bowl being filled from the sink regularly.

As I stood transfixed in the room's threshold, a movement beneath the covers near him drew my attention back to the present chain of events. Again, something twitched under the blanket and I slowly stepped to the bed. Reaching out in almost slow motion, I gripped the edge of the blanket and in a sudden movement, ripped the covers from the bed. Lying on the bloodstained sheets next to my grandfather was a long, black, segmented worm twisting and jerking about. The worm was roughly two feet long, and its body was more flattened than it was in girth. The parasite was with no form of a head but, instead one tip ended in a large mouth opening that rapidly yawned and closed like that of a fish out of water. Tiny hooks decorated the outside rim of the mouth.

I felt my stomach tighten and my mouth filled with saliva as a wave or nausea washed over me. I backed out of the room and stumbled down the stairs, willing myself not to vomit. Using the walls for support, I trudged into the parlor.

"Grandma, we need to leave! I'm taking you to the hospital now! Pops already-" I started but did not finish the sentence as it died in the air.

She lay sprawled out on the chair in what appeared to be an agonizing convulsion. Her legs twitched about on the ottoman; one shoe had already fallen off in her spasms. She clutched franticly at the front of her flowered dress, tearing it open and exposing her bare torso and bra. Her head, as with my grandfather's, was faced upward to the ceiling. Eyes bulging in terror, mouth opened unnaturally wide as she retched. I took two steps toward her until I saw something that stopped me in mid-step. Some object was pushing itself from inside her chest and forcing its way into her throat. Her neck swelled and a sloshing sound was now emitting from deep within her mouth. As she gagged for air, sprays of crimson blood shot from her mouth and rained down upon her arms and dress. Her back arched in a final contortion as her neck expanded and the tipped mouth of a black worm wiggled up into her mouth and poked out from between her parted lips. Blood spilled freely from the corners of her mouth.

I felt bile rising in my throat and backed up into a small shelf of ceramic knick-knacks. Several tiny statues fell from their perches and shattered on the wood floor. I spun from the room and rushed through the hall, smashing through the screen door and onto the front porch. As I staggered off the porch steps and to my car, all I could think about was my poor grandparents unknowingly consuming that water and ingesting those parasite eggs. The underground aquifer must have been the breeding ground to these unknown organisms, and once the filter had become disconnected, their eggs flowed into their drinking water; probably clinging to their intestinal walls and fertilizing into those... those hideous worms.

Once I crawled into the car, I immediately started the engine and whipped the car around. I hadn't even made it down the long dirt farm road when a sharp pain came from my abdomen. The car swerved at the sudden stab of discomfort and it was then I pictured myself drinking those glasses of water. I panicked and screamed when the pain repeated.

# THE UNLIKELIEST OF HEROES
### By Carlton Herzog

Without sustenance, the mind, like the body, will wither and die. Indeed, protracted immobility and silence, and the boredom they engender, rival Dante's Hell where the damned boil in rivers of blood, fuse with dead trees, and dismember and consume one another. Boredom magnifies and stretches every moment into an empty eternity where time ceases to exist, and sanity is precarious at best.

That was our predicament. The old distractions had vanished. There were no video games or movies to break the soul-crushing monotony, no chats or tweets or texts, to remind us of who we were and what we had lost. Slowly, inexorably, we would have slid into madness had not one of our number suggested story-time.

Great reckonings took place in those tiny rooms. There was something about a whispered tale, often twice or thrice told, that resonated more in our forced darkness than in the light of day. You had to pay attention; you had to listen; you had to milk every detail as if it were the last drop in your desert canteen. There were holes in our minds and souls that needed to be filled. Our minds, so bereft of input, recast the mundane and trivial into the heroic.

Thus, it was that Pablo, who up until now had maintained a draconian silence, chose to grace us with a tale.

He began so:

Some heroes are made; others are born, and some are a combination of the two. This one came unheralded into our world. The heavens stayed mute, the stars did not align, no comets blazed forth, and the moon stayed grey and barren. Neither the spoken nor the written word foretold of her coming. Nor was there anything in her lineage to suggest that she was destined for greatness.

Maria Conchita Guadalupe Gonzalez came from farming stock, a plain looking creature with an unassuming manner. She was barely five feet tall and weighed a mere 100 pounds. But, inside that diminutive, tender frame percolated a keen mind and a warrior's heart. So much so, that in Guadalajara, she had distinguished herself first as a patrolwoman, then as a detective, and later as Chief of Detectives.

To be sure, she earned the respect of her fellow officers and the criminal cabals alike. That all changed after she first displayed her unique power. Then respect became fear. Indeed, the people rarely spoke her name aloud, and when by chance they did, they did so in whispers; such was the sheer terror she inspired among the common folk.

She became the scourge of the cartel. To its members, she was ten feet tall and bulletproof.

Maria had not always been so formidable. Nor, as she later proved, bloodthirsty. When she took the job as chief of police, she refused to carry a gun or wear a vest. To everyone this seemed most unusual insofar as her predecessor—and his—had been gunned down in cold blood outside their homes. Maria believed that if she adopted a less threatening posture, she might survive long enough to do some good. But a series of intervening events completely changed her law enforcement policies.

After she was appointed Tijuana's Chief of Police, she felt she needed to look and act more cosmopolitan since she would be rubbing elbows with important people. Something was needed to compensate for her small size and increase her professional stature.

She traveled to Mexico City. She intended to upgrade her wardrobe. As she wandered up and down the streets passing the various shops and *bodegas*, she noticed a blinking neon sign.  It advertised various medicinal and grooming substances. Something about the place, perhaps the odor of burnt ochre or the resplendent colored knick-knacks in the window drew her inside.

While browsing the shelves of snake oils and potions, a gnarled old woman approached her. She looked positively ancient, as if she had lived during the time of the Aztecs. She smelled of mushrooms, tequila and earth.

"I have what you need right here," she rasped and then handed Maria a small jar. The label read: Super Fantastic Hair Gel—Guaranteed to Change Your Life. Maria looked at her quizzically. She took the jar and rotated it in her hand. Then she opened it. The contents were lime green and smelled of pine.

"Go ahead, take it," the old woman urged. "No charge."

Maria questioned her. "No charge?"

"*Si*—you'll be back for more when that's gone," the crone promised.

Maria took it.

Maria wanted to look her best on the first day. After she showered, she slathered the gel on her hair. Only now it didn't smell like pine. Rather, it smelled like some exotic perfume, pleasantly alluring, and calming at the same time. She noticed that it made her hair look fuller, shinier, bouncier. And it made her look prettier. She chalked this up to her imagination and headed to the office.

But it wasn't her imagination. Everyone from the police officers to the staff commented on how beautiful she looked. And she caught one or two of them looking at her with more than aesthetic admiration. But she chalked it up to a *placebo* effect. She was the same person, but somehow the old lady's words had given her a new confidence.

After the formalities had been concluded, she decided to do a ride along with Officer Juan Tax. Little did she know that the drug gangs had already decided to kill her on her first day.

The patrol car was less than a mile from the station when a hail of bullets shattered the glass and killed Officer Tax. Maria ducked below the dashboard. The gunfire stopped after the car rammed into a pole. The hitmen came up to the car and dragged Maria out of the car with the intention of executing her. Two carloads of gang members watched.

What happened next, happened very fast. Maria had been pulled from the car and was being led to a pole where she would be tied. A makeshift firing squad was checking its weapons while two amateur cinematographers were making ready to film the event for the media.

They tied her to the pole and started walking back. That's when Maria's hair took over. It shot out of her head and attached itself above and below where her hands were tied and snapped the telephone pole in two. It took the upper portion and wielded it like a club, smiting the gang members. A few began shooting. More of her hair shot out and formed a wall between her and the oncoming hail of bullets. Still, more hair shot out and strangled the gunmen and cameramen to death.

But it didn't stop there. The presumed bosses who sat in their cars observing their reversal of fortune were sauce for the goose. After the enlivened hair finished with the lackeys, it attached itself to the roofs of the cars and split them in half, then extracted the kingpins and tore them in half.

In twenty seconds or less, Maria's hair had killed a dozen men and she hadn't so much as worked up a sweat. She felt as though she were in a waking dream but was not so dumbfounded that she couldn't muster a sardonic observation "That old bag was right; that's some kick-ass hair gel."

Over the next year Maria began to purge the cartels. Thus, she had a bounty on her head. Several times she had been completely unaware that snipers had her in their crosshairs. If not for the fact that her hair had lightning fast reflexes, Maria would have been dead.

To be sure, Maria's exploits went far beyond that of crime fighting. On one occasion, her hair caught the falling passengers from a plane that had exploded in mid-air. On another, her hair had rescued thirteen hikers in a collapsed Mexican cave. Its strands, tough as carbon fiber cables, had yanked away the boulders and other debris, then snaked their way in and pulled the hikers out one by one. On still another, her hair had manifested as eight stilt legs, walked into the Gulf of Mexico, and rescued the survivors of a capsized luxury yacht.

Her greatest feat of strength came during a series of earthquakes that devastated Mexico. The Canelo Highway that connected Tijuana to Mexico City had several decayed overpasses. When the first shock hit, it unmoored the pillars and the entire over pass loaded with cars threatened to collapse on the ones passing beneath it.

Maria's hair, like the sensory apparatus of many animals, sensed the incipient seismic event. It did not communicate its intent to Maria. Instead, it expanded itself into an enormous arachnid and bounded toward the coming catastrophe in great aerobatic leaps. It reached the scene just as the overpass folded in on itself. She formed multiple struts that sustained the structure long enough for the people on it and below it to evacuate to safety.

One might have expected that Maria's exploit would make her an A list celebrity. Someone who would grace the covers of *El Mundo, Time,* and *The Economist.* Perhaps even meet the Pope and the Mexican president.

But the hair would have none of that. Somehow it tampered with the minds of those who saw it and rendered them blind to its presence. Who can say whether it was a matter of mass hypnosis or invisibility that kept anyone besides Maria and her adversaries seeing it?

The fewer people who knew the truth, the better. Otherwise, there would be critics. Specifically, those who would claim that the kindness of monsters comes at too high a price. Or conspiracy theorists that believed her hair was a form of weaponized life cooked up in a Chinese laboratory, the ultimate purpose of which was to exterminate Western democracy. Those same people might offer a bounty to anyone who could kill Maria or otherwise neutralize her hair's extraordinary powers.

Doubtless, religious extremists would find Maria to be an agent of the Devil himself. They would label her hair a fiend without a face, besieging human beings by a contagious form of diabolical telepathy.

Although the scientifically literate might not exhibit such profound ignorance, and dismiss a supernatural explanation, it would come as no surprise if the scientific classified Maria's hair as a coalescent organism, possibly pathological. Not the sort of thing you want enforcing the law or operating in the highest halls of government. Certainly, the Mexican CDC would want it quarantined for study.

As for the common folk, they knew something was afoot. While they had no direct evidence that Maria's hair was anything but hair, their legends abounded about something called *Azotar,* which means 'scourge' in Spanish.

Maria enjoyed the lack of publicity her hair received. After all, her ability to single-handedly bring the cartels to heel made her look like a truly exceptional Police Chief. At the rate things were going, she would be out of the trenches soon enough. She began to see herself in the upper echelons of federal law enforcement working out of Mexico City.

For the moment, she felt comfortable with her hair. She remained unconcerned about the very real threats made daily against her. She considered them little more than the sound of barking dogs trying to leap over a high fence. And if by chance they cleared the limit and were foolish enough to come after her, she knew that her super-hair would make them wished they had not.

Nevertheless, Maria wanted to know more about her hair. She returned to the shop and questioned the hag, whom she suspected to be a *bruja,* or witch.

The old woman said this: "Your new companion involved itself in the 1910 Mexican Revolution, which ended the dictatorship of Porfirio Diaz. It protected the women soldiers, or *soladeras*. It did so by bonding with Margerita Nera, a Mayan Indian from Quintana Roo, who became a commander in Emilio Zapata's Liberation Army. She was memorialized in the song *La Adelita* and paintings where she wears a pair of ammunition belts across her chest while holding a bugle in one hand and the Mexican flag in the other. In those paintings, Margerita's head is the epicenter of a swirling black tempest of hair that reaches into the sky and the land around her."

Maria asked, "But what is *it*? An instance of the hidden world manifesting itself as a sentient, creeping ooze? A chemical mind with a dim will and mind of its own?"

"It is all those things infused with the spirit of the Mexican people. We call it *El Azator*, or The Scourge. It is a living thing as old as the earth itself. It is the Immortal Protector of the Mexican People; it will always rise to mete out justice to those who would harm them"

Maria asked, "You gave it to me, but where did you get it?  After all, it's not the sort of thing one can buy on

Amazon. And I'm sure it didn't bounce into your shop on its own."

"It lives deep within the ground, and every so often it pools on the surface where it can take stock of things. It did so was when Montezuma ruled the land. It didn't like what it saw, so it exterminated the Aztecs and made it look as if the conquistadors had done so."

Maria asked, "How do you know that?"

The crone smiled. "Because it told me to take it from the ground, spread it into my hair and go into the city. I can still see the faces of those Aztecs it tore apart. It didn't touch the conquistadors. Maybe it didn't like human sacrifice. Maybe it saw a better future under Spanish rule."

"But when it came to slavery, the Spanish proved far worse than the Aztec rulers."

"I don't know. The Aztecs kept slaves by thousands and practiced human sacrifice. So, perhaps it was question of the lesser of two evils. Whatever the case, it doesn't think like us. How could it? It has no solid body, but one plastic to its intent—indestructible, immortal, and eternal. It is forever."

"How do I get rid of it?"

"You can't. When it's ready, it will leave you. Until then, enjoy yourself. You're a god now. Do some good with that power."

Maria left the shop resigned to her fate. As she walked, she considered that her biological clock would run much slower, probably as slow as the hag's.

"And for a woman, that's a mighty good thing!" she mused.

* * *

After he finished telling his tale, Pablo had a self-satisfied grin on his face. I assumed it was from the whispered congratulations we showered on him. But after a bit, I wondered if there were more to it. So, I said, "Great story. Did you come up with it or are you repeating what you read or heard?"

He looked at me with his disfigured face and said, "Some of it is true; some of it is not. You will see for yourself soon enough, for she has heard my call, and even now makes her way here to help us."

I regarded that as a bit of theatrical buttoning on a good story. A coalescent organism springing up from the earth with a will of its own, one whose chemical mind had secretly guided the conduct of human affairs strained credibility. Crackpot in fact. To my mind, Pablo was either a master raconteur or the cheese had slipped off his cracker from too many run-ins with the cartel.

Besides his wild imagination, Pablo brought a bizarre and, some would say, pathetic physical appearance to the table.

He had neither nose nor ears, and a face disfigured by weeping sores. He had one good eye balanced by a dead one, filmy and bone-white. He had a three-fingered hand that looked more like a claw than a human appendage. Burly, barrel-chested, and gorilla hairy, he could have passed for a bouncer, a thug, or a monster.

I kept myself at a safe distance. As much from the terror his appearance inspired as from the threat of infection.

He had been a detective in Tijuana. His disfiguration did not stem from the current plague, but from the hazards of his job. Notorious for their barbaric torture methods, the cartels had cut off his ears and nose. When he still refused to talk, they began taking his digits. Luckily, the DEA had found the lair and liberated him before any more he lost any more bits.

The sores that riddled his body, most notably on his face and arms, had come from a virulent strain of flesh-eating disease. He could not say for sure whether he had been infected while hunting drug runners in the Yucatan or chasing them in Mexico City's sewers. Suffice to say, that the result would have been the same.

He was the *de facto* leader of our little band of survivors. He was the one who led us to the boarded-up house we now call sanctuary. Our merry band of seven had pulled off the boards and climbed through a window. At first, the owner was reluctant to let us stay. But when he realized that our arsenal would be helpful should the less friendly elements roaming the street try to gain access, he relented.

The owner said he had enough food and other necessities to last his family a year. With the addition of ourselves, and severe rationing, we could last three months. Longer if from time to time we sallied forth on scavenging missions to replenish the stock.

We were like Anne Frank, living in hidden rooms to avoid detection. Not by the Gestapo, but by our friends and neighbors who carried the Killer Bug, classified as *amantem regredior* by the CDC.

There was no mystery as to its source. It was a non-terrestrial invasive species brought back by the Europa sample return mission. Somehow it had escaped the JPL quarantine and spread through the general population like wildfire.

If anything, it was proof of second genesis, one that used ammonia (not water) as a solvent and silicon (not carbon) as a binding molecule. Its genetic code, if you could call it that, consisted of hybrid forms of bacteria and viruses that did the work we normally associate with amino acids and proteins. Hence its resistance to treatment and cure. It was, as one CDC doctor put it, a "quasi-vitalized thing that goes beyond our understanding of plague and pestilence. Its pathology is such that it could called weaponized life created for no other reason than to turn our planet into a mass grave."

The Killer Bug had a disturbingly robust transmission factor that ranged from airborne droplets hitchhiking on dust to sweat, saliva, belongings, and clothing. Isolation was paramount since symptoms did not manifest until the latter stages of the disease. Sometimes that would be the dissolution of the body. Typically, the extremities would be the first to go: fingers, hands, toes, feet, noses, and ears.

The more superstitious claimed that it could pass from one person to the next by a mere glance. Beyond that it was likened to one of the ten plagues of Egypt. In that context, there was an expectation that it would be followed by rivers turning to blood, swarms of locusts and frogs, tempests, earthquakes, floods, and eclipses.

Not surprisingly, people drew parallels between the infected and the demon possessed. Once infected, the carrier would lose all impulse control and higher brain function, becoming a tissue of pure raging emotion. The infected would bark and drool like a dog, spout gibberish, wet themselves, and simply run amuck. To see a person run into speeding traffic or through a plate glass window was the new normal. As was the rise in lethal assaults with bricks, guns, knives, and makeshift clubs.

Nor did the violence proceed exclusively outward. Self-inflicted mutilation had an almost competitive fad like quality to it. What seemed extreme at the outset seemed tame in comparison to the self-directed butchery that followed in subsequent weeks.

The plan we formulated was to remain isolated until everyone else died. We prayed that the crazies would either die from the Doom Bug outright or slaughter themselves for lack of anyone upon whom they could vent their fury.

That hope died when the marauding bands of infected came to our neighborhood. Presumably, they were looking for food, preferably living breathing happy meals. It seems that not everybody went belly up once the bug got hold of them. Some went cannibal crazy. I don't know what was worse: the fact that they ate people or that they disfigured themselves to such a degree they looked more fiend than human. Angels of death afflicted with corrupt flesh sent to pour plague over mankind.

They would cut out their cheek skin, lop off their own ears and noses, shave off their lips, and file their black teeth into a row of jagged fangs. If that were not hideous enough, they had a thing for large gaudy face piercings. Neither fully dead nor alive, they were the biological empty set, the species-of-no-species.

They marched in a procession with a giant skull—painted in blood—emblazoned on a banner. They were monsters in every sense of the word. If cinema still existed, they were a horror franchise in embryo, a Cronenberg's or Tarantino's delight. The stuff of nightmares and box office bonanzas. They made the Mexican drug cartels look like a bunch of snot-nosed Girl Scouts.

We all took turns at watch, two on any given shift. Pablo was my shift mate, a circumstance that simultaneously made me feel safe while creeping me out. With his missing ears and nose, menacing manner, and deep voice, he seemed remarkably akin to the demons currently ransacking the houses in the neighborhood. I prayed that he was not their fifth column.

As they neared our makeshift fortress, we placed ourselves to protect the points of entry. But as we sneaked looks through cracks in the boards, it was apparent they were no ragtag band of twisted souls with perverse artistic inclinations. They were a horde numbering in the hundreds and possibly the thousands.

Even as they marched own our street, groups would splinter off, not just to rummage through houses, but also to fight among themselves. And at times, fall upon one member, kill them, and proceed to make a meal. It was like watching a documentary about chimpanzees gone cannibal. So and such were the devolutionary fortunes of those afflicted with what must surely have been a newly mutated strain of the Doom Bug.

Pablo and I stood guard over the barricaded front door. We didn't have long to wait before the assault began. First, they tore away at the boarded-up exterior. I could hear them growling and cursing in what was once Spanish but now a crude conflation of animal noises and half-human words.

We could also hear them trying the boarded side windows and back door. Then there was gunfire coming throughout the house. The ab-men had breached and were being met with small arms fire.

I steeled myself for the door being torn off its hinges. But Pablo did not. He tossed his gun away and sat down. Then he keeled over, shaking as he fell. His eyes rolled back in his head and he went into a seizure.

I could not help him, my focus being on the imminent entry of the man-eaters. For a moment, I thought he had been infected and these were the symptoms. He writhed and squealed and vomited like a man possessed by the very devil. So, I kept one eye on him and one eye on the door. If I had a third eye, I would have watched my back, for by now, the mad men were surely in the house. The only reason they had not come for me was, I presumed, was that they were occupied eating my friends.

Pablo sat bolt upright. He looked at me and smiled. "She's here. Comes now the reckoning."

I wanted to ask what he meant. But in that instant, I heard crashes throughout the house, like trees falling into it. The battering on the front door stopped.

The sounds coming from the front of the house were a series of squeals and concussions. I looked through the peephole and saw what appeared to be massive legs supporting a raven- haired woman. The legs sprang from her head and cocooned her body.

There were eight legs in all. There were also eight tentacles shooting from the core. One was swatting the mad men away from the front yard like so many bugs. Another had wrapped itself around a truck and was using it to smash the rest.

I could see that the remaining six tentacles extended into the house. Every now and then one would retract with skewered fiends wriggling like worms on a hook.

In the interim, Pablo had gathered himself. He stood beside me. We watched *Azator* finish off the last of the ab-men. We went through the rest of the house to look for survivors. We two were the only ones that had survived. There was no sign of the monsters.

We went back downstairs. Pablo opened the door just as Maria was retracting her tresses and resuming her human form.

"My god Maria, I am so glad to see you."

"And I you. It has been too long. I see that this world has taken its toll on you. I can fix that."

Maria's hair uncoiled and wrapped itself around Pablo' head. When it pulled back after a few minutes, Pablo's missing ears and nose had regrown. He looked younger and now he had two good blue eyes where there had only been one.

I asked, "How do you two know each other?"

Maria said, "Pablo was *Azator's* high priest. He was the original host who made the Aztecs the power they were. Its life enhancing powers continue for some time even after it finds a new host."

Pablo asked her, "Will you help us fight this plague?"

Maria said, "We have been treating the symptoms in Mexico by killing the infected. I think *Azator's* essence holds the key to a cure. Ingesting small amount of its essence would protect an individual. The problem is distribution. She can't divide and spread herself the way a virus can. So, I have been looking for a lab and some skilled microbiologists to synthesize a cure. But not many people are left."

Pablo said, "Well, until a scientific solution is found, I say we team up and save what people we can."

Maria said, "That will have to do."

Then she looked at me and asked, "Are you on board?"

I smiled. "Like a band going on tour: *Azator* and Her Plucky Sidekicks. I can dig it."

Maria said, "Then what are waiting for? Let's get this show on the road."

We hotwired a truck. We had not gotten very far before the infected were upon us. I want to say we fought our way to Mexico City. The truth is Maria did the fighting, while at the same time protecting us from becoming dinner. The mission became a stop and go affair: we would hotwire a vehicle, run into a horde of infected, lose the car or truck whereupon Maria would clear a path, then we would find other transportation, and the process would begin again and again and again.

When the infected came at us, they came in waves. To assist her, Maria manufactured spider duplicates, which turned themselves into perpendicular buzz saws cutting through the less than human obstacles. It was a blood bath on an apocalyptic scale as body parts—arms, legs, heads, and torsos—were shorn off and sent flying amid a spray of sticky black and red blood.

The stench of death, like that of a thousand open graves, permeated the air. Its acridity made my eyes and nose burn. I gagged and stumbled, covering my face as best I could so as not to inhale the mephitic stench.

For her part, Maria was remarkably nonchalant. She was as serene and composed as a landscaper wielding a Weed-Wacker to remove unwanted growth in a garden. Every now and then, she would ask if we were okay. But otherwise, she stayed focused on getting the four of us—Maria was still in there somewhere—to our stated objective.

When we finally reached the CDC, the cadre of Mexican Special Forces was reluctant to let us pass. They pointed their assault weapons at us fearing we carried the contagion. Maria, no doubt sensing time was of the essence, relieved them of their weapons and cracked them in the solar plexus. We walked in, unmolested.

We found six beleaguered contagion specialists in a lounge drinking tequila. From the looks of things, they had given up on any hope of finding a cure or treatment. Maria barked at them to get up and get back to work. They did not move a muscle.

So, she promptly shot out her tresses and lifted them up to the ceiling. "We may have found a possible cure. So quit screwing around and come with me to the lab. You can finish your drink after we have fixed the problem."

Then she unceremoniously dropped them to the floor with a resounding thud. They sobered up after that and led us down the hall to one of the labs. Maria gave them the *Reader's Digest* version of the plan and they got to work synthesizing her genetic material.

We have been here for three days now. Any moment we should hear something regarding the fate of the initial batch of test subjects. I think all will be well. Maybe because Pablo looks so good. When I first met him, he was missing parts and looking like death warmed over. But a little spritz from *Azator* and now the bloom is back on the rose. I just hope that is a sign of things to come.

# A CHRISTMAS CAROL KILLER
*By J Louis Messina*

## STAVE 1
## The Killer

Ebenezer Scrooge, a tight-fisted, grasping, spiteful miser, crouched in his counting house in Newman's Court, a dingy, uninviting passage off Cornhill, reading the headline splashed across the pages of the London Times:

*"THE LONDON BASHER STRIKES AGAIN!" The killer struck in the wee hours of the night with his usual signature death blows about the head, bashing in the skull multiple times, leaving a pool of blood and the victim's face nearly unrecognized. Once again, a wealthy businessman had his purse purloined. At this time, authorities have no clues to go on."*

*Seems I have competition*, Scrooge thought.

Seven years ago, today, on Christmas Eve, Scrooge had poisoned his business partner, Jacob Marley, acquiring all his assets. And every year on this festive night, Scrooge conspired to murder someone, known or unknown, in celebration for the hate he had for the season. He picked out the most cheerful, gift-giving, boisterous, charitable person he could find, then left his own signature mark on them, boiled pudding over the face and a stake of holly in the heart.

With this new killer on the loose, Scrooge could roam the streets, unsuspected, kill anyone he liked, and with his gold-knobbed cane, lay the blame on the Basher with a smash to the victim's head.

Scrooge flung the paper aside and counted a pile of coins on his desk, stacking them, and writing the account in his book.

Although renowned for his parsimoniousness, in truth, it kept people from snooping into his affairs. Scrooge, the old skinflint, used his frugality as a cover to hide his extravagances and corruptions.

Chuckling under his breath, Scrooge recalled the wild night he had in West Sussex a month ago, pretending a business meeting had called him away. Under an assumed name, John Huffam, he'd splurged his money on a six-course meal of cod with oyster sauce, ballotines of duck in Cumberland sauce, roast lamb, a chocolate profiteroles dessert, ordered the finest wines, and ended the evening with his favorite after-meal debauchery, purchasing two of the highest paid prostitutes for several nights of carnality. Keeping money from others was the only way he could afford his indulgences.

This made him think of Bob Cratchit, his abused, underpaid, cowardly, sniveling clerk. Scrooge relished taking money out of the pocket of such a feeble-minded wretch. Cratchit had never once stood up to him. With no backbone to speak of, breaking his back was an easy task. If his clerk knew what he did with the money he pilfered from him, the sanctimonious lapdog would more than likely die of saintly shock.

Cratchit, a scarf wrapped around his neck and dressed in shabby work clothes, tiptoed into Scrooge's office, rubbing his frozen hands. Scrooge looked down at his desk and pretended his clerk was a lamp.

"If you please, sir," Cratchit said, blowing on his hands for warmth. "That is, if you don't mind me asking."

"Yes, yes," Scrooge said, waving his feathered pen around. "What is it? Speak up, man."

Cratchit's small voice grew smaller. "It's rather cold, and my hands are numb, so it's hard to write. May I, if it's not too much trouble, put more coal on the fire?"

"Coal is expensive." Scrooge pointed his pen at him. "You know the rules. If you want more coal, you need to pay for it. Place your money here."

"You see, sir, it's Christmas Eve, and I need the money for my family. We had to scrape three months' wages together to pay for Tiny Tim's crutch, and I need the rest for goose, punch, and plum pudding."

"Then why are you bothering me if you don't have the money? Get out and do your job, unless you want to find employment elsewhere."

"No, no, sir." Cratchit bowed his head and backed out of the room. "Sorry to bother you. I'll put my hands in the candle."

"If you snuff it out, you'll pay for another." Scrooge lifted his head and stared down the quivering clerk, as a snake about to swallow a mouse. "I suppose you'll want all day off tomorrow again?"

"It is Christmas, sir, and it's only once a year."

"If I picked your pocket once a year, how'd you like it?"

"Not much, sir, although there's nothing to pick."

Scrooge slammed his hand down, breaking the quill. "Get out and do your work!" He picked up another pen. "And my broken pen will come out of your salary."

Out scurried Cratchit back to his desk; in strode Scrooge's nephew, Fred, smiling so wide it was a wonder he fit through the door.

Scrooge hated his nephew more than Christmas. Fred reminded him of his sister Fanny's death on Christmas Eve. Moreover, his insipid enthusiasm soured his stomach.

"Merry Christmas, uncle!"

"Bah! No different than any other day, excepting less money to make. Humbug!"

"Come to dinner tonight and feast with us."

"Feast? And you as poor as a church mouse. Shall we resort to cannibalism?"

"We prefer a Christmas turkey, but I shall oblige your culinary tastes. Whom shall it be?"

"Any and all that say, 'Merry Christmas.'"

"Then you will fill your belly until it burst."

"An excellent way to decrease the surface population."

With Fred's pesky smile in the darkened room, his firefly teeth sparkled. He sashayed up to Scrooge's desk. "Why do you hate me so, uncle? We have never quarreled."

Why? If he only knew, Fred's smile would sneer, his cheerful countenance twist to contempt; he may well murder him. Scrooge couldn't look Fred in the eye; his nephew looked too much like him.

Scrooge had seduced his sister, lusted after her. When Fanny gave birth, he rushed to her bedside.

"We must tell our secret, Ebenezer," Fanny said in bed, holding his hand. "Fred is our son. You must look after him."

"It will be the ruin of me if you do." Scrooge looked at the closed door. The doctor paced outside. "We will be ostracized. My business bankrupt."

"My shame kills me. But we must do what is best for our baby."

"Yes. I agree."

Scrooge whipped the pillow from under her head, pushed it onto her face, and smothered her. She struggled and grasped and beat at his arms but soon fell limp. He felt no more compunction suffocating her than exterminating a bug. A cold, hard story crossed his mind. She was always a fragile woman. He tried to revive her, but she died from childbirth.

He wept into his hands. The doctor flung open the door and put his arm around Scrooge to console him. A performance worthy of Shakespeare. In the next room, the baby cried. The one responsible for her murder. He had never looked at Fred since.

"Good afternoon," Scrooge said to Fred's optimistic venom and pointed to the door.

"And a Happy New Year, uncle!"

"Bah."

"The dinner offer still stands."

"Humbug!"

His nephew left as buoyantly and exuberantly as he'd entered. If he were not his son, Scrooge thought Fred an excellent candidate for his Christmas Eve killing; however, he didn't have the money, and Fred's charity prospered from his empty platitudes spewing from his mouth; he was glad of that.

Night seeped upon the streets, and the city soaked in darkness, lit by puddles of light. Scrooge slipped on his gloves and heavy coat and took his cane. His clerk pranced out, a merry elf, into the fog and bitter cold with snow so deep, it devoured your boots, and exchanged snowballs with some boys down the lane. What a simpleton. How anyone could think this a jolly time to celebrate was beyond Scrooge. Winter was a scourge.

Scrooge prowled the streets, looking into the faces of wealthy men for victims. Feeling famished, he stood before a melancholy inn, the George and Vulture Tavern, the front battered and weathered, and went in for a bite. The lighting inside danced and flickered over the customers. He sat and observed one man, a fat gentleman paying for his guests' dinners and drinks, handing out money to the servants, as if he employed them, and giving gifts to all out of a bag at his feet.

"Merry Christmas!" the portly man said. His stomach bounced with his words, giving the impression it talked. "Good will to men!"

Here was his man! This benevolent blackguard deserved to die most of all tonight.

"You make merry this evening," Scrooge said, not as a compliment. "Has someone died and left you a fortune?"

"No, no, nothing so macabre, God forbid." The fellow crossed himself, as if to protect their deaths. "I love my relations. This is the time for giving, helping the poor and destitute. I feel blest at this time for my health and wealth and give the Lord Almighty his due."

"Parting with your money recklessly will leave you destitute in your time of need," Scrooge said. "No one will help you when you're sent to a debtor's prison."

"I toast you anyway, my good man." He lifted his cup and drained it. "Whom do I have the pleasure of drinking to?"

"Ebenezer Scrooge, if that's truly a pleasure." Without lifting it, he sipped from his cup of wine. "I toast to your eventual destitution and demise."

"Yes, Scrooge, richest man in London but can't find his money to spend. Archibald Leech, at your service, good sir. I must make haste, however, as I have an important engagement. I'd offer you a present, but I'm afraid I'm spent."

"The best gift yet."

The man tottered to his feet, swaying, as a sailor on a ship in a storm, steadying himself with his staff. In his cups, a stupid smirk implanted on his face, Leech lurched out the door, watching his every step, as if the ground moved.

Scrooge asked for boiled pudding, wrapped it in paper, paid his bill, and followed.

A fog swirled at his feet. Scrooge swept through the mist, keeping his distance on his prey, Leech. A leech sucked on the blood of men. Tonight, his cane extracted in kind. He needed to steer the fat oaf to cover.

Leech hiked along the path, stamping his big staff into the drifts. The fog rose and covered Scrooge, masking his endeavors. Leech disappeared. Scrooge remembered the Basher. The big staff the man hiked with could crush a man's skull.

What if this man was the killer? What if he walked into a trap? How had this man earned his money? Was it from murdering wealthy businessmen like him? Scrooge's purse jangled on his belt. Had he become the prey?

Scrooge lifted his cane for protection and slinked through the fog. One of them would die tonight. As if parting a veil, Scrooge emerged out of the mist. Leech turned and opened his arms, his staff raised, as if he'd part the Red Sea.

Scrooge staggered backwards and swung his cane, ready for combat.

"There you are!" Leech stomped to two people Scrooge had not seen and wrapped his arms around them. "My two favorite niece and nephew. We'll party at your abode tonight. I've drunk and ate myself to stupor but saved room for your banquet."

Scrooge gathered himself and his dignity. He'd had a fright. The pudding had gone cold and needed heating. He tramped back to his house in Brabant Court, groping his way through the gloomy streets of London to harvest the holly and wrap it around a stake. Whomever the chosen victim for tonight, he had to prepare for his evening kill.

Could he find one before midnight?

## STAVE 2
### Marley's Revenge

Scrooge had taken up residence in his partner's house, having acquired all properties after Marley's untimely, or timed, death. Scrooge had been looking for a new place to live, and Jacob's mansion suited him.

As he withdrew the key from his pocket, a cloud formed over the doorknob. He shook his head, wondering if he hadn't drunk too much wine. Marely's enraged face appeared, eyes wide and fixed, hair blowing as in a breeze, transparent, ghostly.

If a guilty conscious had arisen in Scrooge, the specter of it hadn't appeared, for he shoved the key up the nose of Marley and turned it with intent to tweak it and cause pain. The phantom head vanished. Satisfied he had vanquished his remorseful vision, Scrooge stepped inside, locked the door, lit a candle, and clomped upstairs to his bedroom.

A gruff, low voice broke through the door above. "Scrooge."

"Who's there? A burglar?"

However, Scrooge knew the name of the voice, dared not utter it, and decided to ignore it altogether. Swinging open the door, he plunged through. As no one greeted him, he assumed his meal had played tricks on his mind; perhaps the underdone salmon the inn served spoke to him in such a nightmarish manner. The undigested potato he ate seemed suspect; the curdled gravy may well send him to his grave.

He lit a roaring fire and warmed his body, then set the pudding in a pot and over the hearth. Sitting in his chair, he sharpened the stake with his knife, then wrapped the holy around it.

Bells clanged and struck, wildly and with exhilaration. Scrooge's blood froze. He clamped his ears. The bells terrorized his head. When they stopped, Scrooge looked to the door. An apparition formed and oozed through. A figure in chains clanked across the carpet and stood facing him. Trembling, Scrooge widened his eyes in disbelief.

"Jacob Marley?"

"It is."

"You're a ghost, then?"

"I am."

"Have you come to haunt me?"

"No."

"What then?"

"To kill you."

"And it took seven years?"

"Returning from the dead takes time. I have until midnight, then I must return to my grave forevermore."

"An hour left. Very sporting of you." Scrooge stood and stretched, then walked, slowly, through the spirit, shuddered, stuck the stake in his pocket, and grabbed his cane. "How are you to accomplish this murder if you cannot hold worldly possessions? Do you mean to scare me to death?"

Scrooge sauntered to the door, as if on a picnic, and slyly opened it. Marley's pallid, ill face had not moved, nor had his inert eyes followed Scrooge, nor had the body with the clothes he'd been buried in stirred. However, the opaqueness that gripped the ghost melted off the body, as an ice sculpture in the sun, and Marley inhaled for the first time since his last breath.

"I have been granted life for your death." Marley shuffled toward Scrooge, held up the chains that bound him, and rattled them. "Strangulation is your fate."

"I'd like to stay and chat about old times, catch up on your hellish existence, but I have my own victim to hunt. Farewell, Jacob."

Scrooge dashed through the door, slammed it shut and locked it. Marley shook the doorknob. He rammed it. Skipping down the stairs, Scrooge tipped his hat to Jacob and scampered outside.

"Have a good evening."

The door burst open.

"Scrooge!"

Scrooge spasmed to life, cursed Jacob, and trod through the snowdrifts and the flurries of flakes batting his face. The howling wind whistled a melodious, ghoulish tune. Moaning his own descant, Jacob clattered after him, shaking his chains.

"Help me!" Scrooge waved at patrons, arms filled with packages wrapped in brightly colored paper, streaming from shops. "A man means to murder me!"

"Where?" said a Cockney man selling chestnuts and warming his hands over the coals.

"There, there!" Scrooge pointed at Jacob crashing his way. "Arrest him."

"I don't see no one, Gov'nor."

How could they miss the tall, lanky man in dark, tattered clothes and rusty chains?

"Are you blind? It's the ghost of Marley come for revenge."

"A ghost, you say?" The people laughed. The man addressed his audience. "Aye, I see them now. Three spirits, past, present, and future. One spirit ye drunk an hour ago, one you drunk on your way, and one nip yet to come to keep the ghosts away, as they say."

"You're daft, all of you." Scrooge stumbled away from them. "There's only one that means to do me harm."

Although Jacob was as real as money, no one could see him but Scrooge. He raced to the Royal Exchange, hoping to run out the clock. Lights shone behind the white pillars, and Scrooge thought he might meet some businessman he knew that could help hide him.

Jacob's moans approached. Scrooge clambered up the steps, but slipped on the icy patches and fell facedown, splitting his lip. Scrabbling his way up, he darted into the exchange. He looked around, frantic, jiggled the doors, locked, saw Jacob climb the steps, gasped, and ran to the side and jumped over and tumbled to the ground, caught by the arms of the new snow.

Drenched, Scrooge rocked to his feet and lit out toward Bayham Street in Camden Town, the poorest, most squalid tenements ever built. Scrooge owned them. Bob Cratchit lived there. The chimneys smoked, and the soot choked the air and sullied the streets, burning the lungs as logs on a grate.

Laughter and Christmas carols sang from the impoverished people in the poorest part of the London suburbs.

What could they possibly be happy about? No food or money? Why had he come to this miserable part of town? He'd find no refuge here.

If he could hail a carriage, it could carry him around until the clock struck midnight. However, for a dead man back from the grave, Jacob tramped his way down the street so quickly and quietly, Scrooge thought he must have wings.

When Scrooge came out of the street, he headed back to his home, thinking he might lock himself in and wait it out. As the snow fell and blinded him, he careened over the land in the dark, frozen, horrible night.

He thought he'd found Cornhill and broke through a gate crippled by age. He tripped over stones and graves, bunched together, packed and overflowing. He'd blundered his way into St. Peter's church cemetery. Passing the markers, he read the names of some of the men he'd killed on Christmas Eve's past. He twisted through the stark, dead trees, trying to find his way out of the maze of death, but found himself going deeper, lost and confused.

Then he fell, dropped, plummeted into the darkness, screaming and flailing his arms.


STAVE 3
A Grave Ending

Dirt crumbled onto him. Scrooge floundered on the cold, damp, muddy earth. He had fallen into an empty grave. He scraped the sides to lift himself up. In the distance, Jacob's moans crept closer. Scrooge froze, as in a child's game of freeze tag. If he stayed still enough, quiet enough, pretended he ceased to exist, the vengeful ghost would pass him by.

"Scrooge."

Scrooge took in another big breath and held it, inhaling the decay of the grave. Marley couldn't see him buried six feet under in the darkest, blackest of nights. All he had to do was wait it out. No need to panic. He'd found the best hiding place in London.

His heartbeat thumped, harder and louder. Scrooge fixed his gaze on the opening. The rattling chains echoed.

Where was Jacob? Was he moving on? Had he passed him?

Hidden deep in the shadows, Scrooge felt another shadow fall over him. Standing on the precipice, Jacob looked down on him, silhouetted, like a cardboard figure cut out and painted black. Surely, Marley couldn't see him.

"Scrooge."

Damn! Scrooge was never good at hide and seek as a boy.

Jacob leaped into the grave and pounced onto him. Scrooge broke from his fright and swung his cane, striking Jacob across the temple. Although the ghost showed no pain, Jacob reeled backwards. Realizing he could hurt the apparition, he swung again, whacking Marley's chest, hammering him away.

"I've got you, Jacob! Your flesh and bones can break as well as mine."

When Scrooge lifted his cane again, Jacob grabbed it, whisked it away, and broke it in two. Scrooge's bluster deflated. Jacob wrapped the chains around Scrooge's throat, once, twice, thrice and squeezed. Scrooge's eyes popped out of their sockets. He wheezed; his body rumbled and squirmed.

If the clock struck midnight, he'd live. He listened, intently, hoping for the sound, the savior bells. However, his breath rattled, whispered, left his soul.

Reaching into his pants pocket, Scrooge withdrew the stake of holly. With the last of his air, he shoved it into the heart of Jacob. He pushed, breaking bones, puncturing organs. His vision dwindled. Jacob fell back, loosened his grip, and clutched the stake, trying to release it.

Scrooge took the deepest breath yet, giving life back into his body. He jolted, as if electrocuted. Pushing Jacob off him, he rose to his feet, stepped onto the living corpse, clawed his way to the top and dragged himself up and over and back into the cemetery.

From faraway, St. Michael's ancient clock tower chimed midnight.

Scrooge found a shovel stuck in the pile of dirt next to the grave. Swiftly, and without a moment's break, he flung the dirt until filled to the brim, patted the top, clapped the grime from his hands, and strolled away.

"It was my privilege to bury you twice in your lifetime."

Walking back through the fog and mist, Scrooge massaged his sore throat. He stepped lively, his spirit jovial, as a drunk man tipsy from his first few lagers. He'd cheated death; in fact, he'd killed death. It crossed his mind that Jacob counted as his Christmas Eve murder, and such satisfaction swelled within him that he smiled wider than Fred's grin had ever ballooned. He'd lived to see Christmas. Scrooge danced a jig and hooted. If someone saw him, they'd think him mad.

Having worked up his appetite, he thought he might even visit his nephew, take him up on his dinner offer. Not spending his own money on food appealed to him, and his thoughts drifted to the whores in West Sussex. He sighed, stimulated by thoughts of sex.

Where was he now? The snow rained down, and he couldn't get his bearings.

Scrooge felt a blow to the back of his head. The wind knocked out of him. The blow fell repeatedly. He whirled and spun, then collapsed to the ground, dizzy. A man stood above him with a stick.

"Scrooge?"

It couldn't be Marley. Who had followed him?

The stick crashed down onto his skull, ripping it open. Blood gushed.

Was it the fat fellow from the tavern wielding the staff?

"Who are you? What do you want?"

"I'm the Basher you've read about. I've come for your purse."

The man hit Scrooge against the side of the head. He felt his neck crack.

"Take it!" Scrooge shoved it at the man. "Leave me alone."

The man snatched the purse. "This will buy the prize turkey hanging in Leadenhall Market. My family won't starve tonight."

Scrooge squinted, trying to make out the face, obscured by the storm, his vision jarred and blurred. Bells rang in his head.

"Bob Cratchit? It can't be."

"Yes. You've reduced me to killing to survive. Tiny Tim needs to see a doctor. This amount of coin should do the trick."

"You'll lose your situation for this!"

"Lost."

Cratchit bashed Scrooge's face into mush with Tiny Tim's crutch, leaving no witness and no doubt in his mind that Scrooge had died.

"I need more coal, too, so we won't freeze to death tonight."

Counting the money, Bob Cratchit trekked to the market, teeth chattering, heart and mind thawing with one warm thought.

Old Scrooge was as dead as a doornail.

# 'SIRIUS' MATTERS
### *By Rob Santana*

Cliff Harris, free and thirty-five, promised his eight-year-old daughter Sara a new dog. Not a new Mom. He vowed never to marry again. After a lengthy custody battle, Cliff won. He had Sara to himself. They would share the two-bedroom house in that quiet suburb close to school. Cliff's new Chevy was all he needed for travel. Linda, his ex-wife, was free to hang with whatever bum could satiate her lust for drugs and booze. It was this weird talent she had, hiding her little vices. As District Attorney for the small Midwestern town, Cliff had sent Linda's lover Moe Galileo to jail for selling coke in the park. Linda called it cruel and extraneous. Cliff called it comeuppance. Pot maybe, as Moe had started with. But switching to coke? Please.

Cliff could live with his paucity of good looks, which Moe had in abundance. Cliff's frame toted an appendage of fat that quivered with each step, a head-full of graying follicles, and a double chin that showcased a second smile. Moe, with his dark, lean Mediterranean visage, would merit unwanted attention behind bars.

*Say goodbye to my wife, Moe.*

The irony of having to visit Moe's older brother Victor bothered Cliff. Victor Galileo was one of the town's two veterinarians. He specialized in ailing canines, and the waiting time was shorter. 'Sirius Matters,' the font on his store read. (as in 'Sirius, the God Dog Star') Yes, dogs only. Cliff had decided that Sara's aging pit bull Teddy was gravely ill, despite Sara's protest, and needed to be euthanized. He felt bad for his only child, but he despised the yappy little bastard. Victor recognized Cliff from the local TV news broadcast of his kid brother's arrest a week earlier. His glare was unforgiving as Cliff plopped the pet carrier on his desk. Teddy's whimpering filled the room.

"Put him out of his misery." Cliff told him, not oblivious to Vic's vibes. Cliff guessed that if Vic's eyes were laser beams, he would have been in pieces by now. He studied the dog and looked at Cliff.

"You must be real proud of yourself," he said, "sending my bro to jail." A hint of sneer curled his lips.

"I'm sorry it had to be your kid brother, Vic. But selling drugs to teens? Come on. I didn't have much of a choice"

Vic peered into the carrier where Teddy lay. The dog looked up at him, whimpered at first, then lowered its head. "This dog looks okay to me."

"He's *old,* Vic. He vomits on the rug, won't eat. He's like a garden slug." Vic forged a closer inspection, his eyes narrowing. Cliff might have regarded the motion of his eyes. They didn't rattle, just stayed fixed on a point somewhere beyond the counter.

"He don't look old," Vic countered, adjusting his black wig. His craggy scowl seemed painted on. "But, hey, it's your money." He gently placed the carrier next to his feet behind the counter and wrote up the form.

Cliff had heard stories about Vic the Vet.

The 'Mad Scientist' they called Vic. The fifty-something lab tech who lived alone and liked to experiment on animals, like the Nazis had done on humans. The story originated from a plumber who visited Vic's ancient one-story house that faced a wooded area, an area jammed with dug-up and refilled holes. The story soon spread but no one dared test its scuttlebutt. Vic was a creepy guy, but was an expert handler of afflicted dogs. Cliff wondered what category of utensils ringed Vic's basement in that old house.

* * *


"Dad, I still miss Teddy," Sara said. "I think about him every night. Even in class. Why'd you have to put him to sleep? Did he break a law? All he had was a fever."

Cliff looked up from his modest living room desk. How to mollify your only child. He tried this: "Sweetie, Teddy was dying. And pit bulls make me nervous, anyway. No kid should own a pit bull. They're unpredictable. I'll get you a chow."

It was Linda who had chosen Teddy for her daughter before the messy divorce. She had this strange affliction for pit bulls. She loved how they would lap your face, slobber over it as if it were an ice cream bar. The way their black eyes resembled those of a shark at feeding time, rolling up their sockets as they bit down at your arm or leg. To him, pit bulls were ferocious predators. Once Sara segued to stilled withdrawal, Cliff envisioned a peaceful co-existence with his crestfallen daughter: find a babysitter, mingle with his admirers and staff at the finest restaurants, bask in his courtroom sweeps, and educate Sara on the principles of right and wrong.

Then came the bizarre news.

The blond square-jawed TV anchor had to keep a straight face. "It's been reported that a dog with a 'man's face' had been spotted by a night guard standing outside an apartment complex. According to a witness, the guard screamed and scrammed back into his lobby when the pit bull advanced toward him." The anchor shook his head, his lips curved. Chuckles could be heard off-screen in the studio. He coughed slightly, rolled his broad shoulders, and regained his professional bearing. When they showed a Chihuahua's face transposed over a well-dressed man's face, the studio staff cracked up. The anchor, sniggering, had to hold up a hand as in 'Okay, let's get serious.'

Cliff, not amused, jacked up the volume just as Sara padded in from her bedroom.

The broadcast switched to an interview with the guard, who looked shaken. "This weren't no figment of my imagination," he said. "I saw it. A man's face! On a pit bull body! Blue eyes starin' up at me! And a head full a' black curly hair!"

Back to TV Anchor, again fighting down a smirk: "Slow news night, folks. What can I tell you?"

Sara gravitated toward the HD screen, her eyes wide. "Daddy? Did I hear him say pit bull?"

"Sweetie, go back to bed. School tomorrow."

"Did they show the dog?"

"No, it was someone's idea of a joke, baby. Go to bed."

Cliff had to steer Sara back to her room. He could feel her shoulders trembling. It was past two a.m. He went to bed and gazed at the ceiling.

*Nonsense.*

That guard was on K2 or crack or something, drunk maybe, or feared dogs of that species, or- trick of light. Yes! He concentrated on Linda. Her visiting rights kicked off this weekend. He would never forgive Linda.

*Have Sara back by six, Linda, please. Do not test me.*

Cliff did not like being tested, especially by his ex-wife. She knew what the deal was when she married him. A lawyer's life was unpredictable. Up at ungodly hours, home by whenever his client saw fit. She had to have known that.

As black clouds strangled the moon, he heard a dog bark from outside the window that faced his cluttered back yard.

Another bark. Louder.

Cliff shot up like a coiled spring and listened, frowning. *A stray mutt.* Lost in the wasteland of strewn garbage and parched foliage. Another yelp. More muscular. Cliff shook off the din and chuckled. But there was an image he couldn't dislodge from his rattled brain. That of Vic hovering over that goddamn pit bull's body, gripping a special kind of saw, balancing it over the animal's thick neck. Cliff imagined the smell of death, the soil that still caked Teddy's stiff body from the excavation. He chuckled, just as that smarmy TV anchor had chuckled.

*You dope. The guy's a vet, not a grave-robber, not Friggin' Frankenstein.*

Other sounds penetrated the night: Two cats braying at each other, sounding more like babies in need of a nipple, distant dogs howling at the moon, pretending to be wolves, raccoons and overweight possums overturning garbage cans in search of abandoned food. The wind picked up. It chilled Cliff, the sound of that wind. Its temperate whine jarred his senses. It resonated like a phonetic, cautionary warning. It seemed almost to have shaped an indecipherable voice. It died down, then grew louder; howling, then whispering. Cliff sat up in his bed, his hands folded. He looked down at them. They were shaking.

The barking grew louder. Cliff could hear Sara's response from behind the door. Her thumps nearly drowned out the howling that began outside.

"Daddy, he called my name!"

Cliff swung out of bed and pulled open the door. Sara was trembling. He bent down. "What're you talking about, Sara? It's just a stray dog."

She let out a strangled yelp and pointed to the window. He looked over his shoulder. Only the horizon of distant naked trees met his gaze. "I saw him," she said. "He looked right at me."

"*Who* saw you?"

"Teddy! He smiled at me!"

Cliff shook her and she began crying. "Stop this, Sara! I mean it! Teddy's gone! Go back to your room." She sprang to his bed instead and cowered under the blanket.

"Stay with me?" she mumbled. Cliff stared at her, then at the vista beyond the window.

"I'll go see for myself. Stay put."

He skipped to the kitchen, pulled out the largest knife, and crept to the screen door. His heart thumped like a disco bass as he throttled the knob. He eased open the door. The dog's labored huffs tinged the shadows. Cliff gripped the knife and took a step, his black pajamas soaked in sweat. He froze. A shadow flitted past the crumpled flowerbed that rested against the white picket fence. From behind him, Sara's voice rose above the wind. Common sense told Cliff that it wasn't an invocation coming from his daughter. That it was his mind playing tricks on him. So why was Sara bellowing in a way it could reach a neighbor's ear? Making those sounds in her throat made his hair singe. How could vocal chords coming from a little girl create such an eerie transmission?

He stepped out past the screen door and whirled on the window Sara had stationed herself behind. Her eyes were vast, rattling, focused on the darkness surrounding her father. Her face looked pale, steeped in a strange angle, pressed against the window. He felt as if his own daughter was waiting for something dreadful to happen. To *him*. The wind kicked up as if on cue. A cushioned grunt followed by a sustained growl came from somewhere beyond the fence. How far beyond Cliff could not tell. The vicious gale made for indistinct measuring of sound. For all he knew, the dog, this freak of nature, was five feet to the right or left of him, ready to pounce, its teeth bared. Sara resumed making those noises in her gullet. A nearby cat scooted away, not looking back.

"Sara, I mean it. Stop making that noise in your throat! What is that you're trying to say? Who are you talking to? Stop it, For God's sake. Go to your room!" Something moved at the far end of the fence. He moved closer, his hands sweating despite the cold. His eyes widened.

There it was. *Oh, sweet merciful Jesus.*

The dog's smallish tongue lapped in and out from its thin sensuous mouth, then dangled over a perfectly formed row of teeth. Its human-like ears pricked back upon hearing Cliff's receding footfalls. Its blue eyes were massive and fixed. Sputum rolled down its mouth. Cliff could decipher the stitches on its neck before the half-animal lunged at him.

* * *

By Sunday, Linda Harris held full custody of Sara. The police report was fuzzy. Her ex-husband's throat had been torn open. Loss of blood ended his life. A renegade dog, she'd told them, modifying Sara's account. What a smart little girl, they said, dialing 911 soon after watching her father writhe in a pool of his own blood. Her new pet, however, could never replace Teddy. The pit bull was never found, but Sara peered out the window every night, hoping Teddy would return and smile at her again.

# PILGRIMAGE TO THE RANGE
### By Jay Baird

I didn't think that when I killed myself I would have become a martyr. Didn't think that hundreds upon thousands of people would replicate my journey and exit from stage left. Delusions of grandeur weren't exactly on my mind when I committed suicide, more so the opposite if the truth be told. When you book a one-way flight to Arlington, Texas (because one to Houston is out of your price range) and then go to the first gun range that you can find, set yourself at ease in a booth, place the cold steel barrel of the CZ 75B semi-automatic 9mm pistol into your mouth, making sure to angle it so that the back of your head will soon resemble a blooming poppy, you don't necessarily think this is going to become some kind of universal trend.

After I turned the back of my head into a flesh flower and repainted a portion of the wall behind me with a sloppy coating of blood, brain matter and whatever else, I lay on the floor thinking I had somehow messed up. I lay there paralyzed, or at least believing myself to be. I thought that I had turned myself into a vegetable and had made my life even worse. This wasn't something I had anticipated. I tried to wiggle my foot to see if I still had control over my body. I felt movement and thought that being able to communicate by ankle movement to doctors, friends and family would be something at least. I flexed my fingers, straightened my legs and discovered that I still had movement in all of my limbs. This was a relief, which was odd considering I had just made some modern art out of my brain a few seconds ago. I instinctively brought my hand to the back of my head, preparing myself for the sensation that my fingertips would feel upon touching the new body orifice in place of where the crown of my hair should be. My fingertips only brushed hair though. I ran my hand over the back of my head and felt nothing that would indicate injury. Not even fresh blood.

Slowly, I got up on my feet. Standing up, still curving my arm to probe at the back of my head, searching for the exit wound, I turned to look at the wall behind me and saw the residue of what was once my thought factory. That, and whatever else had stuck to the wall or was in the process of sliding down it. Death can be confusing for the first couple of minutes.

My inspection of the accidental tribute to Jackson Pollock I had made was cut short when I heard a shrill scream from behind. I turned and saw a woman whose left hand was resting on a pair of earmuffs that she had brought back to rest on her neck. I had taken mine off, as I didn't want to ruin them when I ate a bullet. I brought my hand from the back of my head and put it up in a mock gesture of both surrender and introduction.

"Oh no, I'm fine… really," I said while pointing at the wall behind me, then bringing it back and waving it slowly to suggest that worry was not necessary.

Her eyes left the wall and dropped to the floor next to my feet. They widened while her eyebrows rose to the point that they nearly touched her hairline; her lower jaw slacked and then she let out a longer and louder scream than before. At this point, other people were exiting their booths to see what all the screaming was about. Some were in the process of removing their earmuffs, showing that their concentration was no longer focused on the black silhouette targets but, instead, on whatever this woman was reacting to.

"Really," I said, feeling slightly embarrassed. I turned my gaze to the floor, finishing the sentence as I did. "I'm fine," I blurted out as my eyes came to rest on a sprawled figure next to my feet… a person who looked identical to me, except for a hole in the back of their head.

It, no I, lay there, lifeless on the hard ground. The gun was still in my slack hand. Its, no, my eyes were open, staring at nothing down the aisle of onlookers. One of them now had a phone to their ear, calling an ambulance when they might as well have called a hearse. I was standing next to myself, looking down and inspecting the sack of flesh and bone I used to be. Like I said, death can be confusing for the first couple of minutes. I thought this might be some kind of trick the remnants of my brain was performing, my open eyes seeing what was going on around me and projecting myself out of the body that was going to be entering the rigor mortis stage of death in less time than it took for my plane to complete its one-way flight. But then the paramedics came and my body was soon after cart wheeled out of the range in a body bag, and then, when an hour or so went by and I didn't fade into the abyss of unconsciousness, I didn't think that this was some kind of 'death dream' anymore.

It takes about a week to adjust to the afterlife. Takes about another week to see how boring it's going to be. Not much to do except roam around and talk to other dead people when you stumble across them. Chances are slim that you'll find this person again, though; the afterlife is real crowded. People also disappear sometimes too. There are rumors of Heaven and Hell, that the current plane of existence was purgatory and that it didn't have to be forever. This can be as relaxing a revelation as it can be a terrifying one. Especially to those who spend their purgatory spying on people in changing rooms. Consequence and the inability to continue in their voyeuristic activities can reduce Heaven to Hell and Hell… well, to just Hell. Nobody seems to know how to escape purgatory, and if they did, chances are they wouldn't be around to say how.

My death was reported in the news and kind of gained notoriety. I think the determination of traveling to the USA from the UK just so I could die in a quick albeit messy way, really spoke to some viewers. But probably not in the way the media wanted. Within a week of my suicide, another two occurred; both instances were people who had traveled to America from places where there were no guns. They had both gone into gun ranges and blown their brains out. Within a month this had snowballed to the point where an average of sixty-five people were setting out on a pilgrimage to gun ranges across all the fifty states.

My suicide had accidentally made me a martyr to those who were planning on leaving life prematurely. Some people loved me for introducing them to what I thought was a pretty simple idea at the time. Others hated me. The media that first reported my death as tragic, now branded me as a sort of anti-Christ who was the catalyst for the deaths of over a hundred people and rising. Weirdly, no one pointed a finger at the media for reporting my death. They read my suicide note and essentially turned it into a death manifesto when they showed it to viewers all over the world. I may be a ghost and a martyr, but that still heart my feelings. The media's coverage and detailing of my death felt more invasive than the foreign body that I had propelled through my skull

The gun range in which I had submitted my art piece eventually became a gallery. People flocked there from all manner of places in unprecedented numbers. For whatever reason, people taking their life in the gun range where I had taken mine was considered some sort of tribute, from what I hear amongst the rumors of the life-impaired. The owner refused gun access to anyone if they specifically asked to be in the booth where I was situated. Unfortunately, the business eventually went under as people killed themselves at this range more so than any other. The proprietor was in no market to run a suicide hot spot and there was no way he could run his business as he did before I accidentally inspired other artists to submit their own art pieces to a wall that was, at the time, being more routinely scrubbed and cleaned than the average household.

The building is now boarded up and acts more like a tourist destination. The front is graffitied with all manner of odes to myself and to the subsequent pilgrims who took their lives after.

I never meant to be a source of inspiration for depressed and/or lonely people when I killed myself. Never meant to be the reason for people going out of business. For a while I ended up being more miserable in death than I ever was in life. No amount of walking through walls and watching new cinema releases for free could change the state of mind I was in. And it wasn't like I could kill myself again. Not like I could accidentally start another trend.

Gun ranges across the United States essentially went under; they became synonymous with suicide and people who didn't intend on leaving the store in a body bag generally seemed to avoid them. Nobody wants to be at a gun range, shooting in a booth, only to realize that they're the only one firing at the targets. Trauma is something people tend to avoid.

There were numerous petitions and arguments over the Second Amendment, which I felt really bad about. I certainly didn't mean to cause political outcry and start a societal civil war when I made my exit plan.

Airline travel stopped selling one-way tickets and capitalized on peoples' desperation. People had to spend money on a return ticket if they were traveling to any of the states and were not from America. A lot of planes leaving America had more empty seats than the ones that were entering. New policies came into action where no foreigner could handle or discharge firearms at gun ranges. The applications for American citizenships skyrocketed. For sixth months, America closed all gun ranges across the states. The owners were paid for their troubles. Everything had a knock-on effect and the tedium of trying to stop the trend never seemed to end well or do as was intended.

After the six months, when the gun ranges finally reopened, vigorous tests were put in place to ensure that people were not trying to pull a "Kevin Willard." I never thought that my name would become a euphemism for a suicide trend.

People were at first hesitant to attend gun ranges, but after visiting them and leaving with their hemispheres, cerebellums and brainstems all intact, a large number of the populous breathed a sigh of relief. Others sharply exhaled through their nostrils with frustration.

The epidemic has since calmed down; life in the USA and for gun ranges seemed to crawl back to some form of equilibrium. But every now and again, someone decided to shoot themselves instead of the target. The pilgrimage had come to be accepted in a weird way. In the same way that people die during construction work and so on. Chances are it will now be this way forever.

During the height of the craze, when close to two hundred people were dying daily, some would stumble across me in the afterlife and stare at me like I were a celebrity. They would approach me sheepishly and say, "Hi." I'd respond and ask, "Are you another dumb ass who pulled a me?"

The pilgrims who had been inspired by me and who had replicated my suicide seemed to like me less when they met me in person.

Sometimes I hang around the gun ranges. In the event that someone pulls 'a me,' I introduce myself and apologize. I greet them and explain to them the predicament that they are now in. Some take it well. Others don't. Being trapped in purgatory can be quite the confrontation when you originally thought that death would be like sleeping forever. I speak from personal experience. Greeting such people can be quite awkward, but being stuck in the afterlife forever has given me time to work on some icebreakers:

"Hi, so you've decided to pull a me and this is now how you'll likely spend the rest of your existence…"

"Hey, So I see you've pulled a me…"

"Yes, I'm Kevin Willard. Yes I'm dead and so are you…"

"Nice shirt; I like that band too…"

Overall, once I've introduced myself and spoken to the person for a while, things seem to generally play out okay. Apologizing to people who commit a me is something I feel compelled to do. I've made quite a few friendships in the afterlife from doing this. I've met people who were lonely like me. I've made more friends in the afterlife than ever did whilst I was alive, though some people who commit a me act more like irritating celebrity stalkers, following me and my new friends around in the afterlife. I'll ask them to kindly stop following us, and in response they'll put their hands over their mouths and giggle like a child. Apparently, my acknowledgment of the pilgrims in the afterlife is considered the final part of their journey. Upon their untimely deaths at the gun ranges, those who aren't greeted by me or by my friends (we work in shifts) seem to find others who committed a me in the afterlife. God knows there are plenty of them. They usually band together and search for me like a demented pack of paparazzi. They're usually disappointed when they meet me and all I have to say to them at the end of their great journey is, "Do you want to watch a movie with us?"

If you're sitting in a cinema watching a new film release, chances are high that I and other bullet-munchers are taking up all the remaining seats. It's unanimously accepted that movies are a good way to pass the time in the afterlife. I never meant to spend eternity watching movies for free in a theatre surrounded by people who participated in a suicide trend that I accidentally started, but life can take you to strange places... the afterlife to even stranger ones.

# DARK AENEID

## By J.B. Toner

Utquiagvik, America's northernmost point. Polar night, 65 days of dark. My second in command, Camille Ravenna, was the first to die. Yog-Sothoth took possession of all but me.

We fought so hard, we walked so far. After the Battle of the Bering Strait, we thought we could go home. Nyarlathotep touched my mind, Ravenna's mind, in the bleak Alaskan wilderness, hoping to drive us mad, but we survived. And we alone, inured, were shielded from the horrible invasion of Yog-Sothoth. The others—my comrades, my friends—their wills and intellects devoured.

I'm Captain William Peter Outland, United States Marine Corps. Tasked with preserving Alaska from Russo-Chinese incursion. I fear neither death nor pain, but demons from beyond the galaxies have come.

As Ravenna's body hit the ice, Lance Corporal Stetson reeled at me, jaws wide. Stets, my old drinking buddy, thirsting for my jugular. I caught his chin with one hand, the back of his skull with the other, and twisted: *pop*, the cervical vertebrae. Sorry, friend. Private Mox scrabbled at my neck, his pupils leper-white—I shot him with my sidearm through the lung.

So fast, it happened. My men, my men, I should be fighting to free their souls, but a fighter under siege has only one reply. Ryerson flung his arms around me from behind; I knife-hand chopped him in the groin, crotch-clutched, and squeezed, but nothing happened. Pain and self-protection, all were gone—he only breathed in service to the Horror. I emptied the .45 into his torso as the others crowded round, then pulled the pin from my last grenade. Slashing through them with my combat knife, I dove and front-rolled through the snow and vaulted over a nearby Escalade. The detonation rocked the street; glass showered my bone-white hair, so recently red. Viscera came splattering down, and my hair was red again.

From houses, shops, and bars, the people of Utqiagvik came staggering. All inhabited, all taken. If only it were Satan! Something I understood! Not this ghoulish monster-god from space, uninterested in humanity, irrelevant to good and evil, meaningless to life and afterlife.

"Hairworms, hairworms!" I screamed. Was I mad already? A memory from high school biology—that nightmare creature called the hairworm, entering the cricket's brain to seize control, to make it drown itself. Chewing its way out, fucking its hairworm mates, and reproducing from the freakish demise of its host. Was that the destiny of humankind?

Now weaponless. Stomp-kicking kneecaps, snatching out windpipes, I fought through the growing horde of soul-dead foes. Part of me shrieked that someday soon we'd find a way to free these innocent minds and I'd be liable for all the hapless dead—but now, this day of night, I had no time or space to think of mercy. You never touch the enemy; you kill his drones.

Nerve-strikes, pain-holds, reflex-throws, had no effect. My only hope was to traumatize these bodies till they couldn't function. I punched a lunging adversary in the chest, snapping his xiphoid process to puncture his solar plexus, and vaulted over his contorting form, as more enemies closed in from behind. The frantic death-spasm hindered their advance.

There: a pickup with the engine running. The driver was getting out, blank-faced, and reaching for the rifle on the gun rack, when I came sprinting up and smashed his skull with a steel-toed roundhouse kick. Then I was behind the wheel and stomping on the gas.

As I passed the city limits, I glanced to my right. Gasped so hard I nearly swallowed my own esophagus: Ravenna was in the shotgun seat. She was naked, every inch of her as white as bleached bone. Sightless eyes creaked in my direction; pallid lips croaked out a broken sonnet.

> *The polar night has come. Two months of black.*
> *Pale frozen stars long dead. The slopping sea.*
> *The Borealis, flare of lunacy.*
> *Lean ravens pecking at dead Autumn's back.*
>
> *The earth is carrion. The sky is ice.*
> *Seagulls like Grendel shrieking from the Pole.*
> *The dark between the stars. The tomb of souls.*
> *Wolves haggard as the birches, grey as Christ.*
>
> *Cadaverous and gelid universe—*
> *Decomposition—entropy—decay—*
> *Despair and dark and death a world a hearse*
>
> *...the dancing night upon the corpse of day*
> *the fall of all the everlasting curse.*

"Camille," I stammered. "What... how..."

She sighed, an exhalation from Gehenna.

"Staff Sergeant, report!"

I hit a bump, glanced at the road, and she was gone. A final syllable muttered in my ear: *Glorm.*

"Glorm? What the fuck is that? What the fuck does that mean?"

The drone of the engine. Groan of the wind. Thank—whomever—that the highways were plowed and salted. Road maintenance was likely to take a precipitous decline this week.

At last I had a moment to breathe. I clutched the steering wheel and tried to process—no—too damned much—shook my head and tried to focus. Alien horrorgods from some black hole reality at right angles to Reason and Salvation, it was all above my pay grade. All I had to know was, they were enemies.

I checked the radio: Warren Zevon singing *Lawyers, Guns, and Money.* Good. Checked the glove box: a fifth of Jim Beam, three-quarters full. Even better. I gulped about half a pint.

Then I saw the lady in the road.

Slamming the brakes, I shrieked to a halt with my front bumper nudging her patellas. A slender form in the black habit of a Carmelite nun; a waifish azure gaze, yearning in the headlights. She came slowly to the driver's side window, and I rolled it down.

"God help us," she whispered. Her lips were deep, deep pink. "The Devil is here." A wisp of hair strayed out from her wimple, strawberry blonde. "We can't escape."

I tried to… speak…

She was inside. Sweet, hot breath in my ear: "No escape." Sleek midriff pressing on my palms, soft skin over sculpted muscle. "No God, no Devil. Only Yidhra."

I felt my lips move, spoken through. "Yidhra."

"Yes." Tongue like a serpent, coiling over my neck, my chest, keying off pleasure points. My back arched. "For one eternity after another."

Straddled by powerful thighs, I hung in a moment's balance. But I know who I am: a United States Marine. I serve no foreign cosmos—not for an eon, not for an evening. Like a dreamer pummeling himself up from sleep paralysis, I reclaimed possession of my fingers, then my hands, and then my arms. "No!" I pushed her back against the steering wheel. She smiled and snarled and split her skin, and thrashing, snapping vipers filled the cab.

What governs all? Is there luck; is there fate? God knows, or no one. A dozen snake-fangs struck my chest and sank into the Kevlar. Others struck the seat between my legs, the headrest behind me, the windshield and the dash. Clawing madly at the handle, I opened the door and flung myself headlong. Somehow retaining enough presence of mind to vault into the bed of the truck, I snatched the AR-15 from the gun rack before I bounded over the side and sprinted off into the wind and snow. Behind me, the snake-nun hellishly self-immolated, and the truck exploded in a cyclone of flame.

*God, my God, I'm so tired. So tired.*

Weary and wounded. Lost in the Arctic Circle. No food, no water—nothing but a gun that might not even be loaded. No one was coming to help.

Doesn't matter. We don't give up. Right now I had no better plan than to just keep moving, so that's what I would do. What else, lay down and die?

Slogging onward through the winter-blasted wilderness. The cold, fatigue, and pain became a nightmare universe inside my skull, and all else faded. The will, the will, to keep on putting one foot before the other. Wind in my teeth and will in my boots, and nothing more. Where was I going? I couldn't remember. I couldn't remember my name.

A gradual, invisible transition, like the stealing of dawn into a shaded hollow. Slowly, I became aware that the cold had slackened and finally disappeared—that I was trudging onward, but the weight of my body was gone. The dark still enveloped me, but not the tenebrous cloud of exhaustion in my brain. I recollected myself and looked about: up ahead, light glimmered.

I knew, as one knows in dreams, it wasn't the light of my world; nor were the beholding eyes the ones I saw when I shaved. I understood, as I walked onward, that my earthly legs were elsewhere—a biped metaphor, a shadow now transcended, of these spirit legs. I'd tripped and flopped into a deeper, truer realm.

Another blink-transition: I was deep inside a cavern that was deep inside a star. Stalactites of calcified flame, downthrust, surrounded me; smoldering stalagmites, flame-spurts locked in place mid-spurt, hemmed in my path. And as I made my way, I realized the frozen fire had eyes. No hands, no mouths, no ears—just horrified, unblinking eyeballs staring out forever. I met one red-veined gaze, and I swear those lidless orbs belonged to Private Mox.

Up ahead, a form. Familiar compound ghost: my father, my drill sergeant, my grim old sensei. You, here? Treading the sun-cave in a dead patrol. Why, master? There is no why, there's just the fight. We cannot win it, we can never win. But all the same, we fight. I'm lost in snow; I'm good as dead. Oh no, you'll live. You'll live to found the citadel of Glorm.

*Glorm? What is…*

*What…*

I found myself still walking through the snow. Above, the Borealis lit the sky, mysterious and beautiful. I took a deep breath through my nose and let it out. Welp—here we are.

The vision was as clear as a memory. I felt oddly refreshed, invigorated. I popped the clip of my weapon and checked it: thirty-round mag, fully loaded. Damn sight better than nothing. I took a moment to hush my nerves and listen, and I heard the distant anthem:

> *First to fight for right and freedom,*
> *And to keep our honor clean—*
> *We are proud to claim the title*
> *Of United States Marine.*

Yes. I know who I am, and no hell-god from the quasars can take it from me. Fuck Death. Fuck Hell. I will fight forever.

I raised my chin and marched onward through the polar night. Hours went by, and days. And then I saw.

Ahead in the darkness, dully glinting, was a mangled barbed-wire fence. A hidden compound, stone and steel now broken by the demon-hordes of Yog-Sothoth. As I walked through the pavilion, I saw scores of crudely eviscerated corpses. The main building, its security doors turned to scrap, was still dimly lit by LEDs. The reek of gunpowder and gelignite was heavy in the corridors. Heads and limbs and bits of lungs were strewn about the place.

Down the hallway, down the stairs. A metal chamber lit by infrared. A lab, complete with two white-coated bodies, slashed and exsanguinated into the floor drain. Scattered about the room were flurries of handwritten notes, along with shattered microscopes and Petri dishes.

The Hellhounds, my slaughtered battalion, had been the first defense against Sino-Russian aggression. I had clearance above Top Secret, and was read into all manner of clandestine operations in the region of Utqiagvik. And yet, I'd never heard even a wisp of a rumor of this place's existence. What the hell were they doing here?

I gathered up the notes, reshuffled them as best I could. To the scrutiny of an intelligent layman, they yielded little— except that the abbreviation "Nyar." kept jumping out at me.

And I remembered enough from my core courses to know what alleles and nucleic acids were for. Whatever they'd been working on had either gotten loose or been rescued by its freakish confreres. On the upside, one of the workstations contained a bottle of water, a mini-bag of Fritos, and an apple. Valhalla.

A little food in my belly—a warm room and a comfortable chair. The sound of fluttering paper woke me up as the esoteric notes I'd been frowning at redistributed themselves across the gore-painted deck. I took counsel with myself and agreed that I should definitely get to my feet and pick them up. Just—rest my eyes for a second.

They closed.

They opened.

I was standing, weightless. The room was the same—but if I looked to my left, it stretched away into a corridor of men in lab-coats moving backwards, a corridor of workmen building a laboratory, carving a space out of rock, and finally the quiet subterranean stone. When I looked to my right, I saw the corpses on the floor decomposing in fast-forward, the vernal roots piercing down through the old steel ceiling, the earth reclaiming a space we'd briefly held. Then I looked down, and shit got weird.

A centipede of me, a trillionfold queue of Outlands stretching back into the past: every instant, every choice, defining a universe. Entangling with the centipedes of my Marines: a ramifying cosmos of once-possible cosmoi, stretching back to Paris Island, high school, Mama's womb. Everything that might have happened, all the choices we might have made and didn't, all now dark; a single glowing line of destinies, once merely possible, now chosen— leading through all if-worlds to this moment. And glancing up, I saw the transdimensional branching of a hundred kabillion possible realities, radiating outward from Now. All my choices, all my possible futures, intertwining with the choices of every other soul: a beautiful multiform tree of might-yet-be's.

Then a thing like a shadow, a thing like a shadow, a thing like a horrible annihilating shadow. Hopping out of nothingness, a venomous transcendental frog, jumping from branch to branch. Wherever it landed, the future went black: withered potential, wasted promise. The uncreating power of the Outer Gods. With all that I am, I caught hold of it and clung.

*You cannot win. No faith, no hope. You are nothing, all is nothingness. You cannot win!*

*Semper fi, you son of a bitch.*

In the end, it came down to one thing, a force that can't be crafted in a lab: the will to fight. And I've got no godly powers, but I know who I am. I'm William Peter Outland, USMC. I *am* the fight.

Finally smothered, that thing—anti-spirit, anti-will— evaporated like an awful dream. I jerked awake in my chair to hear the static of a radio.

"…say again, is anyone out there? We've been attacked by—by something horrible. Is there anyone left? Come in, please come in!"

With a slow and trembling hand, I reached out and picked up the transmitter. "I read you. This is—" Hello, Destiny. "This is Glorm. 71° N, 156° W. All remaining military and civilian forces, converge on these coordinates. You're not alone. I say again, you are not alone."

# MEDIUM RARE
*By Ken Goldman*

"Fate is never fair. You are caught in a current much
stronger than you are."
— Cassandra Clare, *City of Ashes*

"Life calls the tune, we dance."
— John Galsworthy, English novelist

"Fate is persistent, while Destiny waits."
— Madam Somnala, Medium and Teller of Fortunes

Rick noticed the buzzing neon sign flashing in the
window of the small boardwalk apartment. From its
parlor, MADAM SOMNALA — FORTUNES
READ glowed crimson, the flickering illumination seeming
unnecessary during this sunlit afternoon. But the pulsating
letters stirred his interest, and with bemused curiosity, Rick
passed the cigar smoking, bearded, young man standing near
the screened doorway and entered through it. Sliding his
wire rims up his nose, Rick tried not to sound pompous.
"Your sign out front says you tell fortunes."

Old Somnala didn't move from her chair. Nor did she appear to note her customer's smirk, an irony that didn't escape him. *Some clairvoyant!* But he had an hour to kill before Emma was meeting him at The Beef Bar-Be-Cutie, just down the boardwalk. The kids loved that place for its clown-attired servers, and fun seemed the order of the day even if this carny-like gypsy provided the entertainment.

"Yes, your fortune I tell," she answered in broken English, barely looking at him. Her almost unintelligible response suggested her talents probably weren't worth the $20 Rick handed the medium for her hour of magic. Or maybe witchery. "If you prefer, I can speak to the dead for you. With luck, they may answer. It will cost a bit more."

*Of course it will...With luck!*

"Let's keep it earthbound for now." Rick kept any further wiseass comments in check, but the old Cambridge frat boy urge was there.

Smiling, the woman displayed several missing teeth, the remaining ones yellowed and crooked. Somnala could have come straight from central casting: a ton of cheap jewelry, huge loop earrings that did a real number on her drooping ear lobes, and a necklace that displayed some intricate circular design resembling the moon. Her clothing seemed straight out of Goodwill, and her grey hair looked like someone had gone at it with a weed whacker. She smelled of cigarette smoke, probably unfiltered Camels judging from the pile of butts in the ashtray. There were several cigar butts as well, giving off a stale stink that added nothing to the parlor's ambience.

Somnala gave Rick the once over. "You are young and quite handsome. This is not an attempt at revealing your fortune, young man, merely an observation." Maybe this was her version of a joke. Rick knew nothing of gypsy humor, or if it even existed. He wasn't sure what to say. He hadn't really thought this out.

"I'd like to think my good looks are obvious. So, about my future...?"

The gypsy hesitated, maybe hoping to run out the clock on Rick's paid-for hour. She reached for the kettle on her hot plate behind her, poured its contents into a chipped cup. Rick had to smile.

"Tea leaves, eh? We're going old school, are we?"

The woman didn't smile back, perhaps taking offense. "No tea leaves. See? Lipton's." She took a long sip. "Now, give me your hand." Extending hers across the table, she inspected both sides of Rick's right hand like a classroom nun searching for dirty fingernails. She focused on his palm, then interlocked his fingers with her own. "A strong grip, and an assured one. A married man, yes?"

The gypsy probably noticed his wedding band. Somnala had a grasp of the obvious, for sure—so big fucking whoop regarding her psychic powers. Rick nodded, but didn't embarrass her by mentioning what anyone who wasn't blind could see. Her next observation seemed almost laughable.

"And nearsighted, true?"

A 50/50 shot, there. "What gave it away? My glasses, maybe? But, yes, without my specs, I'm your basic blind bat. Nice try, though."

The gypsy had to have noticed Rick's skeptical smirk. "Very well, then. Your marriage line, here—it appears very deep. Ten—no, twelve years married, happy years, yes?" She pointed to the horizontal line closest to his pinky finger.

A more impressive observation, but she could have calculated his age, then made a lucky guess. Rick nodded.

She studied his palm closer. "And children? Two I believe. A boy and a girl. The boy is older, going on—ten? The girl, she is seven and has asthma. Nothing serious, and otherwise a healthy child. Your wife, very beautiful—not especially religious, but she eats no meat, true?"

"My palm tells you all that?"

"That, and much more."

The woman had pulled that information clear out of nowhere, a neat trick. Emma hated her parochial school years; especially hated the nuns who taught her, so rabid Catholicism meant little to his wife. And, yes, she preferred the vegetable platter at the Bar-Be-Cutie. Old Somnala nailed that one nicely.

"Well, tonight will be different," she added. "Tonight she will eat meat."

"That's not much of a prediction. See, occasionally Emma cheats on--"

"Tonight will be different."

Rick almost laughed but caught himself. "You're sure of this?"

"I feel sure only when all other outcomes are impossible."

Rick's cell buzzed. His wife was on the line. "Leslie and Carter are hungry, honey. We may be a little early at the Bar-Be-Cutie. Is that all right?"

"I'll be there soon. Order ahead, okay?"

"Okay. Love ya!"

Rick returned his attention to the gypsy. "Sorry. The wife. So, anything else you—*see?*"

She gave another cursory look at his palm. "Smiles. Many smiles surrounding you and your family. Very soon."

"That's good, right?"

The gypsy didn't seem to think so. "You were in the military. I see a gun. No, many guns. Your fate line, this one that runs up and down, it appears to twist and breaks--"

"Nope, sorry. Never served. I do own a gun, though. Baretta Nano, 9 mm, practically a peashooter. Not licensed to carry. It's home. But a good guess. Want to throw some tarot cards?"

"I never guess. And no cards. Are you certain you wouldn't like me to speak with the dead?"

Rick shook his head, his skepticism on hold, refusing to release his grip on reality easily. Okay, so he did own a gun and people were always smiling around his kids because they were so damned cute. Check and check. But on the minus side, his asthmatic daughter, Leslie, had whipped out her inhaler while the family strolled the boardwalk earlier, so maybe the old woman was observant of those who passed by her window. A trick of her trade, no more. And many women these days were vegans like Emma. But the gypsy *did* know details about his family only close friends would have known. It could have been some elaborate parlor trick—in this case, literally a parlor trick. A little panache to add to the show. Maybe.

"So, about my future? The dead can wait a little longer." He half expected the woman next to reach under the table for a crystal ball.

She didn't. Instead, she again studied Rick's palm. "One knows the future best when one understands the past. *Your* past—it appears quite clear. May I--?"

"Please do."

She grasped his hand, shut her eyes. "Your name, it's Eric. Rick, your friends call you." She smiled, looked at him with unexpected bravado. "No, Mr. ... Sanbourne, is it? I did not see the name written on your credit card inside your billfold when you handed your money to me, as you are thinking."

That had been Rick's very thought, but her insisting she hadn't noticed his credit card meant nothing. His palm had begun to sweat, and he hoped he hadn't made a mistake entering this woman's parlor because the fun aspect of doing so had disappeared. Clearing his head of any telltale thoughts, he remained silent.

The gypsy added, "You have a beautiful home, a home befitting a high salaried lawyer, I believe. A criminal lawyer—Am I correct?"

Correct enough to detect a scam, Rick told himself. *But you should know I'm thinking that, shouldn't you, Ms. Gypsy lady?* His blue collegiate-type blazer covered a simple t-shirt, and his stylish white khaki shorts possibly revealed his financial status. But an expensive diamond studded Rolex and his fancy wedding band—well, the worth of certain things weren't hard to assess. Not too much clairvoyance required here.

"Okay, you got that correct. But about my future?" he asked again, although there'd be no way to determine the ancient woman's accuracy concerning that, would there? Not until long after the gypsy had packed up her baubles and cash and moved elsewhere for the winter, probably with a trailer full of hags like herself, maybe a dozen little ones too from unmarried daughters, because disappearing into the night was what gypsies did. But then again...

*"Tonight will be different..."*

And what if Emma ordered the vegetable platter at the Bar-Be-Cutie, as always? What kind of jerk would demand his $20 back following that fuck up? Still, old Somnala was on the money with the basics. Or maybe that was her way to jack up her customers' anticipation, with the hope of adding a little more cash to her deep pockets. Offer her visitors some accurate information, and who wouldn't be hooked? And soon after, taken!

*Oh, I could tell you much more, sir, for only a small additional fee....*

Rick's thoughts distracted him while Somnala continued studying his palm, deciphering whatever secrets it held. One brow raised and she looked even closer, seeming troubled. She grabbed hold of both of Rick's hands, held them firmly in her own. Her eyes flickered, then closed tight.

"So, does my love line suggest I visit the pharmacy?"

Somnala seemed somewhere else. She looked about her parlor like some frightened animal.

"Your father, he is dead for many years?" The question came from nowhere.

"Yes--"

"He is here with you now. He seems concerned. He—he wants you to leave—*he wants you to leave now!*"

"That's really funny, considering my father was the one who left *us!* Tell him to go to hell, if he isn't calling from there himself! So, this channeling of the dead will cost me extra, then?"

Somnala went pale, a neat trick if she managed this at will. "You have something to ask him?"

"Ask the bastard if I should have the chicken or the rib platter for dinner."

The woman disregarded the sarcasm, or maybe she didn't understand it. "Your father, he says you must be with Leslie and Carter now. Your children, yes?"

The answer took Rick by surprise. "Yes, but how--?"

He remembered the call from Emma! Maybe the old woman had really good hearing. More likely, a decent hearing aid, its volume turned up. Nothing to see here, nothing at--

"Listen, Madam whatever-you-call-yourself. I'm going to meet my wife and kids for dinner, soon, so--"

*"Shh!!"* The gypsy's head swayed and she said nothing for several minutes.

"Look, lady. No offense, okay? I appreciate the effort you're putting into this, but--" Rick stared at the woman who seemed to have forgotten he was there. But she didn't release his hands; she held them more tightly. Rick winced with the pain.

Somnala seemed to come out of a long trance. "There is something...something I..." Dropping Rick's hands as if she'd held a pair of snakes, the woman licked her lips, offered the $20 back to him. "Take it. Go. Please. Your father, he worries. He is gone from here, says now you should go too. Your children your wife--" The gypsy gave no explanation for her sudden change.

"I don't under--"

"Please..."

Rick refused the bill, leaned across the table holding his palm flat before the gypsy woman's face. "You saw something in my palm?"

"Please go..." The $20 remained on the table while the gypsy attempted to light a Camel. Her hand shook.

"You saw something!" he repeated.

"Yes."

"Something bad."

She took a long drag, whispered, "Your father, he spoke to me of—of—"

"Tell me."

She stubbed out her cigarette. "I will show you." She again took his hand, pointed to the curved line on his palm nearest his thumb. "Do you see this line—your life line?"

"I don't see any--"

She traced the line with her own long finger. "It is here, Mr. Sanbourne. Not very deep, nor is it very long—as you can see."

Rick saw. The line was short, ending well before his thumb.

"What does it mean?"

Somnala looked into Rick's eyes, her expression almost threatening. "The line, it ends abruptly. Very rare. Must I explain what it means? Go, please. The dead speak only truths. Sometimes it is best not to--"

Behind them the screen door opened slowly, squeaking on rusted hinges. Only Rick turned. In the doorway stood a tall figure. A man, but more of a shadow in the glare of a setting sun. Rick could make out his oversized wide brimmed hat and large dark glasses, and a face well hidden behind an unkempt beard. Eyeing the small parlor, the intruder closed the heavy door and approached the table where the two sat.

The dead—channeled, and *voila!*

*Not quite...*

"Don't get up," the stranger said, turning to look behind him. Satisfied they were alone, he pulled a small pistol from a tattered denim jacket. "You, mister, look to be a very wealthy man. I saw that when you entered this place. Your wallet, please. The watch and ring too. Lady, you don't look like you're worth shit." Noticing the twenty-dollar bill still on the table, he shoved it into his pocket and moved closer to Rick. "I'm not going to ask twice, fucker. You hear me?"

*Fockerrr. You hearrr me?*

The stranger spoke with an accent not unlike Somnala's, and he held a gun small enough to be a toy. Standing close to Rick, the familiar cigar smell registered immediately.

*Fockerrrrr*

*Another gypsy. Of course...*

"I suppose you'll have to shoot me," Rick said. "Lady here tells me my life line is for shit and that my dead father confirmed it. So I guess this is it, and that's all she wrote, eh?"

The dark man did a double take straight from a bad Vaudeville bit. He looked to the woman, again at Rick.

"I have a gun," he said. The remark seemed almost pathetic.

"What you have is a cigarette lighter, asshole. It says BUTANE right there on the barrel." Rick turned to the woman. "Your son, maybe? The accent, you know? How many gypsies wander in off a Jersey boardwalk, and this guy waited near the door until you worked your black magic on me—*almost!* This is one piss poor scam, lady. Scare the mark into thinking he'd better pay this creep or his life ends here and now. Very tacky, lady, very tacky." He returned his attention to the intruder, pushed himself from the table. "I've seen enough. I'll take my $20 back, please." He pulled his own gun from his blazer and pointed it at the stranger. "Sorry, Madam, I lied about not carrying. See, I've got no license to carry in Jersey. But I can assure Marcos, Milosh, or whatever the fuck your boy's gypsy name is, this gun is very real. So I think--"

The old woman interrupted. "Mr. Sanbourne... Signore... you are mistaken. This man also holds a real gun--"

Like some dumfounded ape, the stranger could find no words. He handed the bill to Rick, forced an unconvincing laugh.

"Look, mister, I--" He turned to the old medium, whipped out a half smoked cigar and lit it with his ersatz pistol. "He knows, Mother. Signore, my apologies for this foolish--"

"Save it. Madam Somnala, a real pleasure. *Idiots!*" Rick mumbled, pushing past the bearded intruder and out towards the door.

"Signore—a moment, please," the old woman said. "You believe we have attempted to deceive you for your money, yes?"

"Damned right."

"Then I must give you something of value for your money, Signore Sanbourne. You believe it was your choice to come to my parlor. But you were meant to come here, as you are meant to do wherever it is you do next. There are no accidents—there is only fate. But destiny, that is different. Destiny, she gives you choice. Destiny may cheat fate. Fate is persistent, while Destiny waits. Do you understand? Destiny can be changed!"

Rick sneered at the woman's twisted logic. "That's double talk... *signora.* Right now my destiny is to forget that this past hour happened and to join my family for dinner. Oh, and to tell you and your boy to go fu--"

*Choice. Okay, then...*

"...that just for the record, I'm FAR sighted!"

Rick chose not to add the accompanying hand gesture. He'd made his point.

So had Madame Somnala.

* * *

The dinner hour hadn't yet arrived when Rick entered the bistro, but already the boardwalk's Bar-Be-Cutie was crowded and filled with children's laughter. One server clown juggled eight large dinner dishes while his comic partner stood by with two plates stacked with ribs and chicken. Clown #1 put down his empty plates, pantomiming he'd like to try his bit with some plates that were filled. Clown #2 emphatically refused, and served Rick's kids their orders. Laughter filled the room.

Rick smiled at the young waiter/jester and took a seat at the table. "Sorry I'm late. Long story—I'll share after I shove some ribs into my face." He kissed Emma's cheek. "So, where in this greasy feast is my lady's salad?"

Emma grinned. "Your lady is going medium rare tonight." She reached for a meaty red rib, chewed on it still smiling. "Surprised?"

Wiping a thin stream of barbecue sauce from his wife's chin, Rick mumbled, "Maybe not."

*Tonight will be different...*

Rick told himself it meant nothing. Emma wasn't zealous concerning her no-food-with-a-face diet, so breaking her rule wasn't uncommon—although her evident enjoyment doing so was. But... something else...

*I see smiles...*

The server clowns wore smiles, all right, and there were a dozen of them. Clowns were this eatery's big draw to attract the kids, and the gimmick worked well. The place was crawling with children.

*Smiles... Painted ones, but still--*

It meant nothing. Somnala had overheard the call from his wife, knew he was coming here. She knew this place.

"Hey, husband! You snooze you lose, my love. The cuisine is diminishing as I speak!" Emma handed Rick a chicken wing. "This bird gave its life so you may gorge. You can at least honor his sacrifice."

Rick took the wing and chewed at it while Carter wrapped his mouth around a long rib, faking a farting sound. His sister, Leslie, dissolved in hysterics. Rick smiled with the moment's normalcy, but all normalcy ended that moment.

Four server clowns surrounded the room, two approaching the table where the Sanbourne family sat. Rick had no time to adjust his glasses to see what the four held. The gypsy's words reverberated in his brain.

*"I see a gun... many guns..."*

*"Your children... your wife..."*

Rick's brain felt on fire. He adjusted his glasses, but his hand shook and his wire rims fell to the floor. Squinting at the four clowns, he felt his mouth go dry as he heard a loud *pop!* Each held what appeared to be a rifle *(maybe semiautomatic weapons!)* as if--

*Terrorists? Crazed Goth nihilists?*

Crazy! The second time a gun was pulled on him today!

*No! These guns were pointed at his family!*

*Christ!*

Children's laughter continued throughout the eatery, but Rick paid no attention to it. If this were some kind of Columbine moment, then he had no choice but--

*Choice!*

He got to his feet, pulled out his Baretta pistol, aimed it at the skinny clown approaching his family...

*No time, no time!*

*"The life line... it ends abruptly..."*

*"NO!!"*

Rick pulled the trigger. His gun made only a cap-pistol pop, but the entire restaurant fell silent, and the young clown, clutching his arm, fell to the floor. A woman screamed. Other screams soon followed. Children's screams, women's...

"That man, he's got a gun!" someone shouted. From behind him, a huge man's arm elbowed Rick's throat. Unable to breathe, Rick dropped the pistol.

Emma got to her feet. "Let him go. Please! My husband didn't mean-- He's farsighted, for God's sake!"

The young server clown twisted on the floor. Several others came to his aid. The server's arm leaked blood through his party striped costume. Screaming and cursing, he remained very much alive.

"Goddammit, mister!" the kid shouted, his grease painted smile seeming incredibly out of place. "Why'd you do that?"

The beefy man released his grip, turned to face Rick. "Don't you recognize a fucking t-shirt shooter when you see one? It's a goddamn advertising gimmick!"

Trying to catch his breath, Rick couldn't speak. He stood in a dizzying swirl of semi-consciousness. Forcing an unconvincing smile, Emma placed his glasses on his face, then grabbed a tight hold of his hand. Surrounded by a growing crowd of patrons, Rick heard Leslie crying.

His vision came into focus and he noticed the dark figure at the door.

No one else did.

* * *

At sixteen, Francis Buckman was large for his age, tipping the scale at close to 300 pounds. That was, of course, the problem. That, and how much he hated being called Francis, especially because no one ever called him Frank, a more genial name he could have lived with. And the laughter of others—hell, why should he have to put up with a lifetime of that? He wasn't like others, and he'd be the first to admit it. He had no desire to be, because the boy hated everyone. Mostly, he hated the kids, little bastards who held nothing back when it came to making fun. There were many older ones too. Christ, even his own fucking mother--

A *malcontent*, he'd overheard his English teacher call him. Francis had to look up the word. The prick teacher was lucky that malcontent hadn't put the man's balls in a sling.

He buttoned his heavy coat to the top. The dark garment was unusual during summer, but there were crazier things to see on the boardwalk. Climbing out of his old van, he headed up the ramp entrance of the promenade.

He pulled out the clown mask, adjusting it. Although the grinning disguise wasn't as elaborate as the grease-painted faces of the others, it would go unnoticed in this place.

*The Beef Bar-Be-Cutie, a stupid name filled with stupid people feeding their stupid faces.*

At the entrance, young Buckman reached under his coat. A crowd stood clustered around a single table, and for some reason a server clown lay squirming on the tiled floor, an absurd sight. But Francis saw genuine humor in it. An accident or something grisly had brought out the ghouls, and a good number of patrons stood murmuring close together to watch the show.

*Perfect!*

He knew this moment was meant to be. Days earlier, as a lark, he had visited the old boardwalk gypsy who called herself Somnala. She'd read his palm, mentioned she saw danger there in what she called his fate line. Probably the old bitch was trying to scare the hell out of him because adults usually saw his excessive body piercings and tattoos as threatening, and this, of course, had been his logic for having them. But if his fate included danger, then *hot damn! He liked it!*

Francis took a moment to study his palm, then clenched his fist. He felt so damned powerful knowing the damage that hand could do. Near where he stood, a man in wire rimmed glasses seemed to notice him, but the guy just stood there among the crowd holding a woman's hand and appearing dazed. An easy target. Francis decided he would go first.

The boy stepped forward past several emptied tables. Smiling behind his clown mask, he squeezed the trigger of his semiautomatic firearm.

# MANOR OF BONES
### By Thomas K.S. Wake

"Easy money, eh?" Eric hated the fact that he'd been right about Matt being wrong. And now he was fucked.

* * *

The manor's pointed rooftop scraped at the night sky in an apparent attempt to reach the waxing moon. The topiary depicting ancient Roman gods occupying the yard observed two figures sneaking across it, both clad in black. The figures were completely silent apart from occasional muffled clanking sounds of metal hitting metal.

Eric huddled behind one of the said yard plants and scanned the building. It was dark and quiet. There wasn't a single gleam of light in any of its arched windows. The massive manor was a dark silhouette against the only slightly lighter sky.

So far so good, but Eric was also very aware of another saying; too good to be true.

"See?" Matt hollered from behind the topiary shaped in the form of Athena and removed the mask covering his face.

Even in the dark his perfectly white teeth were visible. Eric often joked that Matt's pearlies was eventually going to get them caught by drawing too much attention to them.

Eric had to admit that Matt might have been right. Keeping low, Matt made his way to Eric. His tools jingled in a burlap sack.

"So?" Matt didn't even try to hide the complacency in his voice.

"I think our best bet is just to go through the front door."

"Seriously?"

"Yeah. If your midnight fling was telling the truth, then the house is empty. If she wasn't, makes very little difference from where we enter, correct?"

Matt agreed and smiled from the sweet, sweaty memory of the previous night. They really got lucky; Matt happened to pick up the maid from the house on her leave. And their luck kept getting better when it turned out that the maid was very cross with the owners of the manor. They usually cased the places they were going to rob, but there was no time for that now. The masters of the manor would only be away this one night and if even the half of the rumors about the wealth of the Stanton family were true, Eric and Matt would walk out of the manor the richest burglars in Blackpool.

Draped in shadows, they glided to the front door, keeping a constant eye on the surroundings just in case.

Eric knelt and put his ear to the ornamented oak door and listened. Nothing. It was like the house was holding its breath.

Eric nodded to Matt, who took the lead in unlocking the door. With all his faults, Matt was an expert on prying things open quietly and quickly. The heavy door was no exception as the lock clicked a sound of yielding and the door popped open.

"Easy money, my friend." Matt grinned and gestured Eric to enter. The two burglars slid in and were swallowed whole by the darkness.

The manor seemed endless from the inside. Deep shadows hid every corner from observing eyes, making the building appear to stretch to an infinite darkness, quelling all of the moonlight's attempts to penetrate it. Heavy curtains on all the main windows did their due diligence and held the curious night light at bay.

After almost an hour of rummaging through the darkness yielded no bounty, Eric waded through the downstairs, room by room, while Matt was doing the same on the second floor. Nothing. For a house this luxurious there was very little to steal, unless you counted the massive furniture and countless of books that were spread across several rooms in bookcases. The rumors seemed grossly exaggerated. Even the kitchen was void of any silverware or anything of value.

*So much for the hot tip from a hot maid*, Eric thought. He listened, but the house kept its silence. Passing a room he'd already searched, the sudden shift in atmosphere made the hairs on Eric's arms stand up. He got the feeling he wasn't alone. Something was off. The shadows inside the room had shifted. Something was there that wasn't before; he was sure of it.

"Matt?" Eric whispered, suddenly feeling exposed.

No answer.

He tensed. "Stop messing around. You found something?" The voiceless darkness stared back. Only the ticking of a large grandfather's clock echoing from the main hall occupied the inky blackness.

Eric contemplated going in, but lost his nerve for the first time in his entire adult life. He turned to make his way to the bottom of the stairs. Once he was past the doorjamb, there was a sound of cloth dragging along the floor coming from the room.

Eric turned and backed away from the room; not taking his eyes of the gaping dark mouth that was the door. The dragging sound ceased.

"Matt? For God's sake, stop fucking around!"

No reply.

"Shit." Eric reached into his sack and pulled out a knife he always carried with him, just in case. He was glad he never had to use it before. He was a thief, but he scorned violence. He kept backing up until he reached the bottom of the stairs. He waited for the originator of the sound to bounce to the hallway and come after him.

The *dong* from the grandfather's clock made Eric start and he dropped the knife. It fell and wedged itself into the floorboards.

"Fuckin' Hell." With his heart pounding, Eric bent to pick up his knife and missed a figure scurrying across the hallway from one room to another.

He got up and steadied his breath.

"Get a hold of yourself."

Eric took one last glance at the open door and then sneaked up the stairs.

A hallway opened to the right with half a dozen doors on both sides. The square window at the end of the hallway was a light space in the dark of the hallway it was looking over. All the doors were ajar with a looming darkness inside.

Eric heard a sound. Like pattering rain, but it seemed to come from... under the house? Like the ground underneath it was bubbling.

"Matt? For the love of God, answer me," Eric repeated louder but got the same response as before. Taking light steps, Eric proceeded down the hallway.

Every door he passed was vacant of any light, harboring only impenetrable night. Every passing door made Eric's skin crawl. His momentarily gained courage faded away. He was waiting for someone to jump him from one of the doors or hear the shuffling of the fabric again or worse. He imagined seeing a face in one of the empty rooms staring at him, half covered by the doorjamb, but when he turned to look there was nothing. Did the someone retreat to the dark of the room or was there never anyone there at all?

Repeated calls for Matt disappeared into the hallway.

"Where the fuck are you?"

Eric came to one of the doors and heard the shuffling of cloth inside the room.

"Matt?"

Suddenly hurried steps with increasing *thuds* sprang from behind him. As Eric turned to face the source of the sound, the shuffling from the room turned to a skitter and before Eric had time to react, the door flung wide open and a figure of animated darkness was upon him. Eric threw up his arms in defense, but it was too late. A blow to the jaw plunged him into an even deeper darkness than the one occupying the manor.

He woke up with the feeling of gravel filling his mouth. It took him a moment to realize it was the fragments of his broken teeth making the noise inside his skull. The exposed roots throbbed with pain as the jagged remnants of his pearlies ground against them. He spat out splintered enamel and blood. He had to keep his mouth slightly open to keep the serrated edges from grinding against one another. His entire head was encased in pain.

He scanned the room: stone walls glistening with moisture, no windows and a door made of eight thick metal bars.

"Ladies and Gentlemen!"

The sudden loudness made Eric jump on the bed he had been lying in. The sound was coming right outside his cell and it had the intonation of a ringmaster. The announcement was followed by a large group of people cheering.

"Our next attraction is straight out of the slums of Blackpool. I give you... ERIC!" The announcer stretched out Eric's name into ridiculous lengths and ended it with a high-pitched squeak. There was the sound of a crowd clapping.

Eric peeked through the bars on the door.

The narrow stone passage outside the cell led to the right, opening into a larger space further down the path.

With no other option, Eric stepped out of his cell and made his way toward the sound of the crowd. There had to be a way out.

"What the fuck?"

He found himself standing in some sort of an arena surrounded by an elevated auditorium packed with people in black suits, wearing masks of ivory white with only one eye opening that had a blue rim painted around the hole. Every one of the spectators wore white gloves. A troupe of aristocratic Cyclops.

A gaunt man with a black top hat and purple suit was standing in the middle of the arena.

"Are you ready?" he asked as if Eric was in on whatever this was.

Before Eric could respond, thick steel bars slid screeching into the stone wall, revealing a dark corridor on the other side of the arena. Eric heard an anticipating huff inside. The gaunt man disappeared into the opening and muttered something in a language Eric didn't understand.

"You win; you go free!" the voice shouted from the corridor. "As simple as that!"

There was a moment of silence, followed by thudding heavy footsteps. A thing_emerged from the darkness. Eric shrieked like a girl. The audience erupted in laughter and started clapping. Eric now realized that was the sound of pattering rain he had heard before.

The thing was over ten feet tall and perhaps it was meant to be some sort of a man; it had the resemblance of a humanoid, but all its proportions were off. Thick stitching zigzagged across its bare skin, holding together the parts accrued from several different people. The bulging biceps swung large hands with sharp nails, long as filthy daggers at the end of every finger. The thing emanated anger and violence.

On its left hand hung the remains of a person. The thing's claws were buried deep into the chest of a dead man.

Eric saw what was left of Matt's face. It was chewed almost beyond recognition. He was missing several, large chunks of meat all over his body. Deep dripping craters were gaping like a red mouth caught in a perpetual surprise.

The thing flung Matt's corpse at Eric. He barely rolled away from the airborne cadaver. His friend's remains tumbled like a rag doll and stopped only when they hit the wall.

"Easy money, eh?" Eric hated the fact that he'd been right on Matt being wrong. And now he was fucked.

The thing turned with stunning agility and lunged at Eric like a released spring. Eric threw himself to his left and avoided the claws by only an inch.

The crowd cheered again.

Eric looked around in hopes of finding anything he could use as a weapon. He was out of luck. The odds were stacked against him.

Another desperate roll and the thing's anxious claws *swooshed* past Eric's head. He took of his belt, hoping his pants would stay on. He chuckled at the idea of dying with his pants around his ankles. The chuckle quickly disappeared as the creature charged again toward its prey.

Eric sidestepped and lashed out with his belt as hard as he could. The buckle connected with the thing's face and tore a gash across its cheek.

A small victory, but it filled Eric with confidence.

"Yeah! Fuck you, Frankenstein!"

The thing shielded its face from the relentless assault Eric laid upon it and began to back away.

The crowd gasped as it backed away from Eric and lost its balance stepping on Matt's corpse. Its weight made the dead bones crunch and the body wiggle under its feet. The thing tumbled down, and Eric was immediately on it, pounding the hideous face with his fists.

Eric grinned a maniacal grin as the adrenaline guided his hands and his knuckles descended on the thing over and over again.

A sudden surge of pain turned his grin into a grimace as the thing got a hold of Eric's ankle and, in the blink of an eye, he was flying.

Eric hit the arena wall hard. Blood spurted from his mouth. He took a wheezing breath as the thing's massive hands grabbed him by the neck and turned him around to face it.

Its breath reeked of copper and putrescence. It snapped its yellow stained teeth at Eric.

Eric took a swing at its face, but the thing caught his hand in mid-punch. Eric howled in pain and his world darkened when the thing yanked and separated Eric's arm from the elbow joint, leaving the bone sticking out of the stump.

The thing squeezed and Eric's vision was fading. In a frenzied desperation to live, Eric jammed the ragged bone protruding from his flesh into the thing's throat. It howled and started to gurgle as the blood was flowing into its windpipe.

Eric screamed, grabbed the back of the head of his assailant and pressed harder, driving the bone deeper into the thing. The giant staggered, its hold loosened, and it fell like a tree of meat.

The audience went silent.

Eric panted, grasping to hold on to his consciousness. He fumbled around the stump with his good hand, trying to keep the blood inside. He had dropped the belt and couldn't see it anymore. He could have used it as a tourniquet.

"I am free, right?" he spat to the audience.

"If you win, yes," the voice in the darkness said. The words were followed by the sound of steel grinding against stone.

Massive footsteps thundered in the darkness as something even bigger than before rushed to the arena.

# THE BLACK MARKET PROJECT
*By Chisto Healy*

In the lonely ghost-white halls of St. Joseph's hospital, Dr. Rhine paces back and forth, rubbing the stubble on his chin. He does this several times a day to regain his composure. Behind him a small high-pitched voice speaks his name. He whirls around like he's prepared to fend off an attacker. A short brunette in green scrubs stands before him, her face bent in a frown, marking her concern for his mental well being. "What is it, Lucy?" he asks her.

The girl looks up into his piercing blue eyes, and bites her lip. "Another one just came in doctor."

"I see. They were bitten?"

"Yes sir."

"What did you do?"

Lucy chews on her already well-gnawed thumbnail. "I put him in quarantine."

The doctor gives an obviously forced smile. "Good. Good job. Was there any family?"

She nods shyly. "Mmhmm. I told them that his wound was a side effect of a newly discovered infection, and we don't have the means to cure it yet, but we'll do everything in our power to take good care of him."

The doctor's smile is genuine now. "You are going to go far some day, Lucy," he tells her. "Your loyalty and wit is unmatched within these walls. I'm glad you're on my team."

Blushing, Lucy smiles, and turns her eyes towards the ground. "Thank you, doctor."

"Call me Mark," he tells her. "What room is the patient in?"

Making mince meat of her thumbnail, she responds, "24."

"Very good. Thank you Lucy." With those words, Dr. Rhine heads down the hallway, this time with a purpose. He doesn't get far.

"Doc- um… Mark?" Lucy calls out behind him. "Are you sure this is right, what we're doing?"

Maybe he shouldn't have been so quick to judge her loyalty. He turns around slowly, to face her. His heart thumps hard in his chest. He has trusted her, in confidence, with the truth of what he does here. She could ruin him, very easily. "Are you unsure, Lucy?" he asks her.

"No. I guess not. No. I'm not. It's just… sometimes-"

"Sometimes what? Are you asking for a cut of the money?"

The small girl looks at him, her eyes wide, and mouth agape. "What? No. Oh no. Of course not. I'm just afraid that if it gets out what we do, others won't understand. I just… I guess, I fear the consequences."

Dr. Rhine gives his understudy another genuine smile. "You don't have to worry, Lucy. If the walls should come crashing down here, I won't take you with me. I will assume full responsibility."

"Okay," she smiles nervously. Then the doctor turns back around and makes his way back down the milk-white hall. She watches him go, and then leaves, once he's out of sight.

Dr. Rhine makes his way to room 24, and eases the door open. The patient is lying on a bed. To be in the quarantine room, the doctor is supposed to wear protective gear, but he neglects that fact. He knows that he doesn't actually need it. It's all part of the elaborate ruse. He looks at the stranger, sweating profusely and twitching, in his bed. The doctor takes a deep breath and approaches. "When were you bitten?" he asks the man.

Shivering terribly, the patient looks up at him, peering through watery eyes. "Last night," he says in a little more than a whisper. "Did… Did she have some kind of disease?"

Dr. Rhine smiles uncomfortably. He doesn't like what he does. He doesn't even keep the money. If he were in it for that reason, he wouldn't need to remain a doctor at all. It's his conscience that drives him. Others would call his actions inhuman if they knew, but he can't worry about that. He constantly reminds himself of the consequences should he quit. It's much bigger than him.

"Yes. A disease," he says. He peers at the man's chart. "I'm sorry, David. There is no medical cure for the disease that you've been infected with. It is a growing problem in our area, and we strive daily to find a solution to the problem, but as of yet, we haven't had any luck."

"Am I going to die?" David asks.

The doctor frowns. If the man had a way to see himself, he would definitely realize the seriousness of his condition. His pallor is a sickening bluish white. Veins and arteries are showing through everywhere.

Quickly the doctor retrieves a needle from his lab coat. It's filled with Tetrodoxine, the most powerful poison known to man. It won't kill David, not permanently. It will render him comatose and seemingly dead to those that aren't aware of the chemical in his system. In a few days he will come back to life, miraculously. Some call it 'the Zombie drug' for this reason. Dr. Rhine isn't dealing with zombies though. If he were, he would be less afraid.

"You're already dead," the doctor says grimly as he leans over the bed.

"What are you saying?" David asks before a spasm takes over him. All the muscles in his body strain and tense, then relax.

The doctor quiets him with a finger to his lips. Checking over his shoulder to make sure no one is watching, he administers the shot of poison. David's eyes grow wide enough to be on the verge of popping free of his skull. His fingers twitch uncontrollably, and then his head falls back, and his breathing stops. He is dead…for now.

"I'm sorry," Dr. Rhine tells him. "Please forgive me."

Retrieving a cell phone from his coat, he dials a number. For security purposes, he made sure to memorize the number instead of programming it into his phone. Should someone find his phone, he doesn't want the evidence to be there for them. They've worked hard for years on this, and their work is invaluable to humanity.

When the call goes though, a rough hoarse voice answers, "Hello, doctor. What have you got for me?"

Swallowing hard, Dr. Rhine pays a nervous look around. His heart moves like an express train in his chest. Realizing he's alone, he answers, "Another one came in. He's ready for delivery."

Even though the man is on the other end of the city, in his mind's eye, Dr. Rhine can see him smiling. It nauseates him. If he didn't need this monster, he would never associate with him. "A million, yes?" the hoarse voice says.

"That's correct," the doctor tells him.

"Good. I'll have it ready. Bring him to me now."

"Right," the doctor says, clicking the off button on his phone.

He immediately goes to the outgoing calls list on his phone and deletes the number. Then he returns it to his coat, and pages the ambulance driver. Dr. Rhine had to purchase a gun to make sure the drivers were on board, and he has always been disgusted by such weaponry. Even still, he believes he would actually shoot them if they tried to go to the press. Up until now, the public has believed that creatures like the one David was soon to become, only existed in fiction. Every time one turns up, Dr. Rhine and the others like him, sell them to morbid collectors like Mr. Bosworth, the voice on the other end of the phone.

They try to catch them as they turn, before any damage can be done. That's how Dr. Rhine came to be employed. The Black Market Project is illegal, and would be shut down immediately if ever discovered. A shiver passes through the doctor at the thought of what would happen. May God help humanity if they should ever fail.

The ambulance driver shows up at the room where the doctor is waiting, impatiently as always. "Where am I taking him?" the EMS worker says, paying a glance to David's body.

"Bosworth," Dr. Rhine tells him. "I'll have Lucy inform his family that he didn't make it, and deliver our most sincere apologies."

"Whatever," the driver says, with a shrug. If the doctor didn't display his snub-nosed .38, the man wouldn't even be part of this. He can tell by the look in Mark Rhine's eyes that he is crazy and wouldn't hesitate to pull the trigger. The driver has children at home. He can't take any chances of not coming home to them. Besides, he gets his cut of the money, before the doctor donates the rest of the large sum to a local charity. With his family in mind, every bit of extra income is helpful. So, as usual, he does his job, and makes the delivery, and keeps his secret.

2

David opens his eyes. His whole body aches terribly. He doesn't know how long he was out for, but it feels like years.

He blinks a few times to get his eyes into focus, and sits up. Looking around, he realizes that he is in a cage. He starts to panic. Scrambling to his feet, his legs feel wobbly and almost give out on him. Breathing so hard and quick, he is on the verge of hyperventilating; he rushes towards the gate. Grabbing the bars with both hands, he struggles to break free. A bell dings somewhere, and a panel opens before him shining artificial sunlight into his face.

He's never known light to burn so badly. It is extremely painful, and his flesh actually starts to steam right before his eyes. He stumbles backwards into the darkness of his prison, and falls to the ground. Shielding his eyes from the light, he starts to cry. Where is he? What is happening?

The light blinks off. David hears hoarse laughter come from outside of the cell. A voice says to him, "I see you're awake. That's good. Welcome home."

David squints hard, in an attempt to see who stands before him. His eyes still burn, but after a moment the man comes into focus. He is tall and overweight, dressed in an expensive designer three-piece suit. A shaggy red beard covers his face, and he wears wire-rimmed glasses with a golden frame. His nose is red with the effect of many years of consuming alcohol. "Who are you?" David asks him.

The man smiles excitedly. "My name is Raymond Bosworth, but I'd prefer if, from now on, you refer to me as Father."

"Are you insane?" David says moving into a squat position. "You can't keep me locked up like this. I am a man."

Throwing an index finger up in front of his toothy smile, Raymond says, "Correction. You *were* a man. That was before you were bitten. Now you are a beast, and the newest addition to my collection. Look around you."

David turns slowly, scanning the area surrounding him with his burning eyes. He realizes that the room is filled with cages just like his. All but a few of them are occupied by other men and women. Every one of them looks sickly, their skin as white as hospital bed sheets, and their eyes as red as the blood that smears their lips. Does he look that way? There are no mirrors. "May I see a mirror?" he asks his captor.

The man gives a deep laugh that comes from the pit of his stomach. "It wouldn't do you any good," he smiles. "You have no reflection."

"This is madness," David snaps at him.

"No," Raymond says without losing his smile. "What's mad is how much people are willing to pay to see you, or even more to have you feed on them."

"Feed on them?"

With a small chuckle, Mr. Bosworth says, "The hunger hasn't reached you yet, but it will. It's just a matter of time. Then, some fool will pay me their life savings, thinking you will turn them into one of you. I will let them in your cage, and you will feed on them, killing them savagely. I get the money. You get the food, and the secret remains ours. It's quite perfect actually. I've been doing this for quite some time now. Don't fight it."

"This is inhuman!" David snaps, rising to his feet.

"You *are* inhuman," Bosworth smiles, and gives a shake of his chubby index finger.

"No."

Raymond shakes his head. "Poor thing. You are in denial. You will realize the truth soon enough. I will leave you now to get acquainted with your new brothers and sisters." With that, he turns and strolls to the door, whistling as he goes.

David sits back down on the ground. Tears fill up his burning eyes. He leans his back against a wall. Is this it for him? Will he spend the rest of his life here? How did this happen?

"You know what the worst part is?" a voice says from a nearby cell. "Our lives are eternal now."

What?

David jumps to his feet, and runs to the front of the cage.

"Don't touch the bars!" someone else calls out to him. "There's a sensor. The sunlight will come every time you touch the bars. That's how he keeps us here."

Backing up, David says, "Do I look like you?"

"You do."

"What has happened to us?" David asks, unable to see who he's talking to. The tears exit his eyes en route to his chin. "What happened to us?"

"Think about it, newbie. We were bitten. Now we are ghost white, cold as death, and thirst for blood, until we feel like we're going to come apart inside. What do you think happened to us?"

"No," David says, backing up further. "That is impossible. It's just a myth. I'm still in the hospital. This is a nightmare." Laughter surrounds him. He drops to his knees and begins to sob. "Are we to stay here like this, forever?" he cries.

"Most do. Some don't," someone nearby answers. "Some refuse their food and allow themselves to starve to death. The choice is yours."

David sits in silence as the hours pass by. What will he do when the time comes for him to feed? Can he resist the urge? Can he hold out long enough to actually starve to death? How long will that take? What if he can't? What happens when Bosworth passes away? Will someone else just take over? These are all questions that only time can answer, and in this place, minutes feel like years. David feels he has found hell. Maybe if he thinks along the same lines, he can survive on hope that heaven exists as well.

The next day, when David awakens, his stomach twists itself in knots, as the craving invades him. He thought he'd have more time, but time isn't on his side in this place. He feels like he's going to be sick, like an addict kept from his fix. "Please," he mumbles to anyone that will listen. "Please. It's killing me. Please."

His words are followed by laughter again. After some unknown period of time, Mr. Bosworth is standing outside his cage. "Please Raymond. It's killing me," he whines.

"What is my name?" The red bearded man asks. His smile is not present now.

"Father. Father… please. Feed me, father," David moans.

Mr. Bosworth's smile returns. "You will do well here," he says. "I will bring you your first dish momentarily." He exits the room, and before long, returns with a college aged boy. The boy's face is painted white. He wears black lipstick and nail polish, and clothes to match. "Are you ready?" Mr. Bosworth asks the boy.

The boy nods. He is somewhere between afraid and awestricken. "This is my newest child," Raymond says with a gesture towards David. With a deep breath, the boy nods again. Mr. Bosworth smiles, and opens the cage. "Go on. Eternal life awaits you."

Slowly, and with hesitation, the boy makes his way into the cage. Once he is inside, Raymond Bosworth closes the gate and locks it. The boy whips around, his eyes wide with fear.

"You're gonna let me back out right?" he asks, the chills of his fear causing quivers in his voice.

"Of course," Mr. Bosworth smiles. Then he turns his back and exits the room.

"Stay over there," David growls at the boy. He's backed himself into a dark corner of the cell, and huddles there. The boy peers into the darkness, trying to spot him.

"Are you really a vampire?" the child asks, swallowing hard.

"Be quiet," David snaps at him. "I can smell you. I am very hungry."

The boy swallows hard again. Tears build up quickly in his eyes. He questions his decision to come here. "Are you gonna kill me?" he asks.

"I don't want to, but the pain is excruciating," David says from the darkness. "What is your name?"

"My name?" the boy says. His fear seems to have made him forget who he even is. In a moment when it clicks to him, he says, "Brian."

"Brian," David repeats. Getting to his feet, he steps out of the darkness, and stands before the boy. "Hello, Brian."

"Oh my God," Brian says at the sight of him. "This really is for real."

With a nod, David says, "Yes. It is, Brian. This is real."

"Please don't kill me," Brian pleads as David takes another step forward.

"Maybe just a little taste," David says, licking his lips. "Just to make the pain go away. That's what you wanted anyway, isn't it?" His guts are twisting in knots.

Brian backs up until he hits the bars of the gate. He turns around quickly and grabs hold of them. The artificial sunlight flashes on and David quickly retreats back into the darkness. Realizing that the light keeps him safe, Brian tightens his grip on the bar, and calls out, "Mr. Bosworth! I've got the sunlight on! He's not gonna kill me! Let me out of here now!"

The entrance door flies open, and Raymond storms in. His smile is nowhere to be found. Anger lines his face and brings redness to his cheeks. "Back away from there immediately," he says to the boy.

"Like hell," the boy tells him. "Unlock this cage. I want to go home."

"I don't care what you want," Bosworth tells him. He raises a billy club. "Back away or I'll make you."

Brian looks at the fat man. His own eyes are hard with anger and hatred. He's not going to let go. With a sigh, Mr. Bosworth steps forward and swings the club, bringing it down hard on the boy's fingers. Brian winces, and the tears run freely from his eyes, but he keeps his grip. "This is life or death. You can break my fingers but I'm not letting go," he says.

Then the tall man's smile returns. "Just as well," he says. "We'll make a game out of it. I can't complain about free entertainment." He unlocks the cage and steps away. Brian releases his grip and steps out. He closes his mouth tightly, trying not to be sick. He needs to get out of here, and quickly. "My child," Bosworth says to David, "Your meal is escaping. Catch him. Feed, my child."

David moves faster than he ever knew he was capable. In the blink of an eye, he is out of the cage and on the boy, his stomach twisting and turning, feeling like it's going to tear at any moment if he doesn't fill it with what it needs. With a deep hoarse laugh, Raymond steps over to the artificial sunlight panel. He wants to be able to turn it on quickly, in case his child decides to rebel. He added a manual switch for his own protection. He's no fool. Fools don't make it in this kind of business.

Brian turns his head, and stares directly into David's gleaming fangs. He starts to plead for his life. David leans forward towards the boy's neck. His grip on the boy's shoulders is inhumanly tight. There is no way Brian can get free. He can feel the creature's hot breath on his neck. He begins to lose control of his bladder now that the end is in sight for him.

"We are still men," David whispers in the boy's ear. "This is a disease. We are infected, and kept as slaves. Go. Get help. Tell the authorities. Please. Save us. Bosworth is the only monster here. Tell them it's the doctor. The doctor at St. Joseph's. He does this to us."

After saying what he needs, David thrusts the boy forward towards the door.

"What are you doing?" Bosworth screams at his newest child. He turns the sunlight on. David screams in pain.

"Get back in your cage!" the human monster bellows with fury. He needs to go pursue the fleeing teenager before he gets too far. He could ruin everything, but he's not stupid. He's not going to try to get past the creature that stands in his path. That could very easily mean his own death. He watches as his child's flesh steams and melts. "You're killing yourself, you fool! Get back into your cage!" he screams.

When David can no longer stand the pain, he darts back into his cage, and scurries into the dark corner at the back. He only hopes he bought the boy enough time to escape. Raymond throws the gate shut and locks it.

"I'll deal with you later," he says, taking off out the door.

3

"What room?" Dr. Rhine says to Lucy.

"26," she smiles at him. "Mark? Would you like to get dinner with me later?"

The doctor smiles at her. "Sure, Lucy. I'd like that," he says. Then he turns and makes his way down the hallway. He reaches the rooms where they keep the quarantined patients and looks at the door to 26. He sighs. The stress of this is going to kill him, but what can he do? He couldn't live with himself, if he were to resign. People like Bosworth would probably never let him out of it anyway, if even he wanted to be free. The bite victims aren't the only ones that the rich man keeps as prisoners.

He opens the door to the room and enters, closing it gently behind him. He looks forward at the young blonde girl lying on the bed. Her eyes are deeply sunken and her skin is pale as can be. She is sweating profusely and shaking with internal chills. The humanity is almost gone from this one already. He must work quickly. She opens her mouth in a silent cry, and the doctor notices her fangs. He jumps.

Closing his eyes, he takes a deep breath and removes the poison-filled needle from his coat.

"Put down the syringe," a voice firmly says from behind him. He wasn't careful enough. He's been caught. He places his hand in his coat pocket and wraps his fingers around the handle of his .38.

"Remove your hand from your coat, slowly, Doctor Rhine. Put both hands in the air. Any sudden movements and I will shoot you."

*My God*, the doctor thinks. The police. How? He releases his grip on the gun, and raises both hands in the air. "In the syringe…" he says, his voice shaky, "is Tetrodoxine. It has been known to help cancer patients. We don't know how to treat this disease. I was trying to help."

"Save it," the officer says from behind him. "We know exactly what you're doing. There are four cars on their way to Mr. Bosworth's estate as we speak."

"No." Dr. Rhine turns around quickly and raises a shaky hand, palm out, to say, "Okay. Don't shoot." He starts to pant heavily, feeling as if he's going to pass out. "You have to call them off," he says. "You don't know what you're doing."

"I know exactly what I'm doing," the officer says, without lowering his weapon. "I'm arresting you for selling human beings on the black market to people rich enough to buy them from you."

"They're not human though! They're not human!" The doctor's screams echo through the hallways of the hospital.

4

"My God. Marty. These people look on the verge of death," Officer Ryans says to his partner, as they peer into the cages.

"Probably are," Officer O'Neill says back. "I doubt Bosworth's fed them much. He's kept them like animals in a damned zoo. The guy's a total psycho. What kind of person does it take to work all their life for their fortune, only to spend it purchasing human beings to keep in cages like slaves? What is happening to the world we live in?"

Officer Ryans shakes his head. "Who knows," he answers. "You folks are going to be okay though. Raymond Bosworth is already on his way to finding out for himself what it's like to live behind bars. We're going to get you out of here. We'll get you medical attention right away. You're gonna be alright. You hear me? You're all gonna be alright."

"Thank you," David moans from the darkness of his cell. He doesn't have to try to sound sickly. He feels like his insides are splitting apart inside of him. The pain that comes with the hunger is almost more than he can handle. "Thank you."

The officers, using Mr. Bosworth's keys, start to unlock the cages, and open the gates. David and the others seize the moment and move with inhuman speed. The police officers don't even have a chance to scream. They are taken down, and drained of their lives within a matter of moments.

Once the deed is finished, David stands. He wipes blood from his mouth with his right arm. "Free," he says. "We are free."

David realizes at that moment, that he was right to hope. He knew hell on earth and now he knows heaven on earth. With his freedom comes the true power of his new self. He is a god. "This is just the beginning," he says.

"The beginning," the others agree. One by one, they exit the room, and the building, making their way out into the world.

# HASTINGS
*By Drew Nicks*

Silas awoke beneath his tarp lean-to with the scent of fresh rain and uncollected trash all around him. He rubbed bloodshot eyes and scratched at the multitude of scabs on his arms. After a few moments, he rolled out into the grey dawn.

The sight that greeted him was typical for any regular day on East Hastings Street. While some mild contentment was present, sadness and anger were far more prevalent. Men wandered about in the damp air like zombies; glassy eyed and with a shambling gait. Some of these men had streaks of fresh blood streaming down their arms, evidence of several failed injections. One woman, walking farther down the way, cradled what Silas knew was a plastic baby. Even from his vantage point a half-block distant, he heard her hollering terms of endearment at her "child."

As Silas' world came fully into view, so too did the sweats and shakes. Awake for less than a half hour and already in need of a fix. He fought the feeling back as well as he could. To get that next fix, he'd have to make some quick cash. That might take some work. He adjusted his stained BC parks shirt and torn sweat pants before he set off into the new day.

Passing deteriorated buildings with smashed windows, Silas briefly wondered about their former opulence. Just thirty years prior, these buildings and this area had a very different life. Grand hotels and celebrated storefronts made this place the talk of the town. Now it was the talk for different reasons.

Silas arrived at the tent city in front of the old Astor Hotel. This was the largest tent city on East Hastings. The general consensus was that it had formed twenty years prior, though no one was totally sure. A pecking order ruled this settlement and Silas barely ranked. This was okay. At this hour, the day was only beginning. He watched the rabble roll out from their homes onto the sidewalk. He also saw three unmoving forms lying prone at different points of the sidewalk. Likely victims of overdose. Silas unconsciously scratched his arm.

He was looking for one man in particular: a man who was just as desperate as he. He scanned the crowd looking for the familiar face. He didn't see him until he looked farther up the street.

The man was grubby and encrusted with filth. His torn, army style jacket was covered with variously mismatching and faded patches. His matted beard hung low upon his face. As Silas approached, the man had picked up a thawed Freezie from the gutter. He closely examined its contents. Gravel and dirt floated in the crimson liquid. He brought it to his lips and drained it in one quick sip.

"Andy," Silas called. "How's it going today?"

Andy dropped the empty plastic sleeve into the gutter and turned to Silas.

"I spent last night in a ditch," Andy replied. "But I've had worse nights."

Silas drew Andy into a close embrace. The scent of the two combined would remind one of a restaurant dumpster on a boiling summer day.

"It's good to see you," Silas said. "I've missed you."

Andy grunted noncommittally. Andy had never been one for emotions, at least for as long as Silas had known him. Every now and then, Silas wondered what Andy had been before he ended up here. The shakes hit Silas again. It was time to get to business.

"I don't know about you," Silas said as he pulled away from Andy. "But I'm getting the jitters. I need a fix."

"Me too," Andy replied. "It's been eighteen hours too long, and I've got a hot tip."

Silas stood motionless, listening intently.

"Yep, met this fella last night. Real strange type. Ain't never seen him around before. Kept babbling to himself, like he was fighting with voices in his head. Weird shit, man. Weirdest part was his clothes didn't look that bad. Still had a nice press to his suit. Still had his tie all up. Reminds me of a guy I saw like that a couple-a-weeks ago. Now that guy was something else. He was…"

Silas snapped his fingers in front of Andy's face, trying to draw him back to reality. Andy would wander in his conversations if you weren't on him to stay focused.

"Oh right," Andy said, returning to existence. "This fella was talking about a warehouse not far from here. Wouldn't say what it was but from the way he was acting, it's worth a pretty penny."

Silas looked at Andy with a perplexed expression.

"So why didn't he take it?"

Andy shrugged.

"Don't know. He didn't say that either. Looked like he was riding pretty high when I saw him. Fucking junkies, man!"

A smirk crossed Silas' face as he thought of the irony. But, still, he was intrigued enough to follow up on this story. He nudged Andy.

"Alright, you got me. Let's go have a look."

Andy and Silas turned and made their way up the grunge-laden street.

* * *

The warehouse was like an imposing shadow. Almost like a mountain shrouding a village. Judging from its size and Art Deco design, it had once likely been a high-end department store. One could almost see the specters of men in their finest wares accompanied by their fur-draped women entering through the palatial entrance. Those days were long past and now grime and shattered windows, like defective eyes, gazed upon the neighborhood. She was still a sight to behold though. In places, granite and slate still peeked from beneath their filthy crust.

Silas and Andy stood before the boarded entrance. Silas examined the gang tags and other graffiti while Andy looked about for loose boards or any other point of ingress.

Silas observed tags for the Independent Soldiers, the Red Scorpions, and the United Nations. None were any groups Silas wanted to tussle with. While their artwork was beautiful in an urban decay sort of way, all three gangs were notorious for their brutality and lack of remorse. He recalled how last spring, four of his friends, well maybe not friends, more acquaintances, disappeared one weekend. In this community, people disappear all the time but folks whispered this was different. It was widely speculated that the Red Scorpions had kidnapped them and used them in a sort of bum fight.

"Over here!" Silas heard Andy holler. He looked up and down the street. Andy was nowhere in sight. It was then that Silas spotted the alley. Putting it all together, he headed down the alley. Andy stood close to the wall, a piece of plywood pried up and flapping in the wind. Silas drew close.

"This is our way in, buddy," said Andy. Silas gazed into the near pitch-blackness. He exhaled deeply and went in. Andy followed, letting the plywood snap back into place.

The room they found themselves in was black as night. Silas reached into his pocket and withdrew a lighter. Striking the wheel, a dull light illuminated the two men. They looked about at the polluted walls and broken cabinets strewn about the floor. Silas moved forward to the doorway; Andy followed.

"So where did your guy say we'd find this thing?" He turned back to Andy. Andy wore a dumbfounded look across his face.

"Dunno, but I expect we'll know it when we see it."

The two men made their way down the formerly polished granite halls. Here, light penetrated from various windows like pinholes in black muslin. An eerie silence pervaded the halls and Silas heard Andy withdraw his box-cutter. There were so many open doorways; one could never be too sure what might jump out at you.

When they reached the end of the hall, they found themselves standing in an enormous storefront. The walls stretched far back into the muted black. Silas let out a yelp. The lighter had become too hot to handle and he dropped it to the floor. Now that the only light came from holes in the plywood, the two men could see dust particles dancing in the air. Silas stooped, feeling around for the lighter. He found it and clacked it back to life.

The object of their quest sat in front of them.

At the end of an aisle, flanked by broken display cabinets and various bits of refuse, sat the strangest machine either man had ever seen.

Though neither had ever seen a player piano in person before, this thing looked sort of like one. This machine had far more accouterments and add-ons. As they drew closer, they saw many pneumatic tubes and pipes twisting at odd angles like tendrils of some creeper vine. Silas held the lighter closer, looking at the scuffed wood of the cabinet. Though Silas was by no means an expert on wood, he guessed it was made of oak. *Expensive*, he thought.

Silas raised the lighter to look at the other add-ons. The glass of the cabinet had been smashed out long ago and dust had built thickly on the inner contents. He saw drums, triangles, tambourines, and, in the central place of honor, a Gibson banjo. The machine itself did not look as if it had functioned in many years. It also appeared to weigh several hundred pounds. Silas contemplated what they could do with it. He heard Andy clear his throat behind him. Silas turned back.

"Well?" asked Andy

"I don't think we can move the whole thing," Silas replied. "Even with the two of us, we'll both be crippled."

"No shit."

Silas thought about whether they could break it apart and sell it for scrap. There had to be at least seven hundred dollars of scrap metal in it. However, his eyes kept returning to that centerpiece banjo. It was a thing of beauty. The fingerboard looked to be made of rosewood and the inlays, yellowed by the passage of years, looked like ivory. Silas licked his lips and wiped the foul sweat, which had begun to accumulate on his forehead. He had an idea.

"That banjo," Silas pointed to it. "That's our ticket. That thing's gotta be worth enough to get us both what we need."

Andy grunted noncommittally. He knew what was coming. Both men approached the machine. They each stood on separate sides of it, preparing to break away necessary pieces. Silas reached his hand through the broken glass and grasped the banjo's neck.

Suddenly, lights flickered on in the cabinet. The lid of the piano portion flew open and music began to play.

Both men fell back in shock.

The light and music show baffled the two. An odd, ethereal tune came melodically from the machine. Neither knew the piece but something classical sounded from its chords. A theme played almost imperially. Something like darkly regal importance filled the air.

Another sound crept in, nearly imperceptible to the men's ears. It began as a low shuffle but quickly grew to a crescendo. The sound of feet. Their cadence like the marching of an army. Silas turned back and looked to the hall they had entered through. Shadows danced menacingly along the walls. Their shapes seemed to be humanoid but with exaggerated limbs, which reached forth for the men like tentacles of an octopus.

Silas shot quickly to his feet while Andy still lay on the floor in a stupor. Silas would not lose what they had come for. What they needed. Despite the surreal madness surrounding them, his veins thirsted and ached for the junk. He stepped forward, reaching a shaky hand into the cabinet. With superhuman force, he broke the braces that held the banjo in place. The dry wood snapped like bones. The music reached a fever pitch, hammers striking like blacksmiths, when the banjo was wrenched free.

Now, with the banjo tucked beneath his arm, Silas turned back to look for an exit. The shadows in the hall descended upon the prostrate Andy, leaving the hall open for an escape. Silas couldn't turn away from the horror which befell Andy. The shadow creatures dug their fingers, or whatever they were, beneath Andy's skin. They were peeling him like an orange. Reddish sinew glistened in the muted light.

Revulsion filled Silas' body, but was quickly overcome by the need for escape. He ignored the Boschian nightmare occurring in his wake and ran for the hall. As he passed dust-covered doorways, the sounds of Andy's screams followed, and above it all, the piano kept up its mad symphony.

With the banjo safely stowed, Silas bade a hasty retreat from that den of hell. He pushed past the loose plywood and stood in the moist air, saddened by what had happened to Andy but glad to have something that could get him money.

* * *

Less than an hour later, Silas found himself cold and shivering in a rundown pawnshop. The short, grey, sloppily dressed man behind the chicken wire cage eyed Silas with suspicion.

"And where did you say you got this?" the man asked with a slight lisp.

Silas stood, sweating. He was nearly an indescribable shade of green.

"I got it from a buddy who wanted me to sell it for him."

The pawnbroker picked up his jewelers glass and closely examined the rosewood fingerboard. He marveled at the delicate ivory inlays. He looked intently at the Gibson lettering. All were authentic and accurate for a banjo manufactured in the 20s or 30s. A very beautiful instrument to be sure, but a feeling of wrongness filled the pawnbroker. And not just because the instrument was clearly stolen. Something else flowed through it, something the pawnbroker did not want in his shop.

"Sorry, buddy," the broker said, setting down the jewelers glass. "She's a beautiful little piece but we don't traffic in stolen goods here."

Silas stared with wild, furious eyes. The junk sickness was making him teeter on the brink.

"I told ya, it ain't stolen! You know what? Just give me three hundred for it and I'll walk away right now."

The broker shook his head. This junkie wasn't getting it. He certainly wasn't the first.

"And I told you, buddy," the broker said, more emphatically, pushing the banjo back to Silas. "Take your banjo and go somewhere else."

Silas reached out. He thought about strangling the broker. Choking the life right out of that fat, useless prick. Watching his face turn blue and his eyes turn red, bulging out like overfilled zits. The intense pleasure it would give him.

Instead, Silas took the banjo in his tensed hands. The shakes and quivers were nearly overtaking his body now. He turned and left the shop without making another fuss. After Silas had left, the broker went to the nearest sink and washed his hands. The banjo had left a strong scent of decay upon his person.

* * *

The sun had begun to set as Silas walked out of his fourth pawnshop. Not a single one would take the banjo. Silas' frustration grew with each passing moment and still the sickness raked through his body. The shakes filled his body so thoroughly that he could be confused for a person with Parkinson's strolling down a broken, neon light filled street.

All hope was seeping from his frame. And with what to show for it? He had watched an acquaintance be flayed alive by... by a what, he didn't know. Now he was stuck exactly where he was before. Up shit creek with a banjo for a paddle and a fever which reminded him of descriptions of Malaria.

"Hey buddy!"

The voice caught Silas totally off guard. For several moments, he thought the voice came from inside his head.

"Hey buddy!" it called again.

He knew he heard it this time. Silas shot his head side to side. He peered into a nearby alley, his eyes struggling to adjust to the dimness. A filthy figure in a hooded trench coat beckoned to him. Silas couldn't tell if the figure was a man or woman. At this point, he did not care.

Stepping through strobing neon light, he approached the figure. Silas still clung to the banjo beneath his arm. Even within touching distance, he couldn't make out the sex of the figure; its face was shrouded in the folds of the hood. It held in its outstretched hand a hypodermic full of the black tar he so longed for.

"Give me the banjo!" the figure said; icy blue eyes illuminated beneath the hood.

Hungrily, Silas swapped the banjo for the needle. Without a second thought, he had the needle deep in a vein. He depressed the plunger and slipped away. The euphoria turned to blackness as his consciousness evaporated.

* * *


Silas came to in a large room that smelled of mildew and urine. He thought he was alone until he felt the presence of others around him. He stood; saw the strange machine he and Andy had vandalized. The banjo had been replaced.

Suddenly, the cabinet lit up and out poured its discordant song. Silas looked and found himself as part of a semi-circle of other homeless. All but he were knelt in prayer. A feeling of somberness and sobriety filled Silas as he too knelt in supplication.

# MONSTROUS LOVE
## *By Pamela Scott*

### 1

There are bodies everywhere, corpses piled on top of one another.

I walk through the streets, stepping in pools of blood. I've got clothes on: a white shirt and black trousers, torn into almost shreds and stained with blood. My feet are bare, caked with dirt and blood.

I can taste blood. I can smell it as well. The blood of the dead has a distinctive stink like rot. I can also smell fresh blood.

I keep walking, sniffing the air and following the scent.

I find them, a small group of people, two men, one woman and two small children. They're huddled together in a doorway. One of the men has been hurt. The blood I can smell seeps from an open wound in his side.

I kneel in the doorway and lick my lips.

2

I scream awake, gasping for breath and shaking. My skin's bright red and slick with sweat. The thin sheet covering me is sodden with sweat. I kick the sheet onto the floor. I lay shaking and whimpering. The bedroom door flies open and a shape moves towards me.

My wife, Clara, wraps me in her arms and holds me. Her arms are cool. Her touch is gentle and soothes me. The terror starts to recede, little by little. I stop shaking. My heart stops racing. My breathing returns to normal.

"Another one?" Clara says.

I nod. I still can't speak.

"My poor baby," Clara says.

She holds me in her arms and rocks me gently.

"Will you make an appointment with Dr. Kotz?" Clara says.

"Yes, the dreams are worse this time."

"Okay."

Clara holds me and kisses me.

"Are you okay, Mummy?"

I look up at the sound of the tiny voice. Our daughter, Nicole is standing in the doorway. She's wearing a nightdress: a pink Disney Princess one. She looks tiny and tired.

"I had a bad dream. That's all," I say.

Nicole runs into the room and jumps onto the bed. She gives me a big hug and I sweep her into my arms.

3

"And how long have you been having these dreams?" Dr. Kotz says.

The dreams, violent, awful dreams, filled with death and terror and blood have haunted my sleep for as long as I can remember. They started long before I met Clara and have gotten worse since Nicole was born.

"Did you give birth to your daughter?" Dr. Kotz says.

"I can't have children. Clara is her birth mother."

Dr. Kotz writes something down. "Is there anything about these dreams that makes them stand out? Do you recognize any landmarks? Are the dreams different or do they have any similar features?"

The dreams are both the same but have different elements. They are always set in a large city, somewhere that isn't remotely familiar, different streets and places in the same enormous city. I'm always naked. There are always a lot of dead people, piled on the street around me. The streets run with blood. I always smell fresh blood and follow the scent.

"Do you know why I'm having these dreams?" I say.

"I can't be completely sure, but there are a few possibilities. The most obvious one is anxiety, something is stressing you out or worrying you and is manifesting in your dreams."

"Can it be that simple?"

Dr. Kotz nods. "You said the dreams have gotten worse since your daughter was born?"

I nod. "I used to have them every few weeks. Since Nicole was born I've been having them two or three times a week."

"It could something as simple as anxiety about your new responsibilities as a mother."

A great wave of relief washes over me. "What do I do about them?"

"I want you to keep a dream journal and write down what you remember after each dream. I'd like you to be a descriptive as possible, make a note of any sounds or smells and how you feel."

"Is that all?"

"I'll write you a prescription as well for sleeping pills. Take one when it's absolutely necessary."

He scrawls on a sheet of paper and hands it to me.

"Thank you, Dr. Kotz."

4

I follow the trail of tiny, bloody footprints along the street. They weave in and out of the alleys and doorways, always leading into the darkest places. The bloody prints get smaller and smaller and start to fade, but there are always tiny red spots. And the smell.

"You can't get away from me," I say.

There is no answer, just silence all around. I know there are people still alive, too many, hiding from me in dark and secret places, hiding from the monster with the face of angel who decimated the city.

A smell fills my nostrils as I pass a dark doorway. I freeze and turn my head towards the smell. I can smell blood, fresh blood. I can smell a whiff of urine. The strongest smell is fear. I duck into the doorway.

"You can't hide from me. I can smell you. I will find you," I say.

I see something shift in the darkness. I grab it and yank something towards me. It's a child, a girl not much older than five or six. She's spunky. She got away from me when I ate her parents. She screams and struggles in my arms.

"You smell delicious," I say.

I sink my fangs into her neck and suck.

5

I scream myself awake, sobbing and shaking.

## 6

The TV screen turns black. The words, EMERGENCY BULLETIN, start to flash on the screen, repeating until it fills the whole screen.

"This is an emergency bulletin! Do not be alarmed! Please do not leave your house! You will be removed to a safe area in time!" a robotic voice repeats, over and over.

"What's happening?" my mum says.

"I don't know. Something about an emergency and how we can't leave the house," I say.

"Why?"

"I don't know, Mum. That's all it said."

Mum stood up. It's been years since she really moved. She put on so much weight after Dad left that she's been bedridden for years. She uses the furniture to help her walk and gradually pulls herself towards the front door.

"Mum, I don't think you should do that. The bulletin said we should stay indoors."

"Nonsense."

Mum opens the front door.

The first thing I notice is the smell, the stink of blood and death. There's burning as well. Mum stands frozen in the doorway, her massive bulk trembling.

"Oh, dear God," Mum says.

I go over to her and try to peer around her. She takes up most of the doorway so I can't see much. Mum heaves her bulk down the few steps until she reaches the front garden. She stops and just stares.

I go after her and freeze in horror before I even reach the bottom of the stairs. The stink is overpowering. The street's littered with bodies. The buildings are on fire. The air's thick with smoke and ash. I start coughing and cover my mouth. My face burns with pain.

"We should get back inside," I say.

Mum starts to walk towards me, slowly. Her face is filled with pain and I can see how much of an effort it is for her just to walk. She stops dead in the middle of the garden. She starts to cough and splutter. She falls backwards and hits the ground with a thud, twitching and shuddering.

"Mum!"

I race towards her, oblivious to the burning pain in my own body. My legs give out and I hit the deck. I try to get back up but I can't move. I lie in the grass, in agony, thrusting and twitching. The pain burns and I've never felt anything like it in my life.

The world goes dark.

An unknown time later, I open my eyes. It's dark outside and the sky's full of stars.

The pain's gone. I sit up.

All around me, the rest of the dead sit up as well.

7

"Why do you think you're having these dreams?" Dr. Kotz says.

I stare down at the linoleum on the floor of his office and shake my head. "I don't know. I've been having them for as long as I remember. They haunt me."

Dr. Kotz is recording our session. I signed a form authorizing him to record our sessions so he can analyze the transcript at a later date. I'm happy to let him do what he wants as long as he can help me.

"Did you keep the dream journal?" Dr. Kotz says.

"Yes."

I take the A5 ringed notebook out of my bag and hand it to him. I've written about each dream in as much detail as possible, sights, sounds and smells. I've read over my journal several times. The dreams have similar features but all are different. Dr. Kotz goes through my dream journal. He asks me a lot of questions.

"Do you know why I'm having the dreams?" I say.

"Not yet, but I will help you get to the bottom of this."


## 8


I can taste blood in my mouth. I touch my mouth. It's caked with blood, some of which is still wet. I'm dressed in a white shirt, black trousers and a black pair of boots. The front of my shirt is soaked with blood. I'm cradling a dead woman in my arms. She's limp and lifeless. Her throat's been torn open.

"Where are my Mum and Dad, Miss?"

I turn around and see a small girl huddled into the corner of the room. She's wedged into a tiny space. She's very small, not much more than five or six. She's wearing pink fluffy pajamas and carrying a grey teddy. She starts to scream 'Mama!' when she sees the dead woman in my arms.

I drop the dead woman and walk towards the screaming girl.

I grab her and drag her towards me. She's screaming and thrashing and more fidgety than I can be bothered with. I slap her and she goes limp in my arms.

I sink my fangs into her neck and start to suck.


## 9


I scream myself awake. The bedclothes are wrapped tightly around me. I thrash helplessly.

It takes a few moments for me to realize I've wet myself.


## 10


"How sure are you that this experiment will work?"

Dr. Kotz looks up at his colleagues sitting around the table in the conference room. They're the last of their kind, the last scientists who survived the terrible plague that decimated the world and turned almost everyone into fiends who drank blood. Those who were the first to turn had fed on others and the darkness spread.

"How sure can we be about anything?" Dr. Kotz says.

"There's no point in even attempting to find a cure for this unless the odds are good it will work." Dr. Junger says.

"Enthusiasm is one thing, but this will cost a lot of money, money we scarcely have and cannot afford to spend on a whim." Dr. Bruce says.

"It will work; I'm sure of it," Dr. Kotz says.

"But how sure?" Dr. Junger says.

"I can't give you percentages. This has never been attempted before, not even on test subjects. It's a chance, that's all, a chance to reverse what was done to our world," Dr. Kotz says.

Dr. Kotz's proposal for revolutionary new blood transfusions, clean blood to replace the dirty, corrupted blood and reverse the change receives the full approval of the board. A few days later they start to round up the corrupted souls and bring them to the laboratory under the cover of darkness. The transfusions start right away.

The experiment is a complete and utter failure.

They only manage to reverse the corruption of one soul. The others are lost forever. Many die in agony hours after they receive the first transfusion. Many more die in the following weeks and months.

Dr. Kotz succeeds in wiping out the last of the poor souls who were infected by the plague. In a way, people think he's a hero for making the streets safe again. They have no idea of the awful truth.

Dr. Kotz is given a new appointment: to watch the corrupted one they managed to save.

11

I climb onto the roof of the building that surrounds the market square.

The white nightdress I'm wearing is soaked with blood. I can taste blood in my mouth. My lower jaw's streaked with blood and gore.

I'm cradling the body of a dead girl in my arms, a child no more than four or five. She's the most exquisite meal I've had in days.

I open my arms and let the body fall to the streets below.

A woman looks up, no older than nineteen or twenty. She points at me and starts to scream. Another woman screams. And another. Then the men start screaming.

In mere seconds, the market place is filled with panicked people, screaming and running around but not really doing anything or going anywhere.

I leap and land on the back of the nearest woman and knock her to the ground. She shrieks and tries to crawl away. I tear her throat out.

I leap to a man a few feet away who seems to be paralyzed with fear and chew him open.

12

I scream myself awake, sweating and trembling in fear. I can smell urine.

13

I force myself to stay awake.

The dreams are getting worse. Dr. Kotz hasn't made any progress in helping me find out what the dreams mean and helping me to stop them. He's pretty fucking useless to be honest. He writes stuff down and gets me to keep a dream journal.

So I force myself to stay awake. I'm afraid to fall asleep because I know the dreams are waiting for me.

I always fall asleep eventually. There's only so much a person can stay awake before exhaustion overtakes them. I barely get two hours sleep a night. I'm a zombie, sleep-walking through my life.

14

"Are you going into work today, Darling?" Clara says.

I shake my head. "I already called in sick. I don't have the strength for it today. I can barely lift my head off the pillow. I'm fucking exhausted."

"Do you want to me to phone Dr. Kotz?"

"He's worse than useless. I'll be fine."

15

"Please don't hurt me."

The voice comes from the darkness. The room stinks of death. I didn't have a hand in ending the life of any of these people. The room stinks of decay and rot. The people in this place died from something else, a kind of plague. I can taste bile in my throat.

"Please don't hurt me."

The voice comes again. I search the darkness. I see her, close to death and leaning against the wall at the back of the room. She's a child, no more than five or six years old. She stinks of death and rot and I have trouble believing she's breathing, let alone speaking to me.

"I won't hurt you, child. I couldn't anyway. Your blood is full of rot," I say.

The girl weeps. I turn around and leave this stinking place of rot and death. I search the village for something to eat but there's nothing. I made a mistake coming here. The village is being consumed by a foul plague. I can't risk feeding on anyone here. Their blood would upset my stomach.

I flee.

## 16

I jerk awake in bed, dripping with sweat and trembling.

## 17

I wake up in darkness.

I don't know where I am at first or what's happening. My head feels sore and sleepy like someone's drugged me or I've been hit on the head. The last thing I remember is Mum dying in front of me and endless pain.

Where am I?

What's happened?

Where's Mum?

I'm lying on top of something cold and hard. I touch underneath my body with my fingers. It's metal. A metal table? I sit up. My head's spinning. I close my eyes and take a deep breath. The darkness stops moving and I open my eyes.

"Hello? Is anyone there? Can you help me?" I call out into the darkness.

There's no answer. I stand up on not quite steady legs. I walk forward a few feet. My legs ache and they feel really heavy so it's a huge effort to shuffle forward. I keep moving. I can myself gradually getting steadier. The room's dark and I can't see anything.

My leg bumps into something, something hard. I burn with pain and cry out. I touch the shape with my fingers. It feels like another table. I run my hands up the table. My fingers press into something soft. I keep pressing. My fingers touch bone. It takes a few moments to register I'm touching a dead person. I start to shriek.

Suddenly, lights come on and I can see and hear people running towards me.

## 18

I lie awake long after Clara and Nicole fall asleep.

Clara is on her usual side of our bed, eyes closed and snoring. Nicole is curled into a ball at the foot of the bed, out for the count and sucking her thumb.

I've been struggling to sleep recently, afraid to close my eyes because I know what's waiting for me.

I lie down, curl against Clara and try to sleep.

## 19

I jerk awake.

My heart is racing. I feel quite sick. I'm shaking.

I look around me.

Where am I?

I'm in a field somewhere. I have no fucking idea where. I'm barefoot and my feet are covered in mud. I still have my nightdress on. It's soaking wet.

I start walking.

## 20

I fall asleep on the sofa, curled up in one of Clara's massive afghan wool blankets. Clara is working night shift. Nicole is asleep in bed, curled around her favorite teddy, Mr. Snuffles.

## 21

I wake on the floor of an abandoned, burned out building, some sort of warehouse.

My nightdress is soaked with blood.

## 22

I can't sleep. It's late, almost 2 a.m., and I'm exhausted but I can't sleep. I toss and turn. I'm dripping with sweat. I throw the bed sheet off me because I'm sweating like a pig.

Clara is fast asleep beside me.

I get out of bed; go into the bathroom and splash cold water on my face.

I'm shaking.

I leave the bathroom and walk the length of the hall to my daughter Nicole's room. She's due to turn four in a couple of weeks. She still looks so small and I can't get over how old she is.

I creep into the room, stand over the bed and look down at her.

I sink my teeth into the soft flesh of her throat and suck until I feel her go still in my arms. I go into my bedroom with my daughter's blood fresh in my throat and sink my fangs into Clara's throat. She jerks and twitches beneath me.

## 23

I scream myself awake.

## 24

The girl is unconscious and tied to a chair in a dark room beneath Dr. Kotz's laboratory.

"Untie her," Dr. Kotz says.

"Are you sure?"

"She has been cured. It's fine."

Dr. Kotz's assistants untie her and jerk away as if afraid she's going to wake up. Dr. Kotz kneels on the floor in front of her. He gently touches her knee.

"It's okay, my dear. You're quite safe now," Dr. Kotz says.

They wait with her until she wakes up. It doesn't take long.

"Where am I?"

"You're safe now. You had a terrible accident. You almost died. We took care of you and healed you."

"Can I go home now?"

25

"I want to know why you've been lying to me, Dr. Kotz," I say.

He stares at me, unflinching. "I don't know what you mean, Miss Bruce."

I laugh in his face. "I don't want you to lie to me anymore, Dr. Kotz. You can cut the bullshit now."

Dr Kotz insists he's got no idea what I'm talking about. I must be confusing him with someone else. Did something happen? Did I have another dream? I take my dream journal out of my bag and throw it across the table at him.

"It's all in here," I say.

"What is?"

"The dreams I've been having, Dr. Kotz, aren't dreams; they're memories. But I think you already knew that Dr. Kotz."

He says nothing. He lifts up my journal and starts to go through it. I've filled almost every page. The dreams have increased recently. I dream every night, sometimes two or three different dreams a night. They have gotten more and more violent. Dr. Kotz's eyes widen in shock.

"I've started to dream about killing my family," I say.

"I had no idea," Dr. Kotz said.

"Why did you lie to me, Dr. Kotz?"

"I never lied. I followed orders and did my job, Miss Bruce."

I grab him by the throat and yank him to his feet.

"You did a lot more than that, Dr. Kotz. Your 'cure' did something to me."

"I saved you, Miss Bruce. I tried to save everyone."

I hurl him across the room. He's light and virtually weightless. He slams into the filing cabinets against the wall. I move towards him at lighting speed. He's red-faced and trembling, weeping like a baby.

"Please, Miss Bruce," Dr. Kotz says.

"I think I'm changing back."

The color drains from Dr. Kotz's face. He turns as white as sheet. He's trembling. The small knife is in my hand before I even realize I've removed it from my pocket.

I slit his throat and drink the blood as it sprays my face.

26

"What are you doing?"

I hear Clara's voice and come back to myself. I'm standing in my daughter's bedroom, standing over her bed in fact. I can still taste Dr. Kotz's blood. My mouth and chin are caked with dried blood. There are splashes of blood on my clothes.

"I'm not sure; I don't remember," I say.

Clara takes a step towards me. She sees the blood and her face turns white.

"What are you doing?" Clara says. Her voice sounds small and frightened.

My mouth hurts and I realize my fangs are out and cutting into the soft flesh of my cheek. I look down at the bed. Nicole is asleep. I remember pulling the covers off her and tilting her head slightly so I can see her throat. Oh, God!

"What the hell is going on? Where have you been?" Clara says.

I look at her. "What do you mean? I've been here."

Clara shakes her head. I realize how pale her skin is. Her face is streaked with tears. "You've been gone for almost a week. I filed a missing person report with the police."

Oh God, I can't remember.

"Where have you been?" Clara says.

"I don't remember."

I look down at my daughter. I want to rip her throat out and drink her sweet, sweet blood. Clara touches my arm and I flinch from her.

"Don't touch me," I say.

"Please tell me what's going on. I want to help you."

"You can't help me, Clara. Nobody can help me. Dr. Kotz thought he helped me but he didn't, not really."

"I don't know what you mean."

"I'm damned."

I touch her face. She's scared and crying. I want to kiss my daughter's cheek and tell her goodbye but I can't. I couldn't stop myself from hurting her.

The knife I used to slit Dr. Kotz's throat is in my hand before I even realize it.

I press it against my jugular.

# BLOOD RED ORANGES
*By Barbara Jacobson*

"A ghost?" Madalyn asked the realtor.

"Yes," the realtor assured her. "But this house is the best deal this summer."

"The house is gorgeous," Madalyn explained, "but I don't know if I want to meet any ghosts."

"You won't," her husband, Chad, growled. "There is no such thing as a ghost. You're a psychologist, for God's sake. Control yourself."

Chad stared at her. He wore his police uniform, and he looked like he might arrest her. There was a dead stare in his eyes.

"I have to have this house. We can't walk away from a half-price deal like this! You haven't lost your grip on logic, Madalyn? Have you?"

Madalyn glared back at him.

The realtor interrupted the silence, "A steal like this won't last. Ghost or no ghost."

Madalyn, feeling humiliated by her husband, tried to smile. She pretended she was really agreeable to buy the elegant hilltop house with the dazzling black-and-white décor. "Are the furnishings included in the price?"

"Oh, yes," the realtor replied with a smile. "The owners didn't take anything but some of their clothing."

"I guess they were in a hurry," Chad said, as though he were at a crime scene.

"Enough!" Madalyn said, exasperated.

He shot a smile at her. "Do I have to sleep on the couch tonight?"

"I was thinking in your cruiser."

He smiled and threw an arm around her waist. Madalyn was just the opposite of Chad in appearance. She was petite and had brown hair. Chad was well built, tall and blond. She put her arm around his perfectly trim waist, and they started to walk together.

"Let's check out this house one more time," he whispered into her ear.

Chad had always teased her about her simple tastes. Unlike him, she loved a traditional home with warm colors and human-sized rooms.

She tried to like the over-sized house with its bulky furniture, but it made her uncomfortable. She felt lost under the soaring white ceilings, upon which strange angles and boxes of light moved around as large tree branches moved in the Southern California wind outside.

The kitchen had white cabinets so tall they almost disappeared into the ceiling. As in the rest of the house, there were no drapes or shades to cover the huge windows. The floors were white stained wood. The only color was the blue streak in the marble counter tops and the gleam of the stainless-steel appliances.

In the master bedroom, drawers were left open with clothing strewn over the sides. *They rushed out of here*, Madalyn thought. Chad came into the bedroom. He grabbed her by the arm and dragged her outside into the backyard.

There was a large fire pit on the right side of the pool and a large tree that shaded the left side of the property. Madalyn stopped to take a whiff of the tree. The scent was appealing. Not only was it sweet, it was also inviting.

"Oranges?" she inquired.

"Blood red oranges," Chad answered, knowingly. "Ever have one? They make great cocktails too."

"I bet they're delicious," she enthused.

She pulled away from him and walked under the tree. She rubbed her fingers over the rough surface of its trunk. A warm feeling rushed through her.

"What are you doing? Hugging a tree?"

She smiled back at him. She nodded and laughed.

He stared at her with his hands on his hips, near his gun.

The realtor came outside with her clipboard. "Are you ready to sign an offer?" she addressed Chad.

Madalyn walked up to the realtor, leaving Chad behind her.

"Here, I'll sign," she said.

Two weeks later, the couple took possession of the house. They brought with them only the kitchen furniture from their apartment, putting the rest of their things in the garbage.

* * *

It started the day they moved in, as Madalyn was hanging a painting of blue flowers that her mother had painted. After she stopped banging a nail into the wall, she heard a strange moan coming from the back of the house.

"Chad!" she called out. "Are you okay?"

No answer.

She continued to marvel over her mother's still life of the blue flowers. She missed her mother. Her mother was stolen by a heart attack when Madalyn was just ten years old. She had a lonely childhood growing up with a cold grandmother.

There was another moan. This time it was a little louder. A ghost?

"Chad!" she yelled.

He didn't answer her.

After emptying the drawers of the previous owners' clothing, she unpacked Chad's and her clothes and put them away. When that chore was accomplished, she dragged out a huge vinyl bag that held her new bedspread. The blue flower accent in its pattern almost matched her mother's painting. The pattern had an old-fashioned quality to it.

Madalyn threw the new bedspread onto the king-size mattress. She smoothed out the wrinkles and tossed white satin throw pillows at the headboard. She stood back and surveyed the work. The splashes of blue in the bedspread and painting warmed up the sterile-white room. She was about to open another box when a long moan bellowed through the house.

"Chad!" She jumped at the sound of her own voice.

This time, he came right away. He waited in the doorway. His hands were on the hips of his tight blue jeans.

"Why are you moaning? You sound like a moose."

"I thought *you* were moaning."

She froze.

Chad left immediately to search the house. He returned with his gun in hand and a perplexed expression on his face.

"It's coming from outside, in the backyard. It's probably an animal. Relax. There's nothing to be afraid of."

That night, they made love, but Madalyn was distracted. She was busy listening for that horrible moan to return, but it didn't. Afterward, Chad ran his fingers over the new bedspread.

"This isn't our new bedspread. Is it?"

"It is," Madalyn raised her voice, knowing what was coming next. "It matches my mother's painting."

"That's true," he said, "but I hate it. It's way too old fashioned for this house. The bedspread and painting have to go."

"That's bullshit, Chad!"

"No. Let's not fight. If you can't, or don't know how to, decorate a house like this, we'll get an interior designer."

"Oh, I can't stand you!"

She grabbed her pillow and robe and stormed into the living room to sleep on the sectional. Chad didn't follow her. Madalyn tried to get comfortable on the twenty-foot, black leather couch, but to no avail.

She wondered about the people who used to live in this house. She imagined a man and a woman with black faces sitting on this couch. What had made them leave? Was it the moaning sound? She listened carefully for it, but heard nothing. Somehow she fell asleep.

She wasn't sure what time it was when she was jolted awake. She sat on the edge of the couch and listened for awhile. Silence. She wrapped the robe tightly around herself and lay back down. At four in the morning, the moan returned. It was a long, breathy moan. Madalyn jumped off the couch and ran back into the bedroom, where Chad was asleep. She jumped into bed and pulled the flowered bedspread over her head.

When she woke up the next morning, she realized Chad was gone. *Maybe he went to get groceries*, she thought, remembering the refrigerator was empty. She pulled the bedspread over her head and found her warm impression on the sheets. She could remain in here all day if she wanted because she and Chad had taken a week off from work to put their new home together.

As she lay there, she heard Chad come in through the front door. Shortly after, she heard the kitchen cabinets open and close. *Groceries*, she thought. Soon, Chad walked into the bedroom, dragging a painting in one hand and a vinyl zipper bag in the other hand. There was a naughty smile on his face. He dropped his goods, then tore the bedspread from Madalyn's body and threw it onto the floor. He opened the vinyl bag and pulled out a new bedspread. He shook out the wrinkles and dropped it over his wife.

It fell like a parachute filled with air and landed on her body. It felt like satin. The pattern immediately upset her. There were bands of black and white, and a large red circle in the center.

"Wait, Madalyn. Wait until you see the painting."

He ripped the brown paper off the front of the artwork, revealing a canvas covered in zigzagging lines of black and red on a white background.

"Like it?"

"You bastard." She got up and walked out of the bedroom.

"Wait! I also got black satin sheets for us to slide around on."

"Whatever!"

He followed her out of the bedroom, dragging her blue bedspread and mom's painting with him. He tossed them into the spare room.

"Since you like these things so much, we'll display your taste in this empty room. Maybe it can charm our guests. Love you, Madalyn," he said, walking to the kitchen.

She followed him, brandishing an imaginary knife.

"No bloodshed, my love," he laughed. "I'll make us a great lunch."

He filled the blender with two scoops of protein powder, two glasses of blood red orange juice, a banana and a pint of strawberries. He got out two tall glasses and filled them with the frothy liquid. Before his wife could say a word, he planted a generous kiss on her thick brown bangs.

"Here, a perfectly healthy smoothie. It'll put some badly needed muscle on your little body. Oh, by the way, I invited half the police force over for a party later on. Sort of a housewarming party. I told everyone we're having a barbecue and drinks... and to bring a date."

"Oh my God!" Madalyn cried.

"Don't worry. I shopped for food, and I'll cook everything."

Madalyn spent the afternoon getting ready for the party. She slipped into a light blue bikini. Because she was so small, she could wear a string bikini without drawing too much attention. She thought twice about it, took off the bikini and put on a pair of white shorts instead. She had no plans to swim because it would ruin her makeup and hair, which she spent an hour curling with her electric curling wand.

She didn't know too many of the cops and their mates. A little fear ran through her. *Stop it*, she thought. *You're an accomplished psychologist. You know how to mingle and make a good impression.* Helping Chad with their guests would keep her busy.

By the time she finished getting ready, she heard the doorbell ringing and her husband greeting their guests. She went into the living room and saw two men that she knew. They were carrying a Kegerator of beer.

"Hi, Mark and Jeff," she said, pleasantly.

"Hello, Madalyn," they both said. "You ready to party?"

She followed them to the sliding glass doors leading to the back yard and was shocked to find some thirty guests crowded around the pool and the fire pit areas. A couple was marveling over the blood red orange tree.

"It's so exotic," the young woman said.

Madalyn smiled and approached the woman. She put out her hand and the woman reciprocated. "Hello, I'm Madalyn. Chad's wife." Now Madalyn was in character—self-confident and charming. She greeted everyone else with as much grace. After receptions, she helped Chad, who stood at the barbecue, cooking food he would never eat. The air filled with the smoky scent of sausages, hot dogs and hamburgers.

Chad turned to her and suggested that she pick some oranges and make screwdrivers for their guests. He handed her a large, empty basket. She nodded and grabbed the basket.

She stood under the blood red orange tree and picked the fruit, one by one. The guests cheered and she raised a fist in mock victory. As she proceeded to pick more fruit, she became aware of the aroma—sweet like the pies her mother used to make. The more she picked, the more enthralled she became with the texture of the fruit. The oranges had a smooth, yet bumpy, surface at the same time. The bumps tickled her skin. She couldn't help but to let out a giggle.

Chad stared at her. She waved at him. He looked away as if she disappeared. She didn't care what he thought and continued to pick the fruit, filling the basket until it overflowed. He jogged over to her and grabbed the basket.

"Those are more than enough oranges. Thank you."

Madalyn watched him walk away. When he wasn't watching her, she picked another orange and pulled the skin away, leaving the peels on the grass. Carefully, she dug her thumb into the center of the orange and pulled away a wedge of the fruit. She slid it into her mouth and let it drool onto her chin. The juice was good. No, it tasted wonderful. The nectar made her high, but not dizzy. She was in control.

From the rest of the orange, she took a large bite. It squirted all over her face. She turned to look at Chad. He was staring at her with a stone face. Madalyn burst into laughter. She noticed that everyone was now staring at her. She curtailed her bites to small ladylike nibbles, and they looked away. She knew she should stop eating and join the party, but she never before tasted fruit this delicious. When she finished, she sucked her fingers clean.

*I must rejoin the party*, she decided. She slipped out of her shorts, ran toward the swimming pool and took a huge leap into the water. She made a huge cannonball splash that drenched the chief of police and his wife. Chad glared at her in disbelief, and then looked away in embarrassment. He didn't speak to her for two days afterward and never brought it up. This time, he was the one who slept on the couch.

It was on the second night that everything changed. Madalyn was in the bedroom, tossing and turning. She was staring up at the ceiling when the moaning came back. For some reason, she wasn't afraid anymore. She got up and tiptoed through the living room, where Chad was sound asleep. She opened the patio doors and went out into the night.

The moan came again. It was coming from the blood red orange tree. It was softer this time, but it still radiated through Madalyn's body. She felt fearless, walked over to the tree and sat right next to its trunk, where the smell was intoxicating. When the moan came again, it was so loud she had to stick her fingers in her ears. The next moan was softer. Soon it became a whisper. Madalyn sat up straight and listened carefully. A voice whispered something.

"What?" Madalyn asked. "Please speak louder."

"Maddy," the voice said. "It's me."

"Who are you?"

"You don't recognize my voice, Maddy?"

Madalyn's heart began to pound. "Mom, is that you?"

"Yes, dear."

Madalyn started to cry. Her mother had died when she was a child. She remained lonely until she met Chad.

"Are you all right, Maddy?"

"Yes, Mom."

"Are you happy?"

"I guess so."

"Is it Chad?"

Madalyn waited a few minutes to answer. "Maybe. Where are you, Mom? I miss you terribly."

"I'm right here."

Madalyn looked around in the dark until she saw glowing eyes by the pool. She jumped before realizing they belonged to a neighborhood cat.

"I don't see you, Mom."

"I'm down here."

Against her better judgment, Madalyn believed her mother. At least in her heart she did. She lay in the grass, beneath the tree. In the grass she found an orange and sniffed it. *Oh my God*, she thought, *it smells like baby powder*. She remembered her mother had dusted herself with baby powder after every shower. Madalyn didn't think she could ever eat this fruit again.

"Mom, does your spirit live in the fruit?"

"No, I'm down here."

"In the ground?"

"Yes!"

"If that were true, how can you breathe?"

"It's very hard, but I'll manage as long as I can."

"Oh my God! I'll get help."

Madalyn ran into the house and woke up Chad. He didn't want to wake up and turned over on his side.

"No, get up! My mother is buried under the blood red orange tree. Please help me get her out before she suffocates."

"Are you having a nightmare, Madalyn?"

"No, it's real. Come out and see for yourself."

Begrudgingly, he got up and slipped into his jeans. He stayed shirtless.

"I don't know why I'm listening to you. You must have lost your mind."

Chad was halfway out the patio doors when he ran back into the house. He returned with his revolver and slipped it into the back of the waist of his jeans. He walked into the night with the confidence of a policeman. When he reached the tree, he rested his hands on the trunk. A moan came from the tree. He jumped away.

"When the moan dies down, you can hear my mother's voice. She talked to me."

"Why are you talking like one of your patients?"

"Stop it. I speak the truth."

"Your career will be over if I have to put you in an institution."

"If you don't believe me, why did you come out here and bring your gun?"

"I thought there might be a real person in distress nearby."

"You mean a damsel in distress."

"Don't be a jealous bitch."

"You are such a pig."

He grabbed her by the arm.

"You're hurting me!"

He shoved her backwards and started for the house.

"Where are you going, tough guy?" Madalyn's mother asked.

He jerked around to face the voice. "There *is* someone buried here!"

Chad turned and ran to the garage. He returned with a shovel and began to dig. The ground was dry and difficult to remove. However, he was more stubborn than the soil. He succeeded in breaking the ground and worked tirelessly until he dug down to a coffin.

"Get back, Madalyn. Something looks odd to me."

She peeked into the hole and saw an old, ornate coffin. It appeared to be made of mahogany and silver. Chad forced the lid open and let out a masculine scream. He jumped out of the grave and backed away. Before Madalyn could ask what it was, a skeletal creature sat up and stretched out its long, bony arms. When she looked closer, she was astounded to see the creature had horns on its head.

The skeleton climbed out of the grave. It appeared to be male. It must have stood eight feet tall and had a huge, scaly tail. Its claws were so long, it could have swept a man off his feet with one sweep of its hand. Madalyn gasped and covered her ears with her hands as the monstrosity let out a deep moan. It was nothing like the soothing moans of her mother. This monster from hell had fooled her in order to get Chad to dig him up.

The skeletal abomination stepped towards Chad, dwarfing his well-built, six-foot-tall frame. As it moved closer, both he and Madalyn screamed. Chad raised the shovel over his head and brought it down upon the skeleton's arm. It moaned and took the shovel away from him. The skeletal creature then threw the shovel at the tree, leaving a hole in the trunk. The tree began to drip blood.

Madalyn ran into the house. Tears ran down her face as she helplessly watched from the patio doors. The skeleton grabbed Chad by the neck and throttled him into unconsciousness. The creature then proceeded to throw him over the pool. Chad crashed into the side of the diving board and fell into the water. He came to and swam to the side of the pool, where he climbed out onto the cement. He stood up, reached for his gun and emptied the magazine into the skeleton.

Unhurt, the skeleton went after Chad and lifted him high into the air. It dropped him on its skeletal leg, breaking Chad's back in half. He slid down onto the hard ground. He was dead.

Madalyn escaped and went as far away as possible. No one believed her story of the blood red orange tree and the skeleton that crawled out of a grave. They told her she was crazy when she told them she still hears moaning during the night. She told her story over and over again in the mental institution.

The patients believed every word she said.

# SHADE

## *By Joe Palumbo*

Clyde nervously tapped the middle finger of his left hand against his knee. His eyes flicked from the woman at the opposite end of the conference table to the large windows to his right and saw the sun was setting. He took a nervous breath and looked back at Alicia. He glanced down, checked his watch, and saw it was less than an hour until sundown. He looked back up at Alicia and saw she was still staring down at his file on the table. He took the opportunity of her distraction to reach into his jacket and remove his prescription. Before she looked up, he shook a single white pill out and tossed it in his mouth. His face wrinkled as he swallowed the pill dry. Alicia stood and stared at Clyde for a moment. She then turned towards the wet bar in the corner of the room.

"Mr. Burton," she said as she walked, "your sales here look very good. You have done quite well."

Clyde's eyes flicked towards the setting sun for a horrible moment and then back to Alicia. Her slender back was to him as she filled a glass with tonic water. In the silence of the room the hiss of the carbonation sounded like machine gun fire. He looked at the horrible shadows that were already growing in the room. He quickly wiped sweat from his upper lip and glanced up at the lights embedded in the ceiling. They were off; Alicia had only the soft light lamps built into the table lighting the room. He glanced back at her just as she used a small pair of silver tongs to drop a lemon wedge in the water. The impact caused an explosion of bubbles in the water.

Alicia walked back to the table, sipping her water. She set the drink down on one of the coasters and placed her hands flat on the table. She then stared at Clyde with eyes that were as hard and cold as stone. Clyde swallowed a lump away and willed himself not to look at the setting sun again.

"I read here that, not only did you sell our telecommunication services to Gregory Financing, but they have requested that we take over their I.T. services as well."

"That's right, ma'am." Clyde was impressed with the steadiness of his voice.

Alicia picked up her drink and looked back down at the file as she sipped. Clyde took the opportunity to take another look at the sun. He then observed the shadows again, and they were growing. With terrible inevitability the shadows were slowly consuming the world around them. A fresh layer of sweat trickled down the back of his neck and his temples.

Alicia then looked up and said, "Really, I don't see much to discuss. You have been doing very well and your sales continue to rise steadily. I think we are done here." She then flipped the file shut and leaned back in her chair.

Every fiber in Clyde screamed at him to leap from the chair and race to the door, to get out of this room, the building, and run to his safety. Instead, he slowly rose from the chair and gave Alicia a slight nod of his head. He then turned and, to his amazement, was able to take sure and steady paces towards the double wood doors. His sweaty hand had just grasped the silver knob when he heard Alicia's voice from behind him.

"There is one more thing."

He closed his eyes and took in a breath to steady himself before turning around and asking, "Yes ma'am?"

"There is more to just good numbers to succeed here. It also takes someone who can meld well with the rest of the company." She interlocked her fingers on her lap as if in demonstration of her point. "I asked around a bit about you before we had this meeting. I discovered that only two people on your floor even knew your name or was at least certain of it."

"I am a private person," Clyde said quietly.

"As am I, but people here know me. I interact well with everyone here. I simply advise you to do the same." She then pivoted her chair back towards the table and picked up her drink. "Have a good weekend, Mr. Burton. I hope we can meld a little better come Monday."

Clyde gave another nod and left the conference room. As he walked down the hall towards the elevators, he could feel the surge of energy starting in the back of his legs, the need to run. He took another deep breath and continued his smooth walk down the brightly lit hall. The lights helped him keep this calm. He wondered as he reached the elevator if he was going to do so well on the trip back home. He pressed the call button for the elevator and thought of his father.

* * *

"Daddy," he called. "Daddy come here, hurry!"

Clyde's father swung the door open and flicked on the bedroom light. Clyde was sitting up in bed clutching the Batman sheets to his chin and visibly shaking with fear. His father let out a frustrated sigh and shook his head.

"Buddy, you've got to stop doing this," he said, sitting on the edge of the bed.

"But he was gonna get me."

"I've told you so many times there is no such thing as this shade thing." His father gently worked the sheets away from Clyde's chin. "You're ten-years-old now, and you need to understand that there is nothing in the dark."

"He's not in the dark; he *is* the dark," Clyde countered with panic in his voice.

Clyde's father placed his hands on his son's shoulders and eased him back on the pillow. He then stood from the bed and looked down at him.

"Please leave the light on," Clyde begged.

"No," his father said with a shake of the head, "you've gotten too big for that." He could see tears beginning to glisten in Clyde's eye. He let out a heavy sigh and ran a hand over his face. "I'll turn your lamp on, but that's it."

Clyde nodded in agreement and his father walked around the bed and flicked the lamp on. He then went back to the door and flicked the light switch off. He took one more look at his son who lay in his bed in a circle of white light. He then shook his head and shut the door.

* * *

Clyde climbed in his car and started the engine as he closed the mental curtain on the memory. Just above the front and back floorboards, thin blue LED lights glowed dimly. They were just bright enough to banish the shadows, but not too bright to attract any attention. He reached into his jacket pocket and removed the orange bottle of pills. He looked down at the label.

TAKE ONE AS NEEDED FOR ANXIETY.

He popped the cap and dry swallowed another of the small low-dose sedatives. He then backed out of his assigned space and exited the parking garage. The bright lights of the city made the feeling of panic lessen, but in every dark alley he could see him. He could see Shade looking back at him. He had hoped his mother was right; that this really was something that one could escape from by the simple act of aging.

* * *

"Maybe this is something he will grow out of," Clyde could hear his mother's voice through his bedroom door.

"I want to find whoever told him this urban legend, or whatever it is, and kick the shit out of them," his father growled.

"That won't help anything. Besides I asked him, and I don't think anyone told him. I think it is something he came up with on his own. I even asked around work and no one knew what I was talking about."

"Yeah, I went through his comics when he was at school yesterday and I couldn't find anything. I figured that someone must have told him a scary story since I couldn't find any characters like that in his comics."

"I think we should take him to a counselor, with that and getting older, maybe this will go away." His mother's voice then faded down the hall as they walked away.

* * *

Clyde drove farther away from downtown and merged with the heavy flow of commuters who were also leaving the area for whatever plans they had for the weekend. Knowing that he was surrounded by people made him feel better. He knew they could not see him and honestly could not care less about him, but the fact that other people were around him acted like a safety blanket. He tried to grin, but it felt more like a grimace. His memories continued to come in snippets. College came to his mind. Maggie came with the thought.

* * *

"So, what scary thing kept you up as a child?" Maggie had said, sipping beer from her plastic cup. "For me it was it was the librarian ghost from *Ghostbusters*. Do you remember that?" Before Clyde could answer she said with a fake shiver of fear, "I couldn't go in a library alone till I was fifteen."

Clyde and Maggie sat on the outside steps of their college dorm, passing a joint back and forth and drinking beer. Clyde thought about the question as he watched insects buzz lazily in the heat of the summer night around the blue light of the security lamp across the parking lot. He took a sip of his beer and debated on making something up. She then nudged him in the side with her elbow and he looked over at her.

"You can tell me," she said playfully. "I won't make fun of you. It can't be any crazier than me being afraid of a library ghost."

"I used to be afraid of the dark. It was bad enough to be considered a full phobia. I know lots of people say they have a phobia, but they really don't. A phobia is a debilitating fear of something. Mine was debilitating. I used to think the dark itself was going to get me. I went to a counselor and went through some exposure therapy."

"Are you still afraid of the dark?"

Clyde stared past the blue circle of light and in the darkness beyond it and said, "No, not anymore."

"Well," she said and placed a hand on his thigh, "I'm going to leave the light on for us anyways."

* * *

Clyde pulled into his house at the end of the loop. He looked at his darkened home through his windshield and swallowed hard. After that night in college he was back at square one, but with more therapy he was able to go on and put the fearful thoughts away. However, things had worsened for him over the past two years. The panic, the feelings that the darkness was watching; that Shade was watching.

He reached for his phone mounted to his dash and pulled up an application called Home Control. A diagram of his house filled the screen. One of the buttons just below the diagram was a large red button with the word "OFF" written in bold. He tapped it and the button changed to green with the word "ON." He looked up and saw every window fill with white light, one by one.

He stepped out of his car and turned to look at the city skyline in the distance. He admired all the twinkling lights. Above those lights, forks of lightning danced in the emptiness of the night sky. A distant rumbled of thunder touched his ears. He turned his back on the storm and climbed the steps up to his front door. He took one final look before going in.

Just inside, he shut and locked the door behind him. He then leaned his back against the door and reveled in the feeling of the fear draining out of him. He was home, and he was safe. He was now back in the environment that he controlled, and the darkness could never reach him. He turned and headed to his bright kitchen to cook himself a dinner. Washing his hands in the kitchen sink, he stared at his reflection in the window. The reflection was translucent, and he could see the darkness of his side yard beyond. He thought back to college.

* * *

He leaned on the black metal railing that lined the stone landings of the steps that ran up the side of the dorms. He leaned there, propped a bare foot up and looked again at the blue light with its lazy bugs. He removed a soft pack of smokes from his jeans pocket and lit one up. He checked if anyone was around because Clyde Burton smoking was a rare event that only occurred while drinking or after sex, and people would notice that he was no longer drinking. He took one drag and just as he let it out, he heard a voice from the direction of the parking lot.

"Oh, I know what you did," the voice said in a playful manner.

"Martin, you scared the shit out of me," Clyde said as he steadied himself on the rail.

Martin adjusted his jacket and said, "You had a better evening than me. How was she?"

"You know you are the guys who give the rest of us bad names," Clyde said, shaking a finger at him.

Martin laughed and took a slight step back to let a passing car by. Martin now stood with his back eclipsed by the darkness. Clyde took another drag on his smoke and looked down on his friend from the second story landing. He then saw something just over Martin's right shoulder. His mind wanted to process it as movement, but Clyde could not fully classify it as movement in the true sense of the word. It was as if the darkness shifted. Then Clyde saw it. Two spots above Martin's right shoulder hovered in the darkness. There was no light from them but somehow they were darker than the shadows around them. Like two voids in space had appeared there. Clyde did now know how he knew, but he knew they were eyes, and suddenly he knew what the eyes belonged to.

He tried to call out. He tried to yell, to tell Martin to run, but all he could do was stand there with the cigarette dangling from his lips. Clyde's eyes were covered with a film of terror. Martin saw this and opened his mouth to speak when four bands of blackness wrapped around Martin's chest, stomach, and head. Martin's eyes grew large with shock and then he was gone. Clyde had watched him simply vanished into the night.

* * *

The memory played over and over in his mind as he ate and continued as he cleaned the dishes. Clyde set the last dish into the drainer and heard a bang of loud thunder that sounded as if it were right outside his door. The storm was getting closer. Flashes of lightning illuminated the curtains with strobes of blue light and Clyde could see the slight dimming of his lights. He dried his hands and with fast steps he went to the glass doors that overlooked his back yard. He pulled the shades open and pressed a button next to the sliding glass door. The backyard was filled with white light from three halogen floodlights that were installed above the awning over his back porch.

When he slid the doors open a burst of humid air pushed in, causing the white curtains to blow up in a silent dance. Clyde hurried outside and went to the wooden box that occupied the space where his privacy fence met the back corner of his home. He opened the wooden gate and saw the generator sitting on a concrete slab. He leaned forward and pressed the small plastic button labeled "TEST." Several lights lit up along the top and he was pleased to see they were all green. He shut and locked the gate and went back inside.

Another explosion of lightning lit up the sky and the resulting surge caused the lights in his home to grow brighter before dimming back to normal. Clyde waited for the lights to go out and braced himself for the twelve-second wait till the generator would take over the responsibility of bringing the lights back on. He counted twelve seconds off in his mind and realized that, in the darkness, twelve seconds would be an eternity. He went in the kitchen and removed a large flashlight from the drawer and an electric lantern from under the sink. Another flash of lightning from outside and the lights brightened again; this time Clyde heard a loud pop from his hallway and the tinkle of falling glass. He thought of Martin again.

* * *

Red and blue lights pulsed rapidly, giving the scene in the parking lot a stuttering appearance. Uniformed police officers milled around with large flashlights searching the area where Martin had been standing not an hour earlier. Mixed in with their ranks were campus security and detectives in suits. One of these stood before Clyde with a leather note pad in one hand and a pen in the other.

"What was Martin wearing?" the detective asked.

"Uh…jeans, dark jacket, and a band t-shirt," Clyde said as he lit up another smoke. He decided to add a situation like this to one of his few that called for a cigarette.

"What was on the shirt? What band?"

"A.F.I. The shirt was black and had a picture of three rabbits in a circle on it."

"His jacket?" the detective requested while writing down in his pad.

"It was black. It was one of those Members Only jackets. He got it from his dad. He loved that stupid jacket."

The detective nodded and wrote more in his pad before saying, "Did you get a look at who grabbed your friend?"

Clyde hesitated for a moment. He wondered if he really should tell this office what he believed really took Martin, but instead he said, "It was dark."

The detective nodded in understanding. Martin knew what the detective thought he meant by the statement, but it was so much more than a description.

"Thank you. Get in touch with us if you think of anything else," the detective said before walking away to pursue his case that would never be solved.

* * *

Clyde looked down the hall and saw the back half was covered in a thick wall of darkness. He shook away a wave of gooseflesh that was forming in the small of his back and headed back to the kitchen. He opened the doors under the sink and removed a box of light bulbs that was one of two-dozen boxes. Setting them on the counter, he then grabbed the electric lantern. He then heard another loud pop instantly followed by more falling glass. The entire hall would now be dark. He lit the lantern and removed two bulbs from the box of four and shoved each one in a separate pants pocket. He then picked up the lantern and headed for the hall.

He stopped just at the entrance to the hall when his shoe hit something soft. He looked down and what he saw caused an electric current of panic to shoot from the bottom of his feet to the crown of his head. His mouth became dry and breathing became almost impossible. The shock of it caused him to drop the lantern. It hit with a heavy clang and the light from inside flickered and died. Sitting on the floor, half covered by the darkness of the hall was a jacket. A black Members Only jacket.

Clyde pulled his gaze away from the jacket and looked down the hall. Hovering just at the end were two dark spots like drops of pitch floating in a sea of nothing. They looked directly into Clyde's eyes. Each one brimmed with a horrible and mocking intelligence. Clyde's breathing became loud and ragged and sweat ran freely down his body. Another flash of lightning pulsed outside and the lights above him flickered and struggled to stay on before relenting and shutting off. Clyde was suddenly thrown into a void of nothing but even in the blinding darkness he could still see the black holes in space staring at him.

To the average person walking down the street, twelve seconds is nothing. In the span of time, twelve seconds is just a fleeting moment that, for many, is not long enough for anything to really change. That person does not give that length of time any thought. However, for Clyde Burton, twelve seconds is an eternity, and held plenty of time to feel the tentacles of Shade wrap around his petrified body.

Outside, the generator detected the outage and rumbled to life, restoring power to the home. One by one the lights came on, banishing the darkness in every room. The final lights to come back to life were the living room and kitchen lights. On the floor just in front of the hall were a broken electric lantern and a black Members Only jacket.

# THE WAITING ROOM
*By Jameson Grey*

After a while, you think you know all the stops on the line. As traveling mutates from an exciting adventure into an obsessive ritual, the daily commute does that to you. You catch the 7:19 commuter-rush morning train (if it's on time, or even running). If not subject to any delays, you arrive an hour later at your destination and, if you leave work on time, you do the whole thing in reverse, bagging the first available seat, or, if you are really lucky, a table on which to place your hot beverage. (I'd stop short of calling it tea or coffee, as it often tastes like something in-between.) You might even buy a newspaper. Me? I tend to read books—or doze.

The ritual does not stop there: the calling order of the stations is your next lesson. Learning that by rote enables you to calculate the halfway point of your daily journey—if only so you can look up from your book and think, *Phew, I'm halfway home* or *Hmph, I'm halfway to work* (and I'm sure you actually think the 'Hmph' bit). Eventually you reach a point where the time differences between individual stations are ingrained. Soon afterwards, you begin to recognize your fellow commuters: John Smith, who gets off at Rochdale, Jane Smith who gets on at Halifax—perhaps you will even acknowledge them with a faint smile of recognition. If the train is running particularly late, you might offer a derisory comment to your neighbor. That is rare though, for lone passengers on trains are not social animals. We tend to prefer staring at nothing to conversing with strangers. Or is this just me? If I am not reading or dozing, I find myself sitting waiting or, more often, standing in the crush like a catatonic sardine until it is my turn to peel out.

All of which is a roundabout way of saying I knew that Endslaw station was roughly the halfway point of my daily journey—some five minutes from Hebbleton and two minutes from Calderton. It's why I came to notice the woman sitting in the waiting room at 19:59 every evening. It's why I wondered how come she never boarded the train when only this one route passed through.

I guess I had been gazing blindly out of the train window the first time I saw her. I remember looking up and seeing a woman in a grey coat in the platform's waiting room, her head bowed down. At the time I might have given the matter little thought, and it is only hindsight that lends the moment gravitas, but I must have thought something was wrong; she seemed completely disinterested in the train standing at the platform.

I might have let the observation go, but she was there again the next time I passed through Endslaw at 19:59. Perhaps she met somebody at this time? I found it odd that she bowed her head in the same pose and that she wore the same clothes. Was it a coincidence?

I am not consistent in the trains I catch home: some days I am an hour earlier traveling through that part of Yorkshire—sometimes even later. Maybe it is because of this irregularity that, after the second time I saw her, I noticed she was not on the platform at 18:59 or 19:29 or

20:29 (this would have been the next train to call at the station if she were meeting anyone). Indeed, even when the 19:59 did not arrive at Endslaw on time—which, of course, was often—she was not there.

Yet, two weeks later, I happened to be on a train that arrived punctually at Endslaw at 19:59 and, sure enough, the woman in the grey coat sat in the waiting room with her head bowed down. On this occasion, I realized that no one ever boarded the train at Endslaw. No one alighted either.

I did not know who traveled on the other trains during the day, but it wasn't economic sense for a train company to continue to run a service to a station that nobody used. I should have put the thought out of my head, but, twenty-four hours later, when I again saw the woman and again nobody got on or off the train, I thought I would ask the conductor why the service continued to stop at Endslaw.

He gave an unexpected response. "This service doesn't call at Endslaw, sir. In fact, there's no station there—don't think there ever has been."

"But we just stopped there a minute ago."

"I'm afraid you're mistaken, sir. The last station was Hebbleton; the next one is Calderton. If you'll excuse me…" Shaking his head, he continued up the train on his inspection rounds.

I was more than puzzled. A mysterious woman who never boarded the 19:59 train, in fact paid it no mind at all when it did arrive, yet was always there to meet it and never there at any other time, and now a conductor denying that Endslaw train station even existed… it made no sense to me—no sense at all. I resolved to alight at Endslaw the next day.

*  *  *

These days I live alone—no girlfriend—but I was married in my late teens and throughout university to a fellow undergraduate. Miranda was a brilliant young scientist with a significant research career ahead of her, but she was struck by a rare illness while we were on an even rarer holiday (we were celebrating completing our courses). After spending many weeks recovering in hospital, she died unexpectedly, just two days before her graduation ceremony; the university's vice-chancellor paid her a lovely compliment in his speech, eulogizing that 'Miranda truly was the wondrous one amongst her peers.'

I shan't go into the somber days that followed her death. It is enough to say I loved her very much and still miss her intolerably five years on. Throwing myself in a new direction career-wise—I had originally planned on becoming a journalist—was my way of dealing with the grief.

I have not always been a commuter. I have changed jobs a couple of times and, even when I started my present job, I lived nearer to work than I do now. But a couple of years ago my friends all seemed to go through the marriage-and-babies thing or the changing-city-for-career-reasons thing, so I decided to up-sticks and try a new city myself. Twelve months ago, I moved all my stuff westwards across the Pennines, and have been commuting since.

As the days of traveling the same route mounted, the excitement of travel slipped away and my perception of the stops on the line and the people who used them heightened; I realized that my focus had narrowed to a point where the stations I was passing through and the people who alighted or boarded were one and the same. Towns and villages consisted only of the people who used their respective stations. While commuting, I read books and dozed in a self-contained reverie. I knew the length of time I would be on the train, where I would be stopping, how long it would take to get to the next station, and who I would see when I got there. I had become complacent.

* * *

"Hello there, are you all right?"

At first, it seemed the woman had not heard.

"Hello."

She looked up at me. Dark sad eyes gazed into mine. "I thought nobody would ever see me," she said.

"What do you mean? Why do you sit there every day with your head bowed?"

"I am resting. Originally, I stood on the platform, but when no one noticed me and I got tired, I took to sitting down." The woman sighed. "After a while, hope began to drift away," she added.

"I don't understand. Why do you never catch any of the trains that stop here?"

"The trains do not stop here anymore."

She was mistaken. I knew the guard on the previous day's train had been wrong too. I had even checked my A-to-Z when I got home. The train line clearly passed the southern tip of the small town of Endslaw, and while no station was marked—an oversight I intended to inform Ordnance Survey about—a Station Road was clearly marked next to the station.

The train had pulled into Endslaw on time at 19:59; the woman in the grey coat had been sitting in the waiting room, so I had picked up my bag and alighted from the train.

"But I've just gotten off the train."

"No train has ever stopped here; only people stop here."

"I don't understand. How could I have gotten off the train if it didn't stop here?"

"You wanted to get off the train."

"Yes, but – "

"You wanted to get off the train, so you did."

For a crazy moment, I felt like I had stepped into an episode of *The League of Gentlemen*. I half-expected to see a sign or for the woman to say, 'Welcome to Endslaw—

you'll never leave!' "Who are you?" I asked her. "Why do you wait here?"

"I am waiting for my train."

I did not point out that she had just told me no trains stopped here, that she had told me this despite my stepping off a recently arrived train. Instead, I fished inside my bag for my mobile phone, intent on calling National Rail Enquiries. I did not need to call them (I knew the next train was in half an hour's time); nevertheless, I was less sure of myself than before, less certain that I knew the timetable by rote, despite the frequency with which I traveled. I found my phone buried under some paperwork.

There was no signal—typical! I stepped out onto the platform and walked its length, hoping for at least some signal pickup. There was none.

Suddenly, I realized there was only the one platform at Endslaw. On this stretch of track there would normally be two lines running through the station, and West- and Eastbound platforms. It was not unheard of for there to be only one line running through a Yorkshire station, but it was definitely unusual.

Giving up on my phone, I replaced it in my bag and walked back to the waiting room.

The woman had gone. I had neither seen nor heard her leaving. Although intrigued by the woman's disappearance, I decided to head home.

I looked at my watch: it was 20:28. Where had the time gone? The next train was due in a minute, and as I had not heard any delayed arrival announcements, I presumed it would be on time. Indeed, I could hear the rumble of train on tracks.

I looked along the platform. In the distance, a train was slowing. As it was summer, the light of the sun was still bright. The train's headlights were off. As it neared the platform, I wondered where the woman had gone, and if she would be here the following evening. The train drew level with the platform, and I thought about why she had insisted that trains never stopped at the station yet had added, enigmatically, that she was waiting for her train.

Absently, as the train came to a stop, I reached for the *Door Open* button, reflecting again on the conductor's assertion that the train did not stop at Endslaw. As I somehow slipped through the train and stumbled onto the line below, I wondered, with some amusement, how he could have thought that there was no station at Endslaw, when here I was standing on the platform. Even as my head connected with the steel track below the train, I thought, *how could you miss something for so long?*

* * *

I regained consciousness to find I was lying on the edge of the platform. Unsure how I had managed to climb back up, or even if I had fallen off to begin with, I stood up, rubbing at a sore spot where I appeared to have banged my head.

I wandered over to the waiting room, thinking that, although the woman in the grey coat had disappeared, she might have returned, or perhaps some other enigmatic stranger had taken her place. The waiting room was empty. Strangely, my bag was on the seat where I had seen the woman. Picking it up, I returned to the platform's edge.

Had I really fallen straight through a train like some insubstantial being? If so, who or what had lifted me back onto the platform? Had I, in a daze, clambered back up? As an unmistakable sound impinged my perception, I realized I would not have long to wait for an answer to the first question.

Another train was approaching the platform.

Well, at least, I could hear another train approaching. I could not see it yet. The volume increased and, as it did, I realized with some surprise that it sounded remarkably like a steam train. I squinted my eyes and tried to focus on the distance. (It sounds nearer!) Still I could not see any train. I looked both ways along the track but still saw no sign of it. In fact, the chug-chug-chugging was slowing, as if the train were near the platform.

Like some crazy cartoon character, I closed and rubbed my eyes, hoping that this would enable me to see the train I could hear. All I could see, as the chugging stopped, were empty tracks. I half-expected somebody to step onto the platform from mid-air. *All aboard the invisible train*, I thought witlessly.

I reached out, trying to touch what was not there and felt…something. Not the hard metal of an old steam train, but a presence all the same. It was a cold sensation, like a shiver. I snatched my hand back.

The sound of a whistle jolted me back to whatever reality I had left, followed by a barely audible cry of "All aboard!" The train I could not see began to chug away from the station. I knew at that moment that I had not imagined falling through the first train. Like the phantom steam train pulling away into the encroaching night, it simply was not there.

* * *

Miranda used to tell me I had hyper-selective perception. If my nose was in book, or I was watching TV or playing a videogame, she could scream bloody murder or shout "Fire! Fire!" and I would merrily ignore her. Often times this trait amused Miranda; others it annoyed the hell out of her.

I did not do it consciously. Rather, I seemed unable to widen my focus. Concentrating on one task, I excluded other matters, with apparent disregard for their importance. Miranda, whose aptitude for juggling multiple tasks was towering, used to warn me, in that viciously humorous tone of hers, that one day I would be caught rubber-necking some young thing in a summer dress and walk into a lamppost, or something more terminal, such as a car. I would usually laugh at this and say something corny like I only had eyes for her, at which point she would pretend to stick two fingers down her throat and gag.

I remember one night, after Miranda had gone to bed, staying up to watch some scary zombie movie on TV. An hour or so into the film, I felt something cold touch my shoulder. I leapt off the sofa in terror.

"I thought you were asleep," she had said, laughing as I clutched my chest and tried to calm my breathing.

"I was engrossed—I thought *you* were asleep," I responded.

"I woke up and was thirsty. I was heading to the kitchen to get some water and saw you lying on the couch. I didn't want you to get a stiff neck." She was struggling to contain her amusement but, by then, I was laughing too. I must have cut an absurd figure hopping off the couch at her gentle touch. That's selective perception for you.

I remembered this as darkness finally arrived at Endslaw train station. The dim lights of a third train had passed through by this point; the train had been a new one, built to take advantage of electrical overheads, but its appearance on this line was no less a curio than the steam train that had passed before. This stretch of line, indeed the line in its entirety across the Pennines, was not yet electrified. This no longer seemed an important consideration.

I knew that low-wattage lighting or failing electricity did not cause the dimness of the train. The train was a lucent ghost in appearance and voice. It approached, stopped and exited the station sounding like a record spinning on a powerless turntable, its resonance lost and tinny in the night air. Its whole existence, like memory, was ethereal.

After the third train passed through, I tried to leave the station on foot. I walked off the platform on to what I assumed was Station Road. A couple of hundred yards down the tree-lined road, it curved to the right. As I rounded the bend, I saw I was approaching Endslaw train station on the left once again. Performing a swift one-eighty, I retraced my steps to the station I had left a few moments before.

I continued past the station, following the road as it curved to the left. On my right, I saw Endslaw train station again. I hurried past as Station Road again banked to the left. It was quite dark by now, the trees blocking off what little twilight there was. I broke into a trot, following the road as it continued to bank to the left. On my right, once more, was Endslaw station. I ran, sprinted, as the road ever more banked to the left and Endslaw train station appeared to my right. I thought of turning one-eighty again and running the other way but realized there was no point. I was not getting anywhere; I was running in circles.

I walked onto the platform at Endslaw station and saw my bag leaning up against the platform wall. Seizing it, I ran swiftly out of the station, down Station Road, into the next station, threw my bag into the waiting room and sprinted out onto the road again, hoping that when I arrived back at the station, it would not be where I had tossed it.

The bag was in the waiting room.

After this experiment, I half-heartedly tried running along the train tracks, but as soon as the line curved through the trees, I found myself running back towards the station. I did not bother running in the other direction—the outcome seemed inevitable—so I climbed back onto the platform and returned to the waiting room.

I pulled my jacket out of the bag for warmth and, lying down on the hard bench, told myself it would all be fine in the morning.

* * *

A corpse-cold hand shocked me awake.

"Miri," I gasped, but the hand belonged to a woman in a grey coat.

"I am not she," she said, taking her usual seat.

"What time is it?" I wondered aloud.

"It is twenty to eight."

I stood up, trying to stretch some life into my body. The sun was beginning to dip. "You mean in the evening! How long have I slept?"

"I do not know."

"Where did you go last night? What is this place? Why can't I leave here?"

"I caught a train. This is Endslaw station. You leave when your train arrives."

"You're very succinct. Can't you elaborate? Trains—at least real trains—do not stop here. You said that much yourself last night."

"I cannot elaborate."

"You cannot or you will not?"

"I cannot."

"You mean you don't know."

"That is correct," she said. "Each night I catch the first train I can and hope it is the right one."

"But it brings you back here?"

"I have not caught the correct train."

"How will you know when you've caught the right train?"

"I will have moved on."

"How long have you been returning to this place?"

"I cannot recall. I know only that it is a long time."

The dialogue of questions and ever-more enigmatic answers was interrupted by the shriek of train brakes. The 19:59 had arrived. "Is this my train? Is this my train?" I was almost giddy.

I grabbed my bag and ran out to the platform. I stabbed at the *Door Open* button on the train but kept missing. My hand swept through it. I looked through the window and saw the faces of commuters I had seen every day for the past twelve months: Jane Smith from Calderton, John Smith from Rochdale. I kept trying to hit the button even as I realized that this was not my train anymore. Even if I could get back on, I knew that it would only bring me back to Endslaw.

I returned to the waiting room, where the woman in the grey coat had remained. "Did you ever try to get back on the train that left you here?" I asked her.

"I did," she replied, "and like all the others, it brought me back here."

"How do you get on the trains that stop here? Some of them seem barely even to exist."

"You've got to want to board them. You've got to want to move on. Even that hasn't been enough for me. But I try; every day I try to board a different train, hoping that it takes me home, or someplace else, someplace new." She stood up. "I hear a train now."

I heard nothing but watched her as she walked out to the platform's edge. She waited patiently. I still saw or heard nothing of the train. She turned to me and smiled, a dark sad smile for her dark sad eyes, and I was filled with an unbearable urge to follow her, as I had been drawn to this station, to see where her train would take her. Before I could act, she stepped up an unseen step to board an unseen train and disappeared into the twilight, and I knew that this was not my train.

* * *

That was forty minutes ago. It is getting darker now, but I have seen more trains in those forty minutes than in the corresponding time period yesterday (I saw a faint ghost of the steam train this evening—is my awareness growing?) I say 'yesterday,' but frankly I am not sure how time works in this place. There seems only to be one place for me: this station and the road or track that leads to it. Is there likewise only one time for me: the twilight of the day? I went to sleep last night as the sun had set and woke to find it setting. Perhaps every night has been like that for me since Miranda died.

At first, when I realized that the conductor had been right all along, I wondered how come I had never noticed that Endslaw was not read out when the announcers listed all stations the service stopped at. They could not have used the shorthand 'calling all stations' on every announcement. I realized that I had not missed it, that Endslaw station had never been on any planned timetable of stations on any train journey I had taken; it was just there—a place to be, a time to be.

The woman in the grey coat was probably like me once: some thin specter of a being gazing out of a train window, searching for empathy, perhaps searching for love. I wonder if I shall see her again tomorrow, and whether we really are doomed to this phantom existence, waiting for the right train to take us home and to stop us missing those important connections. I wonder if I should go sit in the waiting room and rest my head for a while—instead of standing on the platform at Endslaw, watching the ghosts of trains pass by.

# FRONTIER FAITHS
### *By Henry Myllylä*

Pastor Francois stares at the funereal passage of a shrouded figure beyond the trees down a rocky hillside. Starving and weak, he'd cry for its attention unless he'd know it as a sinister apparition of the woods.

Francois turns around and starts to follow his own footsteps on a thin, crunching frost. Walking across a little clearing, he imagines the backward prints leading him to anyplace else. Perhaps undoing the stains of their transgression.

Woods thicken at the end of the clearing and roots sprawl like snakes around his feet. Trying to keep his balance, his crude steps are like those of a poor blind man navigating the alleyways of the city. Last night his smallest toes felt as if roasting in a fire. Now they are but a senseless lumps of flesh in his deerskin moccasins. Limping forwards, he pulls his hands deeper into his greatcoat's sleeves and pumps his fists back and forth. His palms and fingers meet like dead lovers in embrace. He could already hear the coarse breath of young Jones from beyond the wooded, downhill passage.

Lying in an almost fetal position, covered in blankets about the tree, Jones' breath is but a thin vapor escaping from under the black hood. As Francois kneels before him and moves the hood aside, Jones' restful face explodes into a frightened grin.

"Just me." Francois brushes his palm across Jones' brow, where sweat has iced into shining pearls about his hairline. Open wound on Jones' lower lip is black. A grave unwilling to seal.

"I thought-" Jones shivers and pulls his form tighter in. His eyes go across treetops and his voice is weak. "It's you." He smiles, now focusing on Francois' face again. He turns a little and gropes the air between them with a feeble motion of his fingers.

Francois takes the cold hand into his and prays in his mind for some warmth, some mercy into the young man's demise. There's still soft youth left in Jones' cold eaten skin. "Keep with us. We'll get you away, son."

Jones turns his head to see their surroundings. His eyes stay in the uphill terrain where increasing boulders and scarcer forest gives way to the pale daylight.

It is the direction where Billy Worrington, the veteran mountain man and the only other soul left of their group, had left at the break of dawn to scout the surrounding area and, if God willed, find something to eat.

Jones' cold fingers convulse against Francois' palms, digging into their skin. "Don't let him-" Jones' eyes break into tears. "Don't, please, I'm begging you." Spit drips from his teeth, flies across his round cheeks and forms glimmering strings between his tattered lips.

"Hush, son. Hush." Francois seals Jones' trembling lips with his finger, feeling the warmth of saliva on his skin. Jones' eyes quiver in terror that Francois feels in his stomach. He utters a wordless prayer to eradicate the stains inside his mouth and bowels. "It won't happen again. I swear."

"Just… bury me whole." Jones speaks in a voice that shatters Francois' heart. Haunts him like a ghost. "Whole." Jones' eyes turn up, reflecting the dark shards of treetops on their blacks. Then he closes his eyes and falls into a sleep.

Francois pulls the hood back over his face and tightens the jacket and thick wool blanket to cover him. Jones hunches like a wounded animal under covers.

Francois stands up. The little droplets of Jones' spit have turned cold on his skin. Wind howls in the trees and a little breeze gnaws his bones. Something snaps. He turns around and looks towards the frozen uphill ravines. *Billy?*

Frozen torpor of the landscape remains unchanged. He bends his knees, sure of hearing something else than his own thoughts or the thin breaths of Jones lying beside him. Another creak sounds from afar. Merely as an echo past the trees. Francois turns around. Facing the encampment again, he realizes the black eyes on him.

It is Joshua, who is looking down at his hunched, barely living brother with soulless eyes. He is completely naked, his pale, rot patched skin a ghostly canvas surrounding his black eyes.

Francois gasps. Breath escapes his grinning lips in strangled clouds.

Joshua raises his chin, opens his posture against the wood behind his back, his toes crawling through the frost like vermin escaping a fire.

"Go back!" Francois spits, his eyes wide in panic. "G-! Leave us, you-. Be gone!" Francois barks with burning lungs.

Joshua's stomach pulls in and his abdominal skin tightens against the ribcage shielding his rotten heart. He slides his hand across his chest, traces his neck with his palm all the way up to his forehead. His black eyes stare at Francois like zenith suns as he lets out a monstrous gasp. Thin lips pull back, revealing a broken pit edged with fangs. With a ferocious gnarl, like a joint separating from a bone, his teeth bite his own arm, sending clotted, dirty blood pouring down across his ghost.

Francois falls to his knees. "We had no choice!" His eyes tear up. He is lying and would do anything to die without blame like Jones. With a glint of redemption in his heart. His stomach burns and he tastes the bitter iron of Joshua's blood and sinewy, cold strips of his inner thighs and calf again on his tongue. He gasps, coughs and bends down crying and purges the bitter emptiness of his stomach into his throat in violent spasms. His very own tongue, that sick, abominable, stained worm should burn. Be cut and not given a single more word to defile. Francois turns aside the hem of his greatcoat and reaches to his belt, grasps the carven bone hilt and pulls out his blade. Through his tears, he sees Joshua's swollen tongue licking the clotted blood that, being dead for a week, doesn't steam nor run, but reaches out of the boiling tatters like black, thick poison.

Francois spits towards Joshua's black eyed, bloodied countenance and raises the blade to his own eye level and presses the cold steel against his own eyelid. The blade shakes in his hand and cuts his cheek. The pain clears his senses for the moment. It is better to go down into a grave muted forever. Bound to deafness with bleeding temples and burning coals for eyes than to be dragged into Hell with one's ghost. His chest burns. Everything is quiet. He steadies the shaking blade, places the tip straight under his right eye and aims towards the socket's deep end. He exhales, lets the avalanche of inner pain pour past his throat. He prepares and gasps. But then a sharp strike sends the knife flying away from his hand.

Another strike blows Francois' right temple and bends his neck. The world blackens momentarily in his eyes. He finds himself from the ground, lying on his side, his temple against the cold ground.

The fur-bound boots step over him and Billy picks up the knife from the ground.

Looking at the blade and then at Francois, Billy lifts his shambled coat pieced together from thick blankets and puts the knife onto his belt. "What's gone into you, priest?"

Francois grins and shoots his head up from the ground. "You damned devil, you shouldn't-"

"Did what I had to." Billy's voice roars, "I shall live and not a priest nor a boy shall cross me!"

Jones lies underneath his covers, seemingly unknowing of the chaos surrounding him. Billy raises his fist at Francois. "Don't tell me you were not in it too, priest. Let me tell you, the winter doesn't care. Nor the mountains." Billy looks into the gloomy gray devouring the mountains beyond the trees, "You become the beast or the prey. You're gone the moment you flinch. Seen it before, seen it now." Billy steps closer to Francois and looks deep into his eyes. His voice is now nearly a whisper. "There's no one to judge. No one cares. Get your head together 'cause the mountains don't ask."

The side of Francois' face hurts in warm waves that remind him of his still beating heart. He sucks the curse from his lips back into his lungs, rises to a sitting position and tries his temple with his hand. His brow is wet and his fingers redden upon touching the searing spot. Keeping his silence, Francois presses his sleeve over the wound. Pain sears past his head all the way to his neck. His jaw aches. He'd never been hit before, nor really brawled; always intended to use his head for things other than stopping blows.

"It's nothing." Billy grins. "Only the living suffers."

* * *

This wasn't the first time Billy was in trouble. Neither was it the last. He'd go out of this world kicking and wasn't gonna admit that he was done. His last shuteye was gonna be his last. Simple as that.

He'd seen men better than him fall in the mountains. Shattering either their bodies or their minds. Those stories made no glory tales.

Bears survived until they didn't. So it was with the other beasts. They don't make a mess of it when things go wrong. Neither did he. The priest is about to lose his mind, so the punch better make him regain his grit. And that young man Jones… They'd soon figure a way to deal with him.

It wasn't gonna look good, Billy admits. But here. Lost. Five weeks since the last known trail and winter breaching in on them. No one is watching. No one cares.

Before arriving back at the temporary encampment and finding the priest crying with his blade drawn out, Billy had taken a few hours to explore the area. He trekked beyond the tree line to the highest possible point and stopped. The landscape continued in rocky ranges of barren tops and forested bottoms against the dismal sky, bloated under the coming winter's weight. The expedition was lost. Utterly so.

Their food was spoiled the moment they entered the trail. The heavens hung low and mountainous passages came out of the mist as if from some godforsaken netherworld. Even the roots and the smallest game seemed vanished, devoured into the bowels of the earth.

Billy heard the laughter of his boys in his mind and he saw his wife chopping wood in front of the terrace. Isaac knew the wilderness already, but would he pass it on to little Abel? The ways of the game and trails. All the lessons that could prove too harsh to learn by mistake if approached without one's smarts. Without one's grit.

He looked at the narrow, wooded passage in the horizon that they passed two weeks ago. Still then sure about the waters of this valley able to provide them with fish and a place to camp before advancing farther.

But things got worse fast. He'd thought the brothers Joshua and Jones were fit for the trial. The priest sound of mind. But he was proven very wrong when the hunger and cold got to their heels. He flinched at the thought of the day Jones would surely avenge his brother, if he ever gain his feet back from the frost. But as swollen as they were, he doubted it. The brothers were gone; the one about to follow the other soon.

He rubbed his hands against each other and blew into them, simulating the warmth of Joshua's steaming innards. Jones shouldn't have refused his brother. The priest was wiser.

Billy's mind wandered about Joshua's opened cavities as he heard the priest's screams through the woods. He turned and began to advance back towards the lower grounds, steadying his hand to his knife. That's when he found the priest battling the loss of his reason. That's when he knew he was about to go on alone.

* * *

Francois and Billy drag Jones on a blanket through the downhill ravines until they reach the rocky, inland riverbank. In front of them, the river runs black and silent towards the mountains, snaking past choking holds of tentacled roots.

Billy kneels by the water and cups his hands. Dipping them into the flow, he raises some to his face and reads the dark gush with his eyes. Behind him, Francois moves the covers aside from Jones' feet and grasps his boot. "Hold still. I need to check."

Jones whimpers as Francois pulls the boot off and reveals the swollen foot. The inflamed skin is blue and black around the toes, the gaps between them already melted into cadaverous orifices.

"It's bad, ain't it?" Jones' voice wavers from under his hood.

Francois pulls on the second boot with both hands. It falls off, scalping away most of the swollen flesh, leaving mere wet, blackened tatters to cover the bones below the ankle. Francois gasps, fighting the rancid, thick sweetness in the air. His eyes wet and he looks at Jones, whose desperate eyes don't want him to say anything.

Jones turns to look at Billy who is still kneeling by the river.

*Whole*, Francois reads a wordless prayer from Jones' shivering lips.

*Whole.*

Billy stands up in a quick leap and turns around. The hem of his coat turns aside from his belt in a single sweep as he nears Jones. He drops to his knees by Jones' head, grasps the hood and pulls it all the way across his face.

Blindfolded and pinned down against the bare rock, weak Jones struggles to free himself but Billy, controlling his covered face with the full force of his upper body, makes the struggle futile. Billy pulls the rest of the covers off from Jones with his other hand, revealing his chest. Then Billy reaches for his belt and pulls the knife out.

Billy stabs. Once, then twice in a row. Then he speeds up, stabs the gasping chest in continuous, swift motion. Jones' screams transform into a muffled, wet gurgle and his struggling arms are but mindless, shaking twigs.

Billy goes on, non-stop, relentless. Jones' chest collapses like a blood-drenched rooftop and his throat spasms under the hood. Billy stops. He grins and takes a long, exploding breath through his nostrils. He pulls his hand away from Jones' face and lets it fall to its side. Billy passes the knife to his other hand, lowers a little to gather his momentum and stabs again. He continues with full force until the knife scratches against the rock under the blood-spurting, nearly decapitated neck multiple times in a row. He stops, looks at the mangled pit of Jones' neck, grasps the hilt with both hands and strikes the knife into the middle of the mutilated chest, leaving it standing there.

"Sons for sons." Billy straightens his posture and turns his blood-sprinkled eyes on Francois. "Them-" he gasps and wipes his bloodied face on his sleeve, "for mine."

Francois struggles to breathe and drops the boot from his hands. Sitting on his knees by Jones' legs, he feels warm rivulets running past his face as Jones' splattered blood pools on his brow and descends down his nose.

The blood forms rivers in crevasses of rocks and little lakes in cracked hollows, still gushing from the human ruins. Francois hears three shallow, mechanical gasps sounding from the chest.

"I met the Devil once." Billy's eyes are nearly black from the blood. As he blinks, the red shifts. Paints strange art on their whites before settling underneath the lids again. "He said there's two things he'd come to take from me, while giving some in return. It left me wondering for a long time. I had no two things that mattered. Years passed and I was still young in those days. But the day my second son was born, it all changed."

Francois stutters, choking on the simple words, "Why … But, Jones?" He looks at the desolate remains between them.

"Go and see for yourself, priest." Billy looks towards the river. "See for yourself."

Francois pushes himself up. Balancing on his trembling knees, he meets his own reflection in the black water. Billy appears in the reflection beside him. Francois' heart fights against his throat. He closes his eyes. Prays this nightmare to end.

"Look deeper," Billy's voice commands Francois out of his inner darkness. He looks into the black eyes of Billy's reflection. They glimmer. There's a star, a slight sparkle in the reflection. A group of them in the black distance. Little, wavering stars. Multiplying, more and more the longer he looks into the water.

Billy kneels and merges his hands under the water. He pulls out watery handfuls of sparkling, shimmering rough and begins to laugh. The black depth sparkles. Wherever Francois looks at the riverbank, it is but an expanse of stars spreading across the riverbed like the veins of the earth itself were bleeding.

Billy smiles. "Priest, this is heaven on earth."

* * *

Francois leaves as Billy immerses himself in the study of golden nuggets. After a ravine-spoiled thicket, the river takes a turn. The rocky bank widens, escorting this black serpent into the gray distance. He rubs his palms together, trying to detach the clotted, deep filth on their burrows, but it only seeps deeper into his skin.

He kneels by the water that licks his hands in cold, razor-like tongues. He rubs and rubs. The serene cold makes his forearms spasm and he bends further down and sinks his face into the water, feeling his skin tightening in the paralyzing stream.

Francois keeps his eyes closed and stands up. Apart from his face, his whole being is weighted by itching bitterness. Thick filth, worms. Flies spawning in his tendons, nesting under his skin in bloated vestiges they'd eaten. He hears their wings rustling in his head, in the hives of his bones.

He opens his eyes and spots a glimmer in the depth on the further side of the river. A marbled shade under the water becoming corporeal as it approaches the surface.

Soon a black, cloaked form crawls up from the water to the opposite bank. In spider-like steps, it turns around and the black robe shifts. Pale, marbled thighs open and reveal a bloodied vulva from beneath the black garment dripping with water.

Francois stares in awe as the thing trembles and screams out an animal wail. Its legs reach out, toes raking the stones as the vulva stretches and opens wide like a bloodshot eye. Then, like ravenous dogs, something emerges from the bleeding mass and flesh separates from flesh. Hands and legs and a head, a complete shape births from the dark membrane over the black, wet hems.

Sour iron taste burns the back of Francois' throat at the sight of the being rising to its two feet and rubbing the tattered, bloody clots on its skin. Violent spasms of revulsion run through Francois' legs and grind his waist in searing beats. He falls down, bows towards the form and gasps in pain. The burning sensation boils in his stomach, radiates across the tip of his penis, which he begins to rub and claw, gasping for air. The stronger he claws himself, trying to reach the middle of his insides, the lesser he hurts. Going deeper, trying to choke the fire burning his insides, he grasps his testicles, thrusts his claws to their roots and pulls. The tissue rips in a frantic surge that sends a fiery wave through his whole body. He falls onto his face against the rocks and smiles. There is a moment of silence. Then darkness covers everything in his sight.

* * *

As Francois returns, nearly crawling past the ravines, his other eye is swollen shut and filled with dirt.

"What's with you?" Billy shakes his head, his hand fidgeting with a piece of gold he had put into his pocket.

Francois smiles at him, blood still dripping inside his pants. "Gonna take you home to your boys." Then he kneels by Jones' brutalized remains and sighs. All the blood, peeled skin and shredded tissue is now at rest. Frozen. Jones' eyes stare into the distance like smoky pearls. Francois covers him, grasps the blanket and pulls.

For a moment, Billy seems like he is about to intervene, but doesn't. Instead, he remains still, fidgets with his gold pieces and looks to the side as Francois pulls the covered remains to the bank and pushes them into the water.

After Jones' dark shape has sailed out of their sight, Francois gestures with his head towards the way he came. "Come."

He leads Billy to the widening riverbank; this time not looking at the other side, but keeping his pace towards the upper stream. His groins have stopped bleeding and there's but a numb pulse and little warmth between his legs. He puts his hand into his pocket, pulls out two soft, bloody pieces and fidgets with them. If he didn't know better, he could have mistaken them for boiled eyes.

It is no good for two boys to grow without a father. Nor a man to walk without a cause. Francois smiles at the endless river and reaches his open palm towards Billy.

Billy looks at the offerings in awe.

"You must eat." Francois offers them to Billy's face. "It's a long way home."

Billy had a chance if he'd ration himself sparingly. He had to stay fresh and walking. Unfortunately, it meant that Billy would have to get by with all the little outer parts first. Toes, nose, fingers and ears. After those, he'd gradually offer his better parts.

# YOU NEVER CAN TELL
### *By Matt Bliss*

Anthony didn't care what his friends and family thought; he knew that Alyona was the one. From all the late night chatting online, Anthony knew she wasn't just using him for a green card; he was confident that she truly loved him.

The polished airport floors reflected the red arrangement of roses that Anthony held cradled in his arms. He did his best to suck in the belly that hung below his belt buckle, but soon put the worry from his thoughts. Alyona saw the pictures he sent. In fact, she often replied with a smattering of kissy face and heart emojis. Unlike the other girls he tried to win over, Alyona loved him for who he was and, for whatever reason, didn't seem to mind his receding hairline or hefty gut.

His heart fluttered at the sight of her coming down the escalator. Not only did she look *exactly* like her pictures, but she was also the embodiment of Anthony's *perfect woman*. The corners of her ruby red lips turned up in a smile when she spotted Anthony waiting for her.

She glided toward him across the terminal on long pale legs. Anthony felt the only thing keeping him from floating away were the roses he held toward her as she approached.

Alyona pushed the flowers aside and pressed her body to his without a word. He squeezed her tight and buried his face in her hair. Instead of the perfumed aroma he dreamed she would smell of, he was greeted with the musk of many hours spent traveling halfway across the world.

"You made it! You're finally here! I... I can't believe it," Anthony gawked at the woman with glistening eyes.

"Yes," she said with an impassive face, "I am here now. Let us go."

Anthony took her luggage, placed a heavy arm around her small frame, and escorted her to the car thinking, *how could I be so lucky?*

* * *

When they arrived at the large, two-story Colonial, Anthony held out his arm in the grand gesture of performing a magic trick.

"Welcome, to your new home," he said with a great smile.

Alyona breezed right past the man on her way to the front door with hardly a glance up. Wrestling with her bags, Anthony hurried to the door to unlock it.

He was so excited he couldn't find the proper key even though it was the same key he used every day. He flipped the *jingling* loop of keys over a second time when he heard the soft pattering of steps behind him. Alyona let out a quick snort and grabbed Anthony's arm. The neighbor's dog came trotting up to the two of them.

"Baxter!" Anthony said, squatting down to pet the floppy eared lab. "You got out again, eh bud?" He patted the pup before looking at Alyona's furrowed brow and tight lips. "It's okay," he said in a calming tone, "he's just a dog. You know…*Dooooggg*." He stretched the word out as if it would make it easier on her.

Alyona moved toward it when Chris, his neighbor, ran up the walkway. "Sorry, Anthony," he said through short heavy breaths. "I don't know how he keeps getting out."

"It's okay; you know he always just ends up here. Ain't that right Baxter?" He pet the dog in a flurry of drool and hair. Alyona watched with flared nostrils and wide eyes. She didn't relax until Chris fixed the leash and waddled around the corner out of sight.

The front door opened to reveal the trail of rose petals awaiting her arrival. Alyona wasted no time at all and grabbed Anthony by the collar with a look of fierce excitement in her eyes. She pulled him to the ground and kicked the door shut. Her hands ripped at his shirt until it hung from his soft chubby body in shreds.

This was quite the change from the quiet girl on the car ride over. For Anthony, it was like a dream come true. He dreamed of the moment he and Alyona could be together and make love for the first time. Only, he didn't expect it to happen so soon or with such a rabid *ferociousness*.

She clawed her nails at his thick torso with grunts of excitement. She mounted him with enough force to bruise his hipbones. Anthony fell into a whirlwind of pleasure and pain that left him bloodied and speechless. It was just what he wanted. A young, beautiful woman that wanted *him* the way he was.

* * *

Anthony kissed Alyona on the forehead before leaving for work the next morning while she was busy eating whatever she could get her hands on. Her lips, still ruby red, seemed to pull back around her teeth as her jaw opened big enough to fit an entire rack of ribs inside. Anthony watched in astonishment as she polished off most of everything in the fridge.

"Wow, you almost eat more than me!" he tried to joke. "Make yourself at home, honey. I'll be home from work before you know it."

After a short car ride, Anthony opened his crowded mattress store and stood out front to catch Morris, the owner of the neighboring barbershop, in their usual morning routine. Over the years, the two friends would lean against the cinderblock wall between their shops and talk until a customer arrived.

"It was amazing!" Anthony later told his friend. "She just attacked me like some sort of...*animal*!"

Morris raised an eyebrow. "That's great and all Tony, but you don't find it a bit *odd*?"

"What do you mean?"

"I mean," Morris stepped closer, speaking in hushed tone, "she's half your age for Christ sake...Let's face it; her home country is going through some shit right now; I've seen it on the news. You don't think she *might* have something else in mind by coming here?"

Anthony let out a sigh and shook his head. "Not this again. You don't know her like I know her. Just look at this." He pulled the collar of his shirt aside to show the deep bite marks in his shoulder. "My back is covered in 'em. She had this...*raw* sexual energy—and it was all her, not me! Why would someone who was just trying to get a *green card* fake *that*?"

"I'm just sayin' that it seems a bit odd that someone who looks like *her*, would go for a guy like..." he waved a hand to Anthony, eyes tracing him top to bottom, "well... *you.*"

"Watch it Morris—"

"I don't mean nothing by it Tony! We've been friends for a long time; I'm just lookin' out for ya. I'm the last person who wants to see you hurt, okay?"

Anthony eased back. "I appreciate it, but it's not like that. Why don't you and Vicky come over for dinner tonight to meet her? You'll see it's not like that."

Morris smiled, "Alright sure, why not? Hell, even if she is a blood sucking beast trying to get after my best friend, I figure I better take a look and see for myself!"

They smiled and slapped each other on the back before leaning against the wall, and waiting.

* * *

Alyona wolfed down her food like it was her last. She cleared her plate almost before the others had a chance to start. Morris and his wife stared in shock that *they too* might get eaten if they got too close. Anthony however was awestruck. *His girl* could keep up with his large appetite, and still looked pencil thin.

"So Alyona," Morris said to the woman licking her plate, "Tell us about your home country."

She dropped the plate and fixed her sharp eyes on him without a word. All eyes watched her, but she didn't answer. Morris and his wife squirmed in the uncomfortable silence, trading awkward glances.

"Uh…she doesn't really like talking about her homeland you see…" Anthony answered for her. "Things are not the best there right now." He smiled, trying to ease the tension while placing a hand on her stiff back.

Morris and Vicky turned back to moving around the food on their plates.

Alyona grunted across the table at them, "Why do you ask this?" She held the seething stare on the couple.

"Just uh…making conversation is all." Morris grabbed his wine glass and downed it in one gulp.

"Is there something that worries you?" she asked.

Morris squinted his eyes at the woman for a moment before answering. "Well now that you mention it—"

"Morris!" his wife interrupted.

Anthony shot him a look to say, *don't you dare,* before trying to change the subject. "Come on guys, drop it."

"So what *worries* me," Morris continued, "is why someone like *you,* would come to *my country*, to be with *my friend.* I worry that there might be an *ulterior motive* here." He leaned back in his chair, as the others waited to exhale. "So Alyona, tell me, why *did* you come here anyways?"

Anthony could feel the woman's tense body start to tremble. All at once, Alyona *popped* up, knocking her chair to the floor before she jumped on the table with a growl and exposed teeth. Morris' eyes went wide as she sprinted across the table in a clatter of dinnerware and jumped at Morris with her nails curled into bony hooks.

Vicky screamed as Morris brought his arms up to block the savage woman. He held his forearms in a cross over his face as Alyona fell on top him. Growls and screams erupted as her teeth sunk into his forearm and pulled away, tearing away a large chunk of flesh.

Morris gasped in shock as Anthony ran at her from behind and grabbed her in a bear hug. He lifted her thin frame easily while she kicked and snarled.

Morris staggered back until he pressed against the wall. The hole in his arm oozed crimson blood onto the floor. "She bit me! The bitch fuckin' bit me!" His other hand held the wound while Vicky ran to his side.

"Let's go, Morris," she squeaked, clearly frightened by the woman flailing in Anthony's grasp.

"You know what?" Morris said heading for the door, "I don't care anymore! Enjoy your freak show! *Crazy bitch!*"

The two pounded out, leaving a trail of red splotches in the carpet. Alyona eased up at their departure.

"What the hell was that?" Anthony said as he let go of her, "That was my best friend! I know what he said was wrong, but you attacked him!"

Alyona grabbed his face and kissed him, shutting him up in one swift move. Her lips were warm, and stained with Morris' blood. "Make love to me," she said, tearing off the man's shirt. "Now!" She threw him to the table that collapsed from his massive size in an explosion of splintered wood. She hissed and snarled, straddling him atop the pile of debris. Her nails carved deep lines in his chest while she slammed her hips into his, again and again. Once again—she was *rabid,* and once again—*Anthony was in ecstasy.*

* * *

When the friends crossed paths the next day, they pretended not to see one another and went about opening up their businesses. After a long awkward moment, Anthony looked over to see the bandage on Morris' arm. Guilt built up inside him at the sight of it, and Anthony decided to say something.

"Morris…I uh…wanted to say something to you," he began while rubbing the back of his neck.

Morris froze with his back turned.

"I'm sorry, for what happened. I know some things were said and—"

"Things were said?" Morris turned and shoved his bandaged arm in Anthony's face. "Fifteen stitches Tony! I had to get fifteen fuckin' stitches thanks to her! Not to mention the weird infection that came along with it. So yeah—I wouldn't say, *words were said,* I would say, *sorry the freak who is playing me for a green card bit you!"*

"You better not start that again! You do know that's why she did it right? Because of what you said. Talking like that, you deserve to get bit! Hell, I almost did it myself hearing you say it again!"

"Tony, you're my best friend; I'm not gonna sit by while some hussy—"

"Who cares, Morris? Who cares if that's what she's after? It's not your place! If you *truly* were my friend, you would support me! You would be happy that *I'm* happy! Because for the first time in my life, I am happy! But my friend is trying to ruin it for me. And if she *is* just using me for a green card, so what? I'll be the first to say you were right. But I don't think that's the case. Something *magical* is happening between us, and I just wish you could support me. So if you want me to feel bad about your arm, all I can say is that you deserved it!"

Anthony started back to his shop when his friend followed after.

"Wait!" Morris said letting out a sigh through the corner of his mouth. "Okay…you're right." He threw up his hands, showing his palms. "I'm sorry. I should've supported you but I just sorta gave you grief. I just didn't want to see you hurt. I'm sorry, I fucked up—I won't do it again, okay bud?"

"Okay, thank you."

He folded his arms, "I guess I owe Alyona an apology too."

Anthony shrugged and gestured to the bandage, "I'd say you're about even now."

"Once everything cools off with her, let me know. I'll swing by and apologize—maybe bring a gift or somethin'. That okay?"

"I think she'd like that. I'd like that," Anthony smiled in relief. "Thanks Morris, it means a lot to me."

The two men leaned back on the adjoining cinderblock wall, waiting for a customer that never came.

* * *

Anthony pulled up to his house like a kid on Christmas morning. Going home to Alyona was a gift, and making up with Morris somehow made it better. Anthony climbed out of his car wearing an eager grin when he saw his neighbor

Chris walking up to him. Anthony smiled and raised a hand to wave as he normally did, but this time Chris didn't return the gesture.

"How's it going, Chris? You okay?"

He walked over with eyes scanning the yard around him, unable to stay focused on one thing. "Have you seen Baxter? He's been gone all day. I can't seem to find him anywhere."

"No I can't say that I have, but I just got home. I'll ask Alyona; she's been home all day. Maybe she's seen him."

"Yeah, okay. It's just odd. I know he gets out a lot, but he usually comes right back or just heads to your house." Chris kept scanning in hopes of spotting the dog.

"I'm sure he'll come right back like always. If I see him, I'll let you know right away, okay?"

Chris nodded and proceeded up the street, whistling and clapping his hands between shouting the dog's name.

Anthony unlocked the door and stepped inside, still grinning at the thought of his woman waiting inside. The door creaked open to a cold darkness that lessened his smile. He turned an ear, listening for her, but only heard his own nasal breathing.

"Honey? Are you home?" He tilted his head to the muffled reply from the bedroom. He shook off his worry and threw his keys into the ceramic bowl on the entryway table. "Hey, have you seen Baxter today? I bumped into Chris and he said the dog got out again. I guess he's getting worried." Anthony slipped off his shoes and dragged his fingers along the textured drywall until finding the switch and flipping it.

He started toward the bedroom when he noticed the trail of muddy paw prints on the carpet. The sight stopped Anthony with a biting fear. "*Honey*?" he said again with a crack in his voice. The trail of paw prints led strait to the master bedroom. He followed along, eyes moving from one paw print to the next until they disappeared behind the closed door. He placed a hand on the doorknob and an ear to the door and listened. He heard the deep reverberation of a growl, one that sounded *painful*.

*Baxter!*

Without another thought, Anthony bust into the room. The small space was in complete disarray. Springs and stuffing spilled from deep gashes in the upturned mattress. The wooden dresser lay in a pile of splinters. Clothes, shredded to rags were scattered all over the room. He searched the mess that was his belongings when Alyona let out a series of high-pitched grunts from the attached bathroom.

Anthony walked to the open doorway and saw Alyona on the tile floor inside. She sat—knees propped up—one hand held the countertop—the other gripping the open toilet. She let out a deep howl while her face contorted in pain. Sweat beaded on her forehead as she shook with each pain-filled growl.

"Wha…what's going on?" Anthony said as he stepped over the empty dog collar, no longer thinking of Baxter. He moved closer, watching her distended belly protruding from her torn-up dress. Thick blue veins raised above her tight skin in a network of crevasses and valleys. Her round belly waved as something inside pushed against it.

Anthony's eyes bulged from his head as the room began to spin. "What's happening?" was all he could say.

Between fits of snarls and moans, Alyona's sharp eyes met his. "I am with child," she said before the movement in her stomach grew worse and her nails dug into the counter.

"That…can't be! It wasn't enough time! Unless…"

"It is yours," she said. "We will be family." Her ruby red lips turned up in a smile showing the points of her teeth.

*Family…* the word rang like a bell in his mind. It was everything he ever wanted, a family of his own—with the woman of his dreams. "*Family…*" he murmured aloud, liking the way the word felt in his mouth.

Alyona locked her eyes on his and echoed the word, "Yes, family!" Another wave of pain broke her away. Anthony felt her rumbling growl in his gut as she tensed up and spread her knees. He moved closer, unsure of what to do. He wondered if this was how all expecting fathers felt.

An explosion of green mucous shot out of her, painting the floor in its vibrant color. She howled in pain as a pale, curved surface began to push its way from between her legs. The large egg shot out of her in a network of green webs. Anthony hesitated before picking up the egg and cradling it in his arms. The shell was thin and soft, like warm leather.

Alyona began grunting again, as more eggs started firing out from between her legs in a lattice of green slime. After the sixth egg, Alyona curled herself around them and let out a soft *purring* sound. Each one pulsed with a heartbeat. Each one *breathed* with *life*.

Alyona looked up at Anthony, still holding the egg. "They will need food," she said.

"Food... yes," Anthony agreed.

"Something big, *fresh…*"

"Yes," he nodded, "*fresh…*"

Anthony watched Alyona run her fingers over the eggs while he pulled out his cellphone and dialed. "Morris? Hey, It's Tony. I was wondering if you still wanted to come by sometime soon? I have some people I want you to meet. *I want you to meet… my family!*"

Anthony grinned as he watched Alyona wrap her arms around the cluster of eggs on the bathroom floor and thought, *how could I be so lucky?*

# GLASS BODIED WOMAN
## *By Josh Darling*

On the corrugated metal steps, she locked the semi-truck's door and slammed it shut. She worried it would pop open after she got a few feet away. Climbing down the driver's side of the truck and into the night, she felt wet, filthy, and satisfied. Wet with sweat, filthy from the act, satisfied from her meal of dopamine. She pulled her skirt down, covering her panties. She couldn't afford getting picked up for indecent exposure. She didn't know how much time she had, but the impulse to fix again would be closing in.

She felt all the cars on the highway speeding by the truck stop in her system. She knew all the drivers and the passengers. She knew their thoughts. And, from the roar of the engines, she could tell their points of origin and their destinations.

That was the fleeting rush of escape.

Time was running out.

Feeling something cold, she touched the crotch of her panties and sniffed her fingers.

"That fucker came in me," she said to the parking lot full of trailer trucks.

It occurred to her someone might be waiting for her to get out of the truck. Truckers were assholes with hard-ons, dollars to spend, and crystal to snort. She'd already been through every crank-addicted shithead in her trailer park. Truckers were the only people she could think of with a ready supply of meth. Speed kept them awake for the two, three, four days of hauling. Starting here, in Dade City, Florida, and arriving in California, New York, Chicago, and other points unknown.

She knew the sexual side effects of speed too well.

Men got hard and stayed hard. It turned her on and dried her out. Making her want sex that let her down.

Feasting on it was amazing.

She checked the front of her red miniskirt for wet spots. She could get the stains out in seconds if she focused.

There were no faces in the darkened truck windows.

No one noticed.

She hungered for her next hit.

The urge was coming on faster.

Minutes ago, she felt good. She wondered how long she could stay stable.

She'd have to find another trick to fill the void or else she'd go to shit.

The Flying J Truck Stop was a series of divisions. There was a parking lot for truckers and a parking lot for regular folks, both coming off the highway for a break. It had pumps for diesel and pumps for gasoline. Inside the truck stop was a 24-hour half-diner/half-convenience store.

A hallway for bathrooms separated the diner from the convenience store. The whole hallway reeked of piss and urinal cakes.

If she couldn't find more crystal soon, she'd become unstable. Before she dropped out of high school, the school psychiatrist applied that term to her. She was "unstable, in both her home environment and mental health."

She wasn't hungry enough to eat other food, French fries, hamburgers, bologna sandwiches, microwavable pizza; but she starved in other ways.

Her luck in finding tricks was holding out in the convenience store. She didn't do anything lame like stand next to the condoms or bend over to pick stuff up. Truckers with wide bloodshot eyes and speed sweat on their brows were so horny she didn't bait them. They came to her.

Entering the store, the fat asshole behind the counter gave her a squint that whispered w*hore.*

She didn't care.

When a man says *whore* what he means is *I am jealous your pussy makes in a day what I make in a week.* It's why all strippers were *whores.*

Before she was a *whore,* she was a *slut,* or *I'm jealous of your ability to attract a bunch of sexual partners when I can't get one woman to fuck me.*

A Pabst would smooth things out and slow her destabilizing.

How much time did she have?

Her body demanded more.

Would she be able to keep her trail clean?

Steal a truck and drive, that's what she'd have to do. That's how she'd escape to the next lot. Could she stay normal and not freak out during the journey from point A to point B? Maybe she could do a little on the road, somehow saving some more for later. Her thinking was getting fucked and she had to–

"Hey, there," he said.

"Am I in your way, Sweetie?" She brushed her dyed ginger hair over her shoulder.

He was good-looking, mid-20s, blond, clean-shaven, white T-shirt. Country meat, he didn't come off as a trucker. The thin gold cross around his neck said pure apple pie and corn fed Christian boy. As her mom would say, *I wouldn't mind having his boots next to my bed.*

His head angled on the isle of chips.

"I wanted to ask you," his hands made slow circles in the air in front of him to coax the words out.

"You want a date?"

"Yes ma'am."

"You at the motel across the way? You ain't local."

"I've got my rig outside."

"You can't be a trucker, you look too-"

"Clean? I get that a lot. I'm Travis, by the way."

"Darla. So, what do you want to do to me?" Her drawl came on thick.

"I was thinking we could spend some time together in a religious way."

She chuckled, "That's one way to put it, you holding?"

"I mean my hands are empty."

"Got any weed, ecstasy, acid or downers, skag, roxi, Percocet, Methadone, Hydromorphone, morphine, oxy, laudanum, or crack, cocaine, crank, any kind of uppers really? I love speed, like dexies, Adderall, methylphenidate—that's the fancy name for Ritalin, all methamphetamines are good, but crystal is better. We can mix them and play baseball, I love baseball. But, you know, you got any *dope* in the grand definition of the word *dope?* Ain't nothing better than getting high while I suck you off at the same time and I'm a hundred times better at giving head when I'm lifted."

She had no idea if that last bit was true, but it always got her drugs.

"Wow, how do you know I'm not a cop?"

"I know the face of every pig in Dade City—all twelve of them. You got dope or what?"

"I got the straight dope."

"Twenty, it's more if you want to put it in my butt or jizz in me; that includes skeeting in my mouth. Cause when you finish, you want me to swallow." She stepped closer to him. "No cum dodging for Darla. Right, Daddy?"

With porn star doe eyes, she pushed the tip of her tongue out from between her lips.

He took a half step back.

She wondered if she'd spooked him. Coming on too strong scared off some guys. Other men didn't get she was hooking until she started rubbing against them and talking money.

He swallowed, "Let's go to my rig and we'll talk about what's in store for you."

"Get me a beer."

* * *

Standing next to his truck, she chugged the Pabst. Finishing, she burped and tossed the can under the truck.

The truck and trailer were white with blacked-out windows. A 6-inch cross was on the driver's side door. In black letters under it, *Jesus Christ is Lord in Heaven,* under that another cross.

"She's an old rig, but I bought her outright with a lot of hard work."

"I bet you did."

He climbed the steps, unlocked the door, opened it, then back down, allowing Darla's assent to the cab. Inside, she scooted to the passenger seat. On the dashboard were a Bible and an 8-inch tall agonized Jesus nailed to a cross. The handle was snapped off her door making getting out impossible. Travis got in, blocking the one escape route. Her hooker senses tingled with an *oh fuck* feeling.

He was a psycho and she'd let her guard down because he looked like someone she'd want to fuck. In her distress for drugs and sustenance she ignored anything that might be a red flag.

In the driver's seat, he locked his door.

He turned to her, "That was missing when I got the truck."

*Bullshit,* "You said you got meth?"

"I have something better."

*Like a 12-inch Bowie knife to skin me with.* "Better?"

"As I said, I have the straight dope, and that's the truth, the straight dope from the Lord."

She clutched the armrest. "Are you a serial killer?"

"What? No, when I said I wanted to talk to you about what's in store for you. I meant it. Darla, this isn't about matters of the flesh."

"Freaky shit costs more. If you want to pee on me, that's an extra twenty, and an extra forty for in my mouth. I'll poop on you, but I don't do people pooping on me."

"I want to take a moment to get freaky and tell you about my lord and personal savior, Jesus Christ."

She wondered if he was going to kill her in the name of god.

"If you don't want to get high and do sex to me, stop. I'll fuck you up if you think you're gonna hurt me."

"Give me five minutes and let me and Jesus change your life."

"Jesus was a bitch. Odin came back after being dead nine days from hanging on a tree. That's more hard-core than three days on a stick."

When one of her mother's boyfriends was released from prison, he was covered in Aryan Brotherhood tattoos. Watching daytime TV and freebasing crystal, he'd spout off about the Viking gods. He sounded like any other idiot Bible thumper.

"You believe in Odin?"

"I don't believe in anything. Mister, I'm asking nice, let me out."

"You know you have an eternal soul? And Jesus loves you and he died for you? Don't you want more from life than drugs and prostitution?"

"I enjoy drugs and I don't have no guilt about whoring. I know women are supposed to cry if they turn tricks, but I got a man's brain about it. When I get paid to fuck, I'm high-fiving myself. And I really like meth–"

"Which damages your brain and rots your teeth and your soul."

"Maybe, let me out, I'm starting to fiend."

"Don't you want freedom from your addiction? In Proverbs, it says a man without self-control is like a city broken into and left without walls."

"That's crazy; you can't break into a city. I ain't a man; I got tits, see?" She pulled down her tube top, exposing her breasts. "And I can't quit drugs, it's like they say in *Ultimate Fighting Championship,* 'Quitters never win and winners never quit.'"

He bowed his head away from her.

"You afraid of my titties? You can touch them if you like. You can even suck on them like you're thirsty for milk."

He shook his head, "I weep for you. In Leviticus, it tells us do not defile your daughter by making her a prostitute, or the land shall be filled with prostitution and wickedness."

"I don't think I can have kids, so don't worry about my daughters making a land of wickedness. But, if I did have daughters, and they was happy hooking, I'd be happy for them."

He gasped.

"What about disease? God created STDs to punish the sins of the flesh."

"I don't think I can get those. Some of the dicks I've seen looked like Freddy Krueger's face and I ain't got no itch."

"You don't get them because God has a special plan for you."

From her pelvis to her rib cage, nothingness consumed her guts. She wanted this to go easy, but she wouldn't be able to keep it together much longer.

"Cover yourself," he said.

"Either you let me go or you make me cover up. Look, they're so big I can get them in my mouth." She raised her breast to her lips and sucked her nipple. It popped out of her mouth with a wet kissing sound. "You ain't the slightest bit hard? I bet you're real big."

"You're acting crass and unladylike."

"Unladylike is for women owned by men, wives and shit. I don't want to be no lady. I ain't sure I'm a person, but it's gonna cost twenty dollars if we get our fuck on or not."

"I'm not joking, I don't want you going to hell and having your flesh roasting in a lake of fire for eternity. I beg of you, save yourself and repent. Beg His forgiveness and you will be forgiven."

"Screw this. Let me out."

"Salvation can be yours."

"What if I can't get saved? If I'm not human, I might not have a soul. What then, Mr. Smartguy?"

He wasn't high. She wasn't high.

Devouring him would be bland.

"That's nonsense and you know it, don't be afraid of the love of Jesus Christ."

The vacuum inside her tore in every direction. No matter how many different things she tried, only one thing stopped it.

Pulling the tube top down further, it hugged the middle of her waist. She got out of her seat and moved for him. Spreading her thighs over his lap, her skirt rode up. Straddling him exposed her panties. His sex pressed under hers.

"You say you ain't interested, but your pecker sure is."

He turned to the empty seat. "That's crass."

She kissed his neck.

"Without endorphins you'll have no flavor." Her hands moved over his fly. "Please, Sugar, give me your giant cock. I bet I won't be able to walk right after you fuck me."

It was average, but telling guys how huge their dicks were helped them get going.

"Stop, it's not too late for salvation." He put his hands under her bust to lift her off him.

Moving with his nudge, her back pressed into the steering wheel.

It didn't hurt until he tried taking his hands off her.

"Told you, I'm not sure I'm human. I could be human, but different, which is what I like to think."

He wondered how she Crazy-Glued his hands to her ribs.

"I'm going to have my turn trapping you, and you can see how you like it."

He jerked his hands back. Instead of freeing them, she fell into him. Her breasts muffled his yelp as stinging bolted through his palms. Pulling his head back, he whimpered, his face adhered to her cleavage, her nipple inches from his lips.

"You ever see Spiderman? The old one, where his fingers got stickies on them so he can walk on walls? I got those all over my body. Now, you nod if you're gonna be good."

Moving his face against her flesh felt like toxic pins and needles. His face released from her chest. His hands remained on her. The more he tried to pull them away, the more it felt like he was dragging them across razors.

Exertion and pain got him grunting.

"Let me free."

She raised her hands, "I ain't holding you."

"Whatever you're doing, it hurts."

"It'll hurt more if you resist. My mom had this one boyfriend, one time he tried to beat me because I wouldn't blow him. I had him stuck to me for an hour. I was trying to wait for my mom to come home. She was out with her other boyfriend at the time, now that I think about it, that might have been her pimp. Anyway, when I finally let him go his hands looked like—you ever see on the Discovery Channel when some dumb shit gets a snakebite and their skin turns black? That asshole never bothered me again. So, don't pull away, cause I'm not sure, but I might be injecting you with venom, real slow like."

"How do you not know what you are?"

"I can't go to no doctor. They'll cut me up because I ain't normal. I never met my dad and, as far as my mom goes, I know I'm a trick baby. Why don't we skip the ancient history and fuck? I got other shit to do tonight. You said you have dope? Don't you be lying to me, Jesus don't like liars."

"The word of Jesus Christ is the only straight dope I've got and I'm high on his word and you can be too."

"Really, Travis? Really? This'll be less painful for you if you're high. I'll like it more if I'm high and you'll taste better."

"One, we're not married. Two, God destroyed the city of Sodom because they practiced sodomy." His index and middle fingers pressed against her, attempting involuntary air quotes on the word *sodomy*.

"Ain't that butt fucking?"

"And using your mouth, so, no tasting me."

"Oh Sweetie, you still think I'm blowing you. When dopamine releases in your brain, you taste better, not your spunk." She reached down the front of his pants. "Damn, you've gone rope on me."

"You're creeping me out."

She put her hands on the sides of his face. "You should be proud of your limp dick. Most guys would still have a boner, but it's nice to see a man with a soft dick for Jesus. I'm so hungry it hurts. I heard fear spoils meat, but think about all them millions of cows killed every day in factory farms. They know they are about to die and I ain't never had a bad hamburger. Think about it."

She winked.

Yanking the fabric of his T-shirt in opposite directions, she ripped it down the middle.

"Come on, I liked this shirt."

"When I got in the cab and saw the door handle was missing, I thought you was gonna kill me. With the tables turned, you still believing in Jesus?"

"How can you not?"

"You think if you pray to him, he'll save you? Like, fly down from the sky?"

She rubbed his chest.

"It doesn't work like that," his tone was annoyed, not afraid.

She wondered if she was wrong and cows at the slaughterhouse were too dumb to know they were about to die and that's why hamburgers tasted good.

"I know," she said.

She put her hands in his mouth. They were tough and rubbery, the bones in her fingers had a flexible give. They conformed to his insides. He tried biting down, but his jaw couldn't close with so much of her in him. Her fingers made it to the start of his throat.

Thick barbed needles slid out of her hands. They went deep into his tongue, the inside of his cheeks, the roof of his mouth, and the backs of his lips. The needles at the end of her fingers hit the back of his throat, triggering his gag reflex.

He shook forward, vomiting. Mouth blocked, it spewed out of his nose. He wheezed, sinuses burning with stomach acid. The chunks of food that didn't erupt onto her stuffed his nose.

He was a fish convulsing at the end of a line struggling to escape the suffering piercing him. Violating him. He bucked. Thrusting her away, she slammed into the steering wheel. He tugged her into him. The whiplash motion didn't free him.

She giggled, "You fight for your life like a pussy."

Whatever had fired out of his nostrils was on her chest and arms. Where it landed, her skin faded into translucency. Her organs floated. He couldn't recognize them. No heart to pump the clear fluid inside her. Her internal parts came in pastel shades, some more solid than others. He could see where her hair sprouted from her head and covered a vanishing scalp. Like her missing heart, other things floated in place of a brain. She was a jellyfish in gutter drag.

His windpipe jammed with his own sick. He kneed her in the ass. Anything to break free before asphyxiating. He snorted out air, sucked in hard, snorted out more. He rocked back and forth, trying to escape the hurt she put on him.

"Fight all you want but I got you."

Pieces of vomit passed into her skin.

"I eat food but I also eat this way."

She pumped herself back and forth priming her muscles. She pushed into him. With a single motion, she pulled down and back. Her arms were free from his body.

A frigid deep breath rushed into his lungs.

Air at last.

His consciousness hadn't assembled the reality of the moment.

Large chunks of meat stuck to both her wrists. She'd ripped his jaw off. In the same action, she divided it into two. On each of her forearms were his muscle, skin, teeth, blood, spit, and vomit. His tongue, most of his jaw, some of his flapping neck skin, and his vocal cords were on her right forearm. The piece of him on her left was smaller. Traveling toward her torso, his flesh sank within her, dissolving into clarity.

He croaked, hissed, and gurgled.

From the crater in his body a geyser rose. The glass bodied woman leaned into him. His fluids entered her. Opaque, they dirtied her like milk spreading in water.

Coated in him, she became invisible, a place keeper for her hair, clothing, and digestion.

He thrashed for a few moments of hysterical pain.

Their bodies relaxing, she felt his death beats. The weak thump of his circulatory system saying, *Fuck it, I quit. I don't care if the brain or the rest of all y'all die, I'm done.*

And then it stopped.

All of him.

Wanting off, she allowed his hands to drop from her. He wasn't that good. She still needed to fix. He wasn't enough. They weren't both high, it was a meal with no flavor. She flopped over to the passenger seat. The desire for a hit of anything interrupted her enjoyment of the sensation of being full.

The fluids on her clothes pulled through the fabric and into her skin. They'd be clean in a few moments. With her hands on her belly, the progression to opacity started.

She wasn't finished assimilating the mess when hunger pangs groaned within her.

*Why am I so fucking hungry?*

She examined the transparent section of her stomach that cried for food.

"Oh shit, I'm preggers."

# ABOUT GERRI R. GRAY

Gerri R. Gray is an American novelist, editor, poet, and short story writer in the horror and bizarro genres. She is the author of seven published books, including her popular debut novel, *The Amnesia Girl* (HellBound Books). Her work has appeared in numerous anthologies and literary journals. A former antique dealer and B&B proprietor, Madame Gray lives in upstate New York in an historic and decidedly haunted nineteenth-century house with her husband and a bevy of spirits. When she isn't busy creating strange worlds filled with even stranger characters, she can often be found rummaging through antique shops, exploring haunted places, dabbling in the occult or traipsing through old cemeteries with her camera in hand. You can visit her online at www.facebook.com/AuthorGerriGray or on Twitter @GerriRGray.

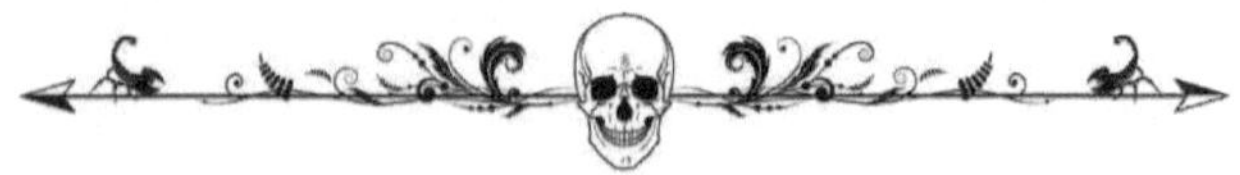

Now wash
your hands

# OTHER HELLBOUND BOOKS

## The Toilet Zone
### *"Restroom reading at its most terrifying!"*

Compiled and edited by the grand master of 80's schlock horror, Bret McCormick, each one of this collection of 32 terrifying tales is just the perfect length for a visit to the smallest room....

At the very boundaries of human imagination dwells one single, solitary place of solitude, of peace and quiet, a place in which your regular human being spends, on average, 10 to 15 minutes - at least once every single day of their lives.

Now, consider a typical, everyday reading speed of 200 to 250 words per minute - that means your average visitor has the time to read between 2,500 to 4,000 words, which makes each and every one of these 32 tales of terror - from some of the best contemporary independent authors - within this anthology of horror the perfect, meticulously calculated length.

Dare you take a walk to the small room from where inky shadows creep out to smother the light and solitude's siren call beckons you?

Dare you take a quiet, lonely walk into… The Toilet Zone

# Blood and Blasphemy

If you enjoy your horror dipped in buckets of blood and sprinkled with generous amounts of blasphemy, then you've come to the right place!

Blood and Blasphemy is a collection of over thirty of the most sacrilegious horror stories ever written.

Within these irreverent pages, you will encounter a priest that keeps his deformed spawn chained in a root cellar, a convent where a poisonous species of salamander is worshiped, a demonic altar boy, possessed religious relics that kill, blood-drinking clergymen, a Son of God who feeds on sin, an unsuspecting couple who run afoul of religious lunatics in a small town, the divine (and deadly) turd of Christ, and other terrifying tales guaranteed to make church ladies faint and nuns clutch their rosaries.

Featuring stories by: Aron Beauregard, George Alan Bradley, Cardigan Broadmoor, Scot M. Carpenter, Myna Chang, Clay McLeod Chapman, Nick Dinicola, Jude M. Eriksen, Michael Martin Garrett, Gerri R. Gray, Christopher Hamel, Carlton Herzog, B.T. Joy, A.L. King, Daryl Marcus, Jeremy Megargee, Donna J.W. Munro, Hari Navarro, Trevor Newton, Drew Nicks, C.C. Parker, Wolfgang Potterhouse, J.L. Shioshita, J.J. Smith, Henry Snider, J.B. Toner, Sheldon Woodbury, Ken Goldman, and Shawn Wood.

**Schlock! Horror!**

An anthology of short stories based upon/inspired by and in loving homage to all of those great gorefest movies and books of the 1980's (not necessarily base in that era, although some do ride that wave of nostalgia!), the golden age when horror well and truly came kicking, screaming and spraying blood, gore & body parts out from the shadows...

This exemplary 80's themed/inspired tales of terror has been adjudicated and compiled by one Mr Bret McCormick, himself a writer, producer and director of many a schlock classic, including *Bio-Tech Warrior*, *Time Tracers*, *The Abomination*, *Ozone: The Attack of the Redneck Mutants* and the inimitable *Repligator*.

Featuring stories from: Todd Sullivan, Timothy C Hobbs, Mark Thomas, Andrew Post, James B. Pepe, Thomas Vaughn, Edward Karpp, Jaap Boekestein, Lisa Alfano, L. C. Holt, John Adam Gosham, Brandon Cracraft, M. Earl Smith, Sarah Cannavo, James Gardner, Bret McCormick, and James H. Longmore.

## Graveyard Girls

*Female authors + Horror = something spectacularly terrifying!*

A delicious collection of horrific tales and darkest poetry from the cream of the crop, all lovingly compiled by the incomparable Gerri R Gray! Nestling between the covers of this formidable tome are twenty-five of the very best lady authors writing on the horror scene today! These tales of terror are guaranteed to chill your very soul and awaken you in the dead of the night with fear-sweat clinging to your every pore and your heart pounding hard and heavy in your labored breast…

Featuring superlative horror from: Xtina Marie, M. W. Brown, Rebecca Kolodziej, Anya Lee, Barbara Jacobson, Gerri R. Gray, Christina Bergling, Julia Benally, Olga Werby, Kelly Glover, Lee Franklin, Linda M. Crate, Vanessa Hawkins, P. Alanna Roethle, J Snow, Evelyn Eve, Serena Daniels, S. E. Davis, Sam Hill, J. C. Raye, Donna J. W. Munro, R. J. Murray, C. Bailey-Bacchus, Varonica Chaney, Marian Finch (Lady Marian).

## A HellBound Books LLC Publication

http://www.hellboundbookspublishing.com

**Printed in the United States of America**

Now wash
your hands

www.ingramcontent.com/pod-product-compliance
Lightning Source LLC
Chambersburg PA
CBHW061301190726
48288CB00002B/307